FLIP THE WITCH SWITCH
A WICKED WITCHES OF THE MIDWEST MYSTERY BOOK FOURTEEN

AMANDA M. LEE

WINCHESTERSHAW PUBLICATIONS

Copyright © 2019 by Amanda M. Lee

All rights reserved.

No part of this book may be reproduced in any form or by any electronic or mechanical means, including information storage and retrieval systems, without written permission from the author, except for the use of brief quotations in a book review.

❀ Created with Vellum

PROLOGUE

SEVENTEEN YEARS AGO

"I hate camping."

Clove Winchester, her black hair pulled back in a loose ponytail, screwed up her face in the most petulant of tween expressions and glared at her great-aunt Tillie. It was the *snine*. The half sneer, half whine. She was good at the *snine*.

Aunt Tillie didn't care how good she was at the expression. The tone of her voice was like vampire nails on a glass window.

"You don't hate camping," she fired back, her agitation coming out to play. "You like camping. Camping is fun. You're just whining because you like the sound of your voice."

"That's what Mom says about you," Bay volunteered. Unlike her cousin Clove, Bay was fair and blond. She also wasn't darting her eyes around the campsite because she feared some unforeseen monster sneaking up on them. She was calm, although pleasant was another story.

"Your mother says what about me?" Aunt Tillie huffed as she dug in the bag by her feet.

"She says that you like the sound of your own voice."

"Well, that sounds just like your mother," Aunt Tillie said primly. "Do you want me to tell you something about your mother?"

"She's going to tell you whether you want to hear it or not," the third young girl, Thistle, announced from her spot across the fire. Her hair was blond, wild and unkempt after an afternoon traipsing around the woods to collect herbs. She didn't seem to care, though, because she had other things on her mind ... like seeing how far she could push her great-aunt. "That's what she does."

"You listen here, Thistle," Tillie snapped, narrowing her eyes. "I'm going to tell you because it's important to what we're doing out here."

"I thought we were lost," Clove groused, her eyes going wider (if that was even possible) as something fluttered from one tree to another. "What was that?"

"I think it was a rabid bat," Thistle replied dryly. "It's going to come bite you during the night and it's going to be all *Cujo* up in here before the sun rises."

"Oh, that shows what you know," Tillie said, making a face. "It takes weeks for rabies to set in. She wouldn't turn into *Cujo* right away. She would froth at the mouth and we would have to lock her in a shed before it got that bad."

Clove, eternally miffed, folded her arms over her chest and glared. "I want to go home right now!"

Tillie was used to her great-nieces making demands. She'd been sharing a roof with them for years — and before that she occasionally volunteered to babysit, but only if she needed the cover toting around three small children could offer should the police come sniffing around asking questions — and she knew exactly how to handle the mouthy little cauldron sniffers.

"We can't go home." She chose her words carefully. "Part of the outdoor experience is sleeping under the stars. As witches, you have to commune with nature. It's one of those rules that you have to follow even if you don't want to."

Clove was having none of that. "I don't want to follow the rules! The woods are full of animals ... and monsters ... and animals."

"What animal are you worried about?"

"The big ones."

"She's worried about Bigfoot," Thistle volunteered, her expression seeming to indicate that she was bored. "She saw this video on some nature show and there was footage of Bigfoot and the lady who was talking said that Bigfoot lived in our area, so ... she's basically scared of Bigfoot."

Clove was officially scandalized. "I am not afraid of Bigfoot!"

"You are so." Bay rubbed her hands over her bare knees and stared into the fire. "How long do you think it will be until they send a search party after us?"

Clove worried about ridiculous things. Bay worried about real things, and Tillie found that far more dangerous. That's why she opted to address both problems with one breath.

"First, you don't have to worry about Bigfoot, Clove. I know what you saw on television, but Bigfoot doesn't live around these parts, so you're safe."

Clove brightened considerably. "Really?" She flicked her eyes to Thistle. "Is that true?"

Thistle made a face. "Why are you asking me? I know what you know."

"You don't know jack, Thistle," Tillie fired back. "But that's neither here nor there. The fact of the matter is, this isn't Bigfoot territory."

Clove drew her eyebrows together. "Where is Bigfoot territory?" She clearly wasn't sure if she should believe her great-aunt, but she definitely wanted a reason to tear her thoughts from a huge apelike creature that might rip her from limb to limb.

"Bigfoot lives in the Pacific Northwest." Tillie was matter-of-fact. "That's his home."

"And where is that?" Clove gnawed a fingernail as she searched the shadows for hints of movement. "Is that a long way away?"

"We're talking Oregon, Washington state and Canada, Clove," Tillie shot back. "Don't you pay attention in geography class?"

"Canada?" Clove's voice turned shrill. "We're really close to Canada."

"Canada is big like Margaret Little's behind," Tillie explained. "It's huge. The part of Canada we're talking about is a long way from here. Bigfoot can't live here, so it stays in the spot where it's supposed to live."

"Are you sure?" Clove clearly wanted to believe, so she unclenched a bit. "Why would people say Bigfoot was hanging around these woods if it's not true?"

"People are morons, Clove. They say stupid things all the time."

"Yeah, but ... you're sure, right?"

Tillie bobbed her head. "I'm completely and totally sure. Bigfoot can't live in these woods because the Dogman owns them."

Clove's mouth dropped open. "Who is the Dogman?"

"He's like Bigfoot's hairy cousin who wags his tail," Thistle offered helpfully.

"Pretty much," Tillie agreed. "The Dogman is better. He can be distracted with Frisbees and when you do that fake throwing balls thing. He's cool that way."

Clove buried her face in her hands and whimpered. "I hate you. I can't believe you got us lost."

"Hey!" Tillie's eyes fired. "I did not get us lost. I know exactly where we are."

"Is that close to the Dogman's lair?" Thistle asked, feigning legitimate curiosity.

"Listen, junior mouth, I might not have a room to send you to, but that won't stop me from cursing you if I feel like it," Tillie warned. "Just ... shut your mouth."

"I would but I'm afraid this is the last time I'll have to open it and your threats have no power on me, old lady." Thistle might've been only ten but she was worldly in a way most kids couldn't claim. She was smart beyond her years, which made her a constant thorn in Tillie's backside. "We're going to die out here and it's completely your fault because you got us lost."

"I don't get lost."

"Really? Then why did you have to magically make a fire?" Thistle challenged. "How come we're eating berries instead of tacos? We're supposed to be eating tacos."

"Oh, it's taco night." Clove sounded mournful. "I love tacos. How could you get us lost on taco night? That is just the worst."

"Oh, suck it up." Tillie made a face. "You're being a bunch of babies. Where is your sense of adventure? We're in the woods, on a beautiful night, and the only thing standing in the way of us and adventure are the stars."

Instead of immediately responding, Bay, Clove and Thistle merely stared at their great-aunt. Thistle, per usual, was the first to speak.

"That is the biggest load of hogwash I've ever heard," she snapped. "You don't like sleeping outside any more than we do. You just can't figure out how to get us home."

"That is not true." Tillie was even more annoyed than usual, which was saying something, because she was the queen of agitation on a normal day. "I know exactly where we are."

"We know exactly where we are, too," Thistle said. "We're lost."

"We're not lost!" Tillie exploded.

"We're lost and the Dogman is going to eat us." Clove openly sobbed. "I'm too young to die. Just think about everything I'm missing out on in life. I'll never get to date ... or wear nice boots that aren't hand-me-downs ... or watch an R-rated movie and actually be able to talk about it without my mother yelling when she finds out."

Tillie's glare was withering. "Listen, drama queen, we're not lost. I know exactly where we are."

"Where?"

"Where I want us to be."

"And where is that?" Thistle challenged. "Where do you want us to be?"

"We're in control of our destinies."

Thistle narrowed her eyes until they were nothing more than glittery slits. "You are so full of yourself, old lady. I can't believe you haven't exploded yet. I mean ... no one should be able to have that much hot air inside of them without blowing up.

"And, just for the record, I'm not disrespecting my elders when I say that," she continued. "I've heard Aunt Winnie say it, like, ten times. That means it has to be true."

"Don't you worry about Winnie," Tillie snapped. "I'll handle Winnie and her runaway mouth just as soon as we get home."

"And when will that be?" Clove queried. "Before or after the Dogman eats us?"

"Clove, the Dogman is not going to eat us. Be practical. He would much rather eat deer and rabbits because they taste better. If he kills us, it's because he simply doesn't like us."

"Oh, well, that is so much better," Clove snuffled. "I want to go home!"

"We all want to go home." Thistle leaned back on her elbows and stretched her legs out toward the fire. "But we can't. We're lost. Aunt Tillie took us into the woods, promised we would be home for the taco bar, and then got us lost."

"Oh, there's never going to be a taco bar again," Clove wailed.

"I'm done talking to all of you," Tillie hissed. "You're all on my list."

"I don't think that threat frightens us as much as you wish it would," Thistle argued.

"Just shut your holes." Tillie held up her hand and stared into the woods, as if willing herself to hold it together.

The foursome lapsed into silence for a long time, the only sound the crackling fire. Finally, Bay was the one to break it.

"If we're not lost, why did we circle the same tree four times before you decided we should make camp?"

Tillie slowly tracked her eyes to her oldest great-niece. Bay was the dangerous one of the trio. Clove was the whiner and manipulator. Thistle was the plotter with more bravado than brains. Bay, however, was the thinker. She worked things over in her mind until there was nothing left but the truth.

"If we're not lost, why are we camping without equipment?" Bay persisted. "You love tacos. You would never willingly miss out on them. That means we have to be lost. That's why we're stuck here with a fire and berries instead of at home with tacos and that tequila Mom doesn't think we know about."

"Tequila she stole from me," Tillie muttered, shaking her head.

FLIP THE WITCH SWITCH

"That wasn't an answer to the question." Bay refused to back down. "If we're not lost, what are we doing?"

"We're camping."

"There are tents when we camp, sleeping bags. There's bug spray and food. There're s'mores."

"Oh, why did you have to bring up s'mores?" Clove whined. "I'll never get another s'more. Why, Goddess, why?"

Tillie rolled her eyes at Clove's diminutive form. "You're seriously on my last nerve, Clove. One more word and I'll take your berries away. How do you feel about that?"

"What I don't get is that if we're lost, why aren't you using magic to lead us home?" Thistle challenged. "You're a witch. Why not just snap your fingers and make one of those orb things and have it lead us back to the house?"

Clove straightened. "Yeah. Why not do that? We might not miss taco night if you can conjure one fast enough."

"I can't do that." Tillie avoided three curious gazes. "Go back to eating your berries."

Thistle was instantly suspicious. "And why can't you do that?"

"Because I said so."

"Why really?"

"Because your mothers will see if I do that and I refuse to explain myself to them," Tillie supplied. "They think they're so smart. They warned me before taking you out that I should be careful because the foliage was extra thick this year and they were worried I would get turned around. I mean ... I've been hanging around in these woods since before they were born. Who are they to tell me what to do?"

"Right," Bay said. "We wouldn't want that. Especially if they were right."

"Stop flapping your gums," Tillie ordered, her expression darkening. "You're fine. The light just got away from me. In the morning I'll be able to see where we are and we'll be home before breakfast. This is not the end of the world."

"And how will you explain to our mothers about our unscheduled camping trip?" Bay pressed. "Don't you think they'll be wondering about that?"

"I'll just tell them you girls needed to be toughened up. They'll believe it because ... well ... look at you." She gestured at Clove, who was still fake crying over the taco bar.

"Why can't you just conjure an orb that gets us close to home?" Thistle suggested. "Then you can hide it before they see it."

"I thought about that, Thistle, but you have a big mouth and will tell them what happened, so there's no way I'll get away with it."

"So ... you'd rather sit out here in the dark all night even though we're going to tell them regardless?" Bay asked.

"Pretty much."

"You suck," Thistle lamented, flopping on the ground. "I mean, you really suck."

"You're an absolute delight, too, Thistle." Tillie stared at the fire. "Now, how about we make the best of this situation? Let's tell ghost stories."

"I know a ghost story," Thistle announced. "Once upon a time, there were three pretty princesses and they were lost in the woods with their great-aunt, the cave hag."

"And Thistle is cut off from telling stories," Tillie announced. "I ... ." She trailed off at the sound of a twig cracking.

Clove squealed as she hunched over and Thistle bolted to a sitting position.

"What was that?" Bay asked, her eyes peering into the darkness.

"It's the Dogman," Clove announced. "He's coming ... and he's hungry."

Tillie rolled her eyes. "How many times do I have to tell you that the Dogman doesn't eat people? He just plays with them with his teeth until they die."

"I don't think that's better," Thistle complained. "In fact ... ."

Whatever she was going to say died on her lips when another twig cracked.

"It's the Dogman," Clove wailed. "We're all doomed!"

"Don't get carried away, Clove," Tillie snapped. "I have everything under control. Trust me. No one will dare cross into our campground as long as I'm alive."

"Oh, well, now I'm torn," Thistle said. "On one hand I want to kill you for making us miss the taco bar. On the other, I want to throw you at the Dogman so he can play with you while we make our escape."

Tillie's eyes flared. "You're definitely on my list."

"Bay?" A distinctly male voice drifted into the clearing from the east. "Tillie?"

Bay hopped to her feet. "Detective Terry." She raced into the darkness before Tillie could stop her, throwing her arms around the broad shoulders of the man who emerged from the trees. Terry Davenport was dressed in a police uniform, the lines on his face deep and pronounced as he hugged the girl and let his eyes drift from face to face.

"I'm glad to see you girls alive," he said after a beat.

"We were almost eaten by the Dogman," Clove announced. "It was the most terrifying experience of my entire life."

"I see." Terry smoothed Bay's blond hair. "So ... I got a call from your mothers. They were worried you might've gotten turned around in the woods."

"And you just magically found us?" Tillie's annoyance was on full display. "I find that hard to believe."

"I saw the campfire from the road and decided to stop. There's a no-burn rule in effect right now because it's so dry."

"I ... ." Tillie pursed her lips and furrowed her brow. "What road?"

"The one right over there." Terry pointed. "You're about a quarter of a mile away from the house."

"Oh." Tillie straightened. "Well, I knew that. I was just teaching the girls about emergency camping."

"Right." Thistle made such an exaggerated face that Terry had to bite the inside of his cheek to keep from laughing. "You knew where we were the whole time. That's why we're eating berries instead of tacos."

"Oh, taco bar." Clove's eyes lit with mirth, the Dogman all but forgotten. "We should get home. I love tacos."

"Definitely." Terry directed the girls toward the road. "Get in the truck and I'll drive you." His gaze was heavy as it landed on Tillie. "Do you have anything you want to say? Winnie, Marnie and Twila were worried."

"There's nothing to say." Tillie was breezy as she blew past him. "I had everything under control like I always do. There was no reason to panic. I knew you would show up exactly when you did."

"Oh, yeah? How did you know that?"

"You're predictable."

"Good to know. I guess I'll be predictable and take you home, huh?"

"That would be for the best."

"I figured you would say that."

ONE

PRESENT DAY

"Are you sure this is it?"

Landon Michaels, his shoulder-length black hair freshly washed and gleaming, pulled into a rutted clearing that only vaguely resembled a parking lot and glanced around at the sparse landscape.

"This is it," I reassured him, smiling as I took a moment to stare at the nearest tree, "This is Camp Mayhem."

Landon arched an eyebrow as he killed the engine and removed his keys from the ignition. "Camp Mayhem? That can't be its real name."

"No, it was Camp Manistee ... because that's the lake – and river – it's closest to."

"Camp Manistee." He smiled. "I didn't remember the name. Camp Mayhem has a nice ring to it, though. Come on. Let's take a look."

He was excited. For some reason, that excited me. I, Bay Winchester, witch extraordinaire, was thrilled to visit an old camp I hadn't seen since I was a teenager ... and I had no idea why.

It was his idea, of course. Once he realized we'd both attended the camp — and at the same time — he insisted we find an opening in our schedules to visit. Lingering snow made that difficult for a bit, but once decent weather arrived he started pressuring me to make it happen. Finally, with the sun shining and the birds chirping, I couldn't think of another reason to put it off.

So, here we were. My boyfriend, the man I lived with and knew I would spend the rest of my life with, was excited to revisit the camp where our paths first crossed ... even though both of us only remembered the event in the vaguest of terms.

"Let's take a look," I said brightly, hoping I looked more excited than I felt. In truth, while I was fascinated with the idea that Landon and I had met and crushed on each other years before we crossed paths again and fell in love as adults, I didn't have the fondest memories of the camp. The first time I visited was as a little kid and my mother and aunts got in a huge fight that resulted in Aunt Tillie lighting the tops of the trees on fire to shut them up. The last time, I was a teenager and my mother insisted my cousins and I were driving her crazy and we needed to get out of the house. I spent a full week trapped at the camp with annoying counselors who allowed my arch nemesis, Lila Stevens, to torture me whenever the whim struck.

Between those trips (and many others, sometimes multiple visits each summer), sure, we had some fun ... and occasionally heartache when the boys and girls were officially allowed to mingle. That didn't change the fact that I had some very bad memories of the place.

"Why did this place close down?" Landon asked, reaching for my hand. He was clearly oblivious to my trepidation.

"I don't know." That was the truth. Once I graduated from high school I left my hometown of Walkerville in the rear-view mirror. Camp Manistee was nothing but a distant memory at that point. When I returned years later, I had an attitude adjustment. I never thought to research the camp, though. It simply wasn't on my radar.

"I don't really remember it." He cocked his head to the side and stared at one of the rundown cabins. "I don't remember it being set up this way."

"You stayed over there," I reminded him, pointing toward the opposite side of the lake. It wasn't an overly large body of water. In fact, it seemed much smaller than it had when I was a kid. That was obviously a perspective thing. "The boys' camp was on that side of the lake. The girls stayed over here."

Landon followed my finger with his gaze. "There's only one cabin over there."

"There used to be more. I think one of them fell down years ago. Chief Terry mentioned it. He was your camp counselor the year you were here, even though you don't remember him."

"I went to a lot of camps when I was a kid," Landon explained. "They all melded together."

"Did you hit on a lot of girls at those camps?" I asked. "Did they all meld together, too?"

"Oh, I'm not falling for that." He wagged a finger in my face and swooped in to give me a quick kiss. "I'm not a complete and total idiot. You were the only girl I fell for at camp. That's why you have such a special place in my heart."

I didn't believe him for a second. Not about having a special place in his heart, mind you. I believed that without a doubt. The part I had trouble believing was the bit about him falling for me when we were barely teenagers. "I think you talk big."

"And I think I had a huge crush on you. I might not remember much, but I remember that."

"Well ... I remember you." That was true. "It's kind of muddled in my head because there was a lot going on then, but I definitely remember you." That was also true ... at least I was fairly certain it was true.

"And I remember you ... and oddly enough, your mother. I remember having a conversation with her, though I'm not sure what I said."

"I asked her about it and she says she doesn't remember. She thought it was cute that we were at the same summer camp."

"Cute?" Landon made a face. "It's kismet, sweetie. We were always destined to find each other."

I snickered, genuinely amused. "You're throwing that word around a lot. 'Destiny,' I mean. You seem to be getting a kick out of the idea."

"Oh, I am. You have no idea." Landon squeezed my hand tighter and then pointed. "Let's check out the cabins."

I followed close at his side, frowning when we approached the first cabin. I had slept under its roof at least twice that I could remember — the same with the other two cabins — but the building felt somehow ominous now.

"It doesn't look safe," I offered after a moment's contemplation. "Like ... maybe the roof is going to fall in or something."

Amusement flitted across Landon's features as he tugged me toward the cabin. "The cabin has obviously stood for a number of years, decades even. Do you think it's going to suddenly fall down now?"

That was a good question. "I don't know. The cabin also hasn't been disturbed for at least five years, I'm guessing. Maybe our appearance will be enough to cause it to cave in."

"Oh, have a little faith." His tone was pleading and he was having too good a time for me to ruin it.

"Okay, but if the roof falls in, I told you so."

"If the roof caves in and we're buried alive, the last thing I will remember is those words," he said dryly, tugging desperately on my hand. "Come on."

The door wasn't locked. There was no reason for it to be. It opened with only minimal complaint, a creak straight out of a Scooby-Doo mystery. There was no electricity. There never was. I remembered carrying lanterns with us when we had to leave the cabin after dark, which was frowned upon.

During the day, light shined into the cabin from every direction through the multiple windows on every wall. The bunk beds we'd slept in — which had a rustic feeling back then and looked like odd skeletons of a time long since forgotten now — remained standing, but I wouldn't risk climbing on one for anything.

"Did you stay in here when we were at camp together?" he asked. He was obsessed with learning everything about that camp adventure. The problem was, I couldn't remember.

"I don't know. You seem to forget, I came to this camp every year for a time."

"I know, but ... are you sure you don't remember?"

I could've lied to him. He never would've known and it might've made him feel better. We'd promised to be as honest as possible with one another, though, and I intended to stick to it. "I can't remember, Landon." I tapped my finger on my bottom lip as I slowly turned. "That was the year Rosemary was here," I noted, referring to a distant cousin I disliked with fiery resolve. "She came to camp only once, and I vaguely remember her being in this building."

"Really?" Landon looked suspicious. "Are you just saying that to appease me?"

"Oddly enough, no. Go check on the wall over there." I vaguely gestured. "If I'm right, Lila carved her name in the wall next to Rosemary's to announce they were best friends forever."

Landon made a face. "Lila and Rosemary were best friends?"

"They were." I nodded. "Once Lila figured out we didn't like Rosemary and that she might have dirt on us, she couldn't make friends with her fast enough. They were joined at the hip the entire weekend."

"That Lila was always a class act," Landon muttered, drawing his keychain from his pocket and using the flashlight to point in the corner I'd indicated. "Oh, yeah. Look at that." He grinned as he focused the beam on a specific spot. "Lila and Rosemary together. That's like the worst horror movie ever."

I was amused despite my memories. "It's like a horror movie reboot, because those always suck."

He smiled as he slung an arm around my shoulders. "Yeah. I'm still sorry you had to put up with it." He brushed his lips against my forehead. "Screw Rosemary and Lila. We're doing better than both of them combined."

He wasn't wrong. "Yeah." I allowed myself a moment to rest my head against his shoulder and then I pulled back. "Let's get out of here. This place is dirty and gross. Plus, I'm still not convinced the roof won't fall in on us."

"Fine. We shall take the adventure outside."

It was spring in northern Lower Michigan, so we had plenty of sunshine when we hit the front porch. It was early in the season, not exactly warm, but the weather was much more welcoming than it had been weeks before.

"We're supposed to have a really hot and humid summer," I noted as I hopped off the porch and hit the ground. "After how crappy our winter was, I'm looking forward to it. I'm sure I'll complain nonetheless."

"Yes, you're nothing if not consistent when complaining about how hot or cold it is," he teased. "Who says we're supposed to have a hot and humid summer? It's a little early in the season to be gauging that."

"The Farmers' Almanac."

"Oh, well, if the Farmers' Almanac says so, then it must be true."

"Hey, don't discount the Farmers' Almanac. There's a reason it's hung around as long as it has."

"Yes, superstitious witches." He tickled me, causing me to squeal and hop ahead of him. "Where do you think you're going, my little witch?"

He was feeling awfully playful. I had no intention of discouraging him. "I want to check out the lake," I replied, without hesitation. "It's pretty out here, even though the lake isn't very big. It's restful. I like restful places."

"Which is why you live on your family's property."

"Hey!" I jabbed a finger at him. "You live on that property now, too. You can't give me any grief."

"I can always give you grief. I'm good at it."

"You're definitely good at it." I swung my arms as I skipped toward the lapping waves, grinning when I reached the shore of the crystal-clear water source. "It's beautiful out here. I always thought it would be cool to live on the water. You have to be rich to do it on the bigger lakes here, though."

Landon glanced around, taking a moment to survey the full property. "Is the area over there part of the parcel, too?" He gestured toward the boys' camp, which looked to be in even worse shape than the girls' camp.

"To my knowledge. You would probably have to check with the land deeds office. Why are you so interested?"

He shrugged, noncommittal. "I don't know. I just am. I mean ... this is where we met."

I arched an eyebrow. "It is ... but I don't see why it's any better than where we met the other time. That was in a corn maze, and you know how I feel about corn mazes."

"Yes, you love them." He grabbed my hand and tugged me away from the water, wrapping his arms around my waist as he swayed back and forth. "As romantic as that corn maze was, this is better. You weren't sure of me at the maze. You were sure of me here."

That was an interesting way to look at things. "How do you know that?"

"I guess I don't know for certain. I just feel it."

"I was certain of you in the corn maze," I offered after a moment's contemplation. "Maybe not that first day, but by that last night I knew I could trust you."

"Was that before or after I was shot?"

He knew I hated it when he brought up that incident. "Before ... mostly." I pulled him away from the water. "It's much too cold to get our feet wet. Let's look someplace else."

"Do you have a suggestion?"

"Well, if I remember correctly, there's a volleyball pitch that way and a pool over there."

"A pool?" Landon knit his eyebrows. "I don't remember swimming in a pool. I think I would have much fonder memories of this camp if there'd been a pool."

"I thought your memories were surrounded in floaty hearts because I was here."

"Cute." He poked my side. "Seriously, I don't remember a pool."

"That's because it wasn't built until the spring I turned sixteen." I started out across the grounds, Landon in tow. "A local business — the one owned by Mrs. Little at the time, in fact — donated the pool."

"She donated a pool?" Landon was familiar with Margaret Little. She was one of his least favorite people, and that was saying something because his list of annoying acquaintances was long and storied. "Why would she possibly donate a pool? That doesn't sound like her at all."

"I can't remember the details." I racked my memory. "I seem to remember some sort of competition with Aunt Tillie — like Aunt Tillie donated a rope swing for the lake and Mrs. Little had to outdo her — but I could be totally wrong."

"Now that I could see happening."

I chuckled as I cut around a large weeping willow. The leaves hadn't filled out yet, but it would be a beautiful tree when it was decked out in all its glory. I remembered it from when I was younger, though it was much larger now.

"They built the pool and we enjoyed it a few years. I don't think the camp stayed open that long after we aged out. I'm trying to remember."

"It's too bad." Landon's expression reflected yearning as he glanced around. "Seriously, this place is really cool. Kids today spend all their time on cell phones and playing video games. They're missing out on all the fun things in life."

"Okay, Grandpa." I snickered as he reached to snag me around the waist, easily evading him. "You sound like Aunt Tillie."

"Aunt Tillie plays video games on her phone."

"She's also trying to devise an app in which she will curse people for money."

Landon slowed his pace. "Excuse me?"

"It's true. She has Sam and Marcus working for her, even though neither of them is an app developer. Her plan is to get people who want to exact revenge on their enemies to pay a fee through the app and she'll curse them."

Landon's mouth dropped open. "You cannot be serious. She won't really do that, will she?"

I shrugged. "You know how she is."

"I do. That's why I'm asking."

"I wouldn't worry about it." I meant it. On Aunt Tillie's lists of threats this week, the Pocket Curser — and, yes, I pointed out how that name could be taken the wrong way — was the least of my concerns. "Besides, once she realizes Sam and Marcus can't really help her she'll give it up and move on to something else."

"I hope you're right," Landon muttered as we came to a gate. "Is this the pool?" He peered over the rusty metal fence and frowned when he realized what he thought was an enclosed field of brush and garbage actually was a covered pool. "Oh, gross. I'll pay you twenty bucks to swim in that." He pointed toward the murky water that showed through a tear in the cover.

I shot him a questioning look. "You do realize I'm not one of your brothers, right?"

"Sorry. I momentarily lost my head. Girls don't play the same games boys do."

"Oh, we would've played the same games," I countered. "We simply would've paid better money for something that stupid."

"Good to know."

Once he'd managed to get the gate open, I separated from Landon and circled the pool. Given the huge amount of brush and garbage that had become trapped inside of the fence, I had to tread carefully so I wouldn't veer too far to the left and risk walking on the cover. I had no doubt that it was weak after years of being left in place and I would fall right through it if I made a wrong step.

"Someone should come out here and clean this up," Landon lamented. "I mean ... it's a total waste sitting out here like this."

"Plus I don't want to know what creatures are living in this pool," I added as I turned a corner at the far edge of the space. "In fact ... ." I forgot everything I was about to say when I noticed something protruding from another hole in the cover. I had to do a double take, but I was fairly certain I recognized the object ... and that wasn't a good thing.

"What were you saying?" Landon was distracted by a large sheet of faded cardboard at the end of the enclosure.

"Landon, I think we should call Chief Terry."

He didn't look up. "Why? I have no intention of molesting you out here ... unless you really want me to, that is. I guess I could take one for the team if you begged."

I cleared my throat and tried to stay calm. "I'm serious. You should call him now."

Landon finally dragged his eyes from the cardboard and focused on me. "Why?"

"Because there's a human hand poking through the cover down here, which means there's a body in the water."

Landon blinked several times before responding. "No way."

"Way."

"I guess that puts an end to the nostalgia."

TWO

Chief Terry wasn't happy. He parked next to Landon's Explorer, hopped out of his cruiser, and immediately headed toward me.

"Do I even want to know what you two are doing out here?" he growled. He looked frustrated, which was very unlike him.

"Walking down memory lane," Landon replied dryly. "We wanted to re-live the day we met at summer camp."

Chief Terry rolled his eyes. "I knew when you told me about this it was going to be a thing. You're an FBI agent, Landon. You know that public fornication is against the law. Besides that, she's my little sweetheart." He helplessly gestured toward me. "I don't like it when you do things like this because it makes it impossible for me to pretend you two aren't just playing house."

Landon's eyebrows lifted. "Wow. That was a mouthful."

"It was," I agreed, moving closer to Chief Terry to give him a hug. "I'm still glad to see you."

I wasn't much of a hugger as an adult, so Chief Terry ran his hand over my back and turned his eyes to Landon. "What's this?"

"I don't know. Maybe she wants to fornicate with you in public or something."

"Don't ever say anything like that again," Chief Terry hissed, extending a warning finger. "I'm deadly serious. I don't like that at all."

"I can see you don't have much of a sense of humor today," Landon drawled, his eyes twinkling. I couldn't figure out why he was pushing Chief Terry so hard. He usually opted to show his fellow law enforcement official respect unless he was feeling particularly annoyed. "Perhaps it has something to do with your upcoming date."

Oh, geez. I'd totally forgotten about that. I turned a set of expectant eyes to Chief Terry. "That's right. You and Mom are going on an official date."

Chief Terry was in no mood to be teased. "I believe you said you found a body. Don't you think you should show it to me?"

"The body isn't going anywhere." As it was, I didn't know how the retrieval team was going to get the body out of the pool. It looked to be tangled with the cover, which had come undone in some places and was sinking in others. It was a true mess ... and I was grossed out by the entire thing. "Tell us about your date. That's tomorrow, right? Mom is all aflutter over it. She's been trying on outfits."

It occurred to me after I opened my big, fat mouth that I probably should've kept that detail to myself. No one in the family could keep a secret to save their lives, though, so I brushed it out of my mind.

"I'm not here to talk about my dating life." Chief Terry was stern. "I'm here about a body in a pool. Maybe. Are you guys even sure you found a body? It could be a twig or something. I'm guessing no one has checked on the pool in at least five years."

"It looks more like ten," Landon replied dryly. "And, yes, we're sure there's a body. I'm not new. Also, as you so graciously pointed out, I'm an FBI agent."

"You're a pain in the butt is what you are," Chief Terry countered. "Now, come on. I want to see this body."

I took a moment to survey the dirt road that led back to the highway. "Didn't you bring the medical examiner?"

"I have to confirm there's a body first."

"Yeah, but ... Landon confirmed it." I pointed toward my boyfriend. "Why isn't his word good enough?"

"She's got a point," Landon noted. "Technically, I outrank you."

"You're an agent. I'm a chief."

"I'm a Fed and you're a local."

"And I'm a witch," I added impatiently, their banter starting to grate. "Can we get this over with? I don't want to stay out here longer than necessary because ... well ... now I'm creeped out because there's a body in the pool."

"Oh, sweetie, don't let it get you down." Landon slipped his arm around my shoulders as we began walking toward the pool. "The camp is still magic. Just because we found a body in the pool doesn't mean this place isn't awesome. It simply means that ... we can never skinny dip here."

I shot him the meanest look in my repertoire. "There was no way you were ever getting me in that pool anyway."

"What about the lake?"

"Oh, well ... ."

"If you two don't end this conversation now I'll thump you both," Chief Terry warned. It was rare for him to threaten me, so I knew he meant business. "Now, show me this body."

Chief Terry made the same face as Landon when he saw the pool, a wrinkled-nose grimace that seemed to indicate his stomach was turning. "This is ... lovely."

"Look at that." I pointed at the rotting sign on the west side of the pool. I hadn't noticed it the first time we entered the space. "It's Mrs. Little's sign."

"Mrs. Little had a sign?" Landon asked, making sure to keep his hand on my arm so I didn't accidentally careen into the pool and ruin evidence.

"She bought her own sign," Chief Terry replied, his eyes flicking to the dilapidated slab of wood. "She paid for the pool, so she dedicated it to herself."

Landon snorted. "Oh, well, that's just priceless."

"I can think of a few other words for it."

I could, too, but we had other things to deal with. "There." I pointed when the hand came into view a second time. It seemed somehow smaller this time, and I was almost certain it belonged to a woman. "I don't think she's been here very long."

"What makes you say that?" Chief Terry asked as he carefully navigated closer. He looked grim as he hunkered down and tried to get a better look at the hand. It almost looked as if someone had fallen into the pool and tried to claw through the cover to get out and froze in a weird position. "Geez. That's definitely a body."

"Yes, I'm shocked, too," Landon drawled. "I can't believe you're confirming it. I mean ... I thought it could be a body, what with my training and all. Thankfully you were here to make sure I was on the right track."

Chief Terry scorched him with a dark look. "Yeah, yeah, yeah. I wanted to make sure. There's no need to work yourself up and get all sensitive."

Landon smirked. "I was just stating a fact."

"You haven't said why you think she's fresh, Bay," Chief Terry prodded, focusing on me. "There must be a reason. Do you see one of your ... you know .... friends?"

It took me a moment to translate what he was saying. "You mean a ghost?"

Chief Terry scowled. "I believe that's what I was referring to, though I would appreciate you not using that word in front of an audience."

I glanced around, confused. "What audience? It's just the three of us, and Landon knows I can see ghosts." Chief Terry knew, too. He was one of the first people who didn't share a genetic link with me who believed, and that was one of the reasons we shared such a tight bond. The other was that he stepped in as my father figure when I was a kid at a time I really needed someone, and he pretty much doted on me.

What can I say? I like being the center of attention sometimes. It's a Winchester family trait.

"You know what I mean." Chief Terry was calm as he stared at the hand. "We have to call the medical examiner out here. I don't want you accidentally slipping up in front of him."

"I'll try to refrain from doing something I've been trained not to do since I was five," I said dryly.

"You've got a mouth on you today," Chief Terry muttered, straightening. "I'm not aware of any missing person reports in the area. Someone has to be missing her."

"How can you be sure it's a girl?" I asked. "I mean ... the hand is small. I'm leaning that way, too. The skin hasn't been ravaged too much, which means no animals have stumbled across her as far as I can tell. It could be a small man, though." I swallowed hard. "Or a boy."

Terry shook his head. "I believe it's a woman. We won't know for sure until we get her out of there. For now, I just know it's a body. We need to get the medical examiner out here now. I have no idea what needs to be done to save evidence on a discovery like this. I mean ... do we drain the pool?"

Landon glanced around. "Where are the pool controls located?"

"How about you guys figure that out while I call for backup?"

"Great. We'll get right on that."

LANDON WASN'T GROUCHY AS MUCH as quiet as we circled the building looking for the pool controls. I knew that was a sign he was deep in thought.

"If you're worried this is going to screw up our memories of each other as kids, don't get your panties in a twist," I offered. "This is just a blip. The kismet destiny talk will survive."

He slid me a smirk as we rounded a shed. "I wasn't worried about that. Nothing can ruin those memories. I promise you that."

"So, what were you thinking about?"

"I'm just considering how difficult it would be for someone to find this location if they weren't already aware of its existence."

"Oh, so work stuff?" I chuckled as he forced open the shed door. There, sure enough, were the controls to the pool, covered in cobwebs and grime. "I didn't think there was electricity out here."

"There's not." Landon pointed to a panel at the far end of the room. "It's designed to hook up to a generator. That means if we need

AMANDA M. LEE

to pump the pool — and if these controls still work, which I doubt because they've been sitting here for a long time — that we'll need to arrange for a generator to be delivered."

"Aunt Tillie has four generators in her greenhouse," I offered, referring to my persnickety great-aunt, a woman who quite often caused Landon to see red because she was such a pain.

"Why would she need four generators?"

"She likes to be prepared. She's like a Boy Scout ... or a witch scout, in this particular instance."

He laughed. "Well, we'll see what the medical examiner says. I think this is going to be a tricky retrieval. I'm not going through the trouble of stealing one of her generators unless I know we really need it."

"Good plan."

The medical examiner was standing with Chief Terry and staring at the hand when we returned to the pool. I'd met Fred Armitage on several different cases. Hemlock Cove wasn't big enough to have its own medical examiner so every community in the county shared the expense.

"Hello, Agent Michaels. Ms. Winchester." Armitage was all business. "I understand you found the body."

"We did," Landon confirmed. "We were out here taking a look around and we happened to head over here. It was pretty obvious we needed to call for help after that."

"What were you doing out here in the first place?" His tone was accusatory, which caused me to purse my lips and glance at Landon.

"We were walking around," Landon replied simply. "Bay and I both attended camp here as kids. I haven't seen the place in a long time. We thought we would check it out."

"I thought you were from the middle part of the state," Armitage challenged as he extended a tape measure.

"I am, but I came up here for camp."

"Huh. That's ... weird."

"We like to think of it as a fun coincidence," Landon countered, agitation flitting through his eyes. "What can you tell me about this situation?"

"It's a hand," Armitage replied.

"Oh, gee, I never would've noticed," Landon shook his head. "Would you care to share with the class how someone managed to get into this pool?"

"That I can't tell you." Despite his superior attitude, Armitage looked perplexed. "There are a number of holes in the cover. I count seven or so. None look big enough for a body to slip through."

"Slip through?" Chief Terry rubbed his chin. "Are you saying this could be an accident?"

"We won't know until we get the body out of here. I'm a little worried that we're going to run into trouble with the water. It's probably not frozen on the top, but it's still dropping into the thirties at night. The water at the bottom is most likely frozen.

"There's every possibility that the body might be stuck, for lack of a better word," he continued. "If it is, we'll have to warm the water to get the body out. We could lose evidence if that happens."

"So, what are our alternatives?" Landon asked.

"We'll need a full crime scene team. You're with the FBI, so you can order that. The thing is, I can't see all that well with the brush on top of the cover. There might be a hole. She could've fallen in. If that's the case, this is most likely an accident."

I couldn't stop myself from asking the obvious question. "Why would someone purposely walk on top of a pool cover?"

"Maybe it's a homeless person who didn't care or saw something on the cover and wanted to take a risk retrieving it. Maybe it's a drunk or an addict who got confused. We can't know until we get access to the body."

"What are our other options?" I asked. "I mean ... if it's not an accident."

"Then someone deliberately put the body here," Armitage replied without hesitation.

"Wouldn't the cover have to be lifted for someone to shove a body under it?" Landon asked. "I'm no pool expert, but don't you need a special tool to handle the springs that hold the cover in place?"

"Yes, but that tool costs like five bucks at any general store. It's not as if it's difficult to find."

"So, what are you suggesting?" Chief Terry inquired. "Do you think someone murdered our victim, placed her body under the cover as a forensic move, and somehow the body shifted until it found an opening and the hand slipped through?"

"That's as good of a possibility as any," Armitage replied. "I'm not sure if it's smart for us to be wondering about possibilities right now. We need to get the body up. Given how cold the water is, there's a good chance it won't have decayed much. That could work in our favor."

His excitement at the prospect made me sick to my stomach. "Maybe I should wait over there," I suggested, pointing toward a spot far from the pool. "I don't want to see under the cover if I don't have to."

"That's a good idea." Landon rubbed the back of my neck. "I'll tell you as soon as we have any information."

"I can't wait."

IT TOOK ALMOST TWO hours, but Landon was true to his word. I knew when he started heading in my direction that things were about to take a turn. The medical examiner called for backup, which consisted of at least eight able-bodied individuals. They'd been steadily working since their arrival.

"Well?"

"It's a woman." Landon was grim. "She looks to be in her twenties, but we can't be sure of anything until we identify her."

"How did she die?"

"There are no obvious signs of distress to the body, meaning no gunshot wounds or cuts. That doesn't rule out murder. She could've been struck over the head or choked for all we know."

"You got the cover off. Do you think it's possible she fell in?"

"You mean slid in, like Armitage said? No. I think someone had to lift the cover and put her under it. We were lucky to have found her at all. By the way, the water is completely black. I don't even want to know what horrible things are growing in there. You can't see the bottom. I have a team coming from the home office to take over that part of the search."

"If someone put her under the cover she had to be murdered. There's no other solution."

"There's one. She could've died of natural causes, or even a drug overdose, and perhaps someone panicked and hid her body to keep people from finding out."

"Why would they do that?"

"Maybe for state assistance programs or something. I honestly don't know. I can't offer information on that until we know who she is. That's not going to happen until the medical examiner can fingerprint her. The body is kind of ... rigid ... because of the cold water. They have special things they need to do before they can warm it up to get fingerprints."

"Do I want to know what those special things are?"

"Nope. I don't want to know either."

"So ... where does that leave us?"

"With the owner of the property. We're heading out to talk to her. I thought you might want to come."

Any excuse to get away from the death permeating the camp. "Count me in. Let's get out of here."

THREE

Chief Terry and Landon opted to drive together to talk with the woman who owned the camp property. They took me with them for the ride, and I was settled in the backseat of Landon's Explorer when Chief Terry started explaining about Gertrude Morgan.

"Gertie and her husband Earl bought the property thirty years ago," he started. "They got it for a song because at that time no one thought building on Manistee Lake was a good idea. I bet if people had to do it all over again they would snap up that property in a heartbeat."

"So ... late eighties, right?" Landon did the math in his head. "That means they came in at a time when the industrial base here was still chugging along."

"Basically," Chief Terry confirmed. "Back in those days, people assumed everything would stay hunky-dory for the foreseeable future."

"I don't know that I'm comfortable with you using the phrase 'hunky-dory,'" I offered. "It makes me respect you just a little bit less."

"Don't push it." Chief Terry growled, but he turned and offered me a wink before continuing. "Technically, Gertie doesn't live in Hemlock Cove. She lives in Harlan Oaks, but that's barely a town. Never was — maybe a hundred people here or there — but it's basically her and a bunch of abandoned homes now."

"You're saying she's on her own?" Landon queried.

"I'm saying she's not really a part of any community," he clarified. "She's kind of a loner anyway."

"What about her husband?"

"Earl passed about eleven years ago. I'll have to look that up. I'm pretty sure it was more than a decade. I see Gertie from time to time, but she only comes into town to shop when she feels like it. She's not exactly the sociable sort."

"I remember her from when I was a kid," I offered, searching my memory. "She was always friendly. She loved it when we were at the camp and hung around quite often even though she hired counselors for most of the work."

"I think she and Earl had big dreams for that camp," Chief Terry said. "They hoped to make it a go-to destination for kids across the state. That didn't last very long. The camp did okay in the early days. I mean ... it was fine in the eighties and nineties. By the time the century turned, things were starting to fall apart."

"I went to camp after the turn of the century," I reminded him.

"You did. I'm sure if you think back to that time, though, you'll realize that the camp wasn't open the entire season. You had to call and rent the space if you wanted to use it, and that wasn't always easy because Gertie was feeling ornery in those days."

I didn't remember any of that. "I ... why?"

"Well, the camp never provided a sufficient full-time income. There were years right after they took over the camp that Gertie was convinced it would and Earl would be able to quit his job at the paper mill. But it never panned out.

"With each passing year, the dreams she had of running around all summer with a whistle while telling ghost stories slipped further and further from her grasp and she became bitterer," he continued.

"She should talk to Aunt Tillie," Landon countered as he navigated the highway. "She runs around with a whistle and tells ghost stories and does perfectly fine. Maybe there's a trick to the lifestyle."

Chief Terry rolled his eyes but otherwise didn't comment. "In addition to the camp not living up to expectations, she lost her son about ten years ago."

"I forgot she had a son," I admitted, sheepish. "He would hang around the camp sometimes when I was a kid, but he never seemed very happy."

"I don't know that much about Joey," Chief Terry admitted. "He would've been older than you and younger than me. He was a decent way behind me in school and graduated when you were still in middle school. He'd be about thirty-five now ... maybe thirty-seven. He wasn't exactly the go-getter type. But he didn't get in any trouble."

"What happened to him?" Landon asked as he checked his GPS.

"There was some sort of fire," Chief Terry replied. "I can't remember exactly how it played out. I'm almost positive it was determined to be accidental. It wasn't my case. Something happened and he never made it out of the shed he was living in on the property. It burned hot and fast. My predecessor handled it because he knew Gertie."

"That was after her husband died, right?" I was trying to remember.

"Her husband and Joey died close to each other," Chief Terry supplied. "It was less than a year. Joey would've been about twenty-five when he died. I'd have to check his records to be certain, but that's pretty close. He was still living with his parents at the time because he wasn't exactly motivated to get a job and pay his own bills."

"Basically you're saying he was lazy."

"Basically," Chief Terry agreed. "He got a few jobs here and there throughout the years. I seem to remember Edward Sherman hired him to help with his fields one year, but that didn't work out because Joey didn't like getting up before noon and his mother was constantly making excuses. Most people figured out quickly that Joey wasn't going to put in the effort."

I didn't understand that. My mother and aunts instilled a dedicated work ethic in my cousins and me at a young age. We all had our quirks — Thistle and Clove mostly — but we were all hard workers. "So, Gertie was paying his way when he was twenty-five?"

"That's how I remember things," Chief Terry confirmed. "Gertie was broken-hearted when Earl died. By the time Joey followed, she was numb with grief."

"And she's been alone out here since?"

"She has. People have tried engaging her to play cards at the senior center and join in with some of the festivals, but she refuses. She lives off Earl's pension and Social Security, barely squeaks by."

"Why doesn't she sell the camp land?" I asked. "I mean, she could get a pretty penny for that property from some developer who wants to build a big house or even condos."

"I know people have sniffed around trying to buy it," Chief Terry replied. "She always turns them down. She says she and Earl had a dream and she's not ready to give up that dream."

"Yeah, but ... that dream is dead," I pointed out. "The whole idea of summer camps like that is dead."

"You don't have to tell me. I agree with you. She isn't convinced that's true, and she has a right to believe what she wants."

"I guess." I tapped my bottom lip as I stretched in the backseat. Something about the story niggled at the back of my brain. "I remember the pool being built after we stopped going multiple times a year. We still went ... but Mom and the aunts could only talk us into it once a summer. If the camp was already in trouble when we were there, why build that pool?"

Chief Terry made a face. "That was Margaret. Go figure. She had it in her head that we could turn that camp into a place where the youth of Walkerville would want to hang out. I tried explaining that the location was too far for kids who didn't have cars to just wander out there, but she wouldn't listen.

"Anyway, she sat down with Gertie and they came up with the idea of making it a community pool," he continued. "The town council was going to pay her a monthly stipend and Margaret was convinced that would keep the gangs from loitering on the streets."

Landon snorted. "Walkerville had gangs?"

"Only in Margaret's head. There was an old pool on the property, but it was empty and covered. You kids were kept from it because it was a safety hazard. That pool was essentially dumped and refurbished in one summer."

"Did the kids visit the camp?"

"Kind of. I mean ... they did for a month or so. It was a big deal. Everyone loves a pool. The problem is that parents got tired of driving their sons and daughters out there, so it really lasted just the one summer. There was a kind of overflow from the first summer to the second, so I guess it's more accurate to say two summers. Then the camp became a ghost town again."

"It's kind of sad," I mused, staring out the window. "Gertie actually wanted to give something to the community. It's too bad it didn't work out for her."

"I agree. Just be prepared, though. Gertie is a little ... nutty ... from spending so much time alone. She's not 'I'm going to kill you' crazy or anything, but she's not 'let's do complicated math problems' sane either."

I pressed my lips together to keep from laughing. His sense of humor showed itself at the oddest of times. "We'll keep that in mind."

GERTIE'S HOUSE WAS ESSENTIALLY A glorified shack in the woods. I'm sure at some point it was a beautiful cabin with lovely accents and gingerbread trim. Now the roof sagged and the front porch looked as if it should be condemned.

"Are you sure we shouldn't send senior services out here to check on her?" Landon asked as he put his hand to my back and glanced around at the cluttered parcel. "This can't be safe or sanitary. I'm pretty sure there's a nest of raccoons living in that old truck."

"That's Earl's truck," Chief Terry said. "She pitches a fit if you mention getting rid of it ... so don't do that."

"Duly noted." Landon held my hand as we climbed the rickety steps that led to the front door and then gave me a reassuring squeeze before releasing it. He was in work mode when he knocked on the door.

Curiosity had me giving the small woman who wrenched open the door a few minutes later a long scan. Gertie looked as I remembered her ... only more disheveled ... and grayer ... and maybe a little unhinged. I could understand what Chief Terry was saying about the isolation causing her to act strangely. The way her eyes bounced between our faces reminded me of a bad horror movie, one in which an elderly kook lives in a house at the edge of the mayhem and serves as a harbinger to warn partying teens that they're about to die. That's how I felt now.

"Hello, Gertie." Chief Terry adopted a pleasant smile as he clasped his hands together in front of him. "How are you today?"

Gertie didn't return the smile. "I have hemorrhoids, Irritable Bowel Syndrome and heartburn. How about you?"

Chief Terry didn't miss a beat. "I'm managing to skate by," he replied. "This is Landon Michaels. He's an FBI agent who is stationed here these days." He flicked his eyes to me. "And I'm sure you remember Bay Winchester. She's Winnie's girl."

Gertie's eyes landed on me. "I remember. You were one of those heathens who liked to party at the campground when you were a teenager."

Oh, well, I'd forgotten all about that. Apparently she remembered, so we were all good. "I don't think we went out to the old camp more than a few times," I responded. "I hope we didn't cause any damage?"

"Would you care if you did?"

That was a loaded question. "Of course I would." I'd learned to lie from the best, so I delivered the statement with as much gusto as possible. "I would want to make amends. Did we destroy anything? I seem to remember us being respectful partiers."

Landon slid me a sidelong look as his lips quirked.

"I see you have a lot in common with Tillie," Gertie supplied as she held open the door. "You might as well come in. It's not warm enough to let all the heat out."

I followed Landon and Chief Terry inside the cabin and was thankful to see it looked much better inside than outside. It was homey and warm, and Gertie had a kettle boiling on the stove in the kitchen.

"Why don't you tell me what's going on and we'll get this awkward encounter behind us as fast as possible," she demanded.

"We are here for a reason," Chief Terry confirmed.

"I figured."

"It has to do with the camp, Gertie."

She stilled, her hand halfway to the kettle. "Was there a fire? Oh, please tell me it didn't burn down. I don't know that I can take it if it burned down."

"It didn't burn down," Chief Terry said hurriedly. "It's still standing."

"Well, then whatever it is can't be that bad."

"I wouldn't be so sure about that," I muttered under my breath, earning a warning look from Chief Terry.

"A body was found in the pool." Chief Terry opted to blurt it out rather than drag it out. "We don't know much yet. It's a young woman. We're not sure how she died. She was found under the pool cover. There were no tears big enough to suggest she somehow fell through. That means someone had to pull the cover over her."

Gertie blinked several times then snatched the kettle off the stove the second it began whistling. "Well, that is unfortunate," she said finally, shaking her head. "How did you even find a body? I mean ... did you get a call or something?"

"I discovered it," Landon volunteered quickly. "I visited the camp when I was a kid and I asked Bay to take me. I wanted to see it again. We were walking around when we saw a hand poking out of the water."

"You mean you were trespassing."

"I guess, if that's the way you want to look at it."

"There's no other way to look at it," she snapped. "I don't like trespassers." Gertie's gaze was weighted when it landed on me. "I mean ... I really hate trespassers."

"If you would like to press charges for the trespassing, that's your prerogative," Chief Terry offered, calm. "That doesn't change the fact that a body was found in the pool and we need to know if you're aware of how it got there."

"Are you asking me if I put the body in the pool?" Gertie was incredulous. "I'm seventy years old. I already told you about the hemorrhoids. How do you think I managed that?"

"Ma'am, we're not saying we think you killed her," Landon said hurriedly. "It's just ... well ... we're wondering when you last visited the camp. Perhaps you saw someone hanging around that might be of interest to us."

"I haven't been out to the camp in months," Gertie said, bitterness practically wafting off her in waves as she shook her head. "It depresses me to see it how it is. Plus, I have arthritis in my knees. I can't get around all that well."

"Can you be more specific about the last time you were out there?" Chief Terry pressed.

"It was before winter. I checked on the property in the fall, before the snow. I always do. It was quiet. No one was out there. If you're thinking there are squatters out there, I don't see how they would make it work. There's no food source in that area and the heat to the main building has been turned off for years."

"What about fireplaces?" Landon asked.

"There's nothing inside the cabins. There's a fire pit not far from the lake, but it's overgrown with weeds because no one has built a fire out there in years."

"What about neighbors?" Chief Terry asked. "A few people have homes out there. Have you ever asked any of them to check on the camp property for you? That would save you some wear and tear on your knees."

"I don't want nothing to do with those people," Gertie barked, frustration poking through her demeanor. "They keep trying to buy my land from me. They keep saying it's better for me. They don't know. That land is all I have left that I care about.

"We were going to make it a grand place," she continued, turning to me. "Earl and me. We were going to make it one of those camps that people remember forever. You know. You came to camp. You still remember, don't you?"

I swallowed hard at her earnest nature. "I definitely remember."

"It was supposed to be something we could enjoy forever, but it didn't happen the way we thought it would. You want to know why?"

"I'm guessing it had something to do with the changing attitudes of adolescence," I answered honestly. "Children became more interested in television and video games than camp. It's terrible, but it is what it is."

The look Gertie shot me was withering. "It's because of those horror movies. The one with the hockey mask killer who walks around stabbing people. That's why my camp failed."

That was so not where I expected her to go. "*Friday the 13th?*"

She snapped her fingers. "That's the one! Those movies are all about people going to camp and being killed. That ruined my camp. I thought about suing the people who made those movies, but I didn't want to give them more attention than they already had."

I risked a glance at Landon and found him watching Gertie with an unreadable expression.

"I thought those movies came out in the early eighties," I said finally, grasping for something to say. "Your camp didn't close until almost thirty years later. How could the movies be to blame?"

"They're still making those movies!" She spoke harshly and jabbed a finger in my direction, forcing me to hold my hands up in surrender. "Those movies ruined my life. Mark my words."

"I can see that," Landon said, his expression neutral. "I'm sorry that happened. Still, we need to know if you can think of anyone who might be hanging around the camp."

"The camp is off limits. Anyone going there doesn't have permission. Do you think they're going to stop and tell me before they break the law?"

"Fair enough." Landon inhaled deeply and smiled. "It was a pleasure meeting you. I hope we have answers to share about what's going on ... and soon."

"I won't hold my breath."

FOUR

Landon sent me to Hemlock Cove with his Explorer. He stayed with Chief Terry at the campground — the body had been removed, although the members of the tech team Landon sent for were arguing about the best way to drain the pool — and he insisted that it was better for me to head back rather than wait for him.

As owner of The Whistler, Hemlock Cove's only newspaper, part of me felt as if I should stay at the camp to gather information. The other part knew that Landon and Chief Terry would provide me with answers as soon as they had them.

With that in mind, I headed to town. I parked Landon's Explorer in front of the police station and walked to the coffee shop rather than the office, where work would be required.

"Hello, Bay."

"Hello, Mrs. Gunderson." I smiled at the woman behind the counter. She was the friendly sort, unless you tried to dig for information she didn't want to share. Most of the time she was more than happy to gossip about others. When it came to talking about herself, though, she was tighter than a Kardashian jonesing for a camera fix. "How are you today?"

"Can't complain. You want your usual?"

I nodded. "It's starting to get warmer," I noted as she fixed my mocha latte. "Landon and I were out at the old camp this afternoon, looking around. Do you know Gertie?"

Mrs. Gunderson shrugged. "Everyone knows Gertie. She's not exactly the friendly sort. Why do you ask?"

"We found a body out there." I saw no reason to lie. News would spread quickly and it was wise to get ahead of it.

"You did?" Mrs. Gunderson's gray eyebrows flew up her forehead. "Was it anyone we know?"

"I don't think so. I didn't see her come out of the water." I explained about the pool. "Chief Terry and Landon were there and didn't say anything, so that makes me think Chief Terry didn't recognize her."

"So, she might not be a local," Mrs. Gunderson mused as she turned on the steamer for my milk. When she was finished, she combined the ingredients with a conflicted look on her face. "Gertie has never exactly been friendly. She stops by occasionally. I make sure I don't charge her full price for coffee and doughnuts because I know she can't afford it. I think she's just eking by out there."

"She seemed a little off," I said. "I went with Landon and Chief Terry to talk to her. She seemed confused ... except for when she remembered I used to party out at the camp with Clove and Thistle when we were teenagers. That she remembered with absolute clarity."

Mrs. Gunderson chuckled. "Yes, well, she is a bit of a loon. But compared to some of the others in town, I don't think she's the worst of the lot. You don't suspect her, do you?"

"Apparently she has hemorrhoids and an arthritic knee. I don't think she's up to the task."

"That's good to know."

"I doubt she had anything to do with it," I said. "The thing is, if someone is hanging around that camp we should probably figure out who sooner rather than later. It's about the time of year when kids start running into the woods to party and play. If we have a predator ... ." I left the sentence hanging.

"Ah." Mrs. Gunderson knowingly bobbed her head. "I get what you're saying. I don't know anyone who regularly visits that area, especially this time of the year. Some of the locals fish up there, but it's too early in the season."

"Right." I pursed my lips and accepted the coffee cup she handed to me. "I guess I'll leave that to Landon and Chief Terry to figure out. Thank you for your time."

"No problem." She beamed and then held up a hand to stop me before I turned. "Just one quick question."

I sipped the foam on the top of my drink and waited.

"I heard that Terry and your mother have a date tomorrow. Is that true?"

The Hemlock Cove gossip train seemed to be in working order. "I don't know that I'm supposed to talk about that," I hedged. "I don't think my mother will find it funny."

"It's true, though?"

I nodded. "They have their first date tomorrow night."

"All I can say is that it's about time."

I knew an entire family of people who happened to believe the exact same thing.

THE RESPONSIBLE THING TO DO upon exiting the coffee shop would've been to head to The Whistler and start researching the history of the camp. I had no doubt we'd written articles on the business over the years — it was a regular mainstay for fun photos when there was nothing to write about but the weather during the summer — but I was antsy, so I headed toward Hypnotic instead.

The magic store my cousins Clove and Thistle owned was in a state of chaos when I cleared the threshold. Clove, her dark hair pulled back in a loose bun, sat on a couch in the middle of the store. She had garment bags strewn all over the furniture, and it took me a moment to figure out why.

That's when Thistle, her hair a lovely shade of periwinkle blue, stomped to the center of the store. She was dressed in a taffeta monstrosity — orange in color, the trim a vibrant shade of green — and she looked absolutely murderous.

"I am not wearing this!"

I took in the scene with glee as I worked overtime to keep from laughing out loud. "You look marvelous," I enthused, earning a death glare from Thistle and a legitimate smile from Clove.

"Doesn't she?" Clove was on her feet, her hips wiggling as she moved closer to our crabby cousin. "I mean ... check it out. I'm thinking about this design for the bridesmaid dresses. They sent me a sample for you and Thistle to try on, so it's a little big, but you get the general idea."

Did I ever. Thistle was the thinnest of us all and she looked as if she was swimming in material ... and it was material that crinkled when she moved. I was never going to forget this day as long as I lived thanks to that noise anchoring the memory home.

"She looks like a dream," I said, lobbing an evil smirk in Thistle's direction when Clove turned to absorb the full picture yet again.

"I hate you," Thistle hissed, her eyes dangerous slits. "I know exactly what you're doing and I'm going to make you pay."

I feigned innocence. "Our cousin is getting married ... and to the man of her dreams. All I'm trying to do is make sure she has the happiest day in the world. I mean, she deserves it."

"I do deserve it," Clove agreed, her lips curving as she stared at the dress. "What do you think?"

In truth, the dress was what monsters ran and hid from in scary stories. It was ugly, dated and altogether unacceptable. It was also clearly driving Thistle nuts, so that meant I kind of liked it. "There's a nostalgic quality to it," I supplied. "It reminds me of the eighties."

"That's what I was going for!" Clove's eyes sparkled. "It's kind of like *Pretty Woman*, don't you think?"

Not even a little. "Wasn't *Pretty Woman* released in 1990?"

"How can you possibly know that?" Thistle asked as she stared at her reflection in the mirror behind the counter. "I look like the Great Pumpkin!"

I had to bite the inside of my cheek to keep from laughing. She totally looked like the Great Pumpkin. "Mom loves *Pretty Woman*. She has the DVD on the shelf in the living room. Landon and I borrowed it this winter when we were locked in the guesthouse for that weekend blizzard."

Thistle's gaze was withering. "I can't believe I just wasted fifteen seconds of my life listening to that story."

"Oh, you sound crabby." I hid my smile behind my latte as I sipped. "You shouldn't be crabby. This is Clove's big day. You should give her what she wants."

"Oh, I'm going to give her something all right." Thistle slowly dragged her eyes to Clove. "If you think I'm wearing this you're even dumber than you look … and that's pretty dumb. I don't think that's possible, but I wouldn't suggest trying to prove me wrong."

Clove's previously happy expression disappeared. "But … you look like a dream."

"I look like the worst nightmare I've ever had. And, if you try to make me wear this dress, not only will I make you eat enough dirt to choke a giant, I'll also pick a dress that's for skinny people when it's my turn to get married. You know how you hate skinny people dresses."

Clove was shaped like an upside-down pear — extremely top-heavy and short — so Thistle's threat hit home. "You wouldn't dare," Clove hissed. "You know I can't stand those dresses made for walking twigs."

"If you try making me wear this — the color is worse than the fit, Clove! — then I will take things to the next level when it's my turn."

Clove was the first of us to get married. That seemed somehow fitting. She was the one who daydreamed about weddings and princes when we were kids. She wanted to slip a ring on her finger, push out a few kids and live happily ever after. That's all she ever talked about.

Thistle and I, on the other hand, wanted to solve mysteries … and storm castles to save those in need … and take the ring to Mount Doom … and blow up the Death Star. That's simply how we rolled.

Clove getting married first didn't bother anyone. Er, well, mostly. There might've been slight agitation here and there, but Thistle and I were genuinely happy for her and her fiancé, Sam Cornell. The dress fight would turn ugly if a precedent wasn't set early.

"Do you really want to threaten me when I hold your orange dress fate in my hands?" Clove finally challenged.

"Do you really want to threaten me when I can make you wear the color yellow?" Thistle shot back.

Clove visibly blanched. "You know I hate yellow! It's not okay to look like a lemon sponge cake."

"I'll make you wear a yellow lace dress, Clove!"

"Lace? you can't wear lace. That's what hookers wear."

I was already growing tired of the conversation, so I slid into the chair at the edge of the room and propped my feet on the table. "Who wants to hear about my day?"

They ignored me.

"Hookers wear fishnet," Thistle argued. "They don't wear lace. What hooker have you ever seen wearing lace?"

"Oh, hookers wear lace. In *Pretty Woman*, Julia Roberts wore a lace cocktail dress to her first outing as Richard Gere's date."

"I don't think it counts if you saw it in a movie," I offered helpfully.

"Shut up, Bay," Thistle ordered. "I swear to you, Clove, if you try to make me wear this, I'll make you wear lemon lace and learn a line dance."

Clove's mouth dropped open. "You wouldn't dare make me try to learn a line dance."

"I would. It will be the Macarena all over again."

One summer Clove insisted we learn the Macarena after she saw it on a television show. The fad had been over for years, but she misunderstood and thought it was a new thing. Unfortunately, that's when we found out we were rhythmically challenged — except for Thistle, who merely hated the idea of learning a dance designed for the masses — and the fad died a quick second death. It was probably for the best.

"Fine." Clove threw up her hands in defeat. "I won't make you wear the dress. Are you happy? I'll pick something else."

"I won't be happy unless I can pick the dress myself," Thistle shot back.

"That's never going to happen. It's my wedding."

"Well, then you'd better get used to the taste of dirt ... because I am not wearing anything that looks remotely like this."

The conversation was starting to drag now. "Does anyone want to hear about the body I found out at our old summer camp?"

Even though they were in the midst of a fight to the death, they both turned and stared at me.

"You found a body?" Thistle checked the clock on the wall. "It's not even two yet. How can you have found a body?"

I wasn't sure what form of logic she was utilizing. "Well ... Landon and I went to the camp because he wanted to see where our destinies collided — he's seriously convinced we were always meant to find each other, by the way, and it's kind of cute — and when we were checking out the old pool I saw a hand sticking out of it."

The fight over the dress was shelved as Thistle and Clove crowded close to me.

"What kind of hand are we talking about?" Clove asked.

"The bionic kind," I drawled. "What kind of hand do you think? A human hand. It was poking through the pool cover. We had to call the medical examiner and everything. Landon has a crew out there draining the pool for evidence because no one knows what's inside of that thing. Landon said the water was black ... which is freaky when you think about it."

"It's gross is what it is." Thistle made a face. "Still, that's weird. Do they have any idea how it happened?"

"Nope. All I know is that it's a young female and someone had to pull the cover over her body because she couldn't have slipped through a hole or anything. I guess there are no holes in the cover big enough for that to have happened."

"So ... that means someone killed her," Clove said.

"Unless it was an accidental death someone tried to cover up. I doubt that's the case, though. I'm leaning toward murder."

"Oh, well, that's good," Thistle deadpanned. "We haven't had a murder in, like, a full week. We were due."

I ignored the sarcasm. "Landon says he'll let me know when they identify the deceased. Until then, there's not much to do but wait. We don't know how she ended up there or what happened to her. It could be something big or simply an accident."

"It's depressing." Thistle turned her head toward the door when the wind chimes in front of it alerted that someone was entering. "Speak of the devil."

I shifted and smiled when I saw Landon moving toward me. "That was quick. I thought you would be out there the better part of the day. Your vehicle is parked in front of the building."

"I saw it." Landon dropped a quick kiss on the top of my head and settled next to me. "The medical examiner got a hit right away when he scanned our girl's fingerprints."

"Really? That was fast."

"It was. There was a missing person report on her. Her name is Hannah Bishop. She's twenty-five and she disappeared out of Grand Rapids two months ago."

I furrowed my brow, surprised. "Two months ago? Has she been in that pool the entire time? That's not possible."

"I don't know. The medical examiner says the body is pretty much frozen ... except for the hand that was poking through the pool cover."

I didn't want to think about that too much. "Um ... gross."

"Yup. The hand would've deteriorated quickly if we hadn't stumbled across the body. I guess we're lucky a scavenger didn't chew it off or something."

"Are you trying to gross us out?" Thistle complained.

Landon slid her a sidelong look. "Are you auditioning for a play or something? Let me guess, you're the pumpkin princess?"

Her eyes were glittery slits when they landed on Clove. "What did I tell you?"

"Fine. Take the dress off." Clove waved her away. "Do they know how the girl died?"

"No." Landon shook his head and moved his hand to the back of my neck. "We probably won't know that until tomorrow. Bishop's parents are driving up from Grand Rapids in the morning. The medical examiner's office made notification, which I'm not happy about, but we'll be able to interview them before lunch tomorrow."

"That's a good thing, right?"

He shrugged. "We need answers, starting with what she was doing up here. They're our best shot at getting them. For now, we're at a standstill until we get a lead."

I rested my head on his shoulder and looked to Thistle, who was still standing in the middle of the room. "If you put on a green hat you'd look like a carrot."

She glowered at me. "Do you want me to hurt you?"

"I was simply saying that's better than being a pumpkin."

"In what world?"

"It was a simple statement." I held up my hands in capitulation. "Forget I said anything."

Thistle ominously glared at Clove as she headed toward the storage room behind the counter. "Lemon lace, Clove. I will make it happen if you don't make this dress go away."

"I'm on it," Clove called after her, a small smile playing at the corners of her lips. "The next one will be even worse," she said, lowering her voice to a conspiratorial whisper once Thistle was out of earshot. "It'll be pink ... and require a Wonderbra."

"Oh, well, that should go over well," I said.

"She'll be crying by the time I'm done with her."

FIVE

Peg stood on the other side of the door when Landon and I let ourselves into the family living quarters of The Overlook, the inn my mother and aunts ran, shortly before dinner.

The pig – a spotted teacup variety – snorted when she saw us and then proceeded to wiggle her butt as she danced around the room. She wore a camouflage tutu and a rhinestone collar.

"Hello, Peg," Landon greeted the animal with a fond smile. He found Aunt Tillie's new pet much more entertaining than I did. Of course, Peg hadn't crapped in his shoes the first day she joined the family. That distinction was saved for me.

Snort. Snort.

Peg wiggled her butt as Landon leaned over to pet her. She was a baby, which meant she weighed about fifteen pounds. The vet Aunt Tillie called to check her out upon delivery said she could grow to be sixty pounds. My mother and aunts put up a fight, said they wouldn't keep the pig and demanded Aunt Tillie send her back. When they called the sellers, though, they said all sales were final.

Mom decided to take the pig to the Humane Society, but the people there said they weren't equipped for pigs. Then Mom took her to a farm. They were happy to take her. They even said she would make for some fine bacon. Mom couldn't deal with that – not thinking about where the bacon came from was easier for her in that strange land of denial where she enjoyed living – so Peg was now officially part of the family.

She was totally taking over.

"We should get a pet," Landon announced as he sat on the ground and stroked the pig, who couldn't get enough of him. Peg climbed in his lap and rubbed her nose against his face as she continued making her now familiar noises.

Snort. Snort.

"We're not getting a pig." I was firm on that. "Absolutely not. No way. No how. Nothing doing."

"I wasn't necessarily talking about a pig." He smiled as he tilted his head back and forth, as if he was having a silent conversation with Peg that only they could hear.

Snort. Snort.

"What were you talking about?"

He shrugged, noncommittal. "I don't know. What about a dog?"

"We both work a lot of hours and take off in the middle of the night without any notice," I reminded him. "You could be called away for weeks on an assignment."

He shot me a look. "That's happened once since we got together, and I only took that assignment so I could have leverage over my boss to move in with you here."

"Yeah, but it could happen."

"It could, but what the odds? Besides, your mother and aunts live within easy walking distance. If we needed help, or to let the dog out, they could come and get it."

He seemed earnest, as if he was really interested in getting a dog. I had to nip that in the bud. "We can't until I'm positive I'm in control of my magic."

He slid his eyes to me, confused. "What do you mean?"

"Dogs are on a different wavelength than humans. They see and hear ghosts. With my new powers … ." I didn't finish what I was going to say. I couldn't. My necromancer powers were a relatively new occurrence. It was only recently that I realized the ghosts I could always talk to were required to do my bidding if I unleashed my powers. I'd done it twice now – both times to make a killer pay – and I was still coming to grips with my new reality.

"Is that true?" Landon asked.

I nodded. "Why do you think there are such things as dog whistles?"

"That's because they can hear things we can't."

"They can sense things most normal humans can't either."

He pursed his lips, looking me over with a studied gaze. "You could be hosing me," he said. "You might simply not want a dog – which I don't get because they're awesome – and this is your way of fooling me. You're good enough to pull it off."

"Thank you."

"That wasn't a compliment."

"I'm taking it as one anyway," I shot back. "I don't have anything against dogs. I had one as a kid … and I loved him. I was crushed when he died."

"Sugar." Landon bobbed his head. "I've heard the stories. You know, loving another pet doesn't mean you'll forget him, right?"

"I know that, but now is not the time."

"Because of your magic."

"Yes. And the fact that I just bought a new business and I'm working more hours than ever."

"A business you could take the dog to while you work."

Oh, he just had an answer for everything. "And what if I'm right and my magic somehow hurts a dog?"

"I think you're making excuses because you don't want to replace Sugar," Landon countered. "Somehow you think it's disloyal. I'm not sure I'm equipped to deal with that form of neurosis this evening, so we're going to table this discussion. At some point, though, I'm going to want a dog. I'm going to want any kids we have to play with a dog.

That doesn't need to happen right now, though, so I'm going to pick my battles."

"That's probably wise."

"Besides, I have Peg to play with." He lifted the pig and rubbed his nose against the animal's snout. "I'm going to teach you to walk on a leash and dress you in something manly so I can take you in public this summer."

"Please take her," Mom announced as she breezed into the room from the kitchen. She had a spatula in her hand and looked surprised to see us. "Why are you guys hanging around in here?"

"Why aren't you cooking dinner?" Landon countered, looking up from the pig. He shrank back when Mom pinned him with a dark look. "Have I mentioned how lovely you look when you have that 'just baking something good' glow?"

I had to bite the inside of my cheek to keep from laughing at his hangdog expression.

Mom smiled at him as if she was feeling nothing but adoration, but I could read the tension radiating beneath her perfect posture. "Thank you, Landon. You can still take that pig."

"No, he can't." Aunt Tillie, wearing camouflage leggings that matched Peg's tutu, appeared in the doorway. She was dressed for action – I could practically feel the chip digging into her shoulder – and I sensed we'd interrupted some sort of argument. "Peg is a part of the family. You don't just give away family.

"Er, well, we can give away Thistle," she continued. "If Landon wants a pet, let's put a collar on her. She's nowhere near as cute as Peg."

"I agree wholeheartedly with that." Landon gave the pig another pat before standing. "Not the part about taking Thistle. We don't want her. No one is as cute as Peg."

"I think I'm being supplanted by a pig," I muttered, shaking my head.

"I guess that means you're done eating bacon, right, Landon?" Mom asked pointedly.

Landon stilled. He'd obviously never considered the question. "Oh, well ... ."

My lips curved. "Sounds like a good idea," I said. "I mean ... that could be Peg's brother or sister. You don't want to be the guy eating Peg's brother or sister. That's kind of like cannibalism."

Landon made a face. "Are you trying to piss me off?"

"No. I'm being honest. I mean ... look at this face." I bent over and grabbed Peg, ignoring the way she fought my efforts as I lifted her. "How can you eat this face?"

"Put her down, Bay." All mirth fled Landon's features as he glared at me. "She doesn't like being picked up that way."

I acquiesced, but only because the pig was heavy and I had no upper body strength. Holding her was awkward. "She loves you, Landon." I offered up my best pretty smile.

"And I'm done talking about this." Landon refused to meet Peg's forlorn gaze as she tried to get his attention by dancing. She was used to him petting her for extended periods. He had other things on his mind this evening. "What's for dinner?"

"Pork loin," Mom replied without missing a beat.

It took everything I had not to choke on my laughter as Landon's expression fell.

"Seriously?" He almost looked sick to his stomach.

"No." Mom shook her head. "We haven't been able to cook pork products since Aunt Tillie brought her home. We have tacos, enchiladas and burritos, as well as homemade salsa and guacamole. You know ... all your favorite Mexican fixings."

"But no pork, right?" I asked.

Mom shot me a look. "I would let that subject go, Bay."

"Definitely," Landon agreed, slipping his arm around my waist. "Mexican food sounds great."

I was more than happy to let conversation regarding Peg fall by the wayside if it meant I could change the subject to something near and dear to my heart. "Fine. I'm done talking about Peg."

"I wish that could be the rule of the house every moment of every day," Mom said as she strode into the kitchen. "I'm sick of talking about Peg."

"Don't listen to her," Aunt Tillie soothed Peg. "She's just jealous because you're my new favorite and she and her sisters have no way of supplanting you as the queen of the house. In fact ... yeah ... I think I should get you a tiara."

Mom merely sighed. "I hate that pig."

She looked so tired I momentarily thought about letting her slide away without commenting on the big to-do of the following evening. I would've had to turn in my witch card if I did, though. "Let's talk about something else." I clapped my hands to show my enthusiasm. "For example, let's talk about your date with Chief Terry."

Landon brightened considerably. "Yes! Let's talk about that." He grabbed the huge bowl of guacamole sitting on the counter. "Have you picked out a special outfit for your date? Do you know where he's taking you? Have you thought about protection so you don't make Bay a big sister so late in her life?"

Furious, I shot him a dirty look. "Late in my life?"

"That came out wrong," he said hurriedly.

"I would start running if I were you," my Aunt Marnie warned him. "You're in trouble now. You stepped in it with both of them."

Landon decided to prove he was more bravado than brains. "I've got everything under control. Trust me."

"Just in case, I'll take that from you." Aunt Twila, her clown-red hair shining under the warm kitchen lights, plucked the guacamole bowl from his hands. "I don't want to risk you dropping it when the women in this house decide to start smacking you around."

"I think you might've misconstrued what I was really trying to say," Landon said sweetly.

"And what was that?" Mom asked.

"That you're all lovely, the best cooks ever and I'm the luckiest man alive because you allow me to be part of your lives." He sounded so sincere, flashed such a charming smile, it was impossible for the women in the room – including me – not to melt.

Aunt Tillie was the only one who didn't fall for his game. "You're so full of crap you should be dressed in brown and covered in flies."

"And thank you for that lovely visual," Landon muttered. "Can we eat? I think I'm about to die of hunger. That's the only excuse I have for allowing you guys to trap me multiple times in the same conversation."

"Yes, we can eat." Mom gave him a swat with her spatula to get him moving.

The dining room was empty when I slid through the doors. It was early in the week, so that wasn't a big surprise. The Overlook's most popular days are Thursday through Sunday. The other days were something of a dead zone, especially before the summer season kicked into high gear.

"Just us tonight?" I asked as I sat in my usual chair.

"Just us," Mom confirmed, shifting a platter of chopped taco vegetables toward the middle of the table. "It's a quiet night. We're not fully booked again for a couple of weeks."

"That's a nice break for you," Landon noted as he grabbed the container of warm tortilla shells. "It allows you to get caught up on things."

"What things?" Aunt Tillie asked blandly. "What is it you think they need to get caught up on?"

Landon's face was blank. "What do you mean?"

"You said they need to catch up on things," Aunt Tillie replied without hesitation. "You must feel that they're dropping the ball on certain tasks ... that's why they need to catch up. You should tell them all about it."

Landon scowled as he grabbed the platter of seasoned beef. "I'm not falling for that. We need to talk about something else."

I opened my mouth to bring up Chief Terry, but Mom silenced me with a jab of her finger.

"Don't even think about it," Mom warned, steam practically coming out of her ears when she picked up on my intentions. "I brought you into this world. I can take you right back out of it."

She sounded serious. Now probably wasn't the time to push her. "That's not what I was going to bring up," I lied, smoothly switching tactics. "Did you hear I found a body today?"

"Yes, at the camp," Mom replied, not missing a beat. "I think it's horrible that a homeless person broke in and accidentally drowned. I hope things are fixed so that can't happen again."

I knit my eyebrows, confused. "Who told you that?"

"That's what's going around town."

"Well, it's not true," Landon said, handing me the pico de gallo. "The woman we found was young, twenty-five. She was missing out of Grand Rapids. We haven't talked to her parents yet, but we don't see any indication that she was homeless."

"Oh." Mom appeared legitimately confused. "That's what the women at the supermarket were saying. They were all atwitter, said Margaret Little had the inside scoop and that's what she was saying."

Oh, well, that explained things. "You should've learned your lesson a long time ago about listening to Mrs. Little," I pointed out.

"She probably only said that because she doesn't want people to remember she donated that pool," Aunt Tillie argued, reaching toward the condiment platter and grabbing a handful of lettuce. I watched with morbid fascination as she slipped it under the table, to where Peg patiently waited to be fed.

"That's a point I didn't think about," I admitted as I filled a taco shell with my favorite fixings. "The dedication sign is still there, the one she bought for herself ... and then had that weird dedication ceremony to unveil."

"Yes, the ceremony where she was the only one who showed up, so she made all the kids get out of the lake and attend," Aunt Tillie drawled. "I remember it well. She was upset because there was something wrong with the sign."

Now that she mentioned it, the words jogged something in my memory. "Right. Her name was misspelled. Margaret Bitter. She said she double-checked the name and they had the right one and that someone else called and changed it after she placed the order." I slid my eyes to Aunt Tillie. "And I just now realized that was you."

Aunt Tillie adopted an air of innocence. "I have no idea what you're talking about."

"Right."

Landon chuckled as he took the sour cream from me. "We talked to the woman who owns the camp. She seems a little ... out there. I'm not sure she'll be any help. Tracking down anyone who has been hanging around that property won't be easy because of the way it's set up. If someone wants to hide there, there's not much that can be done to stop them ... or detect them, for that matter."

"Gertie?" Mom nodded as she smacked Aunt Tillie to keep her from feeding Peg a handful of tomatoes. "I will lock that pig out of the dining room during meals if you're not careful."

"I'm not afraid of you." Aunt Tillie said the words, but she pulled her hand back. "I wasn't doing anything anyway."

Mom continued to stare at her for a long beat and then focused on me. "Gertie lost everything. It's normal for that to take a toll on people. I mean ... she lost her husband and son months apart."

"And that fire that Joey died in was terrible," Marnie added. "It was a weird shed that he was using as a house, if I remember right."

"Why was he living in a shed?" Landon asked.

"Gertie thought it was time for him to live on his own – at least that's the story I heard – but he didn't have any money, so he moved into the shed. It was a whole big thing and everyone was gossiping about it, something Gertie hated."

"And he somehow set the shed on fire?" I asked.

"He had a lantern out there because there was no electricity. He was reading or something and kicked it over. Apparently the fire spread fast. There was no way for him to get out."

"That's terrible." I made a clucking sound with my tongue and moved to look under the table when I felt a wet nose against my shin. Sure enough, Peg was waiting for a treat. "I think someone needs to take this pig to obedience classes."

"I don't think there are obedience classes for pigs," Marnie argued.

"I bet there are," Landon said, his mouth full of food. "Pigs are supposed to be smarter than dogs. Make Aunt Tillie take Peg to a dog obedience class."

Mom brightened considerably. "Now that right there is a fabulous idea. Aunt Tillie, I expect you to sign Peg up for classes tomorrow. I mean it."

Aunt Tillie glared at Landon. "You're on my list."

SIX

Even though it was spring, the nights in northern Lower Michigan remained cold. There was frost on the windows when I woke, which compelled me to want to stay warm and toasty in my bed. Landon stretched next to me, awake, but he showed no compunction to get up either.

"It will be summer soon," I noted, resting my hand on his chest as I snuggled closer.

"I love summer here," he said, taking my hand and pressing a kiss to the palm. "I like the food your mother and aunts make ... and the fact that everyone gets drunk while dancing out on the bluff ... and that we can take walks at night without having to bundle up."

I lifted my eyes to his. "You like the dancing on the bluff?" I was understandably dubious. "I thought the nudity bothered you."

"Aunt Tillie's nudity always bothers me."

I waited.

"I still like the nights on the bluff." He grinned down at me. "What can I say? I'm a sucker for that wine. It makes everything seem a lot more enjoyable than it really is."

"Yeah." I rolled to my back and stared at the ceiling. "I wonder if

Chief Terry will start spending the night at the inn. Do you think he'll participate in the naked dancing?"

Landon made a choked sound that was somewhere between a laugh and a groan. "I hadn't really considered it. Thank you so much for putting *that* picture in my head."

"It's just ... different."

"I thought you wanted it to be different. You said you wanted him to be happy. You told him to pick a woman and date her, that you wouldn't stand in his way. Then, when he picked the wrong woman, you stood in his way."

Oh, well, that was ridiculous. "That woman was a murderer."

"Yes, but you had no way of knowing that when they first started dating. You were against her from the start."

He wasn't wrong. "I wasn't against her." That made me sound bad. "I just thought he was selling himself short."

Landon's lips curved. "And now he's not because he's dating your mother?"

"I think he's always wanted to date my mother but didn't because the timing never seemed right. This is simply the universe righting itself."

"Oh, well, that was so well stated one might think you actually practiced saying it."

"I have no idea what you're talking about."

"You're such a bad liar." He rolled and started tickling me, causing me to gasp and squeal as I wrestled with him.

I could've run, scampered to another part of the guesthouse, but it was warm in the bed and I had no inclination to go anywhere else. "Stop!" I ordered after a few minutes.

"Only if you admit that Chief Terry dating your mother is the best possible outcome for you."

"That may be true," I hedged. I'd given it a lot of thought the past few weeks and I'd come to the same conclusion. There was a catch, though. "Just because this makes me happy doesn't mean it's not the best thing for him and her."

"I happen to agree."

"You do?"

"I do." He propped himself on his elbow and stared down at me. "I think Chief Terry wants to be part of this family. Despite all his bold words and the faces he makes when talk of witchcraft comes up, he loves you guys."

"But ... do you think he really wants to be with my mother?"

Landon tilted his head to the side, considering. "I think that he fell in love with you, Clove and Thistle first. No, don't argue." He lifted a finger to silence me. "He fell in love with the idea of being a surrogate father to you girls and the affection for your mother came later. I do think he cares about her a great deal. Love is one of those things that happens in its own time. This will be no different."

"But you think it's going to happen?"

His smile was mischievous. "Yes, Little Miss Busybody, I think it's going to happen. I think it's going to be a bumpy road, but it's definitely going to happen."

His answer pleased me. "Good." I wiggled my toes. "I wonder where he's taking her on their date tonight."

"If he's smart it's somewhere outside of Hemlock Cove. I'm not sure he's that smart."

"Why outside of Hemlock Cove?"

"Because it will be like trying to date inside of a fishbowl if he does it here. That can't possibly be comfortable."

I hadn't even considered that. "Well ... I'm sure it will be fine."

"I'm sure it will be, too."

His hands moved to my waist and I shot him a sidelong look. "What do you think you're doing?"

"I'm spending quality time with my favorite girl." He looked aggrieved. "Why would you possibly think I was up to anything else?"

"Because I know you." And, because I did, I recognized he was merely feeling playful rather than lusty. "I've been thinking about the camp." I decided to change the subject. "Do you think it's possible someone has been living out there for a long time?"

Landon stopped his tickling ministrations and shook his head. "I don't know. I've been thinking about that." He flopped down on the mattress. "That area is remote. I mean ... I really like it because it's remote. I think it would be cool to live there. The highway isn't ungodly far away, but that dirt road would need to be paved to live out there during the winter because otherwise it would be too difficult to navigate after a big snowstorm."

I furrowed my brow. "You want to live out there?"

"That's not what I'm saying. It's just ... the road isn't easy to access in the winter. If someone was living out there during the winter, then that means they probably didn't leave. They would've left footprints, and I have to think the people who live in that area year-round would've noticed."

"Only if they bothered to visit the camp. Why would they do that in the middle of winter?"

"Fair point. There are houses around the lake, though."

"Expensive houses," I pointed out. "And there are only a few of them. There are a couple older homes farther back in the woods. The people who live there would've been more likely to see someone."

"Why do you say that?"

"Because those more expensive homes are occupied by people who have money to travel ... and they can't get out of here fast enough before winter hits."

"Ah. Snowbirds." Landon stroked his stubbled chin. "That makes sense. Those are summer houses."

"And probably fall, too. The fall color change is a big deal up here. That's usually in October, and then the rich people are out of here until May or so."

"You're saying that the people in those houses might just be coming back right now."

"I haven't given it that much thought, but yeah."

"So ... maybe no one was staying at the camp. Maybe someone broke into one of those homes and was staying there and dumped the body at the camp because it was convenient. I'm sure whoever hid the body thought no one would ever find it. It was a fluke that we were even out there and the body shifted the way it did."

He had a point, but still ... . "Wouldn't most of those houses have security systems?"

"I would guess that's true. That doesn't mean there's not a way around those systems."

"Does that mean you're heading out there to check on the houses today?"

"I am. I have to check with Chief Terry to find out when the Bishops are arriving. I want to be there for the interview with them."

"This must be horrible for them," I said. "I mean ... part of them probably wondered if she was dead if they were worried enough to file a missing person report. A bigger part was probably hopeful she was alive somewhere, maybe doing something stupid but still alive, and they would see her again."

"I don't know what to expect from them," Landon admitted. "Thanks to the medical examiner calling, we didn't get a chance to form our own first impressions. I'm not a big fan of how that went down."

"Are you going to talk to his superior?"

"I generally don't like doing that, but I don't see where I have much choice." His fingers were light as they trailed up and down my arm. "I haven't dealt with that guy more than a few times since I started spending time here. I can guarantee I'm going to request he never be assigned to my cases again."

"That should go over well."

"I don't really care what he thinks." Landon licked his lips as he slid his eyes to me. "I do care what you think, though."

A chuckle escaped. "Is this the part where you try to charm me into giving you a little morning thrill?"

"I'm always open for a morning thrill, but I was actually thinking about something else."

"What's that?"

"I want you to be present for our interview with the Bishops."

Whatever I was expecting, it wasn't that. "What?" My voice came out a little squeakier than I intended. "What do you mean?"

"I want you to sit in on the interview," he repeated, not missing a beat. "I think you might have unique insight into this case because you're familiar with the area ... and I would prefer knowing if Hannah's ghost is hanging around. She'd most likely show up if her parents were present, right?"

There were so many things about that statement that threw me I didn't know where to start. "I'm not all that familiar with the area. I haven't spent much time there since I was a teenager."

"You're more familiar than I am."

"That's not saying much."

He waited.

"Fine. I'm familiar with the area and I'll give some thought to how I think someone could've survived up there over the winter. If we're talking about an individual who knows anything about survival, he or she could easily make one of those cabins work through the cold months. We have deer ... and smaller game like rabbits and pheasants. There are a lot of turkeys up here."

"So, our killer would've needed a gun," Landon mused.

"Not necessarily," I countered. "People bow hunt all the time ... and actually manage to kill things. There's an actual bow hunting season. Don't forget that."

"What I mean is that our killer probably would've had access to a weapon if he or she was staying in the area," Landon clarified. "There were no obvious marks on Hannah's body to indicate she was murdered with a weapon."

"Oh." I realized what he was saying. "She could've been strangled, though, right? She could've been bashed over the head ... or shot up with something. Her neck could've been broken. All of those things wouldn't necessarily leave a mark that we could see."

"That's a good point." He slid his arm around my waist and tugged me to him. "There's a lot to think about with the logistics out there. I'm guessing it's going to take some time."

"And you want me to help you?"

"I always want you to help me."

That was a big, fat lie. Not too long ago he fought my efforts to get involved in cases. That led to arguments. Lately, though, he'd been eager to hear my thoughts on things. I had no doubt it was because my necromancer powers made it easier to protect myself, which was ultimately a load off his broad shoulders.

"I didn't see Hannah's ghost at the camp yesterday," I pointed out. "If she's hanging around, she's doing it on the down low."

"That might be because she's feeling shy. You said ghosts feel shy."

"Sometimes. Maybe she hasn't been dead all that long and hasn't learned how to control her new reality. I've seen that happen."

"But?"

"But ... I get the feeling she was in that water for more than a day or two. She's been missing two months. I don't know that I believe she was out there the entire time, but she's definitely been out there for a few days.

"If she was killed at the camp, I think that's where her ghost would choose to set up shop," I continued. "The thing is, maybe she wasn't killed at the camp. Maybe she wasn't killed at all. Maybe she died of natural causes and someone panicked and decided to hide her body in the pool. You said yourself that's a possibility."

"I did," he agreed. "I think it's definitely a possibility. I mean ... think about it. Maybe she was hanging around with a rough crowd. They decided to break into one of the mega-mansions out here and party all winter. Maybe she overdosed or drank too much and hit her head. Maybe those she was with panicked and stumbled across the camp when trying to figure out a way to hide her body."

"I guess that makes sense." I rested my chin on his chest. "Are you sure you want me with you for the interview?"

"I do if there's a possibility Hannah's ghost will make an appearance," Landon replied. "She might be sticking close to her parents for all we know. She could've been hiding yesterday and opt to be bolder today. I don't want you questioning Hannah in front of her parents if she is there, but I do want you around."

"I'm not new. I know about questioning ghosts."

"I know you do." He pushed his lips out. "Give me a kiss."

He was adorably hard to resist in the morning. He also knew it, which somehow only added to his charm.

"What if I don't want to kiss you?"

"Then I'll sit here like this until you do." He puckered his lips like a fish, causing me to laugh.

"Fine. I'll give you a kiss." I adjusted myself so I was higher and could meet his lips. Before I got a chance to kiss him, my bedroom door flew open, causing me to instinctively jerk away from Landon and ready myself for battle.

Instead of a monster, I found my mother standing there. Her arms were piled with clothes and she looked as if she was about to melt down.

"Mom!" I whined as I double-checked to make sure I was wearing pajamas. Thankfully I'd covered myself before falling asleep the previous evening. Otherwise things would've gotten embarrassing.

"I need your help." Mom didn't bother greeting us as she threw the piles of clothing on the end of the bed. "I have absolutely nothing to wear."

"For what?" Landon asked. He was shirtless and clutched the sheet to his chest, which I found amusing.

"For my date tonight," Mom replied, lobbing a dark look in his direction. "What do you think I'm worried about?"

"I honestly have no idea," Landon replied, sneaking a gaze toward the clock on the nightstand.

"It's barely seven," I noted. "Why are you thinking about this now?"

"And in our bedroom?" Landon added.

Mom ignored him. "I've been thinking about it for days. I need something nice to wear on my date tonight. At first I thought I would wear my black dress, you know the one I'm talking about, right?"

I automatically nodded. "Your funeral dress."

"It's not a funeral dress." She made a face. "Just because I happen to wear it to funerals does not mean that it's a funeral dress."

"I've never seen you wear it to anything other than funerals," I pointed out, grabbing a black sweater from the top of the pile and frowning. "This is scratchy. You can't wear this."

"Why not?"

"Well, first of all, it's ugly and old and I think there are holes in the elbows here where moths have been getting busy. Yup." I wiggled my fingers through the holes. "Second, it's scratchy. If he moves in to give you a kiss at the end of your date, he's going to be turned off because the sweater is essentially a big sign that reads 'do not touch me unless you want to be scratched' and that can't possibly be a good way to end a date."

Mom's glare was withering. "Really, Bay, do you think I'm going to kiss him on the first date?"

The question threw me for a loop ... in more ways than one. "I hadn't really considered it until right now. It's weird to think about. If you do kiss him, are you going to use your tongue?"

Mom's face mottled red. "I can't believe I thought coming down here and asking for your advice was a good idea." She started collecting her clothes. "This was a horrible idea."

"I agree," Landon supplied. "Next time you should call ahead and make sure we're dressed."

I elbowed him in the ribs and focused on Mom. "I think you're making yourself crazy about this when it doesn't really matter. Just pick out an outfit you're comfortable in. If you're comfortable then Chief Terry will be comfortable and the date won't be a disaster."

"Who said the date will be a disaster?" Mom's eyes were wild as she clutched the clothes tightly to her chest. "Have you been talking about this with your cousins? Do you all think this is going to be a disaster?"

"No one thinks it'll be a disaster," I said hurriedly. "We all think it's going to be great." That was a slight exaggeration, but mostly the truth. "There's no reason to freak out. Everything will be fine." I used my most soothing tone.

"Oh, what do you know?" Mom snapped. "You spend all your time with Landon. You two never really dated. You simply decided to be together and that was it. You don't know anything about dating."

She turned on her heel and flounced toward the door. "And I'll have you know, this dress is a family heirloom," she said before disappearing. "Terry would be lucky to see me in it."

"Of course he would," Landon said.

Mom didn't hear him. She was already gone.

I slid my eyes to him, my lips involuntarily curving. "This is going to turn crazy, isn't it?"

"With your family? Definitely. It's going to be a bumpy ride."

SEVEN

Due to Mom's meltdown, Landon and I decided to eat breakfast at the diner in town. We had a bit of time to burn because Art and Evelyn Bishop weren't supposed to arrive until around ten — it was a three-hour drive from Grand Rapids — and Landon's favorite meal of the day was breakfast ... followed closely by dinner and then lunch and then whatever snacks he could wedge in. He was a very food-oriented individual, which made him popular at the inn.

"I don't know that they'll be able to tell us anything useful," Landon noted as he dunked a slice of bacon in the yolk of an egg. "We need any information we can get, but right now we have nothing."

I watched him with keen interest. "Doesn't it bother you that you're eating Peg?"

He frowned. "I'm not eating Peg. Stop saying that."

"You could be eating her," I argued. "I mean ... Mom wanted to give her to a farm that was going to turn her into bacon. You might not be eating Peg, but you could be eating her brother."

"Just ... knock that off." He was adamant as he bit into the bacon again, but this time he made a face. He didn't look nearly as happy as he did only seconds before when not thinking about the possibility.

"I think I'm going to give up pork products," I admitted, causing him to jerk his head in my direction. "I don't foresee becoming a vegetarian — I mean, I'll still eat beef, chicken and seafood — but I think pork is off the menu."

His mouth dropped open. "You're giving up bacon?"

I had news for him: I was never as attached to bacon as he was. I was more of a sausage person. Of course, that would be off the table, too. "I'm considering it. They have vegetarian bacon substitutes."

"Do you know what those taste like?"

"No." I was intrigued. "Do you?"

"Yeah. I had a girlfriend who was a vegetarian and she made facon in the morning. That's what it's called, by the way. Facon. Fake bacon. It tastes like crispy ass."

I had to press my lips together to keep from laughing at his outrage. "You had a vegetarian ex-girlfriend?"

He scowled. "Don't even. All ex-girlfriends pale in comparison to you. You're the queen of my heart and dominatrix of my soul. You're the heavens, the stars and the best of all worlds."

"That sounds a little rehearsed."

"Only because I say it to myself every single day ... and mean it with my whole heart."

He was too cute to stay angry with. Besides, he rarely brought up ex-girlfriends. I was under the impression he had very few serious relationships in his past. I was happiest when not hearing about them.

"Well, I'm not saying you have to give up bacon," I said, turning back to the original statement. "It's just weird for me to eat it with Peg running around at the inn. Besides, I don't eat that many pork products anyway."

"What about hot dogs?"

"I'll have beef hot dogs."

"Because you don't care about cows as much as you do pigs?"

"Because there are no cows running around the inn in tutus," I replied without hesitation. "If that changes, beef might be off the menu, too."

"I guess I'll have to make sure Aunt Tillie doesn't get any more pets." He finished his bacon and turned to the door when its bells jangled to signify someone entering. The half-smile he'd been entertaining slipped from his face when he recognized the woman standing in the doorway.

"Mrs. Little," I muttered, sinking lower in my seat. The woman was difficult to deal with on a normal day. For some reason, I just knew she was going to be impossible today. "If we're quiet, maybe she'll walk right past us."

"I don't think we're going to be that lucky."

Sure enough, Mrs. Little stood in the middle of the diner scanning the patrons. When her eyes finally landed on us, she immediately started in our direction. "Oh, man." I cut into my pancakes and shoved a huge mound of syrup-covered goodness into my mouth so I wouldn't immediately have to speak to her.

"Oh, good," she announced as she stood next to the table. "I've been looking for you."

Landon pointed at me, refusing to make eye contact as he sacrificed the woman he claimed to love to the whims of a crazed unicorn lover.

"Well, both of you," she said. "May I sit?" She gestured toward the side of the booth where Landon sat and I didn't miss the momentary look of disgust that flashed over his face.

"Why don't you just tell us why you're here?" Landon suggested. "We don't have much time. We have to choke down our meals and run. I would hate to have to hurry you out of the booth."

She frowned, her forehead puckering. "I ... whatever." She shook her head and planted her hands on the edge of the table as she leaned forward. "I want to make sure you're aware of the story going around."

"You mean the story you're telling people about a homeless person dying at the camp?" I asked, remembering that juicy tidbit from the night before.

"That would be the one."

"What about it?" Landon asked as he flipped his egg whites onto a slice of toast and made an impromptu sandwich. He enjoyed mashing his food together into various combinations. We had that in common.

"I want to make sure that's the story that ends up in the newspaper." Mrs. Little's gaze was pointed directly at me.

"I haven't written a story yet," I pointed out. "I have a few days."

"Yes, but I want to make sure the right story makes the newest edition."

I didn't like her tone. "The right story is the truth," I supplied. "I haven't heard any confirmation that the deceased was homeless." I looked to Landon for help. "Was she homeless?"

"Not to our knowledge," Landon replied dryly.

Mrs. Little let loose an exasperated sigh. "Yes, well, I want to make sure that people believe she was homeless whether it's the truth or not."

I had to give her credit. She never thought before she spoke. Even if she did, she simply didn't care how ridiculous she sounded.

"Well, I'm not printing something I know isn't true," I argued. "Right now I'm not writing anything because the newspaper isn't going to print for several days and we're still digging for information."

"When you go to print, she'd better be homeless. And make sure it's written up as a tragic accident."

Her unmitigated gall made me want to smack her around ... or hold her down while Aunt Tillie drew pornographic pictures on her face. What? Aunt Tillie really did that once. She tells the tale to this day. "I'm going to write the truth, no matter what it is."

Landon held up a hand before I could get up a full head of steam. "May I ask why you're so concerned with this, Mrs. Little? It's not as if Hemlock Cove is any stranger to murder ... or killers, for that matter. In fact, given the touristy makeup of the town, I actually think it might benefit you. What's the deal?"

"The deal is that I'm in negotiations to buy that particular piece of property," Mrs. Little replied primly.

"You are?" That was news to me. "Why? You don't like the great outdoors."

"Definitely not," Mrs. Little agreed. "I hate the great outdoors.

However, Manistee Lake is growing in popularity and I have a development idea that could make me a lot of money. I want to build condos out there, the sort that people rent. I figure with the festivals we have here, I'll make a lot of money."

Oh, well, that made sense. "Yeah, but Gertie doesn't want to sell that property." I thought of the woman we'd visited yesterday and felt a twinge. "That's basically all she has left."

"She doesn't have a choice." Mrs. Little was blasé. "She owes back taxes on her own property and doesn't have the money to pay them. She either loses her home or the camp."

"And don't you sound excited about that prospect?" Landon wrinkled his nose as he leaned back in his seat. "Why would you want to ruin that piece of property with condos? That parcel could be so much more."

"Oh, it's going to be more." She looked a little too happy with herself, which turned my stomach. "There's a lot of land to exploit out there. In addition to waterfront condos, I'm also going to design a second fairground. We need it for all the festivals we have. If we play our cards right, we'll be able to host two festivals at a time."

That sounded like a horrible idea. "Why would you possibly want that?"

"Because it's a great idea."

"And because if she owns the land she can negotiate with the township to lease the land for a steep price," Landon surmised. "She'll be making money hand over fist."

"But only if I can swing a deal to buy the land from the bank," Mrs. Little said. "That won't happen if it's mired in a murder investigation."

"Your concern warms my heart." Landon wiped the corners of his mouth and then dumped the napkin on his plate. "Bay is a professional. She'll write the truth. As for me, I'm not beholden to you. When we find the truth, that's the story I will share. Nothing more. Nothing less."

Mrs. Little's eyes filled with fire. "It was a tragic accident."

"That would be nice, wouldn't it?" Landon shot back. "Sadly, I don't think it's true." He extended his hand across the table to me. "Come on, Bay. We have work to do."

LANDON WAS STILL FUMING when we reached the police station. Art and Evelyn Bishop were already seated in a conference room, though, so he didn't get a chance to vent that frustration.

He was a professional, smoothly transitioning from furious to sympathetic as he shook the Bishops' hands. He introduced me, but was careful in explaining my presence. "She's familiar with the area, attended the camp quite often as a child and is helping us with the geography."

The Bishops were so caught up in their own issues they barely noticed me.

"I want to see my daughter," Art announced.

"I'm sure we can arrange that," Landon said. "Right now she's at the medical examiner's office."

Evelyn was a pretty woman, short auburn hair brushing her shoulders as she pressed her shaking hands together. "I don't understand how this happened. Are you sure it's her?"

"The fingerprints are a match," Chief Terry said gently. "You filed fingerprints with the state police when you reported her missing."

"We did," Evelyn confirmed. "I had her fingerprints taken through this event at school when she was little. It was in case she was ever taken. I didn't think I'd actually have to use them."

"Well ... it helped us identify her quickly," Chief Terry noted. "That's little solace for you, but it could be important down the line."

"How?" Art challenged. His face was so red I worried he was about to have a heart attack. He looked furious, as if he wanted to pick a fight, and there were limited options in the room at which to spew his despair.

"Knowing her identity helps us track her movements," Chief Terry said. "The thing is, I just got the preliminary autopsy results back from the medical examiner's office. They're still conducting tests —

she was in very cold water, which means her body was frozen — and they're still performing tissue and toxicology tests."

I spared a quick glance at Landon, who gave me a reassuring nod before focusing on Chief Terry.

"There's no easy way to say this," Chief Terry started. "Your daughter was strangled and suffered blunt force trauma to the head. We believe she was in the water for six to eight weeks. Getting a firmer timetable is impossible at this point. I'm very sorry for your loss."

I knew that Chief Terry had to deliver terrible news to people all the time. He made a point of keeping us away from that part of his job when we were younger, so I'd never really seen him deliver the news in such a fashion before. It was jarring.

"She was murdered?" Tears flooded Evelyn's eyes. "But ... who would do such a thing?"

"That's what we're trying to ascertain," Landon said. "What can you tell us about your daughter?"

"What do you mean?" Art was bordering on belligerent. "Are you asking if she deserved what happened to her? She didn't. She was a good girl. She never gave us a lick of trouble."

"We don't blame the victim," Landon offered "We're trying to find out what happened to her so we can make the individual responsible pay. We need your help to do that. That includes giving us information."

Art straightened his shoulders and sucked in a shuddering breath. "Right. I ... right. What do you need to know?"

"Well, for starters, I'm curious about what your daughter was doing here," Chief Terry prodded. "Did she have ties to the area?"

"Not that I know of," Art replied, rubbing the back of his neck as he stared out the window. "You have to understand, Hannah was a free spirit. She was one of those kids who didn't see danger. She was adventurous, always hopping on the next thing, and she loved traveling to different places."

"She once told me she would be happiest if she could hop a train that made one stop a day and allowed her to explore a different town at each stop, no matter how boring that town may be," Evelyn volunteered. "I always pushed her to find a husband and settle down, to have kids. She said she was twenty-five and didn't want to settle down. She also said she couldn't see herself having kids."

"She was a free spirit," Art repeated, his lower lip trembling. "She was a good girl who loved to have a good time."

"But what was she doing here?" Landon prodded. "Did she come to Hemlock Cove specifically?"

"I don't know," Evelyn replied, shrugging. "She didn't really say. She was writing a book. *A Thousand Little Places*. That's what she was going to call it. She wanted to visit a thousand different small towns with unique offerings. She was starting in Michigan because that was closest ... and she always loved the things she read about Hemlock Cove."

"Like what?" Chief Terry asked.

"She signed up for a subscription to the local newspaper," Art replied, causing me to shift in my chair. "She got it weeks after the fact sometimes, but she didn't care. She laughed at all the stories. She said there was a story in the town because they had a different festival every week."

Landon smiled. "That's true. This town loves festivals. Do you know where she was supposed to stay when she arrived? There are about thirty inns and bed and breakfasts in the area. It would help if we could narrow it down."

"She didn't say and we didn't ask," Evelyn replied. "She always had her cell phone and promptly returned calls and texts. That all stopped when she left home this last time. I know she hit Hemlock Cove. She said the town was just as great as she thought it would be. She didn't tell us where she was staying, though. She didn't tell us what she was looking at."

"All she said was that the downtown was straight out of a movie and she was infatuated with the mythology that was being spun around her," she continued. "You were having some festival. She didn't tell us what you were celebrating. Maybe that can help narrow it down."

Landon looked to me for an answer.

"Two months ago." I racked my memory. "That would've been around the Lucky Leprechaun Festival."

"St. Patrick's Day," Chief Terry confirmed. "There was another smaller festival before it. There wasn't one after it because we figured everyone would need a week to recover from the green wine Tillie sold."

I wanted to smile at the memory, but that seemed out of place. "So it had to be the Lucky Leprechaun Festival or the March Winds Witch Fest," I murmured "I can go back through the photographs that were taken at both festivals to see if she's in the crowd. I'll need a photograph of her." I felt like a jerk when I looked to the Bishops.

"We have plenty of photos," Art said dully.

"Just so I'm clear, she wasn't meeting anyone in this area, was she?" Chief Terry asked.

Evelyn shook her head. "We would've been more comfortable if she had a travel buddy. She said she didn't need one. In our minds she would've been safer. I guess it doesn't matter now." She chewed her lip as Art slipped his arm around her shoulders.

"When can we take our daughter home?" Art asked. "We want to put her to rest."

"We'll get you in touch with the medical examiner's office," Chief Terry promised. "They'll be able to provide you with that information."

EIGHT

Because it felt as if I was intruding on their grief, I left the Bishops to sob together, and invaded Chief Terry's office. I sat at his computer, booted it, and then started searching for information on Hannah Bishop. I had an interesting idea of where to look.

"What are you doing?" Landon asked when he tracked me down. He seemed surprised to find me behind Chief Terry's desk.

"I'm looking for Hannah on this internet message board," I replied simply. "It's for Michigan people who like to travel."

"How do you know about it?" Landon stepped closer, scanning the monitor over my shoulder. "How did you boot up his computer without a password?"

Uh-oh. Any way I answered that was going to come off badly. "Oh, well ... ." I wasn't sure how to respond. Because of that, I opted to change the subject. "When I was a teenager, I was a lot like Hannah. I wanted to travel the world. I wasn't really interested in small towns, but I was interested in visiting a lot of places."

"Yeah?" Landon slid his gaze to me. "How about now?"

"It's funny. I thought I wanted to be anywhere but here growing up. It turns out I was wrong. I felt a little smothered with all the attention from my mother and aunts, but once I was out from under their roof most of that pressure went away. Besides, now I love this area."

"I love this area, too." He kissed the top of my head. "Do you know what else I love?"

I smiled indulgently. "What?"

I expected him to respond with the word "you" or something flirty. Instead he merely grinned. "I love that you think avoiding the earlier question will make me forget I asked it. Seriously, how did you get Chief Terry's password? His computer is supposed to be on a secure network."

Ugh. He just wasn't going to let it go. "If you must know, I guessed it when I was a teenager and he never changed it."

"You guessed it? How?"

"My name is part of the password ... along with Clove's and Thistle's. It only took me twenty tries to get it right."

"Oh, geez." Landon rolled his neck. "You're basically saying you hacked into the chief of police's computer."

"That's an ugly way to look at it," I argued. "Besides, I'm not doing anything bad. I'm just trying to see if I can find that travel chatroom again. I'm guessing Hannah visited a lot of those spots to talk with other like-minded individuals."

"Anything?"

"Not so far."

Thankfully, further conversation about my hacking skills were off the table when Landon's phone rang. He moved away from me to answer it, which allowed me the freedom to haunt my old online playground. Sure enough, I found a woman I was fairly certain was her within a few minutes. All I had to do was use "Hemlock Cove" as a search term. Believe it or not, it's not a happening place with those who are internet savvy.

"What are you doing?" Chief Terry asked as he strolled into the office, sparing a glance for Landon, who was still on the phone deep in conversation.

"I remembered this old travel message board I used to hang around on when I was a kid," I replied. "Look. Hannah B. I'm betting that's Hannah Bishop. She said she had plans to visit Hemlock Cove and Hell before summer. She even mentions working on a book."

"Does she say anything of interest?"

"I just found her. It will take a bit of time to go through all her posts. Oh, and thank you so much for commenting on my brilliance. Most people wouldn't have thought to check on an old message board like this." I tapped the side of my temple and winked. "Good thing I'm a brainiac, huh?"

Chief Terry rolled his eyes. "Yes, that's exactly what I was thinking." He turned his attention to Landon, who was disconnecting from his call. "That sounded intense. What's going on?"

"First, did you know she hacked your computer as a teenager and can get on your computer whenever she wants?" Landon asked.

"Hacked is the wrong word," Chief Terry countered. "I keep my password taped to my desk in case I forget."

I pressed my lips together when Landon slid me a look.

"You left out that part when relating your amazing password detection feats," he smirked.

"I didn't think it was important," I said. "Who was on the phone?"

"That was Leroy Jessup." Landon turned grim. "He's the head of the team I had out at the camp draining the pool."

"And?" Chief Terry prodded.

"And he found another body," Landon replied. "This one has been in there much longer. Like ... probably ten years. It's mostly bones, although Leroy believes there's biological material in the water. Apparently it's going to take some fancy-schmancy process to siphon it out. He's complaining that it's expensive."

"What did you tell him?"

"That he needs to take it up with the boss." Landon's eyes met mine. "I think we need to head back out to the camp. If there's more than one body, that means we're dealing with a different sort of killer."

"Definitely." Chief Terry nodded. "Let's head out there. I'm dying to hear about this."

That made one of us. I was more resigned ... and nervous.

… . .

LEROY JESSUP WAS A BLUSTERY guy and I couldn't help liking him on sight. He was six feet tall, had a huge belly big enough for him to balance a tray on, and had tufted eyebrows that boasted a mixture of black and gray hair. He also talked in a booming voice like Santa Claus when ordering around his underlings and laughed … a lot.

He was fantastic.

"What have you got?" Landon asked as he swaggered in Leroy's direction. "Anything else to report?"

Leroy ignored him and focused on me. "Are you Landon's girlfriend?"

I couldn't stop myself from returning his wide smile. "Why are you so interested?"

"He talks about you all the time. He says Fay can do no wrong."

My smile fell. "My name is Bay."

"Nice," Landon intoned, shaking his head. "You won't win her over if you can't remember her name."

"Fay, Bay; almost exactly the same," Leroy argued. "They're only off by one letter."

"Or one-third of the letters," Landon pointed out. "She has only three letters in her name."

"Oh, stop being a spoilsport." His smile was firmly in place as he glanced at me. "Have I mentioned that I love his stories about you? He can't stop talking about how pretty you are … or what great cooks you have in the family."

And that right there was probably the crux of Landon's conversations regarding me, I realized. As a food-oriented individual who couldn't talk about the magical shenanigans at The Overlook, he had no choice but to talk about the food … something I'm sure he went on and on about for hours.

"The food is definitely great," I agreed, turning my attention to the pool. I almost fell over when I realized one of the FBI agents was using a large piece of equipment featuring a scooper of some sort to retrieve the body, which was hanging over the lip … and the head appeared to be holding on by a thread. "Is that safe?" The question was barely out of my mouth before the head — which appeared to have long dark hair attached but very little skin — snapped off and fell back into the pool. I heard the water sloshing around and felt sick to my stomach. "Oh, geez."

"Well, that was professional," Landon snapped. "What are you doing?"

"Hey, it's not as easy as it looks." Leroy was focused on the job now. "The pool is full of murky water. We've also pulled out a few dead animals, smaller ones that obviously slipped through the holes in the cover. We didn't even realize what we had here until we saw the head. We weren't exactly looking for another body."

"We had no idea it was a possibility," Chief Terry said. "Do you have any idea how long it's been down there?"

Leroy shrugged. "How long has the pool been closed?"

Chief Terry shifted his eyes to me. "About twelve years, right?"

"How should I know?" I felt put on the spot. "I only know it wasn't open very long before it was closed because people stopped coming to the camp. It had one good summer — I was in college that summer, but Thistle and Clove both swam in the pool — and then it was closed."

"Wait ... it was only open one summer?" Landon's forehead wrinkled. "I don't understand. Why would it be open for only one summer?"

"I already told you." I forced myself to be patient. "The pool was donated by Mrs. Little as a last-ditch effort to save the camp. She wanted to keep kids from hanging around the downtown area because she was convinced that when more than one teenager hung out on the same street corner that gang activity occurred."

Leroy snorted. "She sounds like a fascinating woman."

"Then you're not listening to the story the correct way," Landon fired back.

"There was actually a pool here before," Chief Terry said. "It was empty. It was made of concrete and had structural issues. When

Margaret decided to build a regular pool, it didn't cost nearly as much as it would've if she'd started from scratch."

"The pool was built the summer I was seventeen." I searched my memory. "It was closed when I came home after my freshman year. I remember because Clove and Thistle were complaining about having to swim in Hollow Creek."

"Yes, I remember that summer." Chief Terry made a face. "Thistle refused to wear a bathing suit top because she was going through a rebellious phase and Clove wouldn't stop calling 911 to report her because she was afraid Thistle was going to be exploited on the internet with naked photos."

Landon snorted. "Ah, to be young and a Winchester." He offered me a wink. "So the pool closed when you were eighteen." He focused on me. "That was about twelve years ago."

"Eleven and a quarter," I corrected quickly. "I'm not thirty yet."

"You're close." He tweaked the end of my nose. "Between eleven and twelve years." He squinted his eyes and stared at the bones laid at the side of the pool. "Water can destroy a body quickly. It might not be as old as we think."

"The medical examiner will obviously have to decide that," Chief Terry said. "We need more information on who has been hanging around this pool ... and who closed it. I think that means we need to head back to Gertie's place."

"I don't think that's going to be necessary." Landon inclined his chin toward the parking lot, causing Chief Terry and me to turn in that direction. Even though I knew it was her property, the sight of Gertie out and about surprised me. She didn't look healthy. In fact, she looked beat down.

"She must have heard we found another body," Chief Terry mused.

"Or she simply wanted to see the site where the first one was discovered for herself," I said, forcing a smile for the woman's benefit when her gaze landed on us. "This can't be how she wanted things to turn out for this place."

"Definitely not." Chief Terry stepped forward and extended a hand. "It's good to see you, Gertie. We were just debating whether we should visit you again. You saved us a trip."

"How great for you," she drawled dully. "What are you guys still doing here? I thought you were done."

Well, that answered the question about whether or not she realized a second body had been found.

"We've been trying to figure out a way to collect all the evidence from the pool," Landon replied, clearly choosing his words carefully. "Some of the water is still frozen and we need to make sure we don't overlook even the smallest clue. The pool system runs on a generator, so we had to bring in some of our own equipment."

"Well ... you're making a mess," Gertie didn't look happy. "You're disturbing everything. This used to be a quiet and happy place. Now look at it."

Landon and Chief Terry exchanged quick glances. They were obviously at a loss on how to deal with the woman, who seemed to be trapped in her own world.

"They found another body," I blurted out, instantly hating myself for not thinking before speaking. "I mean ... Hannah Bishop wasn't the only one in the pool."

"I'm confused." Gertie screwed up her face in concentration. "Who is Hannah Bishop?"

"She was the first young woman we found in the pool," Landon replied. "She was from Grand Rapids and came to Hemlock Cove because she was going to write a book. That was two months ago. We're not sure what happened to her, or how she ended up in the pool. We're still working on that."

"We're here now because the excavation team found another body," Chief Terry volunteered. "This one has been in the water much longer. I don't suppose you can remember exactly when the pool was closed?"

Gertie stared at the heavy machinery next to the pool. I didn't think she was going to answer. Finally, she merely shook her head. "A little less than twelve years ago," she replied. "It was open throughout that entire summer and I thought for sure it would open the next summer. That never happened. It was only open for a summer and a half. It was a waste."

"That's right." Things clicked into place in my head. "The summer I was sixteen the pool opened toward the end of the season. We got to swim in it a few times. I knew I got to swim out here, but it didn't make sense with the other things I remembered about it closing."

Gertie nodded. "The construction took a lot longer than it should have. There were issues because it ran on electricity and gas — for obvious reasons — and there was no electricity out there. Finally we had to run the lines and then I splurged on a generator. Boy, was that a huge waste of five-thousand bucks."

"Where is the generator now?" Chief Terry asked. "We looked for it when we found the first body but couldn't find it."

"I sold it years ago. I needed the money."

"Ah."

"You could've used a smaller generator," she added. "You didn't necessarily need the big one."

"Yes, well, we managed to figure things out ... mostly." Chief Terry cleared his throat and I knew he was making an effort to turn the conversation back to the body in the pool. "You had the one really good summer and closed the pool at the end of the season. Did you open the pool at all the next season?"

"No." Gertie rubbed her forehead as she looked back. "I wanted to. I was going to pay the money for it. But none of the summer camps were even close to selling out, and I couldn't really focus. That was right after I lost Earl. It was just Joey and me at that point.

"He wanted to sell the property," she continued. "He thought I was dreaming when I said I was going to figure out a way to turn things around. I refused to entertain the idea of selling, and he was mad about that."

"Is that why he moved into the shed?" Landon asked.

She nodded. "Yeah. I kind of wish I'd sold the land now. He'd probably still be alive if I'd made the right choice then. It hardly matters. All of this is in the past."

I licked my lips. "The bank is going to take it, isn't it?"

Gertie slid her eyes to me, suspicion flooding them. "Who told you? That's supposed to be a secret."

"Margaret Little told us," Landon volunteered. "She has her eye on the property. She wants to buy it for condos and a secondary festival location. She has big plans to make piles of money." He sounded bitter, which caught me by surprise.

"She won't be so happy to hear the news that a second body has been found," I pointed out. "Maybe the deal will fall through."

Landon brightened. "That's something to look forward to."

"Back to the pool," Chief Terry prodded. "Who knew how to open and close it?"

Gertie shrugged. "I had a lot of seasonal grounds help. They all knew about it. The cover bit wasn't difficult. You just needed to move the bolt things and then put the springs on the cover around them before lowering them into the ground. It was easy. There was a special tool."

"Do you know what happened to the tool?"

"That tool was the least of my worries." Gertie exhaled heavily. "I can't believe this is all that's left, that this is what it's come down to."

"I'm sorry about it, Gertie," Chief Terry offered. "I really am. We need to figure out how these bodies got in the pool. That means we won't be leaving anytime soon."

"I guess it doesn't matter." She mustered a wan smile. "Everything is in the past and there's no point in looking toward the future. Do what you have to do. I can't stop you, and there's no point in trying."

With those words, she shuffled away from us and toward the lake. She seemed lost in thought, as if visiting happier times. No one followed, and she didn't as much as glance back at us. She was someplace else and it was best to let her visit on her own.

We couldn't help her, and apparently she couldn't help us.

NINE

I tried talking to Gertie away from Landon and Chief Terry. I figured maybe she would be more open to chatting with me because I wasn't a member of law enforcement. I was right ... and wrong.

"I remember when you were a kid," Gertie announced. We were inside the cabin Landon and I had first entered when we'd visited, before we wound our way to the pool and the body ruined our nostalgic trip. "You were always running around with those cousins of yours."

"Clove and Thistle," I supplied. "I still spend half my time running around with them."

"The short one was all right, but she did that fake-crying thing that I found ridiculous. It was the other one that convinced me your family might be off."

"That would be Thistle." I offered up a genuine smile. "She's still basically the same ... and our family is definitely off."

"Yes, well ... ." Gertie gripped her hands together and then turned away to face the ancient bunk beds. "You had fun when you were here, didn't you? You know what I was trying to build."

I rubbed the back of my neck as I debated how to answer. "I did have fun here," I said finally. That was true. I had fun when I wasn't being tortured by Lila ... or Rosemary ... or whatever other girl had decided to make me a target for the day. "I definitely get what you were trying to do here. Camp is one of those memories that you never fully put behind you."

"Kids today don't want memories of camp."

"And that's sad."

Gertie's eyes were thoughtful as they slid to me. "You're with the FBI agent. I've seen you around together before."

"You have?" I couldn't remember seeing Gertie at all since I'd returned to town after my stint in Detroit. "Where did you see us?"

"Some festival or other. He was winning you a stuffed animal. You were laughing. Oh, and he was trying to drag you to the kissing booth."

"That could be any festival. He's a big fan of the kissing booth ... and winning stuffed animals, for that matter."

"Earl won a stuffed animal for me at a festival once." She ran her fingers over some of the names that were carved into the wooden wall. "We had fun back in those days."

"I don't really remember him," I admitted. "I remember you being around, but not him."

"He was around more when the boys were here. When we had dual camps, the girls would always stay on this side of the lake and the boys on the other side. That is much more difficult to get to, and Earl was adamant that boys were made of sterner stuff so they had to make the difficult trip. We were careful to split our time with the appropriate sexes because we didn't want anyone saying things that weren't true."

I rubbed my forehead. That seemed like a weird thing to say, but Gertie was definitely eccentric. There was no getting around that. There was every possibility it wasn't all that weird in her head. "Well ... that was probably smart," I said finally. "Do you have employee lists? I mean ... lists of people who worked as counselors, even if it was only for a short time."

"Why would you ask that?" Gertie shifted so a set of suspicious eyes locked with mine. "Are you saying you think that a former employee did this?"

I shrugged. "It's possible. I mean ... I guess some random person could've stumbled over the camp and decided to use it as a killing ground, but that second body we just found has been here for a long time. Like ... a long time. That means whoever is dumping bodies here is most likely familiar with the property."

"That doesn't mean it was a former worker."

"Definitely not, but it's a place to start."

"My husband kept all those records. I don't even remember most of the workers." Gertie turned her back to me and focused on the bunk. "I don't know what to tell you, but I can't help."

I considered pressing her, but it seemed a waste of time. I'd been dismissed and Gertie clearly was no longer interested in the conversation. I decided to respect her wishes and leave.

I WAS EXHAUSTED AFTER A LONG afternoon at the camp. The idea of putting up with my family over a boisterous dinner at The Overlook sounded like a bad idea, so when Landon suggested a quick meal at the diner I was happy to accept.

He found me at The Whistler — where he'd dropped me once we got back to town — and threw himself on the new couch across from my desk as I finished up a few tasks.

"You sound tired," I noted as I worked on an email. "I'm almost done."

"There's no hurry." He turned his eyes to the walls, to where the art I'd picked out recently stared back at him. It was abstract, bright, and helped me focus on work. "I had to do the same thing when I got back to the police station. Paperwork is stupid."

I smirked. "What kind of paperwork did you have to do?"

"The type where I justify the heavy equipment used out at the camp. It wasn't difficult once they found the second body. I would've had to jump through more hoops if that wasn't the case."

He'd brought up the subject, so I decided to jump in headfirst.

"What are you thinking about that? Do you think it could be someone who used to work at the camp?"

He steepled his fingers on his stomach as he reclined on the couch while tracking his eyes to me. "That's an interesting question. How did you know I'd been considering it?"

"Maybe I'm a mind reader," I teased.

"I wouldn't discount it. You're magical at every turn."

"Ha, ha, ha."

He didn't laugh. "That wasn't a joke. You're getting more powerful all the time, Bay. I know you realize that. If you started suddenly reading minds it wouldn't exactly surprise me."

I was thrown for a loop. "Well, it would surprise me," I said after a beat. "I've never been able to read minds. That's not what I was doing. I was thinking it myself."

"Ah." Landon's eyes gleamed. "Great minds think alike, huh?"

I shrugged. "I don't know. It's just ... two bodies found in the same pool presents a different conundrum. One body could've pointed toward a transitory individual, or someone who stumbled across the pool by accident. Maybe someone who lived locally but panicked after something terrible happened.

"Two bodies is a pattern," I continued, my mind busy. "One of those bodies has probably been in that pool for twelve years. That means someone went missing almost twelve years ago and was never found. I don't think it's a coincidence that a second body was found in that spot. I mean ... what are the odds? That means either the same person committed two murders or one person had knowledge of another person committing a murder and getting away with it and decided to try their hand at the same thing."

Landon was quiet for a long time. When he finally spoke, it was with amusement. "Do you know what I love about you most?"

"The fact that my family keeps you in pancakes, bacon and fresh-baked bread?"

"And pie. Don't forget the pie."

"How could I forget the pie?"

His smile widened. "Seriously, though. I love the way your mind works. I rarely have to explain things to you because you already get it. You could've made a great FBI agent."

He meant it as a compliment, but all I could picture was Aunt Tillie's face if I became a Fed. "'The Man' in the family? Aunt Tillie would melt down."

"Wouldn't that be half the fun?"

He had a point. "Yeah. I think I'm happy being a reporter and letting you do the heavy investigative lifting. It's a nice thought, though, and I appreciate the compliment."

"I love how polite you are." He swung his legs so they hit the ground and rested his elbows on his knees as he regarded me. "We need to talk about something serious and I guess now is as good a time as any."

My heart skipped a beat. Whenever he got that look on his face it meant something was about to go down. "Do I even want to know?"

"I think it's probably best we get it out of the way now. One of the pieces of busywork I had to sign off on this afternoon was a report from the state-appointed shrink. Melanie Adams has been cleared to stand trial."

Whatever I was expecting, that wasn't it. The oxygen whooshed out of my lungs and I pinned him with a worried look. "What? Are you sure?"

"I'm sure."

"But ... ." I felt lost. "I thought she was being medicated." I swallowed hard as I recovered. "I thought everyone believed she was out of her head because she was spouting off about attack ghosts."

"The doctor says she's lucid," Landon replied calmly. "He says that she's making up the ghost attack to try to get off on a technicality."

We both knew that wasn't true. Melanie Adams was a murderer who took out a local radio doctor, her own parents and tried to hurt Chief Terry before I sent the ghosts of her victims to attack her. The takedown had been relatively quick and painless ... but the ghosts were difficult to explain and if Melanie kept telling people I commanded ghosts to attack her, there was always the chance someone — whether it be a doctor or defense attorney — would decide to look into the situation.

"I should've killed her," I muttered.

"You don't mean that."

"I do. She's alive now and she could hurt my family. I definitely should've killed her."

"Bay, you're looking at this the wrong way." Landon was calm as he got to his feet and moved to the corner of my desk. There he knelt next to me and stared directly into my eyes. "No one is going to believe her. She's spouting a nonsense story about ghosts. You're okay."

"Am I?" I wanted to believe him but I couldn't shake the niggling worry that invaded my brain whenever I thought about putting the ordeal behind me. "If my family has to live the rest of their lives under a microscope because of what I did, if you become the laughingstock of your office because you live with a crazy chick, will you feel the same way?"

He collected my hand. "I don't care about that. You heard Leroy earlier today. I talk about you all the time ... with pride. I'll never be ashamed of you. The witch thing is part of who you are."

"You can't want it to get around," I challenged. "I don't care what you say. I know that's not true."

"I don't want it to get around," he confirmed, his fingers gentle as they brushed a strand of hair behind my ear. "Not for the reasons you're imagining. I'm not worried that people will laugh at me. No matter what, I'm always proud of you.

"I am worried that people might find out and believe the rumors," he continued. "I keep picturing that movie *Splash* in my head. The one where they take the mermaid and lock her in a cage because they want to study her. I don't want my witch being studied by anyone other than me."

His smile was so charming I melted a bit. "Melanie could be a problem," I noted. "She saw what I can do. She knows I sent the ghosts of her parents after her."

"Knowing it and proving it are two different things," Landon said.

"Her defense lawyer will insist she stop telling that story. If she doesn't, then he's going to tell her to add to the mess and try to get the judge to declare her incompetent. Both outcomes benefit us."

I wasn't so sure. "And what if the judge believes her?"

"That won't happen."

"How can you be so sure?"

"I have faith." He gripped my hand. "Now, come on. Let's finish the busywork and head to dinner. You'll feel better when you get some fish and chips in you."

I made a face. "I don't want fish and chips. Now that you mentioned *Splash*, it weirds me out."

"Fine. I'll feel better when I get some fish and chips in me."

"Ah, now we're getting to it."

"We are." He pressed a kiss to my palm and lowered his voice. "It's going to be okay. Just ... don't let this get to you. Everything is going to be fine. I promise."

And because he was the one making the promise, I believed him.

WE FILLED OURSELVES WITH homestyle cooking — I went for the hot beef sandwich and Landon the fish and chips — and were in relatively good spirits when we hit the sidewalk outside the diner.

"It's starting to get warmer," Landon noted as he swung our joined hands. He was obviously feeling playful. "Before you know it, your mother and aunts will be dancing naked in our backyard."

"You almost sound as if you're looking forward to that."

"I'm looking forward to sitting outside and watching the stars."

I snorted. I knew him too well to believe that. "You're looking forward to drinking Aunt Tillie's wine and rolling around with me under the stars."

"It's the same thing."

"It most certainly isn't. In fact ... ." I trailed off when I heard a familiar sound, swiveling quickly. Sure enough, the nervous giggle I thought I'd recognized belonged to my mother. She was walking along a side street with Chief Terry — they were holding hands and staring at one another as they conversed about something I couldn't make out — and they looked to be heading in the direction of the diner.

"Oh, man," Landon complained as his hand went to my back. "I can't believe we missed being witnesses to their first date. Actually, I can't believe he didn't spring for a better meal for their first date. Maybe I should talk to him about dating a Winchester."

I slid him a sidelong look, amused. "Oh, really? What kind of advice are you going to give him?"

"I have secrets." He tapped between my eyebrows. "I know the ins and outs of all the Winchester women. I could give him some much-needed advice ... and the first bit of that advice is that you splurge on a first date."

I poked his side. "You didn't splurge on our first date. Of course, we didn't really have a first date."

He frowned. "Yes, we did."

"What are you considering our first date? Are you talking about when I visited you in the hospital after you got shot protecting us or when you showed up and ate dinner at the inn with the family? Either way, those are not first dates."

"I ... huh." Landon worked his jaw. "You know, now that you mention it, we really didn't have a first date. I don't know how that happened. I mean ... we just kind of fell together."

"There's nothing wrong with that," I pointed out. "We fell together and didn't fall apart ... other than that one blip after you found out what we were and needed to think."

"And I came back in record time," Landon noted. "Let's not go off on a tangent about that again. I hate being reminded."

"Fair enough."

He leaned over and kissed my forehead. "I think we should have a first date."

"And I think we're already living together so that's probably a wasted effort. Let's just have a special date or something."

"Like what?" He looked intrigued.

I shrugged. "I don't know. We can talk about it on the way home." I took a moment to rest my head against his shoulder and watch as Chief Terry nervously held open the door for my mother. They didn't even glance in our direction. They had no idea we were there because they were absorbed in their own little world. I found it adorable.

"We can plan a special date," Landon said, moving his arm around my back. "You didn't get a first date, so you can pick whatever you want for our special date."

"Dancing naked with my mom and aunts?"

"Don't push it. We'll figure something out. I want you to have a memorable date."

"I have a memorable relationship. Isn't that enough?"

"Oh, so cute." He wrinkled his nose and smacked a loud kiss against my lips. "It's not enough. I want you to have a date that makes every other man in this town feel stupid because he can't live up to my dates."

"Oh, so this is about you."

"But of course, sweetie. You're going to benefit, though. Don't you worry."

I wasn't worried. Landon liked extravagant gestures and I had no doubt this would simply be another in a long line. "Let's head home. As much as I'd like to spy on them, my mother would kill me. We'll have to wait for the recap tomorrow morning over breakfast."

"Now that's something to look forward to."

TEN

I dreamt I was running.
Not because I had some ridiculous urge to get in shape, mind you, but because someone was chasing me.

I had no idea who it was. I couldn't see in the darkness. All I knew is that I was in the woods and I heard someone behind me. Heavy footsteps grew closer as I crashed through the trees, an errant branch scratching my cheek as I whipped around to see if I could get a glimpse of my pursuer.

There was no one behind me.

My heart pounded as I slowed my pace to get my bearings. The landscape wasn't familiar. I had to know where I was running before I continued. Otherwise I would be running blind, and that was a sure-fire way to make things worse. Aunt Tillie taught me that. It was one of her life lessons when we were kids. It was right after the lesson on how to stalk without getting caught and right before the lesson on how to steal blackberries from the field behind Mrs. Little's house without her seeing us. When I turned back to look in the direction I had been running, a sense of dread overwhelmed me ... and that was before I saw a pair of hands reaching for me.

I bolted upright in bed, gasping as I fought the covers. It was early, the sunlight offering a soft glow as it filtered through the windows. I knew I was safe, yet my heart was hammering at a fantastic rate.

"What's wrong?" Landon murmured from beside me, automatically reaching out.

"Nothing," I lied, my eyes moving toward the window. "What time is it?"

"Early. We don't have to be up for another two hours. Come here." He was warm as he slipped his arm around my back and tugged me close. "Did you have a bad dream?"

"It was just a dream." I didn't want to go into specifics because I wasn't sure what the dream meant. "I'm fine."

"You need sleep." He kissed my forehead and tucked the covers in tightly around me. "Try to turn off that busy brain."

That was easier said than done. I figured I would wait until he drifted off again and then slip out of bed. Surprisingly, though, the sound of his steady breathing lulled me and I conked out a second time.

WHEN I NEXT WOKE, LANDON was awake and watching me. "What?" I asked, rubbing my cheek. I felt self-conscious. "Why are you staring at me? Was I drooling again?"

"I like when you drool," he replied, running his fingers over my cheek. "You have a red mark here." He gestured toward the cheek that was scratched in my dream, causing me to frown. "Did you scratch yourself in your sleep?"

"Not that I remember." I struggled to a sitting position and stared into the mirror on the wall. From this distance I couldn't see the scratch well. "I'm sure I can cover it with makeup."

"I don't care about that." He stroked his hand down the back of my wild hair. Bedhead was the bane of my existence and I had resigned myself to the fact that it was never going away. "You had a bad dream last night." It wasn't a question.

"I had a *weird* dream," I corrected. "I was running in the woods and someone was chasing me. A branch scratched me." I touched my cheek, which felt sensitive. "Someone managed to catch me at the end."

"That sounds like a nightmare."

"It's hardly the worst dream I've ever had."

His eyes were contemplative as they watched me. He looked as if he was about to start an argument — something I really wasn't up for after a poor night's sleep — but he changed his mind. "You didn't recognize who was chasing you?"

"No."

"Well ... maybe the stress is catching up to you." He tugged me so I pressed against his chest and gave me a soft kiss. "What do you have planned today?"

He wasn't the smoothest when it came to segues. I knew what he was really asking. Sadly, I couldn't give him what he wanted. Not today, at least. "I'm going back out to the camp."

He stopped running his hand down the back of my head and frowned. "Why?"

"You know why. Your crime scene team is done out there. I heard you on the phone yesterday. They've finished."

"They have. What does that have to do with anything?"

"If a ghost is hanging around and she's shy ... ." It wasn't necessary to finish the statement.

"Then she's more likely to pop up and converse with you when so many people aren't around," Landon muttered, dragging a hand through his hair. "I don't know, Bay. What if our killer also decides to take a look around now that it's quiet? You'd be alone out there."

"Not alone. I'm not an idiot. I'm taking Clove and Thistle with me ... whether they realize it or not."

He perked up a little. "Really?"

"Yes, really." I poked his side. "Believe it or not, I'm not an idiot."

"You're the smartest person I know," he agreed, grinning. "I knew that from your excellent taste in men."

I rolled my eyes. "You're feeling full of yourself this morning."

"I'm feeling better knowing that you won't be at that camp by yourself. I thought I was going to have to schmooze you so you would include me in your plans."

"Schmooze me?"

"Do you prefer demand?"

"No. That would've caused us to argue."

"I know. That's why I'm glad you decided not to go up there alone. That's progress."

I pursed my lips as I regarded him. The day was young. We could still argue. Ultimately I didn't have the energy. "What do you have planned for your day?"

"Questioning people who live in the area, looking at property deeds, checking local salvage yards for Hannah's car. You know, the usual."

That hadn't even occurred to me. "Oh. She drove up here."

He bobbed his head. "She did. That means her car may still be up here ... somewhere."

"And if you find out where, that might serve as a lead."

"See, you are smart." He tightened his arms around me and cuddled closer. "We should probably get in the shower and head up to the inn for breakfast. I'm hungry."

I waited. There was a "but" somewhere in that statement even though he didn't utter it.

"If we shower together we can conserve water and help the environment," he added, causing me to smirk.

"You're nothing if not a consummate conservationist," I teased.

"I like to do my part for the environment."

"I guess we should put the planet first."

I WAS FEELING LIGHTER WHEN we reached The Overlook. We parked in the front so we could leave for work directly after breakfast. The inn was quiet as we picked our way to the dining room and pulled up short.

It was empty.

Landon's mouth dropped open. "Where is my bacon?"

I inclined my head toward the kitchen. "Maybe they're running late." Even as I said the words they felt alien. I couldn't remember the last time my mother and aunts were late getting a meal on the table. "Hold on." I strode to the door and pushed it open, frowning when I found the kitchen empty. "They're not here."

"And there's no bacon," Landon muttered as he appeared behind me. "I don't like this."

While I didn't want to encourage him to overreact, in truth, I didn't like it either. Aunt Tillie was like a small child. She needed to be fed on a regular schedule.

"Maybe they're up getting the rooms ready," I suggested. "Maybe ... they had a late night and decided to sleep in because there aren't any guests until tomorrow. Maybe ... up is suddenly down and they're not serving breakfast this morning."

Landon's expression was dark. "Bite your tongue." He extended a warning finger. "That isn't even remotely funny."

I wasn't trying to be funny. For lack of anything better to do, I strode through the kitchen and landed in the family living quarters. Aunt Tillie, who usually made a habit of sitting on the couch and yelling at the various morning news personalities for reporting what she referred to as "fluff" stories, was nowhere to be found and it was deadly silent.

I shot a glance to Landon, worry coursing through me. "I definitely don't like this."

"Let's not get worked up just yet," Landon cautioned. "Maybe they went to town for breakfast. They might not have felt like cooking."

That was the most ridiculous thing I'd ever heard and the look I shot him expressed just that.

"I know exactly what you were thinking just now and I don't like your attitude," Landon muttered as he followed me toward the hallway that led to the bedrooms. "There's no reason to panic. I'm sure there's a perfectly acceptable reason for why there's no bacon. In fact ... ." Whatever he was going to say died on his lips when the door to my mother's bedroom opened to reveal Chief Terry.

He stood on the other side of the threshold in a pair of boxer shorts and a plain white T-shirt — clothes I'd never seen him in — and his eyes went wide when he saw us.

"What are you doing here?" he asked as his hands flew up as if to cover his chest.

"What are you doing here?" Landon challenged.

I peered around Chief Terry and almost fell over when I saw my mother was still in bed ... and the way she had the covers clutched in front of her let me know she was naked.

"On the first date?" I screeched, dumbfounded.

Mom's glare was withering. "Don't you knock?"

"We didn't get that far! We thought something was wrong. Why aren't you in the kitchen?"

"We were out late last night," Mom replied primly. I had to give her credit. This was basically the worst of worst situations and yet she managed to muster annoyance with me. That was a marvelous feat. "We just woke up. If you want breakfast, bother your aunts. Or, even better, learn to cook yourself."

"This is not the time for jokes," Landon countered. "Besides, Marnie and Twila aren't in the kitchen. And there's no bacon."

"Ugh." Mom rolled her eyes. "Well ... you know where the stove is."

I thought Landon was going to fall over. I was so uncomfortable with the situation I could do nothing but grab his arm and drag him from the door. "You're grounded," I called out. "You're not supposed to do it on the first date. That's the one thing you all agreed on when we started going out with boys in high school – well, that and the fact that we would kick off the apocalypse early if one of us got pregnant outside of marriage. Just look at you now."

"You're not the boss of me, Bay," Mom countered. "I can do whatever — or whomever — I want. Get that through your thick head."

I felt as if I might pass out ... or throw up. "This is just the worst morning ever."

Landon slipped his arm around my shoulders. "I'm right there with you."

. . .

AUNT TILLIE TURNED UP IN THE inn lobby with Peg on a harness a few minutes later. She didn't look surprised to see us. Of course, very little surprised her.

"Is breakfast ready?" she asked.

Snort. Snort. Peg wiggled her butt excitedly for Landon.

I shook my head. "There is no breakfast."

"No breakfast?" She made a face. "Is it the apocalypse? If so, I'm ready. You can be on my team, but I'm kicking whiners to the curb."

"It's not the apocalypse," Landon replied. "Although ... Bay might beg to differ."

"If there's no breakfast it's the apocalypse." Aunt Tillie handed Peg's leash to Landon. "Spill it. What's the problem?"

"I can't talk about it." I averted my gaze and focused on the check-in desk. "It's too horrible to verbalize."

Aunt Tillie turned to Landon. "Explain ... and don't go on and on like you usually do. Keep it succinct."

He glared at her. "Chief Terry is in Winnie's room. Apparently Winnie is naked. I can't confirm that because I didn't look that far into the room ... and you have no idea how thankful I am for that."

"That's why you're so upset?" Aunt Tillie rolled her eyes. "Geez, Louise, Bay. Grow up. Your mother isn't a virgin. She had you. Of course she's had sex."

I wanted to crawl into a hole and die.

"I think it's more that it was their first date," Landon clarified. "No one was expecting it."

"Why?" Aunt Tillie wrinkled her nose. "This relationship has been decades in the making. The hurdle was getting them to admit they had feelings for each other and to get this one to move out of the way." She jabbed her thumb at me. "Once Bay stopped being a baby — er, well, the grating sort of baby she was before because she's obviously still being a baby — then it was over and done. All that's left now is the gooey looks and rampant sex.

"Hey, it's just like hanging around with you guys," she continued, offering up a faux smile and fake clapping. "You're just as perverted as your mother now, Bay. How does that make you feel?"

Yup. I definitely wanted to die.

"I think I'm going to be sick," I said finally. "Maybe I should go home and spend the day in bed."

"If I thought you were serious I would be all for that," Landon said. "But you're not. You'll bounce back. That throwing up thing is in your head. Besides, we haven't eaten since dinner last night. There's nothing in your stomach to throw up. There's certainly no bacon."

Snort. Snort. Peg stared at Landon with accusatory eyes. It was almost as if she understood what he said.

"Oh, geez." He looked away from her and focused on me. "Get it together, Bay. We have bigger problems. There's no breakfast."

"I still don't understand why there's no breakfast," Aunt Tillie complained. "Where are Twila and Marnie?"

"Not here, as far as we can tell," Landon replied, moving his hand to my back so he could rub at the tense muscles. "Maybe they freaked out about the sex, too. They've always had things for Chief Terry. Maybe they're so jealous they moved out and didn't leave forwarding addresses."

"Oh, good grief." Aunt Tillie cuffed him. "How many soap operas do you let him watch, Bay? That is the most ridiculous thing I ever heard. Marnie and Twila didn't really like him. They were just trying to irritate Winnie."

"It worked," I said weakly, swiveling quickly when I heard voices behind us. Sure enough, Mom and Chief Terry appeared in the archway. Chief Terry looked embarrassed, but the expression on Mom's face could only be described as fury. "Someone put a bag over my head and maybe she won't realize I'm here," I suggested.

Landon snickered. "Be brave, champ." He kissed my cheek before turning to Mom. "I see things went well last night. I'm happy for you. Perhaps next time we can come up with a plan for breakfast, though, huh?"

Mom folded her arms over her chest as Chief Terry uncomfortably shifted from one foot to the other. "What did I tell you?" she challenged. "If you want breakfast, you can cook it yourself."

"See, that's not generally how it works in this family," Landon complained. "I've never once been here and breakfast wasn't ready promptly at eight. I mean ... this is the end times or something."

Aunt Tillie elbowed me. "I told you it was the apocalypse."

"You get the ark," I muttered. "I'll get the animals."

Snort. Snort. Peg rubbed her snout against my knee, causing me to frown as I stared into her eyes. She was a smart little thing ... but there was no way I would admit that to Landon.

"Now, I'm going to make breakfast for Terry and me," Mom started, tightening the sash on her robe. "I'm willing to include the three of you in those preparations if you stop being babies and grow up. Everyone here is an adult. You didn't see me freaking out the first time Landon spent the night, did you, Bay?"

Actually, I remembered things differently. "I don't remember you being happy about that," I argued. "I believe there was talk of a brothel or something."

"You barely knew him. I've known Terry for decades. Get over it."

Her tone told me she meant business. I swallowed hard. "I can help with breakfast." The words hurt. "Landon can, too." I gripped his hand.

"I'll make the bacon," Landon offered lamely, ignoring the way Peg nudged him with her nose. "Or ... maybe we can go without bacon this morning."

I pressed my lips together and moved my hand to his shoulder. "Suck it up, big guy. There are other breakfast meats."

"Name one that's not a pork product," he countered.

"Um ... turkey bacon."

He glared. "That's not real bacon. It tastes like ... some horrible thing that bad people created to punish fans of good cooking."

"I have to agree with 'The Man' on this one," Aunt Tillie said blithely. "Turkey bacon is something grown in the devil's armpit. We'll just go without meat this morning. Eggs, hash browns and toast will be enough."

"Eggs, hash browns and toast it is." Mom's smile was so broad when she turned it to Chief Terry that I thought it might swallow her entire face. "I think this is going to be a wonderful new family tradition. Who agrees?"

I glanced at Aunt Tillie and found her scowling.

"It had better not," Aunt Tillie muttered. "I don't care if they hump each other like bunnies. I hate cooking. That's never going to change."

I had different reasons for hating the set-up, but I kept them to myself. This morning was simply not going as I'd thought.

ELEVEN

Clove and Thistle turned up at the inn just as we were finishing history's most uncomfortable breakfast. They sauntered into the dining room, chatting about ... something, and fell silent the second they saw the configuration around the table.

"Nice boxer shorts, Chief Terry," Thistle greeted him.

Landon leaned back in his chair and slipped his arm around my back as he looked away from my mother and tried to hide his laughter.

For his part, Chief Terry remained stoic. "Thank you, Thistle. I'm a fan of them."

"They have lobsters on them," Clove noted, scratching the side of her nose. "Is there a reason? I mean ... are you a fan of lobsters?"

"They came in a three-pack and I didn't look at the design." Chief Terry put both hands around his coffee mug and glared at my cousins, practically daring them to say what was really on their minds. Clove had the grace to keep her mouth shut. Thistle, on the other hand, enjoyed a challenge.

"On the first date, Aunt Winnie?" She chortled as she grabbed the coffee carafe. "I'm shocked. Shocked, I tell you. That's not how a good girl acts."

I pressed my lips together to keep from choking on what I was sure would be a mixture of a sob and a laugh. I remembered well the "good girl" talk my mother had given us after we were caught skinny-dipping at the lake.

"Is there a reason you're here, Thistle?" Mom asked dryly. She clearly wasn't in the mood to play games. "If not, you can leave."

"We're here because Bay called us," Clove replied, grabbing a slice of toast from a platter and taking a big bite. "She says we have to go on a ghost search at the old camp. She can't go alone because Landon will whine like a girl, so we're going with her."

Landon slid his eyes to me. "I don't whine like a girl."

"You sound like one of those Real Housewives you're so whiny," Thistle countered. "It doesn't matter. We'll be with Bay to keep her safe. You have nothing to worry about."

Landon narrowed his eyes but otherwise remained passive. "Thank you for keeping my whining at a minimum. It's a great relief."

"What do you expect to find out there?" Chief Terry asked. He seemed thankful to be able to talk about something other than the fact that he'd had sex with my mother on the first date. "Wouldn't a ghost have already shown herself?"

"Maybe," I replied. "I can't be certain. All the activity might've scared a ghost away. It's worth a shot. We need to find out what happened to Hannah Bishop, and this is the best way I can contribute."

"What about the second body?" Thistle asked, glaring at Peg when the pig started rubbing herself against her shins. "Why is the pig wearing a skirt?"

"She likes it," Aunt Tillie replied simply. "She likes being dressed up, and she can't wear leggings."

"Why can't she wear leggings?" Clove asked. "I think a pig in leggings would be cute."

"That's what I said before I forgot about the bathroom issue." Aunt

Tillie turned grim. "She's litter box trained but she can't pull down her leggings. That's why she has to wear a skirt."

"Oh, well ... ." Clove smiled brightly at Peg, but the animal showed no interest in leaving Thistle's side. She was sort of like a cat. It was as if she picked up on the fact that Thistle liked her least and wanted to take advantage of that situation to continuously irritate her.

"I want to go to the camp with you," Aunt Tillie announced. "I haven't been out there in a long time. It would benefit my memory if I could look around."

"And why would we want to benefit you?" Thistle challenged.

"Because otherwise you'll end up on my list, mouth."

Thistle didn't look as if that bothered her, but when she flicked a look to Mom and Chief Terry and found them gazing into each other's eyes as they whispered something only they could hear, she shuddered. "You just want out of here because you're afraid Aunt Winnie's bad first date behavior will carry over to them doing it on the table or something. I'll bet that's why Mom and Marnie aren't here. They fled in terror."

Mom pinned Thistle with a murderous look. "You and I are going to have a talk later, Thistle. Be prepared."

As usual, Thistle's bravado took over for her brains. "I'm looking forward to it," she said, smiling brightly. "I can't wait to bring up all those old sayings you used to spout ... like that giving away the milk for free one. I think we're going to talk and talk until there's nothing left to talk about."

Mom's eyes flashed. "Won't that be fun?"

"It definitely will."

LANDON WAS RELIEVED WHEN I kissed him goodbye in the parking lot. It was clear he needed to put space between Chief Terry and himself so he could clear his head before they met for work later. He was distracted, but not so much he didn't admonish me to be careful and stick close to my cousins before disappearing.

That left Thistle, Clove, Aunt Tillie and me to drive out to the campground. Aunt Tillie put Peg on her harness and dragged her along for the ride, so it was four witches and a pig on our excursion, and I couldn't help thinking that would make a fabulous television show.

"So ... what are you going to say to your mother next time you see her? I'm guessing a lecture on condoms is going to be uncomfortable."

Thistle waited until we reached the campground to ask the obvious question. I had a feeling that was on purpose because she wanted to make sure she had room to run and wasn't trapped inside a vehicle in case I decided to make her eat dirt.

"Do you have to keep talking about it?" I knew I sounded whiny, but I couldn't stop myself. "I want to forget what I saw. I mean ... I'm going to have nightmares." I thought about my dream from the previous night and ran my fingers along the scratch I'd covered with makeup. "Even worse nightmares than usual."

"I think we should talk about it," she countered. "I mean ... holding your emotions inside is never a good thing. If you don't vent with us, well, you're going to blow with them. Tell us how you really feel."

"I feel like I'm going to drown you in that pool," I growled, pocketing my keys as I moved to the front of my car. "Seriously. I will leave you out here if you don't shut your mouth."

Thistle was unruffled by the threat. "We both know that's not true. You're far too responsible — something your mother wasn't last night when she had sex on the first date — to leave me out here with a killer on the loose."

Sadly, she was right ... about all of it. "Someone find a hole for me to crawl in," I muttered under my breath, causing Clove to snort.

Aunt Tillie, surprisingly, paid very little attention to our conversation. Instead, she walked with Peg toward the cabins. That was unusual for her, because she never met a spirited taunting session that she didn't want to dominate. Her reaction made me suspicious.

"What are you really doing out here?" I asked after a beat, watching as she moved toward the first cabin Landon and I had entered during our initial visit. "You don't care about the ghosts."

"I care about the ghosts," she shot back, her eyes firing. "I don't like anyone in my town being killed ... unless I'm the one doing the killing. But I do have a few other things on my mind."

"Like what?" Thistle asked. She was keyed into Aunt Tillie's moods and I read the suspicion on her face. Trusting Aunt Tillie was difficult on the best of days. Today was definitely not one of those days.

"Did you know Margaret Little is trying to buy this property?" Aunt Tillie asked, her eyes drifting to the cabin's roof. "I mean ... actually trying to buy it. She thinks there's profit to be made from owning this place."

"I did know," I confirmed, folding my arms over my chest. "The question is: How did you know?"

"I know all and see all."

That was her patented answer, and I didn't believe it. "How really?"

"I have spies in her inner circle. All she can talk about is this property. She's going to build condos out here. I don't think that should be allowed."

"Why?" I asked, genuinely curious. "Are you afraid she'll spoil the property's rustic appeal?"

"No." She made a face. "I just don't want her to be happy. Spoil the rustic appeal? Who taught you to say things like that?"

I flicked my eyes to Thistle and found her grinning.

"This family makes me tired," I said. "I mean ... really, really tired."

"We're very good at doing that," Thistle agreed. "It's genetic."

WE DECIDED TO TAKE ON the search in an orderly fashion. That meant working together to attack each building. We started at the nearest cabin, even though I'd already been inside, and worked our way through the other two before we took a break to get some air.

"I don't remember those cabins feeling so claustrophobic," Clove complained, shaking her head. "I mean ... seriously. In my memory those ceilings are like twenty feet high. What happened?"

"You were shorter," Aunt Tillie replied simply. "Those cabins were always holes. I remember that weekend your mothers made me come with them to help run the camp — that was the one where Bay found the body — and I thought then the cabins were falling apart. Now they're literally falling apart. I don't see why Margaret would want them."

"She'll tear down the cabins," Thistle said.

"That camp you're talking about is the one where Landon and I met," I supplied. "That's why we came up here in the first place."

"Do you wish you hadn't?" Clove asked. "I mean, you wouldn't be on a ghost hunt if you'd stayed away."

"And then there would be a father and mother still wondering why their daughter wasn't calling home," I pointed out. "I'm not sorry we came here. We were having a good time before we found the body. Besides, it's better to know if there's a predator in our midst. We obviously have a killer up here."

"But how could someone live here?" Clove made a face as she scuffed the ground and looked around. "There's no power. There's no place to shower in the middle of winter."

"I don't think showering is at the top of the list for homeless people," Thistle pointed out. "That's what we're talking about, right?"

"Maybe," I hedged. "I don't like blaming homeless people for murder without actual proof."

"We should blame Margaret," Aunt Tillie suggested. "That would stop her from buying this property."

"Why are you so fixated on Mrs. Little?" I asked. "I mean ... other than your usual reasons. It's not as if you're attached to this property or anything. You hated it when we went to camp."

"I didn't hate it when you went to camp," she countered. "Those were glorious weeks when I didn't have you three running around and getting into my stuff."

"Oh, admit it," Thistle teased. "You cried when you didn't have us around to entertain you."

"I threw naked dancing parties on the bluff," Aunt Tillie fired back. "No, seriously. Every year we sent you to camp we had a big witch retreat. We're doing that again in a few weeks."

"Mom mentioned that," I said, rubbing my hands on the seat of my pants to wipe away the grime I'd picked up in the cabins. "Do you really think we should invite real witches to Hemlock Cove? That seems somehow dangerous."

"We haven't held a solstice celebration since Walkerville became Hemlock Cove," Aunt Tillie pointed out. "It's our turn."

I still didn't think it was a good idea, but the solstice was weeks away. I had time to argue with my mother about that later ... when I could look her in the eye again, that is. "Well, as long as you're happy." I rolled my neck and blew out a sigh, frowning when I realized there was a second vehicle parked in the overgrown lot. This one was a dated Bronco ... and I had no idea when it had arrived.

"Do you see anyone else hanging around?" I jerked my eyes to the left and right as I looked for the driver of the vehicle.

"Why?" Thistle asked, her eyes automatically going to the parking lot. "Oh. Someone is here. When did that happen?"

"Why do you think I'm looking around like an idiot?" I asked, irritation rushing through me.

"Maybe it's the killer," Clove said, her voice ratcheting up a notch. "Maybe we're about to be thrown in the pool like the other women. Maybe there's some sort of ritual attached to what's going on ... like a reverse baptism."

Aunt Tillie shot her a withering look. "How are you even related to me with deduction skills like that?"

"It's entirely possible," Clove snapped.

"It is not." Aunt Tillie shook her head. "That's Randy Weaver's truck. He's the caretaker out here."

Caretaker? This was the first I was hearing about that. "I didn't know Gertie had a caretaker."

"Someone has to occasionally check on the property," Aunt Tillie explained. "That's Randy's job. I know because Elroy Daughtry ran into him up here before winter and asked him about it."

I knew very little about Randy. He was in his thirties, appeared to be one of those guys who had ten different side hustles going at the same time, and boasted what always seemed to be a lecherous gaze when it came to young women. He had a full beard that made me think he was hiding a weak jaw, and eyes that naturally squinted. As far as I knew, he was a looker, not a toucher. He'd been in town only five years, and I had a feeling I would've heard if he did more than look. Still, if he was spending time out here he might be worth a quick chat.

"Where do you think he is?" I asked, spinning. "I ... ." I broke off, almost yelping when I caught sight of Randy standing on the porch of the nearest cabin. He'd apparently been listening to us because he looked amused as he leaned against the structure and stared.

"Good morning," he drawled, his blond hair gleaming under the sunlight. "I didn't realize ya'll would be out here today."

"We're reminiscing," Clove lied.

"We're looking for something the cops might've missed," Thistle corrected.

"It's none of your business what we're doing," Aunt Tillie challenged, sliding in front of the group and directly facing off with Randy. "Do you have a problem with us being here?"

Instead of reacting with anger, Randy snorted. "I don't care. It's not my property. Gertie doesn't pay me enough to chase people away. I just thought I should stop by when I heard about the cops being up here."

"How often are you up here?" I asked. He didn't seem like a man worried about our presence. I took that as a good sign. That didn't mean I trusted him.

"I'm supposed to come once a month."

"How often do you really come?"

Randy flashed a charming grin and held out his hands. "Not as often as I should."

"Before today, when was the last time you were here?" I asked, suspicion niggling at the back of my brain.

"It was before winter." Randy didn't look embarrassed by the admission. "I'm not the most diligent of employees. Gertie knew that before hiring me. Besides, she pays me, like, thirty bucks a month. It's not as if I'm making bank on this gig."

"Still, if you promise a service, you should provide it," Thistle said. "It sounds to me like you're taking advantage of her."

"And it sounds to me as if she's getting what she paid for," Randy countered. "Either way, it doesn't matter. This place is going to be sold. Gertie told me that herself. I just wanted to see for myself what they tore up."

"And probably check to see if there was anything worth taking," I added. "If the camp is really going to be torn down, everything here is up for grabs, right?"

"It can't hurt to look."

His smile made me sick to my stomach. "Yeah, well, that's what we're doing. Don't mind us."

"I don't mind you at all." Randy offered me a wink. "In fact, maybe we should break into teams and search the cabins together. That will allow me some one-on-one time with you girls."

Aunt Tillie glared at him. "Sure. I'll be on your team, Randy. How does that sound?"

Randy cringed. "Oh, well ... maybe you want to keep looking around yourselves."

"I think that's probably best," I agreed. I waited until he gave up trying to flash "come hither" eyes at Clove, Thistle and me when Aunt Tillie wasn't looking and disappeared behind the cabins to speak again. "I don't know that I believe he's a killer, but we should definitely mention him to Landon and Chief Terry."

"Definitely," Clove agreed, shuddering. "He's gross."

"He's all sorts of gross," Thistle agreed. "But he's a looker. I don't think I've ever heard of him actually having the guts to put his hands on a woman. And a story like that would spread like wildfire."

She wasn't wrong. "I ... ." Whatever I was about to say died on my lips when the hair on the back of my neck stood on end. Slowly, I turned in the direction of the pool as I felt a pair of eyes on me.

At first, I thought those eyes belonged to Randy. He was a pervert, after all. It would be just like him to hide and spy on us. It didn't take me long to realize it wasn't him, though. The second I caught sight of an ethereal figure by a tree I recognized we'd found what we were seeking.

"What is it?" Thistle asked, picking up on my mood. "Do you see something?"

I nodded slowly as I met the ghost's gaze. She looked timid, as if she was afraid of her own shadow – if she'd cast a shadow. She had dark brown hair and ducked her head to avoid eye contact. Still, there was something familiar about her.

"It's not Hannah Bishop," I said after a beat. "It's someone else. I think I've seen her before, but I can't remember where."

Aunt Tillie, who could also see ghosts, stared in the same direction. "I kind of see her," she said. "Her essence is weak."

"She's hiding."

"And yet you can still see her. I barely see a shimmer."

"Maybe Bay is more powerful than you on that front now," Thistle argued. "She's a necromancer, after all. She would have to be more powerful."

"She's definitely more powerful," Aunt Tillie agreed, her gaze thoughtful. "Do you want to try talking to her?"

"That's why we're here," I replied. "She might have answers."

TWELVE

The ghost didn't want to talk. She played a rather intriguing game of Hide and Seek that lasted a full hour ... and then she completely disappeared. Thistle was annoyed that I didn't force her to stay and answer questions, but my necromancer powers were a work in progress and I had no inclination to play master and commander over what I assumed was a traumatized soul.

Thistle was still complaining about it when we reached downtown in time for lunch.

"I'm just saying that you wasted our time," she complained as we exited my car in front of the diner. "You could've forced her to answer questions and we might already have a killer in custody."

She had a point, but still ... . "I don't like forcing them unless I have no other choice." I was uncomfortable having the conversation in the open in case someone was eavesdropping. "Let's talk about something else."

"Like what?" Thistle made a face. "Should we talk about your mother having sex with Chief Terry on the first date? That's the only other thing I can think to talk about."

Ugh. I didn't want to talk about that either. Instead, I turned to

Aunt Tillie and found she was edging away from the diner. "Where are you going?"

She adopted an expression of faux innocence. "What do you mean? I'm not doing anything."

"I didn't ask what you were doing. I asked where you were going."

"Oh, well, you're clearly going into the diner. I can't take Peg in there. Her feelings are hurt by that, for the record, so I'm going to take her for a walk to make her feel better."

I narrowed my eyes. Aunt Tillie was a masterful liar, but she didn't put much effort into this one. "Where are you really going?"

"Nowhere you need to worry about." Her eyes flashed with annoyance. "Don't you have your own stuff to freak out about?" She didn't wait for an answer, instead barreling forward. "I guarantee you do, what with your favorite father figure spending the night with your mother and your refusal to embrace your new powers because you're afraid. Those are better things to waste your brain power on."

I worked my jaw. "I'm not afraid." I darted my eyes around to make sure no one was within hearing distance. "And don't say 'powers' like that. You know I don't like it."

"I know that you're being a big baby," she clarified. "You have to get over it. Your powers wouldn't have advanced the way they have if you weren't ready to use them. Stop being a ... well, a Bay."

I glared at her. "You're trying to change the subject because you don't want to tell me where you're going."

"It's none of your business."

"She's going to spy on Mrs. Little," Clove interjected. "We all know it. She'll never admit it. Why does it matter? She's going to do what she's going to do."

Aunt Tillie's gaze was speculative when it landed on Clove. "It's a sad day when I find myself agreeing with you. I don't even know how this happened. The world is topsy-turvy."

Clove beamed at her. "Maybe I'm the smart one and you never realized it."

"Or maybe the world is suddenly spinning backward. Either way, don't concern yourself with me or what I'm doing. I'll find my own way home." She clutched Peg's leash tighter and turned to leave. "By the way, don't tell Terry and Landon that I'm downtown. Make sure they think I'm back at the inn."

That didn't bode well. "Why? What are you going to do?"

"Don't you worry about it, Little Miss Busybody," she shot back. "You mind your business and I'll mind mine. How does that sound?"

It sounded like a recipe for disaster, but I was incapable of controlling her. "If you get arrested, I'm not bailing you out," I warned.

"The cops have to catch me to arrest me. I'm way smarter than them, so it's not going to happen."

That wasn't a comforting answer. "Just ... don't get caught. We have enough going on right now without you making things worse."

"I never make things worse."

Thistle snorted. "Making things worse should be listed as a bullet point on your résumé."

"And having the biggest mouth in the world should be on yours. Now, stop talking to me. I can't fade into the background like a ninja if you're yelling at me across the street. You're ruining my street cred."

I pursed my lips as I watched her go. "Is anyone else afraid she's going to do something stupid?"

"No." Thistle shook her head. "We *know* she's going to do something stupid. Worrying is a waste of time."

Sadly, she was right.

LANDON AND CHIEF TERRY WERE already seated when we entered the diner. They wordlessly made room for us as we crossed, and I was careful not to meet Chief Terry's gaze as I slid into the spot next to Landon.

"Hey." He leaned over and gave me a kiss. "I'm glad to see you're still in one piece. How did your visit to the camp go?"

"It was ... interesting." I shrugged. "By the way, have you guys considered looking at Randy Weaver? We ran into him out there."

Landon furrowed his brow. "Who's Randy Weaver?"

"A local pervert who has like fifty part-time jobs because he refuses to hold a full-time job," Thistle replied as she grabbed a menu from the center of the table. "He's all sorts of lazy."

"He's a pervert?" Landon looked to Chief Terry for confirmation.

"He's got a wandering eye that likes to mentally undress women," Chief Terry replied. "We've never had a report of him actually touching anyone. I've had plenty of complaints about lecherous gazes."

"And you ran into him at the camp?" Landon prodded. "He didn't touch you, did he?"

"No. He tried to get us to go into a cabin with him, but Aunt Tillie changed his mind on that front. He was clearly terrified of her and disappeared not long after."

Chief Terry tapped his bottom lip. "I forgot that he was paid to look after the camp. My understanding is that it's a sporadic thing. He's supposed to go out there once a month or so. He'd make a likely suspect."

"Except he claims that he hasn't been out there since before the snow fell," I said. "I asked. He wasn't ashamed at all of the fact that he hasn't visited. He said Gertie pays him thirty bucks a month and he goes out there when he feels like it."

"I can see him shirking his duties," Chief Terry said. "Killing someone is work. Opening that pool and closing it again was work. I don't know that he would put in that amount of work."

"Well, he's still worth considering." Landon rubbed his hand over my back as I snagged a French fry from his plate. "Where is Aunt Tillie? I thought she was with you."

"She was, but she lost interest once we got back to town. She said she had other things to do." I avoided his gaze as I dunked the fry into ketchup.

"What other things?"

Crap. I didn't want to answer that question. "She didn't say."

"What Bay is trying to avoid telling you is that Aunt Tillie took Peg to spy on Mrs. Little," Thistle volunteered. "Aunt Tillie told us to lie to you, which means she's probably going to do something illegal, and Bay is squirming because she doesn't want to lie but can't exactly tell the truth without risking Aunt Tillie's wrath."

Landon arched a speculative eyebrow. "Is that true?"

"Have I ever told you how handsome you are?" I asked, ignoring the question.

He grinned. "Yes, and that's a game I love playing." He leaned closer so our foreheads were almost touching. "You better hope Aunt Tillie doesn't do something big that forces an arrest. I'm fine with her terrorizing Margaret Little. In fact, I encourage it because she wants to buy the camp. Keep her distracted."

I knit my eyebrows, confused. "Why do you care so much?"

"Because I do."

"But ... why?"

"Because I do." Landon was firm. "I like that camp. It's important to me for a number of reasons."

"Even though you didn't know it existed until a few weeks ago," Thistle muttered.

"I heard that." Landon shot her a look. "It doesn't matter what I thought then. It matters what I think now. I don't want Mrs. Little owning that place. I don't care if you believe that makes me weird."

His expression — bitterness tinged with proprietary bravado — made me smile. "I think it's kind of cute." I leaned closer and kissed his cheek. "You've attached sentimental value to the camp because that's where we met. I get it."

He met my gaze. "If you're laughing at me, I'll make you pay later." He grabbed a fry from the plate and shoved it into my mouth before I could fire back a smart response. "I don't want Margaret Little owning that camp. I'm not going to change my mind."

"No one wants her owning the camp," Chief Terry said darkly. "For years people have been whispering about her trying to buy up pieces of the town. I know she wanted to buy The Whistler after William Kelly died, but his will didn't allow for that."

I jerked my head in his direction, surprised. "I didn't know that."

"She said she wanted to bring the paper to glory." He grimaced as he shook his head. "We all know she would've used it as a propaganda machine for herself and as a way to advertise her businesses above those of all the others in town. I was originally glad when I heard Brian Kelly was coming to town. That was, of course, before he tried to screw you over." He offered a kind smile, which caused me to relax a bit. Sure, he'd slept with my mother on the first date. He was still Chief Terry. He was the man who strong-armed Brian into selling me the newspaper and fleeing town after the transaction was complete. He was the man who rallied the town behind me when Brian tried to erase my position. He was my hero. Nothing had changed that.

"Well, I'm glad that didn't work out for her." I wiped the grease from the fry from my chin. "I remember when she wanted to buy the cemetery. She said she wanted to make sure only the right people were buried in the township limits."

Landon frowned. "You're kidding me."

"No, she's always been a terrible person," Thistle said. "Just when you think she can't possibly do something worse than she's already done, she proves you wrong."

"She's the devil," I agreed, shaking my head. "Maybe we should try to figure out a way to keep the camp from her. I don't know how we'd manage it."

"That's not a concern right now," Chief Terry said. "I talked to the bank manager today. I made sure he realized that loaning her money to buy the property now would be a mistake given the investigation. He's agreed to hold off, at least for the time being."

"That gives us time to figure out a way for someone else to buy it," Landon mused. "Maybe Marcus needs a spot for more animals." He looked toward Thistle, hopeful. Marcus, her boyfriend, and Thistle lived in a converted barn. He ran the stable and a petting zoo. He fancied himself an entrepreneur of late, though I doubted he would want to add more stress to his life now.

"He doesn't have the money to expand anytime soon," Thistle replied. "Sorry. He probably would like the land. It's going to take him two years to pay off the loan he took out for the petting zoo expansion."

Landon made a face and glanced at Clove. "What about Sam? He's doing well with the Dandridge and the haunted tanker."

Clove's fiancé was also a businessman. I knew that he'd gone deep into debt to buy the Dandridge. The business was doing well, but he wouldn't be able to acquire another loan for some time.

"Sorry." Clove flashed him an apologetic smile. "That won't happen anytime soon. We already have enough on our plates."

"It's not your fault."

Landon remained moody while we placed our orders. Once the waitress left, the spirit of the table changed.

"So, Chief Terry, what are your intentions toward Aunt Winnie?" Thistle asked, her eyes gleaming with evil delight.

Chief Terry glared at her. "Don't you worry about it," he snapped. "It's none of your business."

"I don't know." Thistle wasn't the type to back down, no matter who ordered her to do so. "I didn't think it was any of your business when you interrupted my high school dates. You did it all the same."

"That's because you were underage and that boy you were dating was not," Chief Terry fired back. "Also ... you were better than him. You don't see me interfering with your relationship with Marcus, do you? No. Do you want to know why? He's age-appropriate and you're an adult. Plus, he's a good guy. I only stuck my nose in when you were making bad decisions."

Thistle opened her mouth to argue and then snapped it shut. Apparently she didn't have an argument, which made me laugh.

"Oh, look at that." I giggled maniacally. "She's speechless. Somebody take a photo for posterity."

Landon snickered as he moved his hand to the back of my neck and started rubbing. "I never thought I would see the day," he teased.

"Shove it." Thistle leaned back in her chair and kicked out her feet. "Let's talk about something else. Tell them about the ghost you saw."

I wanted to strangle her, but when I risked a glance at the neighboring tables I realized they'd cleared out and nobody had overheard the reckless statement. "Talk a little louder," I hissed.

"Shh." Landon grabbed my hand and pressed a kiss to my palm. "It's okay. Tell us what happened. I didn't realize you saw anything."

"I don't know much." I continued to glare at Thistle as I talked. "It was a woman. Dark hair. We couldn't get close enough to see her because she was shy."

"I told Bay to make her stay, but she refused. She said it would make her feel icky." Thistle rolled her eyes. "I think finding a killer is more important than her feeling icky, but what do I know?"

"Not much," Landon answered, his eyes on me. "It's okay that you didn't want to force her, Bay. I know you don't like that. Do you think it was Hannah?"

I shook my head. "I've seen photographs of her. It definitely wasn't her."

"Then it's probably the other one," Landon said. "What did you say her name was again?"

I realized he was looking at Chief Terry. "Wait ... you guys identified her?"

"We have," Chief Terry confirmed. "Vicky Carpenter. There was a missing person report from more than a decade ago. We managed to match the dental records."

"Vicky Carpenter?" My stomach made an uncomfortable roll. "She was a counselor at the camp the last summer I was there. I think she was there the last summer Clove and Thistle were there, too."

Chief Terry arched an eyebrow. "You're right. I had to pull her missing person file. She lived in Traverse City but worked here that summer. How did you remember that?"

"She was the counselor in our cabin," Thistle replied for me, all traces of mirth missing from her angled features. "She was a lot of fun. She didn't like Lila, which meant we liked her. She was staying the entire summer and came back the next year. Clove and I got to see her again and we were supposed to meet her in town for coffee at the end of the season before she left. We promised to bring Bay with us."

"Oh, I remember now," Clove said, leaning forward. "She never showed up for the coffee. We were upset and went to check at the camp. One of the other counselors said she'd left a day early without saying why."

Chief Terry's expression was thoughtful as he leaned back in his chair. "Apparently she never left after all. She would've disappeared right around the time they closed the pool."

"That's not a coincidence." I thought about the smiling counselor and the way she laughed at every joke, even if it wasn't funny. I was always somewhat upset that I never got to see her again. Apparently she didn't ditch us. She was ripped from her life instead. "We have to figure out what happened to her."

"We will, sweetie." Landon flashed me a reassuring smile. "We'll find out what happened to both of them. I promise you that."

THIRTEEN

Clove and Thistle were eager to open Hypnotic after lunch. They didn't come right out and say it, but the pall that had settled over us after realizing we knew the dead woman in the pool was enough to shake everyone and they couldn't wait to get away.

Landon, on the other hand, was insistent as he followed me to The Whistler. "Why won't you talk to me about this?" He was plaintive as he waited for me to unlock the door.

"I don't know what there is to say," I replied. "I thought I recognized the ghost at the camp. I told myself I was imagining it — I mean, I would know if someone disappeared back then and probably died, right? — but I clearly wasn't."

"You're upset." Landon made sure to lock the door behind us before following me toward my office. I was still getting used to the new configuration of the building — I'd occupied a small office before I became owner — and I started left before I remembered I needed to go right, so I ultimately completed a large (and unnecessary) loop around the front desk. "You're so upset you forgot you're the boss."

I forced a smile for his benefit. "I will never forget that. Would you like me to boss you around?"

He didn't return the smile. "Maybe later. Right now I want you to tell me why you're so worked up."

How could I explain it to him when I didn't understand it myself? "I don't know." I opted for the truth as I shrugged out of my coat. "It's just ... shouldn't I have known she was missing?"

"Weren't you, like, nineteen at the time?"

"So? She was still a person. I knew her. When she didn't show up for coffee I thought some rather unpleasant things about her."

"Ah. That's what's bothering you." He snagged me around the waist and pulled me down on the couch with him. He insisted I needed a comfortable couch so we could nap together during the day — something I thought ridiculous, but we'd ended up enjoying several long lunches since I'd purchased it — and he sighed as he snuggled me close. "It's not your fault this happened. You couldn't have known."

"I don't think we did anything when she didn't show up."

"What could you have done?"

I shrugged. "We could've called Chief Terry. Even if he thought we were being alarmists he still would've gone out there looking for her. She might not have been dead then. Maybe someone was keeping her locked away. We might have been able to discover her before it was too late."

"Bay, you'll drive yourself crazy with what might've been. You can't go back in time and change things. She's dead. It's not as if you're to blame."

"Still ... it seems like I should've known."

"Well, you didn't and we have to move past that." He pressed a kiss to my neck and made me squirm. "Why didn't you order her to stay and answer questions while you were out there?"

"You know why."

"It makes you uncomfortable."

"It does. I've ordered ghosts around three times now. The first time was to save myself. I reacted out of instinct and I don't regret it."

"I don't regret it either. You could've died if you hadn't sent those ghosts to attack. You did the right thing."

"The second time was with Dr. Lovelorn."

Landon made a face. He hated the dead radio personality who'd haunted us weeks ago. Thanks to my new power, I made him visible to Landon, which meant he had to listen to the good doctor wax poetic about any number of ridiculous things for several days. He was still bitter.

"I forced him to answer questions," I continued. "He was lying and hurting people, so I didn't feel all that guilty about what I did to him. The same with Melanie's parents. She killed them and I used their spirits to haunt her. She had it coming ... and they were mostly willing."

"So, what's the problem?"

"The problem is that Vicky was clearly not willing. I didn't even know she was Vicky at the time. I don't want to force a traumatized murder victim if I don't have to."

"I think that's fair." He exhaled heavily, his breath tickling the ridge of my ear. "What are you going to do with the rest of your day?"

"Are you asking because you're a concerned boyfriend or an FBI agent?"

"Concerned boyfriend. Although ... the FBI agent is curious, too. I know you're going to do something about Vicky. I would like to know what."

"I'm going to research her," I replied simply. "I'll bet she's in some of the photographs from the camp back then. There might even be other information."

"Okay." He gave my ear a kiss and then released me. "I'll help."

I was caught off guard. "You're going to go through old files with me? Isn't that a waste of your time?"

"No. We're waiting on information on Vicky's next of kin. I don't have anything to do until then. You might be onto something, and we can discover it together. It will be romantic."

I rolled my eyes. "You just want to make sure I'm not sitting over here pouting."

"Ah. Two birds with one stone. I'm a great multi-tasker."

I couldn't help but smile. "You're ... something."

"So, it's agreed? We're working together."

I heaved out a sigh. "It's agreed. I wouldn't want to partner with anyone else."

"Right back at you."

"THESE OLD FILES ARE SURPRISINGLY thorough," Landon noted after we'd found the camp file consisted of three large folders and moved our operation into the kitchenette so we could sit on the floor and spread the clippings over a larger area.

"William was nothing if not diligent about making sure we had three copies of everything cross-filed," I replied as I held up an old photo of the camp. "He was crushed when things started going digital and there was no need to keep hard copies. He kept it up several years even after it wasn't necessary. I helped him when I came home from college during the summers. He must have quit at some point, because there was a big stack of newspapers that spanned several years when I returned to town."

Landon tilted his head as he regarded me. "You filed them all, didn't you?"

He knew me too well. "It's what he would've wanted."

He grinned. "Come here." He leaned forward and smacked a loud kiss against my lips. "You are a wonderfully moral creature. That's why you couldn't order the ghost around when it wasn't necessary and that's why you probably spent weeks filing articles that could've been accessed with a simple online search."

"I don't think I'm that moral," I hedged. "Aunt Tillie said I was the best liar she ever trained."

"Aunt Tillie is full of crap. You're a terrible liar."

"I managed to hide who I was and what I could do for years before you entered my life. I think I'm just a poor liar when it comes to you."

"I guess I can live with that." He went back to sorting through the articles. "I'm not sure exactly what I'm looking for."

"Me either," I admitted. "Look at the photos. I'm sure Vicky is in there somewhere."

"Yeah, well ... hey, it's you!" He brightened considerably as he held up a photo. I snorted when I saw it. "Look at those long legs and how blond you were."

"It was from the pool," I noted. "I was extremely blond that summer."

"I like you the way you are now." He shot me a flirty wink as he sifted through more articles. "Here's something. There's a list of four counselors, kind of like thumbnail bios. Vicky Carpenter is one of them. It says that she has a sister, lives in Traverse City, and wants to be a teacher when she finishes college."

I exhaled heavily. "I guess that never happened."

"No. The sister is named Stephanie. I bet we can track her down thanks to this. If she's still in the area, we can arrange to talk to her."

I couldn't hide my surprise. "We?"

He grinned. "We're partners, aren't we?"

"Is this just a way to keep me close to you because you're afraid I'm going to feel sorry for myself all day?"

"You knew Vicky. Taking you with me makes sense. Besides, Vicky's ghost might be hanging around her sister's house. You told me yourself that ghosts can go wherever they want, so maybe Vicky splits her time between the camp and her sister's place."

That was a legitimate possibility. "Well ... then we should do a search for her."

"That's the plan. You keep going through the photos and I'll see if I can find Stephanie. I told you this was a good idea."

"Yes, you're handsome and wise."

"And don't you forget it."

STEPHANIE CARPENTER-CREWS WAS NOW a married mother of three girls. The oldest girl was blonde and the frame on the wall of Stephanie's house proclaimed her name to be Victoria.

"I knew Vicky was gone," Stephanie said as she delivered a pot of tea to the table and sat next to us. Her two older children were at school, but the younger one, a toddler, was busy sitting on the floor and making flirty eyes at Landon.

He grinned at the little girl before sipping his tea. "Are you the one who reported her missing?"

"I'm the only one who was left to report her missing," Stephanie replied. "Our parents died when she was in high school. I was three years older, so she was allowed to stay with me, but we were watched closely by Social Services. We had to walk a fine line to make sure we weren't separated."

I couldn't drink my tea because I was certain it would make me heave. "She was the only family you had?"

Landon slid me a look. I could tell he wanted to pet me, but he wisely refrained. We weren't on a date.

"She was." Stephanie's smile was rueful. "She was always a free spirit, that one. She had big dreams. They were almost as big as her heart."

"I knew her." The words escaped before I thought better of them. "She was a counselor at the camp I went to when I was a teenager."

"That's why I brought Bay with me," Landon said hurriedly. "She was with me at the camp when the first body was discovered. Then, when we got confirmation on the second body, she remembered your sister and wanted to come."

If Stephanie was bothered by a civilian being present, she didn't show it. "It's nice that she made enough of an impression that you wanted to be here." Her smile was sincere. "My oldest daughter looks like her. I found out I was pregnant a month before she went missing. That was the only thing that kept me going while we were looking for her.

"I didn't want to believe she was gone back then," she continued. "I thought something had happened. I convinced myself that she went on an adventure and didn't tell me. I kept sending her messages so she would know the baby was close. And then, when I went into labor and there was still no notification from her, I knew she wasn't coming back. The moment I saw my baby I knew that Vicky was gone and that I would have to accept it."

Tears pricked the back of my eyes. "You named your daughter after her."

"It seemed the only thing I could do."

"Did you have your sister declared dead at some point?" Landon asked.

"I didn't see a reason for that. I guess there was still a modicum of hope she was out there. It seems silly because I just told you I knew she was dead when I saw my baby, and that's true. The longer she remained missing, all that hope fizzled, but before ... . It's weird to know she never left the camp. I kept imagining her on the road, traveling and seeing new places. She wanted to visit so many places."

It was only when her voice cracked at the end that I realized she was crying. "I'm so sorry," I said. "I feel I should've known something bad happened to her. We were supposed to meet her for coffee in town, but she never showed. We assumed she forgot.

"When we went to the camp to make sure, the other counselors said she'd left," I continued. "We didn't think to question why. If she really said that or just didn't return to her bunk the night before, I have no idea ... and I'm so sorry."

"Oh, you shouldn't blame yourself." Stephanie was sincere. "She wouldn't want that. She was a good girl with a giving heart. She wouldn't want you carrying this around."

The fact that she was consoling me when she'd just found out about the death of her sister ripped a small tear in my gut. "Thanks, but I still feel guilty."

"We're going to find who did this," Landon promised. "The thing is, we need information. We're working under the assumption that one person is responsible for both the bodies we found in the pool. The problem is that we don't have proof of that and we're dealing with a huge time gap."

"I don't know what I can tell you," Stephanie said. "Vicky wrote me once a week while she was serving as a counselor. I think it's because she thought it was the thing to do and liked to get mail. I always wrote her back, and sent care packages. She was technically an adult, but I knew how much she loved those care packages, so I had as much fun putting them together as she did opening them."

"She must have told you about the people she worked with," Landon pressed. "Did she mention having any trouble with anyone? Or perhaps seeing someone following her? Was she dating anyone?"

"She wasn't dating anyone that summer," Stephanie replied without hesitation. "I know that for a fact. Once the summer was over she planned to travel and she thought it was a waste of time to start a relationship with someone because it would have to end before she hit the road.

"Her plan was to travel and then be back in time for me to give birth," she continued. "I was on her to get a permanent job, something that could lead to better than minimum wage. She had wanderlust, though, and she didn't want to settle for a job when she could sample the world."

"She sounds like a lovely individual," Landon noted. "I wish I could've met her. Still, she must've said something. Can you think of anything that stands out about the correspondence she sent you that summer?"

"Not offhand, but I can look. I have the letters stored in my safety deposit box. I didn't want to lose them and keeping them around the house with small children seemed risky. I can go to the bank and get them tomorrow."

"I would appreciate that." Landon leaned back in his chair. "I won't lie. Right now, we're at a loss. We don't know who could've been at the camp ten years ago to kill your sister and again two months ago to kill Hannah Bishop. The entire thing is ... something we're trying to untangle."

"I have no doubt you will."

Stephanie was so serene I had to ask her the obvious question. "You don't seem upset. Why is that?"

"Oh, I'm upset." Her eyes flashed sad. "I don't want to cry in front of my children." She inclined her chin toward the toddler on the floor, who was peeking through her fingers at Landon and smiling. "I don't want them to associate Vicky's name with tears because then they'll never bring her up.

"They didn't get a chance to meet her, but I make sure they know her," she continued. "I have photographs and we talk about her all the time. I will save the tears until my husband is home and can give me a few minutes away from them."

"You are very strong." I slowly got to my feet. "Your sister was lucky to have you."

"No, I was lucky to have her. Hey, now that you mention it, I do remember Vicky writing about one of the other camp counselors. She didn't like him. The only reason it stands out in my head is because she liked everyone. She didn't mention him being inappropriate, just that he had a bad attitude."

"Did she mention a name?" Landon asked.

"Not that I recall. I'll check the letters again and let you know."

"I greatly appreciate that." He dug in his pocket and pulled out a business card. "Call me anytime if you remember anything."

"I will. Um ... about my sister's body; when will I be able to claim it so I can have a proper funeral?"

"The medical examiner has her right now. Call me tomorrow and I'll have more information for you. I'll make sure that you get your sister in a timely fashion. I think you've waited long enough."

"Thank you."

I managed to hold it together until we were in Landon's Explorer and then I started to cry. He was expecting it, so he pulled out of Stephanie's driveway and parked down the block, out of sight from her home. There, he pulled me in for a hug.

"I feel so sorry for her," I admitted. "Her sister was all she had. I never realized Vicky was alone."

"You couldn't have saved her, Bay. You were basically a child. You couldn't have known what was going to happen to her."

I didn't know if that was true, but I mourned her all the same. "Can we just sit like this for a minute?"

"As long as you want."

"Maybe five minutes."

"It's okay." He smoothed my hair. "I need to think anyway. There's something off about this entire situation and I'm not sure where to look next. Go ahead and cry. I'll be here."

"Thanks."

"That's what I'm here for."

FOURTEEN

Landon left me at my office once we returned. He didn't seem keen on it, but I needed some quiet time. He was there to pick me up promptly at five, though, and I smiled when I saw him waiting for me in the parking lot. He wordlessly grabbed my computer bag, kissed me and then helped me into the passenger seat.

He seemed to be in good spirits as we drove, which helped bolster the sagging ones I was struggling with. I figured now was a good time to drop a difficult decision I'd made on him.

"I need to spend the night at the camp."

Landon kept his eyes on the road, but I noticed the exact moment his shoulders tensed. "Why?"

"I need to talk to Vicky. She's obviously hanging around out there. She wasn't at her sister's house, which makes me sad. She might be happy if she hung around there. Instead, she's obviously haunted by her death ... and traumatized. That's why she refuses to talk to me."

Landon let loose a long sigh. "I don't understand why that means we have to stay the night."

I didn't miss the fact that he changed "I" to "we." That was so ... Landon. Even before I broached the subject, I knew he would include himself. There was no way he couldn't. I was fine with that. In all honesty, I would rather have him with me.

"She's more likely to come out if we're there for an extended period," I replied without hesitation. "Plus, tomorrow is the waxing moon. That's the strongest celestial occurrence we're going to have for a long time. I need to try to make contact then."

He was quiet for a long beat. "You know that you could just go out there tomorrow morning and force Vicky to talk, right?"

I immediately started shaking my head. "No."

"Because you knew her?"

"That and it's rude. Most ghosts only stay behind because something traumatic happened to them. Something so terrible it ripped their souls from their bodies and confused them enough that they had no choice but to stay behind, often re-living what happened to them over and over again. I don't get pleasure out of traumatizing them twice."

"I know that, Bay, but it's for a good cause. We have a killer to find."

I folded my arms over my chest and stared out the window. "You don't have to come. I know you have work to do. I figured I would go up there tomorrow — I'll ask Thistle and Clove if they want to come, but they might not be able to join me until later in the day — and try to get her to materialize. The longer I'm there, the more likely she is to trust me.

"I understand you have other things to do," I continued. "I don't expect you to sit up there and hold my hand. I'm a big girl. I'm not going to cry or anything ... at least not again."

"Oh, don't be like that." He made a face as he turned on the highway that led to The Overlook. "You're allowed to feel what you feel, Bay. I have no problem with a few shed tears. I get it. You knew her and you feel guilty. That guilt is misplaced. There was nothing you could've done to save her. She was gone before your scheduled coffee appointment. I get why you feel guilty, and I don't blame you for it."

"But you're clearly angry."

"I'm not angry. I'm thinking."

"About what?"

"How I'm going to explain to Chief Terry that I'm spending the entire day — and apparently the night — at the camp with you. He's going to think I've lost my mind or something."

I slid him a sidelong look. "You don't have to go."

He snorted. "Please. We both know I wouldn't have it any other way. There's a potential killer up there."

"I can take care of myself."

"I'm well aware of that. There's strength in numbers. Besides, I wouldn't mind a chance to give that entire area a good search. We had a team up there and they took a cursory look around, but they were obviously focused on the pool. This would allow me a chance to branch out."

"So ... you really want to go?"

"That's a hard question to answer. I really want to spend time at the camp ... but the aftermath of a murder isn't exactly what I would call an ideal time. I really do want to look around to see if I can find anything in some of those other buildings. I really don't want to be separated from you."

"You're not exactly a fan of camping."

He made a face. "Who said anything about camping? They have beds."

"They have bed frames," I corrected. "There are no mattresses."

"And I have one of those inflatable air mattresses. Before I bought an actual bed, I slept on it for a month. It's fairly comfortable."

I was surprised at the way he smoothly changed the topic to the mundane. "Why did you sleep on an air mattress for a month?"

"I was so excited to start my new job that a bed didn't seem important."

"Are you still excited about your job? I mean ... I know you're good at it. I know you get a charge out of being the hero. Are you still as excited as you were at the start?"

He shrugged. "I don't know. Are you still as excited about your job as you used to be?"

"I like being the boss."

He grinned. "I've noticed. It's not the same as when you first started, though, is it? As you mature, the excitement wanes. I still like my job and want to be good at it. But other things excite me now."

"Like bacon?"

"Bacon has always excited me. I was talking more about you."

He was open with his feelings, which I appreciated. Still, the simple statement caused my heart to flutter. "Are you saying you're more excited about me than work?"

"Yes. That's not even a hard choice."

"Oh, that's kind of sweet."

He snickered as he shook his head. "I like how I can still woo you with words."

"I'm not sure I like you using the word 'woo.' It seems dated."

"Suck it up."

"Okay." I exhaled heavily to center myself and then turned back to the earlier conversation. "Are you really okay with us going out there? I don't expect you to spend the whole day with us. You can go to work and then join us after if you want."

"I need to talk to Chief Terry, but we'll figure it out. I'd prefer being up there with you guys for the duration. It's not that I don't trust Clove and Thistle. I simply would prefer you have more backup if we can work it out."

"That's kind of sweet."

"I'm a sweet guy."

THE INN BUSTLED WITH activity when we arrived. No guests had checked in yet — although from the way Marnie was carrying on behind the front desk that was imminent — but the family had taken over the main floor and apparently the Winchesters were in a yelling mood this afternoon.

"I didn't overbook," Twila screeched from somewhere deep within the inn. "I know how to use the computer. Stop saying I overbooked."

"You overbooked," Marnie snapped. "We have an extra couple,

which means we're going to have to use the attic room. We haven't been up there to clean it since Belinda moved out."

Belinda Martin was a part-time maid who started her own business. She lived in the inn for months so she could get back on her feet financially. Then, because she figured it was more "normal," she took her daughter Annie and moved to a place not far away. Annie was still a popular figure at the inn, but Belinda was strict about only bringing her to work on weekends. She obviously wasn't here to take a side in the argument.

"I'm betting Annie cleaned her room before she left," I offered as I slipped out of my hoodie. "It probably won't take much to get it to your lofty heights."

Marnie shot me a pointed look. "I wasn't talking to you."

"No, but you're my favorite aunt, so I decided to answer anyway." I beamed at her. "That's how much I care about your emotional well-being."

"I heard that crack about her being your favorite aunt," Twila snapped, poking her head into the lobby. "Don't think I'm going to forget it."

"You're my favorite aunt, too," I reassured her. "It's Marnie only fifty percent of the time."

"Whatever." Twila didn't look as if she had the patience to play games. Instead, she pinned Marnie with a dark look. "I don't overbook. You're counting wrong."

"I know how to count." Marnie rolled her eyes so hard I thought she might fall over. "I'm the one who taught you to count."

"Right. You taught me to count." Twila's reaction was so exaggerated I had to bite my lip to keep from laughing. "You were a year older than me and an educational genius. You got your teaching certificate when you were four."

I left them to their bickering and nudged Landon out of the room. He appeared ready and willing to sit around and watch them snipe at each other, but I had other plans.

"I want a drink," I announced.

"Now we're talking." He slipped his arm around my waist and led me into the library. There, Thistle and Marcus were already seated in chairs and entertaining their own argument.

"I'm just saying that a wolf would be a cool animal to have at the petting zoo," Thistle said. "I've always thought my spirit animal is a wolf, so we should definitely get one."

Marcus didn't look impressed with the suggestion. "No offense, but if my insurance is off-the-charts for a goat, what do you think it will be for a wolf?"

"Those goats are menaces," Thistle argued. "They butt people with their heads and chew shoes. A wolf wouldn't do that."

"Right. A wolf would just rip your throat out." He flicked his eyes to us as we walked into the room and immediately headed for the drink cart. "Would you guys tell Thistle that a wolf is a bad idea for the petting zoo?"

"I think it's a fabulous idea," Landon countered. "I've always wanted to see a live version of *Little Red Riding Hood*. How many people do you think a wolf could eat before you get arrested?"

"Ha, ha, ha." Thistle glared at Landon. "You're supposed to take my side when conversations like this pop up. Just for the record."

"I had no idea that was the rule." Landon mixed two martinis before directing me toward the couch. "I'll keep that in mind from now on."

"You should definitely do that," she agreed, moving her eyes to me. "Where did you spend the rest of the day? I stopped by the newspaper office to see you but you weren't there."

"I went with Landon to talk to Vicky's sister," I replied, my heart giving a small jolt at the memory. "She named her oldest daughter after Vicky. She knew she wasn't coming back."

"She said she was convinced she wasn't coming back," Landon corrected. "She also acted sad because she could no longer imagine Vicky out in the world having adventures. She might've known the truth, but part of her still had a sliver of hope Vicky was out there and just took off for no apparent reason."

"Not knowing is the worst," Thistle mused. "Still, there's hope. Once you know the horrible truth, that hope evaporates, so the not knowing seems preferable in that case. Still, she'll be able to move forward and bury her sister. That has to make her feel better."

"She was strong," I noted. "She had a toddler in the room. A little girl who kept making eyes at Landon. She didn't break down in front of her daughter because she said she didn't want her children to associate Vicky's memory with tears. I think that's a remarkable feat."

"It's pretty good," Thistle agreed, leaning back in her chair as I sipped my martini. "Did anything else happen?"

"We know that Vicky mentioned she didn't like one of her male co-workers," Landon replied. "She didn't say it was for a sexual or violent reason, though. Stephanie kept all Vicky's letters from that summer. They're in a safety deposit box. She's going to read them again and tell us if there's anything of interest. We're heading back out to the camp in the morning."

"We're going to spend the night," I added.

Thistle made a face. "Why would you possibly want to spend the night?"

"I want to make contact with Vicky's ghost," I replied without hesitation. "And, before you suggest that I simply force her to answer questions, I'm not going to do that."

Landon rested his hand on my knee. "Bay has made her decision on this and I think it's a good one. She doesn't want to force Vicky. I'm behind her. That means spending a lot of time at the camp so Vicky can settle down and feel comfortable approaching her."

"I thought maybe you and Clove might want to tag along," I added hopefully. "If she sees the three of us together, it might jog her memory."

Thistle didn't look thrilled with the suggestion. "Why would we possibly want to do that? You know how I feel about camping."

"It won't technically be camping," I hedged. "We have cabins. Landon and I are taking an air mattress. I figured you and Clove might want to do the same. You can bring Marcus and Sam if you want."

Thistle narrowed her eyes. "Camping is stupid."

"It is, but we liked Vicky." I refused to back down. "I don't think spending one night at our old camp is too much to ask. I mean ... she's been dead for ten years and we didn't bother to notice."

"Oh, geez." Thistle's face turned mottled red. "I hate it when you do things like this. I mean ... seriously. How am I supposed to say no when you put it that way?"

"Don't say no."

Instead of immediately answering, Thistle merely shook her head and averted her gaze.

"I can't take the afternoon off tomorrow," Marcus interjected, drawing my eyes to him. "We have a big group of tourists hitting in the afternoon and I guarantee I'll be busy. I can spend the night there if it helps. In fact, to save on the food situation, because I know how Thistle hates cooking by a campfire, I can pick up takeout and bring it with me."

"Now we're talking." Landon brightened considerably. "Burgers, fries and s'mores. That sounds like the perfect combination. I'll be there with Bay all afternoon if the others need to work. You don't have to come right away, Thistle. Bay would like it if you're there later. She really wants to contact Vicky and thinks you and Clove are her best shot of doing that."

"No, she's the best shot of doing that," Thistle argued. "She's the one with the power to bend the will of ghosts. I don't understand why she's not using it."

"You understand," Landon snapped. "She doesn't want to. It makes her feel bad. In this particular case, it will give her nightmares because she knew Vicky. We both know it. Stop being a pain and just agree to help. You're going to do it. You're only arguing so you can say you put up a fight."

"I'm arguing because camping is stupid," Thistle fired back.

"Oh, suck it up." Landon gave my knee a reassuring squeeze. "You're not going to leave Bay to do this on her own. I'm not either. Clove will whine so much we'll feel like gagging her, but she'll be there.

"Whether you guys come in the morning or later in the afternoon, it doesn't matter," he continued. "I'll be with her from start to finish and you guys will show up as soon as you can swing it."

"Which won't be until later in the afternoon because of the tour," Thistle said.

"That's fine." Landon kept his tone light. "Just message us when you have a firm schedule and we'll make it work."

"Fine," Thistle grumbled as Marcus offered her a soothing pat and private whispers.

"You kind of bullied her into doing that," I noted to Landon as I got comfortable. "I'm impressed with the way you handled it. You didn't manipulate and instead took her head-on. That was the opposite of how Aunt Tillie would've handled it."

"Which is why she responded. If Aunt Tillie would've been the one handling negotiations, there would've been no chance of sleep. The arguments would've carried on well into the night. That's not how things needed to go this time."

"You still have to convince Clove."

"She'll be the easy one."

"How do you figure?"

"Clove has a soft heart and she'll want to help Vicky," Landon replied without hesitation. "All we have to do is tell her that Vicky's soul can't be put to rest until this is solved and we need to be at the camp for an extended period to solve it. Easy-peasy."

"I don't think it's going to be as easy as you think."

"Just you watch. I'm awesome when it comes to negotiations."

I was almost looking forward to watching him work. Of course, that could've been the martini talking.

FIFTEEN

Chief Terry was already seated at the expansive table talking with Clove and Sam when we entered the dining room. I hadn't heard him when he arrived, so I was understandably surprised ... until I realized he'd entered through the back door.

"Terry, I put the bag you brought in my room in case you're looking for it," Mom announced as she breezed through the swinging door. She shot me an absent look as I sat in my usual chair. "I didn't realize you guys were here. Dinner is about ten minutes out."

That was it. She didn't say another word. She didn't mention that she was sorry for traumatizing me earlier. She also didn't say that she'd thought long and hard about what had happened and was sorry for being a hypocrite and sleeping with Chief Terry on the first date.

None of that occurred.

"Thanks." Chief Terry's cheeks burned bright when I shifted my gaze to him. He sat to my right — that was the usual configuration — and Landon to my left. Apparently Chief Terry wasn't quite ready to meet my gaze, because he opted to continue his previous conversation rather than say anything to me. "I definitely think we can work something out with patrols around the Dandridge during busy festivals, Sam. I'll talk to my men."

"What's happening out at the Dandridge?" I asked.

"Nothing," Sam replied hurriedly. "It's just ... I found some weird footprints by the tanker and there are new tire prints in the mud on the road that leads to the Dandridge. I think it's obvious someone parked out there and walked around. It must have been last night after we went to bed. I want to make sure it's not someone planning something dangerous."

"I told him it was probably kids," Clove offered. "He agrees, but we want to make sure."

"That used to be a party area," Chief Terry said. "I'll send a few patrols out just to be on the safe side."

"I would appreciate it." Sam rubbed his hands over Clove's shoulder. "Now that I'm getting married to the prettiest woman in the world, I want to make sure she's safe at all times."

Clove beamed at him as Thistle mimed throwing up.

"Oh, that's sweet," Landon intoned. "He's going out of his way to make sure his woman is safe and I'm taking mine to spend the night at a camp where a killer might be hanging out. That makes me feel like a bit of a dolt."

I frowned. "Did you just refer to me as your woman?"

"No. You're hearing things." He didn't meet my gaze. "But speaking of that, I need to talk to you guys." He launched into his spiel, which took only a few minutes, and by the time he was finished Sam was already bobbing his head.

"That's a great idea," Sam enthused. "I haven't seen a ghost myself in some time and I've yet to see Bay in action with her new powers." Sam's mother was a witch and he, too, could see ghosts. "I won't be able to help until the afternoon because I have some deliveries arriving at the tanker tomorrow morning, but we'll definitely be there."

I didn't miss the way Clove moved her jaw. She didn't argue, but it was obvious she wanted to.

"I already told them we need to be at the store for the tour, Clove," Thistle offered. "We'll pick up dinner and head out there once we're finished."

"Right." Clove's expression would've been hard for a stranger to read. She was trying to figure a way out of this conundrum. "Are we sure it's safe to stay at the camp? I mean ... two bodies have been found out there. That doesn't sound safe."

"There will be six of us," Landon pointed out. "One killer would be stupid to take on six of us ... especially when three of you are magical and I'm armed."

"Of course." Clove made a face. "Still, what if the killer decides to hide in the woods and shoot at us?"

"Then we'll duck and run," Landon replied without hesitation.

"But ... ." Clove slid her eyes to Sam, looking for help. He was either oblivious or purposely ignoring her. I had no idea which. "I don't want to camp," she said finally, saying the one thing everyone at the table already knew. "I hate camping. It's one thing to sleep on the bluff after a night of drinking and dancing. It's quite another to purposely stay at the haunted campground with no electricity that's housing a killer."

"You'll be fine." Landon refused to back down. "Speaking of that, I understand you have generators in your greenhouse, Aunt Tillie. We need to borrow one for tomorrow. I want to fire up the electrical out at the campground and see if that helps with the search. I'm also going to need to take some lightbulbs for those old fixtures."

"We have old lightbulbs in the basement," Twila offered "They're just sitting there since we switched over to LED bulbs. You can take them."

Landon grinned. "Thank you very much. That will save some time."

"I don't understand," Chief Terry argued. "Why would you possibly want to spend the night out there?"

"Because Bay thinks it's important," Landon replied simply. "I'm with her, so I think it's important, too."

I felt warm all over. "Thank you."

Landon smirked. "What did you think I was going to say? You need to talk to her. I want to make sure you're safe and look around. It's a meeting of the minds, so to speak. Everyone else will be there to spend the night. No one would dare move on a group like that. Everything will be fine."

"Yeah, but ... ." Chief Terry trailed off and shifted his eyes to me. "What do you think she's going to tell you, Bay?" He looked plaintive. "Do you really think she's going to help?"

"I think she's the only one who can help," I replied without hesitation. I'd given this a lot of thought during the drive back from Stephanie's house. "She's stuck out there for a reason. She wasn't at her sister's house. That means she's probably emotionally anchored to the camp.

"I want to talk to her, figure out what happened and then free her," I continued. "I remember her as a nice young woman. She had a lot of energy and was fun. She didn't bully anyone ... or judge anyone. She was welcoming to all the girls."

"She was also mean to Lila," Thistle added. "That's why I'm going. She caught Lila being mean to Bay that first summer and took her down a peg or two. Like Bay said, she was welcoming to everyone ... but she recognized Lila for what she was. To me, that means she was a good person, and I want to help her."

"And there will be s'mores," Landon added. "We'll build a fire and have a good time while helping a woman who helped you a decade ago."

"Oh, geez." Clove whined as she dropped her head into her hands. "Did you have to put it that way? Now I'll look like a jerk if I don't go."

"You will," Landon agreed. "Do you want to be the family jerk?"

"Not particularly."

"Then we'll see you in time for dinner."

"I guess." Clove huffed and glared at Sam. "I blame this on you."

He didn't appear bothered by the statement. "You'll be fine. I want to see the ghost."

"I'm not sure it's a good idea, but it's not as if you guys will be out there alone," Chief Terry said. "I guess it's not the worst idea."

"Oh, such high praise." Landon rested his hand on my back and smiled. "So ... you're spending another night, huh? You guys aren't wasting any time. Does that mean we're on our own for breakfast again tomorrow? What? I'm just asking so we can plan accordingly. Bay and I have a busy day tomorrow and it's going to require nourishment. I'm not trying to be a jerk. No, really. Oh, don't look at me that way."

Even though I was uncomfortable with the turn of events — mostly that it happened so fast and I didn't have a chance to brace myself — I couldn't stop myself from laughing. Landon always knew how to lighten a mood.

"Don't get between him and his bacon," I warned. "He'll never let it go."

"You've got that right." He winked at me and leaned closer when the table occupants started talking about other topics. "I told you it was going to be okay. Everyone will be there. All you have to worry about is doing your own thing. We'll handle the rest."

"Thanks. You always know exactly what I need."

"Not always, no. In this particular case, yes. We'll figure this all out and help Vicky. None of us will rest until it's done. I promise you that."

I believed him. Tomorrow was going to be a big day.

"EXCUSE ME BUT ... what?"

Mom ambushed me in the kitchen when I arrived for breakfast the next morning. The back of Landon's Explorer was already packed with things we needed and all we had to do was load up on breakfast (and pack a basket full of snacks to see us through until everyone else showed up with dinner) before saying goodbye and heading out.

My mother had other plans.

"You're taking Aunt Tillie with you," she repeated. "It will be good for her ... and you. Think of it as a bonding exercise."

I could think of a few more ways to look at it. "But ... why?"

"Because I said so."

I glanced over my shoulder, hoping to find Landon ready to help, but he wasn't there. He was in the dining room talking over a few things with Chief Terry, making sure he would be available if something popped up. Mom knew what she was doing when she waited for me to be alone to broach the Aunt Tillie subject.

"I don't think it's a good idea." I licked my lips and searched for a way to gracefully bow out of this situation. "She'll be stuck up there all day with us and there's no comfortable place for her to sit." I decided to go with her advanced age first. "Plus, what if she trips or something? We'll be far away from a doctor. That can't possibly be good for her."

Mom was blasé as she whipped her pancake batter. "Your aunt has been walking for a very long time. She doesn't trip. Even when she's drunk, she doesn't trip. She's the steadiest member of this family on her feet ... which is a sad, sad fact."

"Yes, but she could trip. I don't want to be the one who is supposed to be watching her when she finally breaks her streak. I think she should stay here."

"She wants to go ... so I think she should go."

I sucked in a calming breath. Yelling at my mother would only cause her to dig her heels in. If I wanted to escape the inn without Aunt Tillie in tow, I would have to appeal to her keen love of family ... or simply trick her. I was fine with either option.

"I don't think it's smart for us to keep Aunt Tillie with us all night," I persisted. "It's barely getting out of the forties once the sun sets. We'll have a fire, but that won't be enough to warm her and keeping her warm inside the cabins is going to be uncomfortable. I don't think Landon is up to cuddling with her."

Mom's expression never changed as she started ladling the batter onto the griddle. "Take extra blankets."

She was killing me! "What about Peg?" I hoped I sounded rational instead of desperate. "If Aunt Tillie comes with us you'll have to take care of Peg. You don't like her and that will be a hardship."

Mom scowled. "I don't dislike Peg. I think she's a lovely animal. I just happen to believe Aunt Tillie should've asked before bringing an animal into the home. Teacup pigs live about five years. That's not a long lifespan, and she'll be devastated when the pig dies.

"Of course, there is the off chance that your aunt will go before

Peg," she continued. "Then we will be left to care for Peg, and she didn't bother asking if we would be up to that. Our problems are not with Peg but the manner in which your aunt brought her into this house."

Ugh. I hated it when she used her pragmatic voice. That meant she was willing to argue for the long haul, something that didn't bode well for me.

"Mom, I'm not trying to be difficult." I opted to change tactics. "You know I love Aunt Tillie. I take her quite often to give you guys a break. I don't think this is the right time, though. We're going to be dealing with a traumatized ghost and a potential murderer."

"Oh, puh-leez!" Mom rolled her eyes, which told me I'd already lost the argument. "There's no way a murderer is going to be hanging around the camp at the same time you and Landon are setting up shop. If he is out there, he'll leave as soon as he realizes he's not alone.

"That is if he hasn't left already," she continued. "Between the cops running around and you guys showing up willy-nilly, that camp would be a stupid place for a murderer to stay. He's probably already moved on."

I hated that she had a point. "Mom ... ."

"Bay, your great-aunt doesn't have many years left on this earth," she said, spatula in hand. "She loves a good adventure. This adventure is relatively safe in the grand scheme of things. Plus, she loves you girls. She wants to spend time with you. I can't believe you would deny her this.

"I hate to say it because you're my child, but it's selfish," she continued, barely taking a breath. "The fact that you won't give of yourself for your elderly great-aunt speaks volumes about your character ... and it's something I never saw in you. I feel ashamed."

My cheeks flushed hot even though I couldn't help feeling she was manipulating me. "Fine. She can come." I barked out the words before I thought better of them. "Are you happy?"

Mom instantly smiled. "I knew you would see things my way."

The drastic change in her demeanor confirmed my suspicion. "Oh, you just manipulated me."

"I have no idea what you're talking about. I simply think it's good for you to spend time with your elders. Aunt Tillie won't be around forever. The more memories you have of her, the better."

It all sounded perfectly reasonable. But I knew better.

"Stuff it," I hissed, keeping my voice low. The rest of the family was in the dining room, but they would come running the second they realized we were fighting. "You want a break from Aunt Tillie and you're pushing her on me because you think this is the easiest way to get what you want. Don't bother denying it."

"I think you're starting to show signs of paranoia. You haven't been in Aunt Tillie's special crop, have you?"

Aunt Tillie grew pot on the side, something that was illegal in Michigan until the most recent election. Now she could have up to twelve plants legally. That was going to change the makeup of her greenhouse, even if my mother and aunts put up a fight. That wasn't the debate for today, though.

"Just admit what you're doing," I insisted.

"I'm making sure you spend quality time with your great-aunt. I have no problem admitting it."

I tried for another five minutes, but Mom brushed me off and then ordered me out of the kitchen. Chief Terry and Landon had turned to other topics when I landed in my seat.

"What's wrong?" Landon asked when I slouched in my chair.

"Mom says we have to take Aunt Tillie with us."

"Why?"

"Because she doesn't think we spend enough quality time with her."

"Why really?" Landon asked, flicking his eyes to the woman in question. She looked smug as she sat at the head of the table.

"Because I interrupted Winnie and Terry when I conducted my monthly fire drill last night," Aunt Tillie replied, unruffled. "Terry doesn't sleep in anything but his skin, just for the record. He was not expecting a fire drill and I caught him unaware."

I was mortified when I turned to Chief Terry. "Aunt Tillie saw you naked?"

"That's a wonderful two dates you've had," Landon drawled. "You got naked with Winnie and Aunt Tillie in less than forty-eight hours. That has to be some sort of record."

"Stuff it!" Chief Terry's neck was so red it looked as if it burned to the touch. "I had no idea that monthly fire drills were part of the deal here. I mean ... how could I have known that?"

"You could've asked," I muttered, narrowing my eyes. "You're the reason."

"I'm the reason for what?" Chief Terry sputtered. "I didn't do anything. I was minding my own business."

"His own naked business," Landon echoed, grinning.

"You're the reason Aunt Tillie is being forced on us," I said. "Mom wants to give you a chance to get over your embarrassment, so we have to take a shift as babysitters."

"Hey!" Aunt Tillie was obviously affronted. "I don't need a babysitter. I'll be a great help to you at that camp. Just you wait and see."

Oh, I had no doubt I would see exactly what she had to offer ... and for hours on end. Suddenly our casual outing was turning into something more, and I didn't like it.

"This is going to suck," I complained.

SIXTEEN

By the time we added all of Aunt Tillie's "necessities" — including four pairs of shoes, three pairs of leggings, an ax, an extensive lunch spread, a kazoo and a fifth of Jack Daniels — it was well after ten before we made it to the camp.

Landon, who often had trouble maintaining his cool, was a complete and total bear by the time we parked.

"Let's look around and decide where everything is going to go before we start unloading," he suggested, his voice low and gravelly.

I thought about pressing him on the issue, insisting that he perk up, but he clearly wasn't in the mood. To be fair, neither was I. Aunt Tillie was never part of my ghost-wooing plan. We had to deal with her, though, so there was no way to get around it.

"Fine." I hopped out of the Explorer and pulled open the rear door so Aunt Tillie could exit. "Come on. You can come with me and decide where you want to sleep," I suggested.

Aunt Tillie didn't argue, instead handing me Peg so I could ease the pig to the ground. "Make sure you have her leash," she ordered. "I don't want her to take off. I'll make you catch her if she gets away."

"I've got her leash. I ... ." I turned when Landon snagged the leash from me and started walking toward the water. "What are you doing?"

"Spending quality time with Peg while I get myself in order," he replied without hesitation. "I won't be gone long. Don't wander too far away."

I watched him go, a mixture of trepidation and amusement washing over me.

"What's his deal?" Aunt Tillie asked as she came up beside me. "Why is he so grumpy? He was in a good mood last night."

"That's because he assumed that with three couples and three cabins the sleeping arrangements would lean toward the romantic. Your arrival throws his plans into disarray."

"He doesn't have to worry. I have no intention of sleeping with you guys. I brought my tent. Peg and I are sleeping close to the fire."

"You brought your tent?" I slanted my eyes to her. "I didn't see a tent."

"It's in there, and don't worry, busybody. I don't want to be anywhere near Landon and his lusty lips. I can guarantee that. Besides, I have my own list of things I want to do while we're here."

That was worrisome. "What list?"

"Don't worry about it."

I considered arguing and then let it go. "Fine. I'm sure it has something to do with you casting spells and drawing wards to mess with Margaret should she get this land. I don't particularly want her to have it either, so I suggest you make sure the curses won't affect others should someone else manage to buy the land ... and make sure nothing can be tracked back to us."

Aunt Tillie mock saluted. "I've got it all under control."

WE SPENT THE NEXT HOUR wandering from cabin to cabin. Aunt Tillie lost interest in them relatively quickly, but the office — which was on the far side of the parcel — held her interest for an extended period. So long, in fact, I felt the need to go looking for her.

"What are you doing in here?" I asked when I found her flipping through the old file cabinets at the back of the ramshackle office. "What is all that?"

"Old camp records," Aunt Tillie replied as she sat on a padded chair, which I eyed dubiously.

"I can't believe you're sitting on that. Aren't you worried rats have nested in there and something is about to come alive and bite you in the butt?"

"Rats aren't scary. In fact, they make great pets. They only live two years, though, and I don't want to say goodbye to a pet after only two years."

I thought about what Mom had said about Peg. "Did you know that teacup pigs live only five years?" I asked finally.

"I know that the internet says a lot of things that aren't always true. Trust me. I tried that Pop Rocks and soda thing with Margaret. Total bunk. That's how long a teacup pig lasts if you don't take care of it. I plan to spoil Peg rotten so she'll last as long as me."

"Good to know." I removed the pad from a nearby chair and sat on the bare wood. It was uncomfortable but better than worrying about what might be crawling around under my posterior. "Is there anything good in these files?"

"I guess it depends on what you're looking for. I'm looking for a reason to make sure Margaret can't get her hands on this property."

"Like what?"

She shrugged. "I don't know. Maybe it's ancient Indian burial grounds or something."

"This isn't *Poltergeist*."

"That was a cemetery. Ancient Indian burial grounds is *Pet Sematary*."

"Is that better?"

"Definitely. Who doesn't love a good zombie cat?"

I laughed at her response. "Fair enough." I grabbed a nearby file and flipped it open, frowning at the contents. "Holy ... this is a list of kids who stayed here in the summer of 1987."

Aunt Tillie's expression was blank as she lifted her eyes to me. "So?"

"So, maybe there's one of these files for every year ... including the last one when Vicky was here."

"Do you think one of the kids killed her?"

"Probably not, but I'm not ruling it out. I mean ... we were teenagers. The boys were always kept on the other side of the lake — we should probably head over there and take a look, by the way — and it's entirely possible that a teenaged boy lost his cool and did something to her. Whether it's probable, who can say?"

"Well ... if you head to the other side of the lake I'm not going. I'm more interested in this side of the lake. Margaret isn't interested in the parcel on the other side of the lake."

"Has anyone ever told you that your infatuation with Mrs. Little is unhealthy?"

"The same could be said for your infatuation with Landon, but it has cleared your skin right up." She shot me an exaggerated wink as I glared at her. "Now, shush. I'm reading."

"Yeah, yeah, yeah."

We lapsed into silence for a long time. I moved to the floor so I could start spreading out the files. I'd managed to find five years' worth of records. Unfortunately, I couldn't find the year I was looking for and the files were tossed about as if they'd been purposely strewn in a hundred different directions during a search years before.

One file I found was of particular interest. It held a series of glossy photographs — the sort that had been hand-developed in a darkroom on old paper stock — clumped together in a heap. Some of the photographs were stuck together, so it was slow going as I tried to separate them without destroying them. Still, as I went through them I found numerous photos of Vicky ... and myself.

"What are you doing?"

I'd been sifting through the photographs so long I forgot it had been a while since either of us had spoken. "Just looking." My voice cracked, taking me by surprise. Was I crying? When did that happen? "I guess I got a little emotional seeing all the old photos. Look at this one." I held up a photograph so she could see it. Clove, Thistle and I stood together as kids — we were probably thirteen, twelve and eleven at the time — and our arms were linked. It was in pristine condition. "I'm going to keep it and frame it."

When Aunt Tillie didn't immediately respond, I turned to find her staring at a spot behind me. She was barely paying attention to me, which made me wonder if the question had even been directed at me.

"Who are you ... ?" My heart skipped a beat when I caught sight of Vicky floating behind me. She was almost invisible, her countenance flimsy and weak. The tears running down her ethereal face threw me for a loop. "Vicky?"

She jerked up her head and met my gaze, surprise wafting over her features. She didn't stay long. She didn't wait for me to ask a question or remind her of who I was. Instead, she simply disappeared, leaving no trace that she'd ever been present.

"What the ... ?" I shifted my head and found Aunt Tillie watching me with unveiled interest. "What? I'm not making her stay no matter what you and the others think. She'll come around on her own. I know it."

"I didn't say anything," Aunt Tillie said finally, her expression thoughtful. "Why were you crying?"

"I ... don't know." I honestly didn't have an answer to the question. "I didn't realize I was until you said something."

"I wasn't looking at you when I asked the question," she admitted. "I saw the ghost. She was watching you, looking over your shoulder at the photos. She was crying ... and you were crying."

"Maybe we were both lost in the moment."

"Or maybe you were picking up on her emotions."

The simple statement shouldn't have shaken me ... and yet it did. "I don't think that's possible."

"Of course it's possible." Aunt Tillie straightened, her hunt for documents to drive Mrs. Little crazy temporarily forgotten. "You're a necromancer. I should've considered the possibility before this. It makes sense."

I was bewildered. "What makes sense?"

"The fact that you've been picking up on the emotions of ghosts for a long time. I first noticed it back when Landon was on his undercover assignment. You were weepy and morose. I don't think that was a coincidence."

"I was being a baby," I countered. "I was feeling sorry for myself because I missed him."

"That might be part of it, but that wasn't all of it. I thought it was strange at the time – even considered that you were pregnant – but that was before we realized you were a necromancer. You had a lot going on then and it was easy to explain away your raw emotions thanks to what was going on with Landon. I think it was more, though."

Even though I didn't like being reminded of that particular meltdown, I was intrigued. "Have you heard of other necromancers absorbing the emotions of ghosts?" The idea troubled me ... and yet it also made sense. "I'm only asking because, when Melanie took Chief Terry and I thought there was a chance he might not be found in time, I felt ... rage. It wasn't just normal anger and fear. It was rage and I thought for a few minutes that I was feeling what the ghosts of her parents were feeling. I pushed it out of my mind, because I assumed I was being ridiculous."

Aunt Tillie licked her lips as she leaned back in her chair. "I think it's definitely possible. In fact, there are stories about necromancers being taken over by ghosts. They're old stories, mind you. Necromancers are rare. Not everyone who can see and talk to ghosts becomes a necromancer. I'm living proof of that."

"Right." I rubbed my cheek and flicked my eyes to the door, almost coming out of my skin when I saw Landon standing there with Peg. He'd obviously been listening for a bit because he looked engrossed in the conversation. "Hey." I swiped at my cheeks and was happy to find my tears had dried. "How long have you been standing there?"

"Long enough to hear some of your conversation," he replied honestly, handing Aunt Tillie Peg's leash before moving closer to me. "Are you okay?" He looked sincerely worried as he knelt in front of me and met my gaze.

"I'm okay. Are you okay?"

"Yeah." He moved his thumbs over my cheeks. "You've been crying."

"I ... ." I had no idea what to say.

"It's okay, sweetie." He leaned in and gave me a hug. "I'm just thinking about what Aunt Tillie said."

He wasn't the only one. "Do you think it's possible?"

"I don't know." His smile was firmly in place when he pulled back. "I'm not an expert on ghosts. I think where you're concerned, anything is possible. Maybe we can do some research."

"Like with books?" The idea held little appeal. Still ... . "I guess it's worth a shot."

"Definitely." He kept his hand busy on my back as he turned to Aunt Tillie. "What do you think?"

"Are you seriously asking me?" Aunt Tillie didn't bother hiding her surprise. "I don't think you've ever asked me about anything of consequence."

"I want Bay to be okay."

"She'll be fine." Aunt Tillie sounded sure of herself, which was a relief. "She's strong. She'll get control of this like she does everything else. We simply need to watch her. If she is picking up on ghostly emotions, that could affect her in a multitude of different ways."

"Like how?"

"Like ... if she came into contact with a poltergeist at the wrong time, she could turn into the Hulk or something. Maybe not the actual Hulk, but the witchy equivalent. I don't know a lot about necromancy. I've invited the leading authority to the solstice celebration. She's a necromancer, too."

Something occurred to me. "Is that why you're so keen on hosting the celebration this year?"

Aunt Tillie averted her gaze. "It might be one of the reasons. There are more than one, I promise you that."

"Why didn't you just tell me why you wanted to have those witches descend on the area?" I challenged. "I mean ... you could've told me. I probably would've been better off knowing."

"I don't believe that's true," Aunt Tillie countered. "In fact, I believe the exact opposite. You're the self-conscious type. You need to absorb things on your own before you share your feelings with others. You've always been that way.

"You were seeing ghosts for years before you admitted it," she continued. "Don't bother denying it. I saw you talking to nothing in the garden several times when you were little. The first time you were six ... and you had the fortitude to lie and say you were talking to the garden gnome. I knew that wasn't true because I saw you were talking to Gary Steinbeck." She turned to Landon to explain. "He was a neighbor for a few years. He was friendly with the girls, gave them candy and watched them when they played in the yard to make sure they never made it too close to the road."

"That's fascinating," Landon deadpanned. "I love hearing about long-dead neighbors."

"I'm just saying that she's always been the sort to internalize things, smart guy," Aunt Tillie snapped. "The same thing has been happening this go-around. She doesn't want any of us to worry so she keeps things to herself. Occasionally she snaps because of that tendency. That's probably why we assumed her meltdown a few months ago was a snap when it was something else."

Landon opened his mouth to argue and then changed his mind. "Basically you're saying that she's susceptible right now and she wasn't before. Do I have that right?"

Aunt Tillie nodded. "Her powers advanced within the past few months. I'm guessing it started around that time. We just didn't realize it because she didn't overtly start controlling ghosts until that day with the crazed gamer. She sent those ghosts to attack. Heck, she's the reason those ghosts stayed anchored the way they did in the first place. She was exerting power and we didn't even know it."

"So ... what happens now?" Landon looked legitimately concerned. I wanted to reassure him, but I didn't have the appropriate answers to soothe either of us.

"She needs to get control of her magic," Aunt Tillie replied simply. "Her guard was down while looking through the photos." She leaned forward and snagged the snapshot that had me crying. "She was emotional when she saw this, which created an opening. Vicky was emotional when she saw it. It was her emotions Bay was feeling when I looked up. That much was obvious."

"How can you be sure?" I asked. "How do you know she wasn't feeling my emotions?"

"Because you weren't in control. I could read your aura. She briefly took you over. You can't let that happen, Bay. I know you didn't realize you were doing it, but you need to keep it together and make sure that you don't allow yourself to be vulnerable."

"That's easier said than done," I argued. "I didn't even know it was happening."

"You know now. Just ... be careful. This is like all the other magic in your life. You had to learn to control it. This is no different."

I wanted to argue but there was no point. She was right ... and I felt awkward given the way she and Landon were watching me. "I'll be careful."

"You will," Landon agreed, catching my gaze. "You didn't know it was happening and now you do. We'll figure out a way to handle it, just like we do everything else. It's going to be okay."

"You sound like a broken record repeating that mantra these days," I noted. "Don't you ever get tired of it?"

"Nope." His smile was heartfelt. "I happen to like a good mantra." He leaned in and kissed my forehead. "It's okay to feel things, Bay. You just can't let other beings feel things for you. We'll figure it out." He wrapped his arms around me and held tight. "This is just a new wrinkle."

It felt somehow direr than that, but I held it together. "Yeah. I'm going to be completely wrinkly by the time I hit thirty at this point."

"I think you still look young and hot."

I laughed despite myself. "Yeah, well ... ." I jolted when the open door banged against a wall and drew attention to the figure standing in the doorway. I hadn't seen Randy Weaver coming until he was upon us, and he didn't look happy when he realized we were encroaching on his turf ... again.

"Exactly what are you doing out here?" he bellowed. "This is private property. You have exactly thirty seconds to vacate or I'll make you vacate. Starting now."

SEVENTEEN

Randy apparently didn't like visitors at the camp and stopped by more frequently than he intimated when I'd questioned him the first time.

"This is private property," he announced in a self-important voice when we didn't immediately hop to our feet and flee. "You're trespassing. Trespassers may be shot on sight."

"This isn't your property," I pointed out.

His eyes flashed with annoyance. "I've been hired to protect it."

"You told me you got thirty bucks a month and it wasn't enough to make sure you dropped by regularly."

"And who are you again?" Randy adopted a quizzical expression, as if he thought that would be enough to dissuade me from asking the hard questions. Before I could answer, Aunt Tillie pushed herself to a standing position and glared at him.

"She's with me," Aunt Tillie announced in a grave voice.

Randy swallowed hard when he saw her. He was at least a foot taller and almost five decades younger, but he shrank in front of her. "Ms. Tillie, I didn't know you were here."

"Ms. Tillie?" Landon sent her a sideways look. "Do I even want to know what you've done to make this guy fear you?"

Aunt Tillie ignored the question. "We're here looking for a killer, Randy. What are you doing?"

He was obviously caught off guard by the question. "I just told you, Ms. Tillie. I'm here to make sure no one trespasses."

"That probably would've been more helpful if you did it before the body ended up in the pool," Aunt Tillie noted.

Randy made a face. "Yeah, well ... I only make thirty bucks a month."

"Which makes me wonder why you're back here after the fact," I admitted, folding my arms across my chest. "What good does patrolling do now?"

"Well ... ." Randy looked uncomfortable with the question.

Landon stood, his shoulders squared, and faced down Randy with his best "I'm an FBI agent and you have no choice but to answer my questions" stare. "Do you know who I am?"

Randy nodded. "You're Bay's boyfriend. Everyone knows that."

I pressed my lips together to keep from laughing. Landon seemed genuinely amused.

"Perhaps I should get one of those 'Hello, my name is' stickers," he suggested. "I can write 'Bay's boyfriend' and there will never be another question as to my identity."

"I think that's a fine idea," I offered. "I can have a shirt made up for you. What a fantastic birthday present."

His lips quirked. "Sure. I'll wear it on special occasions."

"Like when we're snowed in and can't leave the guesthouse."

He shot me a thumbs-up and focused on Randy again. "In addition to being Bay's boyfriend, I'm an FBI agent. I'm investigating the two murders that happened here."

"Two?" Randy furrowed his brow. "How are there two murders?"

"Another body was found," I supplied. "I thought you knew that."

"No." He scratched at his facial stubble while adopting a far-off expression. "I did not know that. I thought it was just the one."

"The other body has been here for more than a decade," Landon supplied. "Where were you ten years ago?"

Clearly surprised by the question, Randy made a hilarious face. "I don't know. I ... how am I supposed to remember that?" He looked to me for help. "No one could possibly remember that."

"I don't think he's asking where you were specifically," I countered. "It's more of a generic question. Like ... were you in Hemlock Cove ten years ago. You know, something like that."

Randy frowned. "Hemlock Cove wasn't even a thing ten years ago. I wasn't in Walkerville. I was probably down south. I think I was in the Detroit area at that time ... but I did visit a few times before I decided to relocate here for good."

"And what were you doing during those visits?" Landon asked. "You weren't hanging around out here, were you?"

"Absolutely not." Randy was firm on that point. "There's no way I would hang around out here when I could hang around at the bar and get laid." He realized what he said too late. "Not that I would ever do that, because women should be treated in a respectable manner." He offered Aunt Tillie a lame half-bow that made me roll my eyes.

"Oh, please." Aunt Tillie shook her head. "Everyone knows that you have never treated a woman with respect, Randy. In fact, I seem to remember you sneaking onto my property with a few of the less savory women who frequent that hole out on the highway just last year. The fact that I had to chase you off with a gun was hardly respectable."

"You chased him off the property with a gun?" Landon shook his head. "I really wish you wouldn't tell me things like that. You're not allowed to just pull a gun on people willy-nilly. I could arrest you for that."

"Right. Like any judge or jury in Michigan would lock me up for protecting my property."

Landon rolled his neck. "Randy, I'm not going to lie. I find it strange that you're out here given what happened. I would've thought you'd call it a day."

"Gertie wants me to watch her investment. She made that clear."

"When?" I asked, my mind busy. "When was the last time you saw Gertie?"

"Yesterday. She was out here. You saw her, too."

"I did. I didn't realize you two talked."

"She wanted to know why I didn't realize there was a body in the pool. I told her I couldn't watch the property twenty-four hours a day. She didn't think that was an acceptable excuse and yelled at me. I said I would do better. This is me doing better."

"But ... ." I honestly had no idea what to say.

"Tell me about your visits here," Landon prodded, using his most official voice. "How often did you visit?"

Randy looked pained. "I don't know. I swung around when I could manage it."

"And when was that? Once a week? Once a month?" When Randy didn't answer, he kept going. "Once a year?"

"I mostly stopped by when I was in the area checking on other things," Randy replied. "I didn't mark it down on a calendar or anything."

"He told me he hadn't been here since before the snows," I offered helpfully.

"So ... since before October?" Landon did the math in his head. "It's May. You were getting paid to check in regularly, but it has been seven months since you visited the property."

"I've been here twice in two days now," Randy pointed out.

"Yeah, but that's after a body was discovered. That's essentially showing up after the party is already over."

"Whatever." Randy took a moment to glance between Landon and Aunt Tillie, and then focused on me. "You get it. I'm a guy trying to survive. I have a lot of jobs. Sometimes things fall through the cracks. You own your own business."

I wanted to laugh at his newfound serious expression. "Well ... um ... I still show up at the office whenever possible. I might go a few days working at home, but I still show up."

"I can't be here every day," Randy argued. "It's thirty bucks a month, for crying out loud. Besides, no one ever comes here. I can't remember when I last saw someone out here."

"That's the sort of information we're interested in," Landon noted. "When was the last time you saw someone out here?"

"It would've been the fall," Randy replied. "I came out in early October to check on things, and there were three people already here. I didn't know what to make of it."

"Did you recognize them?" I asked. "I mean ... were they locals?"

"I recognized two of them. I don't know who the third one was."

"Well, we're dying to know who you recognized," I prodded.

"Margaret Little and Kevin Valentine."

Landon flicked his eyes to me. "Who's Kevin Valentine?"

"He's the bank manager," I replied grimly. "Obviously they were out here so she could float her plan to buy the property for condos and a second festival location."

"Is that why they were out here?" Randy almost looked relieved. "I figured maybe they were dating. Mrs. Little is old enough to be his mother, so I thought that was gross. But I don't judge. I never judge. Lord knows I've made a few mistakes picking women to spend the night with. They always look better through the beer goggles."

"You're a prince among men," I muttered, causing Landon to smirk.

"What do you know about Kevin Valentine?" he asked. "I mean ... is he a pervert like this one?" He jerked his thumb toward Randy.

I shrugged. "He's divorced. Has two daughters, but they live a few towns over with their mother. They would be teenagers now. Heck, they might even be in their twenties."

"Like the victims?"

I understood what he was insinuating. "I guess, but I've never seen anything in Kevin's personality that would suggest he's a killer. I know my intuition isn't infallible or anything, but he seems pretty normal. I've never heard of him going after women."

"Me either," Aunt Tillie said. "He's not a pervert like this one." She tilted her chin in Randy's direction. "I once caught this one trying to peek through the windows on the main floor of the inn."

"I wasn't peeking at you," Randy said hurriedly. "I'm not into grandma porn."

Aunt Tillie's mouth dropped open as I desperately tried to swallow my laughter. "Grandma porn? Did you hear that?" She looked to

Landon and me for confirmation. "I'll have you know I'm in my prime."

"Of course you are," I soothed. "You're still young and spry."

"You could be a model," Landon automatically added. "Professionally."

"See." Aunt Tillie was practically snarling when she faced off with Randy. "You owe me an apology. Grandma porn my big, fat ... ."

"Back to the campground," Landon prodded. "Have you ever seen anyone else hanging out here who shouldn't have been around?"

"Just you guys," Randy replied. "No one cares about this property except Margaret Little, Gertie and ... well ... you. I don't know what you guys are looking for, but I can't help you."

Well, that was a bit of a disappointment.

THISTLE, CLOVE, SAM AND MARCUS SHOWED UP with dinner shortly after six. They had packed for camping, including warm blankets and snacks, but Clove and Thistle clearly weren't happy.

"I blame you for this," Thistle muttered when Peg started begging for food from her plate. "Seriously, Bay, wasn't this entire thing bad enough without including Aunt Tillie?"

"It's not my fault," I countered as I finished off my hamburger and fries. "Mom insisted because she wants private time with Chief Terry."

"Oh, naked time?" Thistle wrinkled her nose. "I am so grossed out thinking about the things they're going to do tonight. I mean ... do you think they're going to be wandering around the inn naked?"

The thought hadn't occurred to me, and I was horrified she would dare say anything of the sort. "Why would you put things like that in my head?"

"Because they're in my head," she replied simply. "If I have to think about them, so do you. Those are the rules."

"Ugh."

We lapsed into uncomfortable silence for several minutes. I knew what everyone was thinking — Mom and Chief Terry naked together was the sort of visual that would blind mere mortals — and my stomach twisted before I could finish my food. "I think I'm done." I closed my container and dropped it in the garbage bag Marcus brought for refuse. "I'm going to have nightmares."

"Speaking of that, I thought we could get the generator hooked up before it gets dark," Landon suggested. "That will allow us to keep looking around the cabins after dark ... once we get all the lightbulbs screwed in."

"I can't help but feel there's a joke hidden in there somewhere," Thistle said. "I guess it can wait until later."

Landon and Marcus handled the generator, leaving the rest of us to check the cabins and screw in lightbulbs. To my surprise, the system still worked and we were bathed in light relatively quickly. That propelled me to return to the office, where I found Aunt Tillie going through files.

"You're determined to find something to stop Mrs. Little, huh?" I said as I sat on the floor and resumed flipping through personnel files. "I thought maybe you would've given up by now."

"I will never give up when it comes to Margaret. I enjoy taking her down too much. Besides, if she wants this property, there has to be a reason. I want to know what it is."

"I thought she wanted it because she'd be able to make a profit on it."

"That's possible, but I'm betting it's more. There's a secret. I'm sure money is involved, but my guess is she's trying to sneak in and scoop this place up before a developer can. Then she will try to flip the property for a big profit. This whole second place for festivals thing is a smokescreen if I ever heard one."

"Unless it's not," I countered, grabbing a new file. "I can see Mrs. Little being interested in the property because of the condos she wants to develop and the idea of leasing specific areas to the township for festivals. That's continuous income for very little investment if she can get the property on the cheap. I have to figure that's why she's working with Kevin."

"I guess." Aunt Tillie didn't look convinced. "I still think she must have another plan. It doesn't matter. I'll thwart her if it's the last thing I do."

I snickered. "You do that, Lex Luthor. I ... ." I forgot what I was about to say when I ran across a date on one of the documents. "Hey. This is the attendance sheet from the last year of the camp. This is what I've been looking for."

"What is?" Landon asked, appearing in the doorway behind me.

"This." I held up the sheet of paper. "This is a list of people who attended camp the last year."

"Good find." He sat with me on the floor, knee to knee, and leaned over to read with me. "Do you recognize any of the names?"

"Yeah. Clove and Thistle are on here. I was hoping to find something that listed the counselors so we could track down the one Vicky didn't like. I know it's a long shot, but I figured it would be valuable if we could find it."

"Definitely." He pressed a kiss to my temple and took the file from my lap. "While you're reading that, I'll keep looking."

It was a cozy moment. We enjoyed sharing resources and working together. The only thing ruining our romantic interlude was Aunt Tillie, who kept muttering as she plotted against Mrs. Little in her head. The warm atmosphere didn't last long, as Landon straightened.

"Here. Counselors are listed here." He ran his finger down a short list. "There are, like, ten listed. That can't be right. You said there were only four, two men and two women for each camp."

"Each summer saw at least three camps, though," I reminded him. "There were different age levels for the kids. "Sixth and seventh grades were grouped together. Eighth and ninth grades. Then everyone else."

"I get what you're saying. You don't want some seventeen-year-old boy hanging with a fourteen-year-old girl."

"Basically," I agreed, bobbing my head. "So, what does the list say?" I took a moment to read it. "It looks like Vicky was here for each female camp. That makes sense, because she liked the money and was gung-ho about camping. It also looks like several other local girls were counselors, though most of them took on only one or two camps."

"What about the boys?" Landon queried. "I don't want to be sexist, but they're the ones we're most interested in."

"Because you suspect sexual assault?"

"I honestly don't know. The bodies were in water. That often washes away all traces of sexual assault. Plus, well, with Vicky's body ... ." He didn't finish the sentence. He didn't have to. I understood what he wasn't saying.

"Is that the motive you're leaning toward?" I asked. "I mean ... I guess it makes the most sense. I don't like the sound of it, but I get it."

"That's only one motive. Something else might've triggered the murders. We have very little to go on. The camp is off the beaten trail, so to speak."

"It has to be a local, right?" I pressed. "With two bodies, that's the only conclusion we can reach."

"I don't know that I agree with that," Landon hedged. "It's possible that the women weren't killed by the same person. Remember, the first killer could've told someone else where to hide a body."

"But they say the only way to truly get away with murder is to tell no one. Why let something like that slip?"

"I don't know. I'm not willing to assume anything at this point. When you assume things, you make mistakes."

"And you're nothing if not a diligent investigator," I teased.

"Exactly." He moved his finger down the list I held and stopped at the last name. Unlike the others, it was written in red ink rather than black. "Joey Morgan," he read aloud. "That's Gertie's son, right?"

I nodded. "That's weird. I don't ever remember him being a counselor. I guess it's possible, but ... I think I would remember that."

"Maybe he filled in for someone else who canceled at the last minute."

"I guess. I mean ... it's possible. People said he was lazy and never wanted to work. Maybe Gertie forced him to earn his keep."

"Yeah, but I'm interested if someone else was on the list before him. I'm also interested in tracking down these other names." He snagged the list and pushed himself to a standing position. "Come on. I think we should be done in here for the night. It's getting dark and the others are building a fire. It's time for s'mores."

"I thought this was a work excursion."

"It was a work trip. Now it's time for s'mores. I can multi-task."

"You heard him." Aunt Tillie was already standing, Peg's leash clutched in her hand. "It's time for s'mores. That's the only part of camping I like."

That was true for me, too. "Okay. But I still want to think about that list."

"Deal." Landon grinned as he pulled me up beside him. "Let's get you sugared up and in flirt mode. Then you can think as much as you want."

"That sounds like a plan."

EIGHTEEN

"Did you guys find anything?" Thistle asked as we made our way back to the bonfire, which seemed too large for seven of us. I wasn't going to put up a fight, though, now that the invading chill was pervasive thanks to the setting sun.

"We found a list of counselors for that last summer," I replied. "I don't know how much good it'll do us. I also found a list of all the campers that summer." I handed the file to Thistle.

"Where is Aunt Tillie?" Clove asked, glancing around. "You didn't ditch her, did you? Our mothers won't like it if we don't bring her back. If you go into the woods with Aunt Tillie, you're supposed to come out with her."

"I don't remember that being a rule when we were kids," I argued. "The opposite was true. I remember the time Aunt Tillie brought you and me back from the woods and left Thistle out there because she was complaining. She said that two out of three was a perfectly respectable percentage. Twila didn't think so when she had to go find Thistle, but everyone else thought it was funny."

"Yeah, yeah, yeah." Thistle made an exaggerated face. "I was perfectly fine in the woods by myself. I would've found my way home without help. I was six, mind you, but gifted even then."

Marcus chuckled as he slipped an arm around her shoulders and kissed her cheek. He was the amiable sort, more laid back than his temperamental girlfriend could ever hope to be. That didn't mean he was opposed to a "Thistle loses her cool" story. "I can picture the meltdown that must've caused. Did you yell at Aunt Tillie when you got back?"

"I don't remember. My mother was crying when she found me."

"You were, like, five-hundred feet from the back door, so she didn't have to look very far," Aunt Tillie noted as she appeared at the edge of the bonfire ring. "It's not as if I left you miles from home. You were in the backyard."

"I was not in the backyard," Thistle argued. "I was pretty far from the backyard."

"You were barely out of the yard." Aunt Tillie handed Peg's leash to Clove and focused on what looked to be a lopsided nylon bag. "I'm the reason you're as strong as you are, Thistle. You should bow down and thank me."

"I'll keep that in mind," Thistle said dryly, rolling her eyes.

"I'm surprised we're still alive," Clove announced, snuggling closer to Sam as he tucked a blanket around her. "We were basically left on our own when we were kids. I mean ... anything could've happened. We raised ourselves."

That wasn't exactly how I remembered it. "How do you figure? Our mothers fed us, put a roof over our heads, made sure we did our homework, dropped us off at school and even gave us chores that helped turn us into responsible adults."

"They also left us alone for hours on end, had us working twenty hours a week before we were out of middle school and let Aunt Tillie babysit us three days a week," Clove argued. "She could've gotten us arrested on any one of those days. She thought it was funny to get us to do illegal things."

Now that I did remember. "They weren't big things." I had no idea why I felt the need to stand up for Aunt Tillie, but I couldn't stop myself. "It was only little things."

"Yeah," Thistle murmured. "Misdemeanors, not felonies. Although there was a bit of larceny, arson and home invasion in there."

"All against Mrs. Little," I told Landon helpfully. "It wasn't serious arson or anything. Aunt Tillie just made a burning fake ghost appear on her front lawn. She was never in any danger."

Instead of admonishing Aunt Tillie, who was pulling her tent out of the bag, Landon merely shook his head. "Sometimes I wish I would've been around to date you during your wild teenage years," he said. "Other times I'm glad I wasn't, because I would've been scared away."

"That's because you're a good boy," Thistle teased. "You always follow the letter of the law."

"I do indeed," Landon agreed. "I like being a good boy. In fact ... ." He trailed off when Aunt Tillie pulled out a series of ancient-looking stakes. "What are you doing? How old is that tent?"

"Don't worry about it," Aunt Tillie challenged. "I've got everything under control."

Landon was understandably dubious. "Do you need help?"

I thought the offer was funny coming from him. "Have you ever put up a tent?" I was legitimately curious. "I mean ... you guys stayed in tents the summer we were here together. I remember that. I thought Chief Terry put up most of the tents, though. I remember him complaining about accidentally hitting his thumb with a mallet when pounding in stakes."

"We did stay in tents that summer," Landon confirmed. "I helped put mine up. I shared it with my brothers. As for Chief Terry, I've tried remembering him from that trip and I can't. The counselor is just a pleasant blur in my memory."

"Do you remember Bay?" Marcus asked, frowning as he moved to stand. "Aunt Tillie, let me help you."

"I said that I have it!" Aunt Tillie's eyes fired. "I'm not so old that I can't put up my own tent. I've been doing it since I was a kid, for crying out loud."

"Is that when the tent is from?" Sam asked. "I mean ... it looks old. Did you keep it from your childhood during the Civil War?"

The look Aunt Tillie shot him was withering. "I only kept the butter churn from my childhood."

"Really? Did you churn your own butter?" Sam obviously missed the signs that he should shut up because he kept barreling forward. "I would love to see a butter churn. I find antiquated tools fascinating to study."

Aunt Tillie made a face and glanced at me. "What did he just say?"

"That he's willing to help you put up your tent if necessary," I replied. I didn't want to call her capabilities into question — she'd lived a long time and succeeded at a lot of tasks, after all — but I had my doubts when it came to the tent. "Are you sure you don't want help?"

"The next person who asks me if I need help is going to have to sleep in the tent with me," she growled, causing the men to shrink back in unison. "Yeah, that's right. You'll be cuddling up next to me."

"She can obviously do it herself," Sam said after a beat. "Go women's lib." He thrust his fist in the air, causing Landon to choke on a laugh before turning his full attention to me.

"Tell me about Joey Morgan," he instructed, retrieving the sheet of paper he'd earlier removed from the file and unfolding it. "You said it was unusual for him to be a counselor here. Why is that? I would think that as Gertie's son it would've been a regular occurrence."

"I didn't know him well," I replied, searching my memory. "I already told you that he was older than us and younger than our mothers."

"Still, Walkerville wasn't very big."

"No, but ... you've seen Gertie's house. They lived out in the middle of nowhere."

"Still, she had to shop in town. You guys saw her when you visited camp. She was always here, right?"

"Not always," I countered. "She wasn't here that weekend we were both here together."

"How can you be sure?"

"I remember that weekend well."

"Because you met me?" His wink was charming, but that wasn't the reason.

"No, because I was upset that Mom, Marnie and Twila were running the camp that weekend. The woman who was supposed to be running it — she served as a counselor quite often to make money — disappeared. She was dead and I knew because I saw her ghost."

"You've told me this story." Landon moved his hands to my shoulders and shifted so he was sitting behind me and massaging my tense muscles. "You disappeared from camp because you went off to find her body. Your mother and Chief Terry followed. You got in trouble and the counselor was put to rest. Am I leaving anything out?"

"No."

"What did the counselor have to do with Gertie?"

"Nothing that I can recall." I looked to Aunt Tillie for confirmation and almost fell over when I realized her tent was erected. "How did that happen?"

"I'm good," Aunt Tillie replied as she ushered Peg inside the tent. "Looks good, doesn't it?"

That was an understatement. The tent looked miraculous, which made me suspicious. "Is this like Harry Potter? Did you magically put up that tent when I wasn't looking?"

"Oh, geez." Aunt Tillie zipped up the nylon door to the tent and took off in the direction of Landon's Explorer. "I have to get my sleeping bag and pillow. Continue with your discussion."

"I just asked if Gertie and Donna Wilder knew each other. Do you remember if they were tight?"

Instead of answering, Aunt Tillie disappeared into the rapidly-dwindling light.

"I don't think she's going to answer," I muttered.

"It probably doesn't matter, but we'll follow up on it," Landon said. "Is there a reason Gertie wouldn't have been at the campgrounds for some of the events?"

"I seem to recall that Gertie had another job for a bit ... but I don't know if I'm making that up in my head or it was real."

"We'll ask her." Landon kept rubbing, his eyes moving to the right at the sound of shuffling feet. "Would you like help carrying your sleeping bag, Aunt Tillie?" he asked when she appeared. She was dragging what looked to be a huge sled behind her. "And when did you load that into the Explorer? I don't remember seeing that."

"Perhaps that's because you were busy pouting about having to bring me along with you," Aunt Tillie suggested. She hauled the sled to the opening of the tent and then plopped down on it, the sleeping bag propping up her back. "I'm exhausted. Who wants to rub my feet?" She looked to Marcus expectantly.

Marcus' discomfort was obvious as he turned to stare at Landon. "You were talking about Joey Morgan, right? I heard about the fire that killed him. That was a big deal back then. My uncle was a volunteer firefighter, and he told me about it."

It was obvious he was desperate to change the subject, so I decided to oblige him. "We were kids when it happened. I remember everyone getting really excited because the fire trucks were only taken out for parades and to rescue cats. That was the joke anyway."

"That's true," Aunt Tillie said as she grabbed the bag of marshmallows resting near Landon's feet. "There are very few fires in this area. Do you want to know why?"

"Are you going to tell us there's a magical reason?" Landon asked.

Aunt Tillie shrugged. "Where's the chocolate?"

Thistle grabbed the bag that contained the chocolate bars and graham crackers and tossed it toward Aunt Tillie. "I hate to admit it — mostly because it will just make your head grow to unnatural proportions — but I don't remember a lot of fires around here now that you mention it."

"Aunt Tillie started all the ones I remember," Clove added.

"Okay, you've got us curious," I offered. "Why aren't there many fires?"

"Because I can control the weather and I make sure it never gets too dry."

She said it in such a manner that it was difficult to question. Still, I had my doubts. "Are you sure that's true?"

"Ask your mothers when you get home tomorrow. It's most definitely true."

I pursed my lips and glanced at Landon over my shoulder. He looked more amused than suspicious, so I decided to let it go. "Tell us about the fire that killed Joey. I don't remember much about it. All I know is that people were talking about a fire and thought it wasn't a big deal because it was a shed ... and then it turned into a big deal."

"I don't know all the specifics," Aunt Tillie cautioned as she brandished a metal stick and shoved marshmallows on the sharp end. "I heard about it secondhand. I was never all that close with Gertie."

"Was she close with anyone?" Landon asked. "I got the feeling that she was pretty isolated when we talked to her the other day."

"She's certainly isolated now," Aunt Tillie agreed. "I don't know that she's always been isolated. Once Earl and Joey died she seemed to figure she was better off on her own."

"Some people isolate themselves after a tragedy because they don't want to risk growing close to others that could result in another loss," Sam noted. "Perhaps that's what she was feeling."

"How would I know that?" Aunt Tillie challenged. "I'm a witch, not a psychologist. I can't tell you what Gertie is thinking. All I can tell you is that there was initially hope that Joey wasn't in the shed because Laura Preston swore up and down she saw him the following day. That hope didn't last long."

"Wait ... how could there be hope?" Landon queried. "A body was found, right?"

Aunt Tillie nodded. "The fire burned hot. All that was left was blackened bones. I saw them myself."

"And how did you see them?"

"I went to the house to see what all the hoopla was about and saw them being removed. Gertie was a sobbing mess. I sent your mothers to deal with her because you know how I feel about crying."

"Yes, we do," Thistle said. "It's only useful if tears get you out of a parking ticket."

"You've got that right." Aunt Tillie winked at her and fired a cutesy finger gun in her direction. "You're smarter than you look. Of course, that's not saying much."

Thistle glared at her. "Listen, old lady ... ."

I cleared my throat to get her to stop. "Do you want to entice her to curse you while we're stuck in the middle of nowhere?" I challenged when it looked as if she was going to start in on me. "She'll make you smell like Brussels sprouts and then we'll all be in a world of hurt."

"Ooh, make them smell like bacon," Landon suggested. "There's nothing better than bacon around a bonfire."

I slid him a sidelong look. "When have you ever eaten bacon next to a bonfire?"

"When I was here," he answered without hesitation. "I remember we had to row across that lake so we could eat every meal. I guess Chief Terry wasn't big on feeding us ... which means your mother was feeding me even then." He looked enamored with the memory. "I remember there was bacon and it was pretty much the best bacon I ever ate."

"Wait a second." I held up my hand. "You remember the bacon, but not me?"

"I remember a very pretty blonde who stole my heart. I don't think I was meant to remember you because I would've pined terribly for a number of years and that wouldn't have been very healthy, would it?"

I wanted to maintain a stern face, but it was impossible. "That was a nice save."

"I thought so." He linked his fingers with mine and pulled me against him, my back to his chest so he could keep me warm. "I still don't understand why there was confusion about Joey Morgan's death if a body was a found."

"I told you that Laura Preston saw him in the woods," Aunt Tillie said. "She swore up and down that he was trying to hide, bending so she wouldn't see him. Apparently he wasn't doing a very good job of it."

"Did anyone look to make sure there was no one hiding the woods?"

"I have no idea. Joey was dead so it couldn't possibly be him. You should know that Laura is a freaking drunk. Not a fun one either.

She's the sort who carries a case of Milwaukee's Best wherever she goes so she can wet her whistle."

"Uh-huh." Landon tilted his gaze to me. "Do you think it's possible this Laura Preston confused what she saw?"

I shrugged. "I don't really know her well. She's never struck me as crazy, but I honestly can't recall having more than a five-minute conversation with her here or there. Why? Is it important?"

"I don't know. It just bothers me."

"Maybe it was his ghost," Clove suggested. "Regular people see ghosts sometimes. It's mostly witches and other magical sorts, but Sam is only one-quarter witch and he can see them. There's always the possibility that Laura has some witch in her genes, and that's what she saw."

"Wouldn't she know that?" Landon pressed. "She would've started seeing ghosts at a young age just like Bay."

"Not necessarily," Sam countered. "I always saw ghosts, but I didn't realize I was seeing them until I was older. Laura might not want to believe, so she convinces herself she's seeing real people."

"I guess." Landon rested his chin on my shoulder. "If Joey's ghost is around, wouldn't you have seen him by now, Bay?"

"That depends on where he's hanging out," I replied. "I didn't see him at Gertie's house. I wasn't really looking then. If it's important to you to talk to his ghost, we can go back out there and look around."

"I guess it's not important." He kissed my cheek and then shifted his eyes to the marshmallows Aunt Tillie had set on fire. "Don't eat all of those. I want a s'more, too."

"Then you'd better hurry up." Aunt Tillie snapped the fingers on her free hand and killed the flames. "I don't know about anyone else, but the best thing about camping is getting hopped up on sugar."

"I can think of a few other things," Landon whispered in my ear. "I'm looking forward to camp nookie. Of course, s'mores are a nice appetizer."

All I could do was shake my head. "Don't you think you're getting ahead of yourself?"

"I guess we'll just have to see."

NINETEEN

We got hopped up on sugar and whiskey — some of us more than others — and stayed up far later than we normally would have. Aunt Tillie got drunk, something I knew she'd deny the next day, and Thistle wandered around on unsteady feet.

Landon pulled me to a standing position so I could dance with him. There was no music, but we swayed all the same. He also insisted on kissing me over and over again. I thought it was romantic and cute until I realized I had chocolate on the corners of my mouth.

It was after midnight when we broke apart to sleep. Each couple took a different cabin — Landon and I opting for the first one we'd entered on our initial visit — and Aunt Tillie rolled into her tent to sleep with Peg. For a moment I wondered if it was wise to leave her exposed and on her own. Then I remembered she was Aunt Tillie and a person would have to be stupid to mess with her, even drunk, and left her to sleep. A quick glance inside the tent told me Aunt Tillie was sharing her sleeping bag with Peg, both of them snoring away.

"They're fine." Landon wrapped himself around me from behind and kissed the back of my neck. "No one will mess with them."

"You're the one who keeps reminding me that we have a killer on the loose," I pointed out.

"She may be a pain, but if I don't come home with her Mom and my aunts will stop cooking for us."

He chuckled. "She's fine," he repeated. "I very much doubt our killer would be stupid enough to come back right now."

I wanted to agree with him but there was an uneasiness streaking through me. I couldn't quite put a name to it — when I watched the shadows for hints of movement I didn't find any — but I remained nervous.

"Let's go to bed," he suggested, his lips moving to my ear. "I have a few ideas for you."

Despite the chill coursing through me, I warmed all over and laughed. "Oh, yeah? What kind of ideas are we talking about?"

"Well, we met here, so I think it's only fair that we solidify our relationship in the very spot we realized we were destined to be together."

I slid him a sidelong look, amused. "You're drunk."

"I am tipsy," he corrected, making a silly face that caused me to grin. "There's a difference."

"What's the difference?"

"If I was drunk, I wouldn't be able to romance you in the manner to which you've become accustomed. Because I'm tipsy, I'll be a romance machine."

I laughed. "I can't wait for you to romance me."

"That makes two of us."

TRUE TO HIS WORD, LANDON was a romance machine. He was sweet, funny and full of himself. He also passed out five minutes after we cuddled in our zipped-together sleeping bags on top of the air mattress.

I dozed lightly, lamenting the fact that I hadn't imbibed more and passed out. Landon snored beside me, one arm thrown over his head, not a care in the world. I, on the other hand, could not embrace full sleep. It wasn't that I sensed something was wrong, mind you, it was more that I felt as if someone was watching me.

It was that thought I couldn't shake when I climbed out of the sleeping bag and headed outside.

I was quiet when I shut the cabin door. Landon was a heavy sleeper under normal circumstances. He had a few drinks in him, so I was doubtful he'd wake. I didn't want to needlessly worry him either way. I was the restless one, after all. If I took a look around and determined everything was quiet, I was more likely to be able to fall asleep.

At least I hoped that was true.

I slipped past the other two cabins, stopping long enough to listen. I heard nothing inside, which made me think that everyone had already passed out. That was for the best, of course. I didn't want my cousins to suffer with me. Still, I wouldn't have minded if one of them was awake so I wouldn't have to wander around the camp alone. No such luck, though.

I was wise enough to keep away from Aunt Tillie. We left the bonfire burning low. It was the wet season, so out-of-control fires weren't a worry. It would burn itself out in the next hour or two. There was no noise from Aunt Tillie's tent, so I knew she was dead to the world. That was definitely for the best.

I was the only one who couldn't sleep. That knowledge only made me more restless.

So I walked the camp, from one end to the other and back. It was dark. It was quiet. I felt as if I were alone. And yet there came a point when I knew I wasn't alone.

I felt Vicky's presence before I saw her. She materialized in the tree line on my left. I was careful not to change my pace. Finally, I decided to talk to her without looking at her. I figured that might be the best way to keep her from rabbiting.

"My name is Bay Winchester." I didn't bellow the words, instead keeping them light and conversational. "You know me. We met a long time ago."

Vicky didn't say anything. Out of the corner of my eye, I saw her shrink back a bit. She didn't disappear, though, so I took that as a good sign.

"I was one of your charges when you were a counselor here," I continued. "I attended with my cousins Clove and Thistle. I wasn't here that last year — I was in college — but we were still going to meet for coffee. Thistle set it up. Do you remember?"

I wasn't really expecting her to answer, so when I heard a whispered word I almost fell over.

"I remember you."

I slowed my pace. "You do?"

"You were going to be a reporter. That's what you were going to school for."

"I am a reporter." Carefully, I turned to face her. I kept a safe distance between us — for her benefit rather than mine — and offered a friendly smile. "I own The Whistler now."

"You do?" Vicky appeared surprised. "I can't believe that William Kelly sold his newspaper to a teenager." She faltered a bit as she looked me up and down. "But ... you're not a teenager any longer, are you?"

"I'm not," I agreed, nodding. "I'm an adult."

"That means I've been here a long time." Sadness flitted over Vicky's face as she looked around the campground. "How long have I been here?"

"A long time," I replied, unsure how much detail I should give her. "You should be in your thirties now."

Vicky's eyes widened as she snapped her head back to me. "Thirties? But ... no."

I felt sorry for her. She was very clearly lost. She'd spent all her time isolated at the campground. It would be easy to lose track of time under those circumstances. "I saw your sister this week," I volunteered, opting to change the subject. "She lives in Traverse City."

"Stephanie?" Vicky perked up. "How is she?"

"She misses you."

"I should visit her."

"You should," I agreed. "She can't see you, of course. You'll have to accept that. You can see her. You can see your nieces, too. You have three of them."

"Nieces?" Vicky furrowed her brow. "I ... have ... nieces. How can that be? My sister was pregnant when I came to the camp. She shouldn't have had a baby already."

Vicky's confusion wasn't out of the ordinary. Most ghosts were confused by their predicament. That was expected, especially right after the individual passed. Vicky, however, had been around a long time. She should be more aware of her reality.

"You realize you're dead, right?"

"Dead?" Vicky's eyes widened to saucer-like proportions. "That can't be right."

"But it is." I was firm with her because I knew it was necessary. "You died that last summer. You never made it to the coffee date Thistle arranged. You didn't ever leave this place, but if you try, you can now. You don't have to stay here."

Vicky's expression reflected horrified doubt. "No. That's not true."

"It is." I couldn't back down. She needed to understand the truth. "You've been gone for a long time. Twelve years. I guess it's kind of like eleven and a half. That part doesn't matter. The part that's important is that you don't have to stay here. I can help you move on."

"Move on?" Vicky shook her head. "I can't move on. I have to get home to see my sister. I'm going on a trip after camp, but I have to see her first. She needs to know that I'm coming back, that I'll be there for the birth of the baby."

"You already missed the birth of the baby." It was harsh, but I needed to snap her out of her confused state. "Her name is Victoria. I saw a photo of her on your sister's wall. There are two other little girls. One is just a toddler. I don't know their names. She named the oldest after you."

"Victoria." Vicky ran the name through her memory. "That can't be right. I wouldn't miss the birth of my niece. I promised Stephanie I would be there. We're the only family we have."

"And she's never forgotten you," I promised. "She still misses you with every breath."

"But ... no!" Vicky's fury flashed hard and fast. "I don't believe you. I wouldn't miss the birth. I promised. I always keep my promises."

I felt sad for her. "Stephanie isn't angry that you didn't keep your promise. She knows you would've been there if you could. It's not your fault that you didn't see your niece born. That's on whoever did this to you."

"Did this to me?" Vicky glanced down at her ethereal form, her expression hard to read as she moved her hands so she could look through them as she lifted them to the moon. "This isn't right."

"You're dead," I repeated. "I'm so sorry. I know that's not what you want to hear. You're dead, though, and you need to get it together. I have questions for you. I want to know who did this to you. Someone should pay for ending your life."

"This isn't right," she echoed, shaking her head. "No. I can't be here."

I was losing her. "Vicky ... ."

"I can't be here," she repeated. "No. I definitely don't want to be here!" She practically screamed the last sentence.

I took a step toward her, though I had no idea what sort of comfort I could offer. She was already gone before I completed the step. She'd disappeared into nothing again.

"Son of a ... !" I cursed under my breath as I swiveled, frustrated. "I hate this." I wanted to mope and lament my bad luck, but a flash of light out of the corner of my eye caused me to forget the dead and focus on the living ... because there was absolutely no doubt the shadow racing away from the records office and toward the water belonged to a living individual.

"Hey!" I yelled out before thinking better of it. I was alone, after all. Everyone else was asleep. If this person — and I was almost positive it was a man thanks to the glimpse I got of broad shoulders — decided to come after me I would be on my own when it came to fighting him off. I was fine with that, ready even.

Then the unthinkable happened.

I didn't understand what I was looking at. The figure ran from the records office, which meant he'd probably been inside. There was no time to figure out why, because a burst of flames at the top of the building made me realize a hard and terrible fact ... the cabin was on fire.

"No!" I raced forward, momentarily forgetting the man running toward the water. I had no idea what to do when I reached the cabin. The roof was on fire and the building was so old I had no doubt it would fall relatively fast. There was no hose to douse the flames, and my mind was too jumbled to come up with a spell.

Then I caught movement to my left and swiveled quickly. For a moment I thought the arsonist had returned to silence me, but the person racing through the crisp night air was Aunt Tillie, and she had her hands above her head.

"*Perfuro!*"

I recognized the word was Latin in origin but didn't know what it meant. Aunt Tillie repeated it two more times and then the meaning became clear when a lightning bolt split the sky. It was followed closely by a deafening roar of thunder.

"Aunt Tillie?" I never got a chance to ask a follow-up question. She never got a chance to answer. The rain followed a split-second later and I was absolutely drenched within three seconds. "Oh, well, of course."

Aunt Tillie kept her eyes on the cabin. "What happened?"

"I don't know. I thought I saw someone running from the cabin and then it erupted in flames. I ... hmm." I turned to look at the lake. I didn't see any movement, but that didn't necessarily mean anything. "I don't think I imagined it."

"I doubt you did," Aunt Tillie agreed. She was soaking wet, but didn't seem to care. "What were you doing out here?"

"Talking to Vicky. She didn't realize she was dead."

"That's not that unusual, especially for a spirit that's been isolated."

"Yeah, well ... ." I made up my mind and started striding toward the lake. "Whoever did this ran in that direction. I have to look."

"He's gone, Bay." Aunt Tillie sounded certain of herself. "There's no way he stuck around. It wouldn't be smart. This guy didn't get away with two murders for as long as he did by being dumb."

I couldn't stop myself. "I have to see." I made it to the shore of the lake. The water was dark, especially now that the moon was obliterated by the clouds Aunt Tillie had conjured. Still, I felt ... something. I peered into the darkness, reaching out with my senses. I almost jolted out of my skin when I brushed against something that could only be described as a panicked mind. "Holy ... !" I jerked when I realized Aunt Tillie had followed. "There's someone out there."

"He must've brought a rowboat or something," Aunt Tillie mused, narrowing her eyes when a bolt of lightning lit the sky. For a brief moment I thought I caught sight of a small dot on the water. When the lightning flashed again there was nothing on the water. "Someone obviously didn't want us digging into the records."

That made sense. "Do you think he was watching us all afternoon?"

"I think he knew we were here," she replied. "I don't know that he could've gotten close enough to really watch us without us figuring it out. I'm a really powerful witch, after all. I would've known."

"Yes you're a very powerful witch," I muttered, shaking my head. "There's no way you can cast a spell and force him to row back here, is there?"

"I'm powerful, not omnipotent."

"It was just a question. But the way you talk, one would think that you're the most powerful being in the world. I'm pretty sure if that were true the most powerful being would be able to make that guy row back to this beach so we can question him."

"Keep it up," Aunt Tillie warned. "I'll put you at the top of my list if you're not careful."

"It was a simple suggestion."

"Yeah, well ... it's something I can't do. Especially when I can't actually see anyone to curse. He might not even still be out there. He might've landed in another spot and escaped. We don't know."

She had a point, still ... . "It's got to be a local." The thought made my stomach dance. "It has to be someone we know. I don't see another explanation."

"It's definitely someone we know," Aunt Tillie agreed, turning her eyes back to the cabin. The storm had doused all the flames. "We need to ward that so it can't catch fire a second time. Just to be on the safe side, I mean. We haven't gone through everything yet."

"Good plan." I fell into step with her as we headed back to the cabin. "I guess the good news is that the constant upheaval out here will keep Mrs. Little from being able to buy the property."

"Oh, she's not getting her hands on this property." Aunt Tillie sounded sure of herself. "There's very little that gives me true joy in this world. Messing with Margaret is one of those things. She'll get this property over my dead body."

"That might be an added benefit for her." When Aunt Tillie didn't immediately respond, I risked a glance at her. "I was speaking about her perspective. From our perspective, we don't want to ever see your dead body."

"I know what you meant."

"I just thought I would spell it out for you."

"That was nice of you." Aunt Tillie scuffed her shoes against the ground as we walked. "You're still on my list, Bay."

I groaned. "I figured."

"Your punishment won't be pretty."

"I figured that, too."

"Prepare yourself."

TWENTY

Landon was furious the next morning when he heard what had happened. His anger was pointed inward.

"I shouldn't have drunk so much. I'm sorry." He pulled me in for a hug as I sat cross-legged next to him on the air mattress. "You should've woken me up, Bay." He kissed my temple and rolled so I was snuggled in at his side.

The morning sun filtered through the old windows and cast an eerie light over the inside of the cabin. From our vantage point on the floor I could see all the names carved into the walls, and it made me nostalgic for my childhood ... even though one of the first names I caught sight of was Lila's.

"You were out cold. Besides, when I first went outside, it was simply because I couldn't sleep. I didn't know I was going to run into a ghost and an arsonist."

"Ugh. That freaks me out." He brushed his hand over my hair. "I don't suppose you can give me a description of the guy?"

"He looked like a shadow."

"A shadow?"

"Yes. Put an APB out on Peter Pan's shadow. That's what I saw."

"I get it. There's no need to get snippy. It was dark."

"I'm not trying to be snippy." I buried my face in the hollow between his neck and shoulder. "I'm just tired. I didn't sleep well. I kept thinking I heard something outside even though Aunt Tillie and I warded all the cabins."

"What time did you finally get back to bed?"

"Around three."

"So ... you only got a few hours of sleep." He tightened his grip on me. "I'm sorry. I really wish you would've woken me."

"What could you have done that we didn't do?"

"I have a gun. I could've shot the guy running toward the lake."

There was a point. "You were also drunk. You would've lost your job if you did that, and we both know it."

"I wasn't drunk."

"You were tipsy. I know."

"I was tipsy and gifted in the romance department. Don't leave that second part out."

"Never." I was so comfortable getting up seemed like a huge ordeal. I didn't see where we had a choice, though. "We should get moving. I don't know that it's wise for us to stay out here another day."

"Are you afraid?" He met my even gaze. "Do you think this guy is going to come back? If so, I can arrange for agents to stake this place out for the foreseeable future."

That sounded like a potential nightmare. "And what happens when I have to come back to talk to a ghost? How will I explain that? Your co-workers will catch me, and then you'll never hear the end of it. You'll be Agent Michaels, the guy whose girlfriend sneaks around in the middle of nowhere talking to her imaginary friends."

"First, I don't care what other people say about you," he argued. "I only care what I think and I happen to believe you're the prettiest witch in the Midwest."

I was in a bad mood and didn't want to encourage him. It was difficult, though, because the simple statement filled me with warmth.

"Second, my co-workers already think I lucked out because they've seen photographs of you," he continued. "I have a framed one on my desk at work. Everyone who sees the photo comments on how pretty you are."

"They could just be placating you," I countered. "I mean ... I don't know anybody who is going to say to a guy, 'Man, your girlfriend looks like her mother and father were brother and sister.'"

Landon laughed as he pulled me tighter. "That's a point, but it doesn't matter. I don't care what anyone else thinks."

"Then call them."

"No, that's not a good idea."

I propped my chin on his chest and stared down at him. "You just went on a diatribe about how you didn't care what they think. Have you already changed your mind?"

"Essentially," he confirmed, nodding. "I don't care if they think you're out here talking to yourself. That will cut down on any trips you can make to talk to your ghost, no matter what.

"When you add to that the fact that we may need to come here for another reason — and, no, I'm not sure what that reason would be at this point — then I don't think it's a good idea," he continued. "I think it's smarter for you guys to set a few magical traps if you can manage it."

"I'm sure Aunt Tillie is already doing just that. We should probably check on the main cabin. I think Aunt Tillie put out the fire before it did too much damage."

He kissed the tip of my nose. "We'll pack up, check the cabin and then head to town for breakfast. I'm starving and I have no intention of eating a granola bar. Only pancakes will do."

I grinned. He was such a food-oriented individual that his reactions were easily telegraphed. "You just don't want to talk about bacon in front of Peg."

"You're not wrong about that." He gave me another quick kiss and then released me. "Come on. Let's get this show on the road. I want to see how much damage was done, and then I want to get out of here."

"The camp isn't as romantic as you thought it was going to be, is it?"

He shot me a quick look. "It's plenty romantic. And I still want to spend time out here. I just want to catch the killer first. I don't want to have to worry about you accidentally getting set on fire when you wander outside to talk to ghosts after dark."

I had to press my lips together to keep from laughing at the absurd statement.

"I never thought I would say anything even remotely close to that," he said after a moment's contemplation. "You've changed my life, Bay."

"You've changed mine, too."

The kiss he graced me with this time was softer. "We'll figure it out. This place is always going to be important to me. And, for the record, I'm always going to be a romantic dynamo, even if I'm tipsy. Neither one of those things have changed."

"Good to know."

GERTIE WAS AT THE OFFICE CABIN when we finished loading our gear into the back of Landon's Explorer. I wasn't expecting her — my understanding was that she rarely visited the camp and she'd already been here once this week — but it was hard to miss her furious countenance as she stalked the front of the cabin and glared at the scorched roof.

"How could you do this?" she seethed when she saw us approaching. "How could you set fire to my property?"

"We didn't," I replied hurriedly, increasing my pace. "Someone else came from the lake and did it."

"Someone came from the lake?" Gertie was understandably dubious. "Why would someone do that?"

"That's the question we're trying to answer," Landon replied. "We're not certain who it was. Bay and Aunt Tillie were outside and saw someone fleeing toward the water. They could not make out his features, but they're fairly certain it was a man."

"And he ran toward the lake?" Gertie's forehead wrinkled as she looked toward the water. "I'm not sure I understand."

"That makes two of us. We were just coming to check out the

cabin to see how much damage was done. We lucked out when that storm came through last night and put out the fire."

"What storm?" If Gertie was bewildered before, she was positively dumbfounded now. "It didn't storm by my house."

"It must've been a quick cloudburst," I smoothly lied. "It sparked up and died here very fast."

"A storm?" Gertie shook her head as she rubbed her toe over the wet ground. "I guess you're right. It obviously did rain here. I don't get that."

I glanced over my shoulder, hoping for a glimpse of Aunt Tillie so I could keep her away with a look. "You can never explain the weather in Michigan. What's that old saying? If you don't like it, just wait five minutes."

"I guess." Gertie was dejected as we let ourselves into the cabin. She spent all her time looking at the roof while I studied the files strewn about the floor. I was convinced they were in a different configuration than how Aunt Tillie and I had left them the previous afternoon.

"Someone has been in here," I muttered.

Landon briefly looked to me and squeezed my hand before moving closer to Gertie. "Does anything look out of place?"

Gertie shrugged. "I haven't been in this building for years. I have no idea."

"We could ask Randy," I suggested, bending over to study a scattered stack of papers. It was the tower I'd built when looking for lists from previous summers. Someone had obviously gone through the files before setting the fire. "He might have checked inside the buildings during one of his stops out here."

"Randy who?" Gertie asked absently.

"Randy Weaver."

"Why would Randy Weaver be out here?"

I stilled, surprised. "You hired him to watch the grounds."

"I most certainly did not." Gertie turned haughty. "I don't have enough money to hire anyone to do anything. If I did, I most certainly wouldn't hire Randy to do anything. He's a complete and total waste of space ... and I know that because the people at the grocery store constantly complain about his shoddy work."

"But ... we've seen him out here." I looked to Landon for help. "We've seen him more than once. He said that he was here on your orders and even apologized because he said he wasn't checking in as often as he promised you."

Gertie let loose a derisive snort. "You're saying he admitted to falling down on a fake job? That sounds just like him. He's such a lazybones. That's what Rhonda at the grocery store says. I've never actually met him. I think I saw him across a parking lot once. He wasn't much for talking. Still, I can't believe he's been out here. I bet he's been sleeping in the cabins or something. Heck, I bet he's been stealing items from the cabins to sell."

I wouldn't put that past Randy. The guy was a total loser. He never met an opportunity he didn't want to exploit. Still, this made zero sense.

"Was there anything worth stealing out here?" Landon asked. "I mean ... what could he have stolen and gotten money for?"

"How should I know?" Gertie's temper came out on full display. This very clearly wasn't her week. "There are all sorts of black markets out there. I mean ... whatever happened to my copper tubing? I keep hearing about thieves trying to steal copper tubing."

"This camp was built decades ago," I pointed out. "I don't think there is copper tubing. I mean ... that's plumbing, right?" I glanced at Landon for confirmation. "There are only old outhouses out here. You don't have plumbing. I mean ... the showers were really old even when we were visiting, and essentially the water was pumped from the lake."

"Thank you, Bay," she said dryly. "That's obviously important to this conversation."

Landon smirked when I raised my eyebrows and then gently nudged me to increase the distance between Gertie and me. Clearly he was convinced that my proximity was agitating her.

"Gertie, if you didn't hire Randy Weaver, why would he be out here?" Landon queried. "I mean ... it doesn't make much sense that he would want to hang out here willingly. I very much doubt there's anything of value to steal. There has to be another reason."

"And thank you for that," Gertie muttered, shaking her head. "It's like you two are getting off insulting me. If I didn't already have hemorrhoids you would've just given them to me, along with agitating my ulcer."

"It's not like that at all," Landon argued. "I need to understand why Randy would want to come here. There's no gold hidden on the property, right?"

Gertie's expression was withering. "Yes. I hid gold out here. That's why I'm in financial trouble. I have gold and don't want to spend it."

"It was just a simple question."

"Yeah? Well, there is no simple answer." Gertie's tone had bite. "I don't know why anyone would hang out here. Have you considered Randy was hiding bodies? He's been in the area for more than five years, which means he's familiar with it. He's never worked for me, but he's obviously familiar with the property. Perhaps he's your killer."

"I guess that's possible." Landon rubbed his chin as he regarded me. "Do you think you saw Randy last night? I mean ... he knew we were here. He even knew we were going through the files in that cabin."

I thought about the furtive figure I'd witnessed fleeing toward the lake. "I guess," I said after a beat. "I didn't see a face, but Randy has the right size and build."

"Then I guess we need to find Randy."

LANDON DROPPED ME AT the newspaper office after breakfast. I really needed a shower — a night spent drinking by the fire and being rained on had left me disheveled and dirty — but Landon wanted to track down Randy as soon as possible and didn't have time to head back to The Overlook. I would have to muddle through the day and then take the longest bath ever later.

The newspaper's resident ghost Viola — a woman who died months ago but absolutely refused to move on because she was afraid she might miss something — was waiting for me in my office when I arrived.

She wasn't alone.

"Vicky?" I didn't bother hiding my surprise at the appearance of the ghost. "What are you doing here?" I didn't realize how hostile the greeting sounded until it was already out of my mouth. "I mean ... do you need something? Have you remembered something helpful?"

She looked like a woman on the edge when she slowly turned her eyes to me. "You're right. I'm dead."

Sympathy rolled over me. "I'm sorry I had to be the one to tell you."

"I'm sorrier that I'm dead," she replied ruefully. "I thought about what you said last night, about how I've been gone for more than ten years. I didn't want to believe you, but it makes sense. I think I've been floating for a long time."

I kept my attention on her as I sat in my desk chair. "Is that what it's been like for you? Have you been floating?"

"That's what it feels like. I mean ... I knew that things weren't right. I couldn't seem to get my brain to work the correct way. It didn't seem weird to me that I was constantly hanging around the camp even though no one else was there.

"There were times people came to visit and I watched them," she continued. "Like ... once there was an older woman who wore a sweatshirt with a unicorn on it. She came with a man and another woman, and they were talking about something serious."

"Like real estate?" I asked, already knowing the answer.

"That sounds right."

"Mrs. Little," I muttered, shaking my head.

"Oh, is Margaret finally putting her plan into action?" Viola asked. She was a former cohort of Mrs. Little's and knew a lot about the woman. "I'm not surprised. She's wanted that parcel for years."

"To build condos on?" I asked.

"That and a few other things. She has big plans for that land."

I had big questions for Viola, but now was not the time to dwell on the camp. I needed to focus on Vicky. We had a murderer on the loose. That was definitely more important. "Vicky, I know it's difficult, but I need you to think back to your last days at the camp. I'm talking about your last real days, when you were alive."

"I don't remember dying," Vicky pointed out. "How can I know when I was last alive when I can't remember dying?"

That was a fair question. "I don't know," I said. "I know that you were making plans with Clove and Thistle. You were supposed to meet us for coffee. You never made it. We assumed something came up and you left the camp early.

"We went to the camp and asked the other counselors if that was true," I continued. "We talked to a young woman with red hair and green eyes. She told us people assumed you'd left early because Gertie came through with payment and there was only one day left ... a day without any campers. Do you remember that?"

Vicky looked as if she was thinking hard. "I vaguely remember that," she said after a beat. "I mean ... I remember we were supposed to have coffee. I don't remember dying."

"Your sister said that you disliked one of the male counselors," I prodded. "Can you remember which one you didn't like?"

"Oh, that one I can remember without any problem." Vicky's lips curved down at whatever memory bombarded her. "There were two of them, in fact. Both were jerks ... and perverts. I even caught one of them peeping through the bathroom window when I was trying to shower one day."

Now we were getting somewhere. "Who was that?"

"Lance Saxon." She grimaced when uttering the name. "He wasn't alone. He had another counselor with him. They were both laughing and leering. I was mortified."

I didn't blame her. "Who was the other guy?"

"Joey Morgan. He was filling in that summer because one of the other counselors didn't show up. Gertie tapped him because she said he was her only option, but I never got the feeling she was happy about hiring him."

"Because Joey was a poor worker?"

"And a pervert," Vicky replied. "He was peeping at all the counselors that summer. It wasn't just me."

"And he wasn't alone?" I wanted to make absolutely certain that she was remembering correctly so I didn't track down the wrong potential suspect. "He had someone else with him. That's what you said."

"Lance Saxon. They were thick as thieves."

"I don't suppose you know where Lance Saxon lived? I don't remember that name and I'm pretty sure he's not a Hemlock Cove local."

"I think he lived in Bellaire," Vicky said. "I'm not a hundred percent sure, but I think that's right."

"Then that's where we'll start looking." I was grim. "Thank you for finding me. I finally have hope we're starting to look in the right direction. We'll make sure whoever did this to you pays."

Vicky shrugged. "That won't help me."

"No, but it's better than nothing."

"I guess."

TWENTY-ONE

I considered calling Landon, but I knew he had his hands full with tracking down Randy. Vicky disappeared not long after unloading the names of two counselors she felt uncomfortable with. One was dead. The other was a man I didn't know.

Without a doubt, I recognized Landon would be frustrated (and most likely furious) if I tracked down Saxon on my own. Still, I wanted to talk to him. I was trying to get a feeling for Vicky's movements that last summer. If Saxon wasn't a suspect, he might know something. That didn't mean Landon would whistle a jaunty tune and smile like a moron when I told him I questioned a possible murderer.

That meant I couldn't go alone.

Clove and Thistle were tied up with tourists at Hypnotic thanks to the large group that had hit town the previous day. Clove wasn't keen on questioning suspects anyway. Thistle was more game, but she couldn't leave Clove to handle the store herself.

Sam and Marcus had jobs of their own, so we rarely took them along for adventures. If they happened to be with the group when the curse hit the cauldron, that was one thing. They didn't appreciate being dragged into things out of the blue, though.

Mom, Marnie and Twila weren't high on my list of cohorts. They were busy with guests ... and whatever else they did during the day, which I suspected revolved around baking. That left one person with an opening in her schedule ... and I realized just how far I'd fallen when I called Aunt Tillie and told her what I had planned.

"That's a fabulous idea," she said over the phone. "I love grilling perps. Pick me up at The Overlook in an hour. I'm looking forward to meeting this guy. I'll bring my cuffs."

Her enthusiasm gave me pause, but there was very little I could do about it. Landon was busy with other things and I couldn't simply ignore the name once Vicky provided it. Because I had time, I browbeat Thistle into driving me home so I could shower. She groused the whole way, but it was only a five-minute ride. She completed her taxiing duty and disappeared.

My car was parked in front of the guesthouse, per usual, so I hopped inside once I'd finished cleaning up and drove to the inn. I felt ten times better once I was in fresh clothes, hair washed, and I didn't even cringe when I found Aunt Tillie scowling as she waited for me. She carried a large bag slung over her shoulder and wore combat boots and a blue jacket that oddly looked like something a police officer would wear.

"What is that?" I was instantly suspicious when she climbed into the passenger seat.

"What?" She looked around the car, as if genuinely searching for a point of interest. "Do you see something?"

"I see you."

"Then it's going to be a good day for you." She clapped my arm. "Let's find a murderer."

I couldn't stop frowning at the jacket. It wasn't until she moved her arm that I finally managed to see the left breast panel. There, in big letters, was WBI. Her name was embroidered above that and she had what looked to be a badge affixed to the coat.

"Where did you get that jacket?" I asked, dumbfounded.

"Oh, this old thing?" She feigned being perplexed. "I stumbled across it somewhere. I really can't remember where."

"Uh-huh." I didn't believe her for a second. She had a shopping addiction, which meant she enjoyed buying things that drove the rest of us crazy. That included leggings, scorpions, guns and a set of drums that mysteriously disappeared from the inn less than a week after they appeared and Aunt Tillie announced she was going to be the next Tommy Lee. "What does WBI stand for?"

She shot me a "well, duh" look. "I would think that's rather obvious."

"Witch Bureau of Investigations?"

"Oh, don't be a ninny. I don't want to announce to the perps that I'm a witch. That will make them more nervous than necessary. It stands for Winchester. Winchester Bureau of Instigations."

In my book, that wasn't any better. "Investigations," I automatically corrected.

Her eyes flashed. "I know what I said."

We lapsed into silence as I navigated toward the highway. The more I thought about our trip, the more I realized it was a bad idea. Still, I couldn't force myself to turn around. I wanted to see Saxon for myself. It somehow felt important, even though I couldn't put my finger on why.

"Do you have anything else in that bag I should worry about?" I asked after a few minutes.

"Of course not. I just have my necessities in here."

"Like what?"

"Don't worry about it."

That's exactly what I was afraid of. "If you have a weapon in there, tell me now. We need to leave it in the car when we question this guy."

"I am a walking weapon," she reminded me. "I don't need anything other than my wits and magic."

She sounded full of herself, which was always a warning signal. "Aunt Tillie ... ."

She cut me off with a shake of her head. "Bay, you came to me because you wanted backup when it came time to question this guy. I'm here to help even though you're a big, fat whiner and absolutely no fun sometimes. I mean ... seriously. How can you not be fun after all the valuable lessons I gave you as a kid?"

Even though I understood what she was doing, I was agitated by the remark. "I'm tons of fun."

She blew a disdainful raspberry. "Please. You're nowhere near as much fun as you should be. You're a powerful necromancer who picks up on the emotions of ghosts. You should be a laugh riot every minute."

"And you think I'm not?"

"I think you're a good girl who wants to help the world and do great things. I get the 'doing great things' part. I really do. I want to do great things, too. The other part is what gives me indigestion."

"First, there's nothing wrong with being a good girl."

"If you say so."

"There's not."

"Keep telling yourself that."

Her flippant response and refusal to meet my gaze was beyond annoying. "Second, I'm not a good girl. I'm bad to the bone."

"Right."

"I am."

"Yes, you're the terror of Hemlock Cove in your Ford ... with your FBI boyfriend ... with your doting police chief father figure following close behind. You're the worst witch of us all."

Oh, now she was just trying to irritate me. "I think I'm done talking to you for the day."

"That's too bad. You're a witty conversationalist."

I frowned. "I'm not a good girl."

"Sure, sure, sure."

"I'm not."

"If you say so."

It took everything I had not to blow up. "I'm not."

"Keep your eyes on the road, Bay."

LANCE SAXON WASN'T HARD TO track down. He worked as a clerk at Bellaire City Hall — something I found through a simple

Google search, complete with photograph — and he was leaving to go on a break when Aunt Tillie and I entered the building.

"Is that him?" she asked, her eyes narrowing as she looked him over. "He looks like a murderer."

I frowned. "How can you say that?" I studied the man in question as he spoke quietly to the woman taking his place at the window. He wore khaki pants, a plaid button-down shirt, and combed his hair in such a manner that I had to wonder if he was prematurely balding. "He looks like a normal guy to me."

"Ugh. You're such a rube. He's clearly a killer."

"Did your training at the WBI teach you that?"

"It did. But I didn't have to train because I was naturally gifted in that department. I do the training because I am bursting with wisdom that needs to be imparted to others."

She was clearly feeling full of herself today. The spell she cast to conjure the storm that saved the records cabin was puffing her out a bit. "Yes. Your academy helped me beyond words when I was a child."

"It certainly did," she agreed. "Now, come on." She tugged me toward the door we'd just walked through. "We need to head outside."

"Why? The guy we need to talk to is inside ... and he's going on break. This is perfect timing."

"He won't be taking his break inside."

"How do you know that?"

"He's a smoker."

I was confused when I turned back to Saxon. "He's not holding a cigarette."

"No, but his fingers are twitching and he looks like a smoker."

"What does a smoker look like?"

"You know."

"No, I don't."

"Yes, you do."

"No, I don't."

"Oh, don't be daft, Bay." Aunt Tillie's eyes flashed with annoyance. "You're purposely being difficult. I hate it when you're difficult."

"Right back at you."

"Yeah, yeah, yeah."

SURE ENOUGH, SAXON WAS indeed a smoker. Aunt Tillie was right. Not only that, she seemed to know where the county workers went to smoke when they were on break. It was a small enclosure behind the building, close to the dumpster — which smelled picturesque, let me tell you — and there were benches and those tall ashtrays spread about when we crossed into the area.

"You're not supposed to be back here," Saxon announced, his eyes going wide when he saw us. "This is a restricted area."

"No, it's not," I countered, shaking my head. "There are no signs and this is government property. Outdoor government property at that. You can't restrict the general public from crossing into this area."

Aunt Tillie shot me an appraising look. "That was excellent. Maybe you're not a lost cause after all."

I ignored her. "You're Lance Saxon, right?"

He raised an eyebrow, surprised. "I guess that depends on who wants to know. I don't believe I recognize you."

I saw no reason to lie. "My name is Bay Winchester. I live in Hemlock Cove. Two bodies were discovered in the pool at a local campground the past few days. One of them has been identified as Vicky Carpenter. It's my understanding that you knew her."

Saxon blinked several times and then sucked on his cigarette, long and deep. When he exhaled, he was more in control. "I wondered if it was her."

It was a simple statement, but it conveyed a lot. "Vicky?"

He nodded. "The body discovery has been all over the news. There's not a lot going on at this time of year, so two bodies being discovered in a small town like Hemlock Cove is a big deal. That's all any of the stations have been talking about."

I hadn't watched much television the past few days, so I would have to take his word for it. "You didn't know it was Vicky until we told you?"

"I only heard about the second body yesterday. They didn't release a name."

That made sense. Landon would've wanted to wait until Stephanie was informed. He might not have released the name until today for all I knew. "I'm sorry to be the bearer of bad news."

"I suspected it was her," Saxon countered, pressing the heel of his hand to his forehead. "She just disappeared that last summer. The other counselors didn't seem worried, so I pushed it out of my head. I never thought she was the type to take off without saying goodbye."

"What can you tell me about that time?" I prodded. "I mean ... when was the last time you saw Vicky?"

"I don't really remember. The last day of camp is always hectic. Besides, I was staying with the boys across the lake. That camp was set up so the boys and girls were separated. It would've made more sense for a camp in the fifties – I mean, how weird is it to separate boys and girls like that? – but I wasn't in charge, so there wasn't much I could do about it."

"So ... you didn't see her the last day of camp?"

"I saw her, but I didn't really talk to her," he countered. "She was helping the girls and I was helping the boys. The goal was to search the cabins and make sure nothing was left behind. Gertie was adamant when she stopped by that morning. She didn't want to pay us extra to contact the parents so they could claim the missing items."

"Gertie was there?"

"She came every day when camp was in session. She didn't always stay — she was upset in those days because Earl had died a few months before — but she always stopped in. The morning of that last pack out she was agitated."

"Did she say why?"

"Just that she wanted to make sure that nothing was left behind because she had other things to worry about besides crazed mothers looking for their kids' retainers."

That sounded about right. "You're sure you saw Vicky?"

"Oh, I'm sure." Saxon turned rueful as he took another puff, his cheeks coloring. "I had a horrible crush on her. I mean ... it was ridiculous. I swear my tongue tied itself when she was around and I sounded like a blooming idiot.

"That last day with the kids was not our last day," he continued. "We always had to stay an extra day to clean up the cabins and the campsite. I never minded because those days were more relaxing. In fact, I was looking forward to it that year because I'd planned to ask out Vicky on that last day when there was no one else around to distract her."

I glanced at Aunt Tillie and found her watching Saxon with rapt attention.

"Did Vicky know you had a crush on her?" I asked finally.

He shrugged. "I don't think so. She was always in her own little world. She was one of the few counselors who actually enjoyed spending time with the kids. She legitimately liked her job. The rest of us were doing it for money. I mean ... there's a reason I don't have kids. I don't really like them."

"Join the club," Aunt Tillie intoned. "Kids are the absolute worst."

I shot her a look. "You said you didn't see her that final day. The other counselors said she left. Do you happen to know if someone packed her things?"

Saxon shrugged. "I'm assuming they did. I mean ... why would they say it if she didn't pack them herself?"

That was a very good question. I had another. "Vicky mentioned to her sister that you made her nervous," I supplied. "Why do you think she would say something like that?"

"Probably because I couldn't stop staring at her." If he was embarrassed, he didn't show it. He was more sheepish than guilty. "Like I said, I couldn't stop salivating over her. I mean ... I was freaking in love with her. She had really long legs and was nice to everyone. I swear my heart hurt whenever I was near her."

"And you didn't do anything to her?" The more I talked to Saxon, the less he seemed a suspect. He could've been a good actor, though.

"Me?" Saxon's eyebrows flew up his forehead. "You think I hurt her? I loved her. Er, well, I thought I loved her. I'm older now, so that seems ridiculous in hindsight, but I definitely had a crush on her. Why would I hurt her?"

"Because people are sick and they hurt the people they're supposed to love," Aunt Tillie replied, matter-of-fact. "Are you sure you're not some sicko pervert who killed her because she turned down your advances? I mean ... you look like a pervert. Who wears plaid shirts, for crying out loud? I'll tell you who. Perverts."

My mouth dropped open. "Um ... ."

Instead of freaking out, Saxon merely shook his head. "I'm not a pervert. I had a crush on her. I never would've done anything to her. I expected her to say no. She had plans to go on a trip. She told me that. I had to ask her anyway. I would've always regretted it if I hadn't.

"I always assumed she left early for her trip," he continued. "I did regret not asking her out ... but not for as long as I thought I would. I met someone that summer and we dated for a bit. That helped me forget about Vicky.

"Had I known she was dead all that time, I doubt I would've moved onto someone else so quickly," he said. "I'm guessing I would've pouted a lot longer. That's how I rolled back then. I was an emotional basket case."

I wanted to believe him. Part of me did believe him. The only hint of nervous energy he showed was when I mentioned Vicky was dead. He seemed genuinely surprised and shocked to find out she was discovered in the pool. Otherwise, he appeared to be sincere.

"What about others at the camp that summer?" I prodded. "Did she mention not liking anybody else?"

"Just Joey ... but everyone hated Joey. In fact, he was so unpopular Gertie showed up and yelled because she thought we should be nicer to him. She said it wasn't fair that we were cutting him out of activities. The guy was weird, but I was so afraid of Gertie I started hanging out with Joey just so she would like me."

"Weird how?"

"Like ... weird. I don't know how to explain it. He spent all his time staring at the girls and disappearing into the woods. We assumed he was smoking pot out there because he always came back with glassy eyes and acting slower than normal. No one said anything, because we didn't want to take on the boss's son. He was unhappy being there as it was. He didn't like working."

"Believe it or not, you're not the first person to tell me that," I muttered, rubbing the back of my neck. "Can you think of anyone else who would want to hurt Vicky?"

"I can't. She was the nicest person in the world. Everyone loved her. I can't believe she's dead. Do the cops believe she was in the pool the entire time?"

"That's the working theory. Do you remember when the pool was closed for the season?"

"The day the kids left. The workers were there when we were loading them into cars and buses. They were done by the time we were done."

"So ... the pool was closed before you were finished with your chores."

"It was definitely closed by the time we were finished with all the kids. I remember being disappointed because I wanted to take one more dip."

"Well, that means someone had to open the pool and put her inside after the fact. It had to be someone who knew the camp."

"Definitely," Aunt Tillie agreed. "But it's not this guy." She jerked her thumb in Saxon's direction. "He's clean as a whistle. Really, Bay. I can't believe you thought he was a murderer. Have I taught you nothing?"

I narrowed my eyes to dangerous slits. "Are you trying to irritate me?"

"Of course not. I'm trying to teach you."

"Well, you're irritating me."

"You shouldn't jump to conclusions. Ah, well. You'll learn." She turned a blinding smile to Saxon. "I'm glad you grew out of your pervert stage. Give up the smoking and then come see me in Hemlock Cove. I'll find a girlfriend for you ... after we de-plaid your wardrobe, that is." She slapped his arm. "Good job on not being a pervert. I can't tell you how relieved I am that we didn't have to shoot you."

Saxon's bewildered expression was almost too much to bear. "I'm happy you didn't have to shoot me, too."

"That makes three of us," I said dryly. "We'll get out of your hair. I'm sorry to have bothered you."

"Don't apologize. I'm glad to know someone is out there fighting for Vicky. She deserves it."

On that we could agree.

TWENTY-TWO

Landon was not happy when I told him about my afternoon.

"So, let me get this straight," he said when he met Aunt Tillie and me by the front door of the police station. "A ghost told you the name of a counselor from eleven years ago who could potentially be a murderer and you packed up your eighty-something great-aunt and drove to Bellaire to question him without telling anyone else where you were going. Do I have that about right?"

Ugh. When he put it that way, I came off sounding like an idiot. "That's basically right," I hedged. "But I don't particularly like your attitude."

"You tell him." Aunt Tillie, still wearing her WBI coat, was focused on the porcelain unicorn store across the road. "I think I'm heading out to take a walk."

"No, you're not." Landon grabbed the back of her coat before she could scurry away. "I'm not done expressing my dislike for how you spent your afternoon."

"You act like I care, Skippy," Aunt Tillie challenged, squirming against his firm grip. "For the record, I don't. We didn't do anything wrong."

"You questioned a potential murderer," Landon argued. "That was all kinds of wrong."

"This is why you're such a goody-goody, Bay," Aunt Tillie muttered, lashing out with her foot and catching Landon in the shin. He grimaced but managed to keep hold of her without crying out. "He makes you want to be a cloying suck-up. Think about that next time you want to follow the rules."

I sighed. "I don't want to be a cloying suck-up. I didn't even know you knew what that meant."

"Oh, I know." Aunt Tillie's expression darkened. "You're definitely on my list now."

I balked. "Why? I didn't do anything."

"You think I'm stupid."

"That's not what I said."

"It's basically what you said." Aunt Tillie turned to Landon for support. "That's what she said, right?"

"Only if you're going to dole out punishment in the form of bacon. I want her to smell like it for the entire night."

Aunt Tillie narrowed her eyes. "Consider it done."

Landon immediately released her and pinned me with a look. "You shouldn't call your great-aunt stupid like that. It's not fair or right. She's a human being."

"A genius," Aunt Tillie corrected.

"That's pushing things," Landon countered.

"Do you want your bacon-smelling girlfriend or not?"

He shrugged. "She's the smartest woman I know, Bay. The fact that you would call her stupid is ... well, frankly, it's disappointing."

"Nice delivery." Aunt Tillie's grin was smug. "I told you before, Bay. You're living your life the wrong way. You should stop focusing on being a good girl and embrace your inner bad girl. That's what I did and I've never looked back."

I folded my arms over my chest and glared at Landon. "Is this your payback for me interviewing Saxon?"

"I don't want payback for that. I want you to be safe. I thought we

FLIP THE WITCH SWITCH

agreed we were going to talk about stuff like this before you ran off half-cocked."

"I didn't run off half-cocked."

"Only a whole cock will do," Aunt Tillie intoned, her eyes back on Mrs. Little's shop. "I have things to do. I'll leave you two to your argument."

"We're not going to argue," I shot back.

"Oh, we're going to argue," Landon countered. "I think it's best if Aunt Tillie goes about her business. She has a curse to cast, after all."

I wanted to shake him. "She's not casting that curse. She's messing with you."

"A deal is a deal, Bay," Aunt Tillie argued. "I made a promise, and I keep my promises. Now, if you'll excuse me ... ."

Landon grabbed the sleeve of her coat before she could depart. "Just one question. WBI. That stands for Winchester Bureau of Investigations, right?"

"Instigations," Aunt Tillie corrected. "I perform a specific function for those who can afford my services."

"And this is a new business you're running?"

"Pretty much. I got the idea when I was watching a show on Netflix a few weeks ago. Private investigators make a lot of money. I've been looking for a side hustle now that pot is legal in Michigan and the snow no longer needs plowing. I'm now a private investigator."

She was opening up to Landon more than she did to me ... and her responses were frightening. "You didn't mention that during the drive. I thought you bought the coat as a joke." Something occurred to me. "What's in your bag? You've been keeping a firm hold on it since I picked you up."

As if to prove my point, Aunt Tillie gripped her over-sized purse tighter. "Don't you worry about it. You're a busybody ... just like your mother. Has anyone ever told you that?"

"That means you have something hot in the bag," I muttered. "It's not explosives, is it? You didn't finally find a way to get C4 delivered to the inn, did you? Oh, don't bother answering." I pressed my eyes shut. "I don't want to know."

"I think everyone is better off not knowing," Aunt Tillie agreed. "I'm off. You don't need to worry about taking me home. I'll handle my own transportation."

"Whatever," I muttered.

"Hold up." Landon didn't release Aunt Tillie's sleeve. "I notice you've got a badge there. You slipped it into your pocket when you caught me looking at it. I'd like to see it before I let you go."

"Badge? What badge?" Anyone who didn't know her would think Aunt Tillie was an innocent senior citizen caught in a web of suspicion by her belligerent great-niece's bossy boyfriend. Anyone who knew her, however, would recognize the truth behind her acting skills.

"Let me see it," Landon repeated.

"Oh, geez." Aunt Tillie made a face and dug in her pocket. "Here. Are you happy?" She shoved the badge I'd only caught a glimpse of earlier in his direction.

"This looks pretty good," Landon noted as he released Aunt Tillie and stared at the badge. "Who did this for you?"

"What do you mean?" Aunt Tillie refused to meet his gaze. "I made it myself."

Landon was understandably dubious. "How did you manage that?"

"I'm gifted."

"Seriously."

"I am serious." Aunt Tillie's gaze fired. "I know how to do a variety of things. Making badges is one of them."

Landon pursed his lips and stared at her for a long beat. Instead of asking further questions, he slipped the badge into his pocket. "I'll hold onto this. We'll talk about you getting it back later."

"That's mine," Aunt Tillie protested. "You can't just steal my stuff."

"I said we'll talk about you getting it back later," Landon reiterated. "How Bay smells will play into that conversation."

"Hey!" Now it was my turn to be frustrated. "I don't want to smell like bacon. You know I hate that."

Landon ignored me and leaned closer to Aunt Tillie to whisper something I couldn't quite make out. I tried to move closer, but he was already done, and Aunt Tillie was walking away from him before I could uncover their dastardly plan.

"Don't even think about cursing me," I yelled at Aunt Tillie's back. When she didn't turn around, I swiveled toward Landon. "What did you say to her?"

"Don't worry about it." Landon tucked the badge into his pocket. "If you can find out who made this for her I'd appreciate it. We've had a lot of fake licenses and identification cards show up over the past few weeks. Whoever made this badge is good. I'd like to talk to him or her."

He couldn't be serious. "You think I'm going to help you after what you just pulled?" I was incredulous. "I hate smelling like bacon."

"I happen to like it."

"You're not the only one. Every man in town likes it when I smell like bacon. As my boyfriend, you should hate that."

"I like it when people are jealous. Sue me."

I wanted to do more than sue him. "Landon ... ."

"Bay, let it go." He didn't smile when he folded his arms over his chest. "I'm not happy that you talked to this Saxon guy without me. What happened to us being partners?"

I hated — I mean absolutely *hated* — his tone. "We are partners," I reassured him quickly. "I knew you were busy. I wanted to talk to him. I felt it was important."

"Even though you're now convinced he's not the guilty party?"

"I don't know that I'm convinced he's not guilty." I chose my words carefully. "If he's acting, he's very good. In fact, he's so good he missed his calling. He should be in Hollywood.

"That said, I figure whoever did this — whoever got away with murder for so long — has to be a masterful liar," I continued. "Does that mean I think he's guilty? No. I don't know that he's innocent either. I figured I would leave that to you to figure out."

"After you've already questioned him, thus tipping him off that we'll be tracking him down."

Crap. I hadn't considered that. "Well ... I just wanted to see his reaction. I'm sorry if I got in the way. I took Aunt Tillie. I wasn't an idiot about it. I was perfectly safe the entire time."

Landon rubbed his cheek as he regarded me. "We'll have to talk about this later. I need to make sure Saxon hasn't bolted, which means a drive to Bellaire. I would appreciate it if you would tell me before questioning my murder suspects."

There was a chill to his words that I recognized. He was angry but didn't want to fly off the handle in the middle of town. "I said I was sorry."

"And I heard you."

"Are you going to stay angry all day?"

He shrugged, noncommittal. "I have no idea. I guess we'll have to see if you smell like bacon when I see you next. That could have an effect on my mood."

Ugh. That was so ... Landon. "Fine." I blew out a sigh. There was nothing more I could do. "If I have to smell like bacon all night, I expect you to get over yourself and forgive me."

"We'll see how I'm feeling after I talk to Saxon. Until then, please stay out of trouble. I would greatly appreciate it."

His tone was exaggerated, telling me he was deadly serious. "I'll stay out of trouble ... until dinner. I can't make any promises beyond that."

"I guess I'll take it."

"Great." I leaned in to give him a quick kiss. "On a different note, Aunt Tillie says I'm a goody-goody and I would be better off as a bad girl. Do you think that's true?"

"I like the girl you are. I don't want you being something other than what you want to be. That said, you've been pretty bad today. Perhaps I shall spank you when we get home."

"You're just saying that because it turns you on."

"I have to get my thrills where I can. Now, get out of here. I have to find your buddy Saxon. If he has run, even the bacon scent won't save you."

I had no doubt that was true. "He didn't run. I have faith."

. . .

FOR LACK OF ANYTHING BETTER TO do, I trudged over to Mrs. Little's store to ask her a few questions. My relationship with the woman was strained — and that was putting it mildly — but she was the town busybody. She had information other people didn't ... and it was exactly the sort of information I needed.

"Hello, Bay." Mrs. Little looked annoyed when she realized I was the one entering her store. "What are you doing here?"

"I have a few questions for you."

"Does this have anything to do with the camp?"

Of course she would jump to that conclusion. She was a businesswoman at heart. She wanted to make sure her potential investment was still a sound idea. That was all she cared about.

"Kind of," I replied, moving toward the counter where she was unboxing new merchandise. "What can you tell me about Gertie and Earl?"

Whatever she was expecting, that wasn't it. "Why? Do you think Earl killed the first girl? That body was there a long time."

"That body was there from the final summer," I confirmed. I saw no reason to lie because the information would come out eventually. "From the timetable we've been able to put together, the kids left the camp the same day Vicky Carpenter disappeared. The pool people were also there at that time to close the pool for the season.

"Another counselor told me that the pool was closed before Vicky went missing," I continued. "That means someone killed her and understood how the springs holding the pool cover worked well enough to shove her body in after the fact and close the pool a second time."

"I hate to be the bearer of bad news, Bay, but I'm familiar with pools," Mrs. Little pointed out. "They're not difficult to cover. There's a special tool for those pegs that come out of the cement. All you have to do is twist them."

"Yeah. I get that." I rolled my neck. "Still, most people wouldn't know where to get the tool. That means it likely had to be someone who worked there regularly."

"And you're leaning toward Earl?" She screwed up her face in concentration. "No, that's not right. I remember that summer. Earl was dead by then. He was alive when we started work on the pool and died not long after. He definitely wasn't there for the pool's last hurrah."

"What about Joey Morgan? What do you remember about him?"

"Joey Morgan would've still been alive. He didn't die until the fall."

"Yes, but that wasn't really an answer to my question," I prodded. "What do you remember about him?"

"I remember that he was lazy." Mrs. Little adopted a thoughtful expression. "That was all anybody ever said about him. He was lazy and didn't want to work. That was surprising because his parents were hard workers. They both had issues, don't get me wrong, but they weren't lazy."

"What issues did they have?"

"Well, Gertie was the overbearing sort." If there was one thing Mrs. Little loved, it was gossip. She delved into stories from decades before with gusto. "She always bossed Earl around. He was a nice guy and a good worker, but he needed a firm hand. Gertie was more than happy to provide that hand."

"So ... she bossed him around."

"She definitely bossed him around," Mrs. Little agreed. "Earl needed constant supervision. He wasn't slow or anything. I mean ... not in a mental way. He was just the sort of guy who couldn't think for himself and needed someone to constantly direct him. Does that make sense?"

Oddly enough, it did. "Joey was one of the counselors that last summer. Someone said that Vicky — she's the girl who was killed — didn't like him. Do you think she could've had a valid reason for her feelings?"

"Are you asking me if there were any rumors about the boy being a pervert?"

Mrs. Little was blunt, I had to give her that. "I guess that's what I'm asking," I admitted. "It probably shouldn't matter because Joey is long gone and there's no way he killed both women, but I'm starting to wonder if maybe he had a partner back then. Perhaps he worked with someone to do something horrible to Vicky and it didn't work out as he planned.

"Maybe he killed her — or they killed her — and two people were needed to dispose of the body," I continued. "Perhaps he had a partner and they got away with it for so long the partner decided to go back to killing now. I mean ... it sounds far-fetched, but I've heard stranger things turn out to be true."

Mrs. Little frowned. "Trust me, if the boy hung around with anyone I would tell you. The faster this little investigation is put to rest, the better for everyone ... including me."

Especially her, I silently added. The bank was unlikely to okay the loan when there was an active murder investigation depressing the property's value. I wasn't an idiot. "You didn't know him to hang around with anyone?"

"Not that I remember. He was a loner. He was quite close with his mother and father. When Earl died everyone thought Gertie would fall apart. She didn't because she had Joey to take care of ... even though he was an adult and should've been taking care of himself. When Joey died she became a shell of her former self. I think it was because she blamed herself for what happened."

"Because he was living in the shed instead of the house?"

"Pretty much," she confirmed. "He had a space heater out there and the fire marshal thought that could be the source of the blaze for a time. He couldn't definitively say in the end because there were numerous fire hazards, including gasoline. I mean ... it was a shed. She kept a container of gasoline out there in case of emergencies."

"So ... the fire marshal never ascertained the starting point of the fire?" That was interesting. "Was it ruled accidental?"

"I'm pretty sure it was accidental. The body was burned beyond recognition. It was a horrible thing. There were numerous stories about exactly what happened right after. Now that you bring it up, I'm not sure which one they settled on."

"Numerous stories?"

"That's what I said." Mrs. Little turned testy. "Seriously, Bay. I'm not sure why you're so worked up about this. I understand that you think Joey might've been involved in the first murder, but he's gone. If he had a partner, I can't help you track him down. I do wish you luck. The faster this is solved, the faster I can close on my deal."

She wasn't even trying to hide her greed.

"Well, then I'll let you get back to it. You'll be the first to know when we come up with a culprit. I know how worried you are about a killer being on the loose."

"That would be great." Mrs. Little went back to her inventory. "Watch what you write in the paper, by the way. I don't want a bunch of people trying to buy that property out from under me. I'll be angry if that property slips through my fingers."

"Well, we all know how worried I am about making you angry. I'll do my best to make sure you get what you deserve."

She obviously missed the edge to my words because her grin was fast and happy. "That's all that I ask."

TWENTY-THREE

On a hunch, I went through William's old files in an effort to find something on Joey's death. It wasn't difficult to find. I even discovered an obituary for Earl during my search. His cause of death wasn't listed and only two survivors were mentioned. The small notice – a total of two paragraphs – made me inexplicably sad. Not sad enough to cry, of course, but sad all the same.

When I realized tears were streaming down my face, I grew frustrated. "Vicky?"

The ghost answered before I could turn around. "How did you know I was here?"

"Call it a wild guess." I swiped at my tears. Vicky looked as sad as I felt. "Why are you crying?"

She shrugged. "I don't know. Why are you crying?"

"I'm crying because you made me cry."

"I don't think that's true."

"Oh, it's true. It's a new thing. I felt your emotions and they overwhelmed me because my defenses were down. I need to work on that."

Vicky's expression was unreadable. "I don't think that's what happened."

"It has to be. I had no reason to cry."

"I don't think that's what happened." Vicky was firm. "I started crying because you were crying. I wasn't feeling sad until I stopped by to visit you and the next thing I knew I was crying. Er, well, I was kind of crying. It's weird. I can't cry because I'm a ghost, but I felt those emotions so I was ghost crying. That's a thing, right?"

I didn't see why not. "Sure. You're definitely the one influencing me, though. I don't tend to cry over obituaries for people I don't know."

"Neither do I."

"But ... ." Before I could ask the obvious question, the door flew open to allow Thistle entrance. Her face was red, her hair wild and her expression murderous. I knew right away something terrible had happened. "What now?"

"You'll never guess what Clove did."

She often led with that same statement, so I wasn't exactly braced for the end of the world. "Did she move your fertility goddess statue again? Or, wait, did she put a top on that statue you made a few months ago and keep trying to display outside the petting zoo even though Marcus is appalled by the nudity?"

"That statue is amazing," Thistle snapped. "But that's not what I'm talking about."

"Okay. I give."

"Tell her," Thistle prodded.

I waited a beat, confused. "Tell who what?" I glanced around, but Vicky had been so surprised by Thistle's grand entrance that she disappeared. "There's no one here but us."

"Oh, there's someone else here." Thistle folded her arms over her chest and inclined her head toward the door. "Tell her what you did, Clove."

I tilted my head to the side and waited for my brunette cousin to make her appearance known. When she stepped in the doorway it was obvious she'd been crying. Her makeup was streaked and her eyes red-rimmed. Her hair also looked as if she'd run her hands through it so many times it was about to take off for outer space thanks to the static electricity.

"What is going on?" I was starting to worry. "Oh, geez. Aunt Tillie didn't follow through with her threat and curse a bunch of seagulls to crap on Mrs. Little's store, did she? I was just over there and everything looked fine."

"Oh, this has nothing to do with Aunt Tillie," Thistle hissed. "This is all Clove. Tell Bay what you did. Tell her right now."

A small sob escaped Clove's throat but otherwise she held it together.

"What's wrong?" I asked, my mind going a mile a minute. "You're not sick, are you?"

"I'm not sick," Clove said hurriedly, moving into my office on hesitant feet. "At least not the way you think I am. It's something else."

"What?" When she didn't immediately answer, I prodded further. "What is it?"

"Well … I'm pregnant."

Whatever I was expecting, it wasn't that. I honestly thought my legs were going to go out from under me as I struggled to absorb her words. "W-what?"

"You heard her." Thistle's expression was dark. "She's pregnant. Not only that, she's, like, four months pregnant. I just thought she put on more winter weight than usual and was having trouble shedding it, but no. She's freaking pregnant and she's been keeping it from us. I mean … can you believe that?"

I swallowed hard as Clove sank onto the couch. People say pregnant women have a glow. That wasn't true about Clove. She looked as if someone had run over her favorite pet and left her to find it by the side of the road.

"I meant to tell you," Clove muttered, avoiding eye contact. "I wanted to tell you as soon as I found out. I was embarrassed."

I rubbed my cheek as I debated what to say. "Why were you embarrassed?"

"You know why."

AMANDA M. LEE

Actually, I did know. Our mothers were sticklers about birth control. The absolute worst thing in the world, as far as they were concerned, was getting pregnant before marriage. They were old-fashioned that way, an opinion that used to make us laugh. Clove, of course, was the most sensitive of our little trio. It only made sense that she was terrified to tell our mothers. Still ... .

"I get why you didn't want to tell your mom ... and my mom. I especially get why you didn't want to tell my mom, but why didn't you tell us? We could've helped you with this."

"I didn't want you guys to be mad at me," she admitted, her lower lip trembling. "The longer I waited, the worse it got. I'm only telling you now because Thistle went through my purse and found my prenatal vitamins. This was after she realized I wasn't drinking around the campfire last night and tried to shame me, saying Winchesters always drank around the campfire and I was embarrassing the family. She's been melting down most of the day."

That was obvious. "Well ... ." I forgot about the file on the floor and dragged a hand through my hair. "When did you find out?"

"Not long after Thistle moved out of the guesthouse," she replied, her eyes glassy with unshed tears. "I was feeling weird that entire time – like I wanted to constantly cry but had no idea why – and then I realized I was three weeks late. I took a home pregnancy test and it came out positive. Then I took seven more just to be sure."

"Obviously you told Sam," I noted.

"He came home when I was sitting in the bathroom with all the tests," she said. "He was really happy but insisted we go to a doctor before we told anyone. He said it was the smart thing to do. I told him I'd never done the smart thing before so I had no idea why I had to start doing it now, but he insisted.

"When we were at the doctor she suggested I wait until I was three months along to tell anyone," she continued. "She said that was standard because most miscarriages happen in the first trimester. That made sense. Plus, well, it gave me time to think about how I was going to tell my mother.

"But the three-month mark passed five weeks ago," she continued.

"I'm like ... really pregnant now." As if to prove it, she lifted her shirt and showed off a slightly-rounded belly. "I can't believe you thought this was my winter weight." Her glare was accusatory when it fell on Thistle. "That is just ... ridiculous."

"It's not as if I've seen you in your pajamas or anything," Thistle shot back. "We don't live under the same roof any longer. I mean ... I didn't want to be the one to say, 'Lay off the doughnuts,' because it sounds mean."

I blew out a sigh as Clove wiped her cheeks. "Well ... this is not the end of the world." I meant it. I wasn't simply saying it to bolster her feelings. "You're engaged. You're getting married to the father of the baby. Wait ... Sam is the father, right?"

Clove scorched me with a murderous look at the same moment something hard slammed into my chest.

"What the ... ?" I put my hand to the spot where I felt the impact and frowned. "What was that?"

"What was what?" Thistle shot me a dubious look. "Are you feeling left out or something? Do you want me to start paying attention to you instead of Clove? I have plenty of anger to go around, if that's the case."

"It's not the case, you ninny," I snapped, my hand busy on the spot where I'd felt the blow. Something occurred to me. "Were you crying right before you stormed in here?"

"Me?" Thistle's eyebrows hopped. "I wasn't crying. I have no reason to cry. I'm not the one who will be raked over the Winchester coals when news breaks of a baby."

"I think you're making too big of a deal about that," I countered. "Our mothers threatened us with great bodily harm if we came home pregnant as teenagers. We're adults now. It won't be as big of a deal as you think."

Thistle wasn't about to be placated. "Oh, we'll just see about that."

I ignored her and focused on Clove. "I was talking about you. Were you crying right before you came here?"

"Yeah. Why?"

"Were you crying yesterday? I'm talking about in the afternoon, before you headed out to the campground."

"I was. I hid in the bathroom so Thistle wouldn't know what was going on. My hormones are all over the place."

"Is that what you were doing in the bathroom for an hour?" Thistle screwed up her face. "I thought you were taking a gigantic dump."

Clove was appalled. "Why wouldn't you suggest more fiber in my diet if you really thought that was true?"

Thistle shrugged. "I didn't want to upset you."

I snorted as I briefly pressed my eyes shut and rubbed my forehead. "You said you were upset right before Thistle moved from the guesthouse. I was kind of watery during that time, too. Son of a witch! I think I've been feeling your emotions. Either that or Aunt Tillie is right and I'm absorbing the emotions of the ghosts around me. I'm not sure which freaks me out more."

"My emotions?" Clove was taken aback. "Why would you be feeling my emotions?"

"Because I'm not the only one with growing powers," I replied without hesitation. "You are, too. At least … I think you are." I slid my eyes to Thistle. "I bet you are, too. We just haven't figured out how you're manifesting. It totally makes sense."

"How does it make sense?" Clove asked, her hand automatically going to her stomach. "Why do you think it's happening now?"

"I don't know why it's happening now." That was the truth. "It just is. You were always a touch empathic, picking up on the emotions of others. Now you're broadcasting."

"Why are you picking up the signals and not Thistle?" Clove asked. "I mean … I spend more time with her."

That was a very good question. "I don't know." I licked my lips and regarded our crabby cousin. "Unless … have you been crying for no reason and hiding it from everybody?"

Thistle's mouth dropped open. "I can't believe you would accuse me of that. Of course not."

She was a good liar, but I knew her better than most. She had a few tells, and she was using one right now. "Then why are you looking just over my shoulder instead of into my eyes?" I challenged.

"I'm not."

"You are."

"I am not."

"You totally are," Clove said, brightening considerably. "Have you been crying?"

"No!" Thistle practically bellowed.

"She's been crying," Clove deduced. "She's been emotional, too. She's just been hiding it better than the two of us."

That wasn't surprising. "Well, I guess you can't be angry at Clove for not telling us that she was pregnant right away. You've been hiding stuff, too," I pointed out.

"Oh, stuff it." Thistle let loose a dramatic sigh and threw herself in my desk chair. "Do you really think Clove has been making us cry?"

"I was crying a few minutes ago and I blamed it on Vicky. Aunt Tillie assumed I was absorbing the emotions of the ghosts. It turns out that Clove has been forcing emotions on us. I'm not to blame for any part of this recent snafu. What a relief." When I raised my eyes, I found Clove glaring at me. "What?"

"I can't believe you're going to blame this on me," she groused, folding her arms over her chest. "I'm pregnant. And I have to tell our mothers. I think they're going to shun me."

That was the most ridiculous thing I'd ever heard. "They won't shun you." I was almost positive that was true. "This isn't olden times. They might give you a little grief. But if my mother tries that, you can point out she had sex with Chief Terry on the first date and that will shut her up. Clove, they're going to be happy. You and Sam are getting married in a few weeks. I ... wait. That's why you and Sam are getting married so quickly."

Clove nodded, morose. "I want to be married before the baby comes. I also want to be married before I tell Mom and the aunts about the baby."

I wanted to argue with her, but that seemed like a dumb stand to take. It was her decision. And, oddly enough, I understood. "So ...

you're saying we have to keep things quiet for another few weeks. I think we can manage that."

"Really?" Thistle was droll. "When have we ever been able to keep a secret of this magnitude?"

I wanted to give her an example, but I couldn't come up with anything. "Well ... ."

"That's right." Thistle turned triumphant. "We've never been able to keep a secret like this. It's going to blow up in our faces."

I wasn't ready to admit defeat. "Not necessarily." My mind was busy with possibilities. "Clove will just have to be careful about what she wears and when she sees everyone. It's better to see them at night ... and stay at the far end of the table. Thistle and I will block you when we can."

"You will?" Clove brightened considerably. "Does that mean you'll help me?"

"We'll do our very best." I turned a pair of expectant blue eyes on Thistle. "Isn't that right?"

She didn't look happy with the question. "I don't know," she replied after a moment's contemplation. "Who will take the fall if this blows up in our faces?"

"We'll take it together," Clove replied.

"Oh, no." I shook my head. "You'll take the fall alone. That's a house rule. Whoever has the secret is on the hook when things go south. We'll help you as much as we can until that happens."

"Really?" Clove's eyes were glassy again. "Do you really mean it?"

I wasn't surprised when I felt tears prick the backs of my eyes. "We really mean it."

Thistle let loose an exaggerated sob. "Yes, we'll help. I demand to be there when you tell Aunt Tillie, though. I think the news may kill her and I don't want to miss it."

I was certain she was making a joke to ease the mood, so I merely smiled. "We'll get you through the wedding Clove. But you have to tell them right after. We'll be running on borrowed time as it is."

"I'll tell them as soon as we're back from our honeymoon."

"Oh, no." I immediately started shaking my head. "You'll tell them right before you leave on your honeymoon. That way they can stew for two weeks while you're safely out of their reach and they'll be pretty much over whatever dark thoughts threaten to overtake them by the time you get back."

"Oh, wow! That's a great idea." Clove was suddenly bubbly again, which meant Thistle and I were free of tears. "We also have to figure a way for you to control your emotions. I'm hoping this is a byproduct of the pregnancy. If not, you need to work on it."

"I didn't know I was doing it," Clove protested. "I'll start working on it right now. I promise. That's my main focus ... as soon as you tell me how to stop doing what I'm doing."

"If we knew that we wouldn't have an issue," Thistle shot back. "We'll have to research it, which means you have to be extra careful around our mothers until we figure out a way to keep them from spontaneously bursting into tears. That won't go over well when Aunt Winnie and Chief Terry are in bed together."

I frowned at the picture she painted. "Did you have to say that? Now it's all I'll be able to think about."

Thistle was blasé. "If it's in my head, it has to be in your head. Suck it up."

"We'll figure it out, Clove." I moved to her and extended my arms to give her a hug. "This is a big deal. You're going to have a baby. There's going to be a whole new generation of Winchesters."

"Cornell," Clove corrected, accepting the hug. "The baby is going to be a Cornell."

"Oh, please let me be there when you tell Aunt Tillie that," Thistle pleaded. "That will definitely kill her."

"Ignore her," I ordered Clove as I patted her back. "This is going to be great. Just you wait."

"I hope so." Clove sucked in a calming breath and I felt her frown against my cheek. "Do you smell like bacon?"

"Crap! I just knew Aunt Tillie was going to do me dirty."

Thistle chuckled. "Better you than me."

"Better you than me," Clove corrected, shoving me away and hopping to her feet. "I think I'm going to throw up. I can't stand the smell of pork." She bolted toward the bathroom, leaving Thistle and me to eye one another.

"Well, things could be worse," I said after a beat. "At least she and Sam are getting married. If she was going to be a single mother I doubt we'd ever be able to put things back together."

"There is that." Thistle flashed a smile. "So, what did you do to tick off Aunt Tillie?"

"It's not so much what I did as what Landon wants. He made a special request."

"He's kind of a pervert."

"Totally."

TWENTY-FOUR

Landon was full of swagger when he strolled through my office door. He pulled up short when he saw I wasn't alone, his eyes narrowing as he glanced between faces.

"What's going on?"

He was an intuitive guy. He would figure out Clove was pregnant no matter what we did. That meant I had to tell him. We'd already talked about just that, and Clove agreed he could help run interference.

"Clove is pregnant. She's terrified to tell our mothers because they'll probably give her grief about it. We're keeping it secret for her until the wedding, which is only a few weeks away. You're going to help. I don't want any lip about it."

Landon pursed his lips as he focused on my brunette cousin. "Wow."

When he didn't expound, I shook my head. "That's all you have to say? This is a big deal."

"I get that. Are you excited, Clove?"

She held out her hands and shrugged. "I haven't decided yet. I kind of like the idea of a baby. I think I would've liked it better two years from now, but there's nothing I can do about that. I'm terrified to tell my mother."

"We're all terrified for your mother to find out," Thistle drawled as she flipped through the papers on my desk. She was brimming with restless energy and her way of dealing with it was being a busybody. "It's a secret until the wedding. That means no one can find out ... including Aunt Tillie."

"I've got it." Landon's eyes flashed with annoyance. "I'm not an idiot." He was calm when he rested his hand on Clove's shoulder. "This is going to be fun. Once the initial flurry of activity is over, you'll be able to settle in and get a handle on how all of this is going to work out."

"Yeah." Clove pressed her lips together and looked pensive. When she finally spoke, it was to utter something I never thought would come out of her mouth. "I'm kind of hoping childbirth is different for witches. Like ... maybe it won't hurt because I'm genetically blessed. That's possible, right?"

Thistle and I snorted in unison.

"Yeah. That's not going to happen," Thistle said. "If you listen to our mothers, their labor pains were worse than those suffered by mere mortals. Labor is going to suck."

The fearful look on Clove's face told me that was the worst thing to say. "But it's a temporary thing and you get a baby out of it," I said hurriedly. "You'll survive. It'll be okay."

"I just don't want it to hurt." Clove buried her face behind the pillow on the couch, allowing me to focus on Landon.

"It's going to be a rough few weeks," I noted.

"Well, there's nothing we can do about it now," he pointed out. "I was hoping you would be done for the night. I'm starving and want to get out of here."

"We have separate vehicles," I reminded him.

"Yes, but I wanted to check to see if ... ." He shuffled closer and smiled. "And there's my dessert." He hunkered down and pressed his nose into my hair. "That is the best perfume ever. I want to bottle that scent and spray it over my clothes so I can smell you all day."

That was a freaky visual. "Yes, I smell like bacon. You got your way. Happy?"

"I'm always happy with you, sweetie." His smile was broad. "Come on. We should head out to get dinner and then go home so I can enjoy my present."

"It's only a present for you. It's a punishment for me."

"It's the gift that keeps on giving." He squeezed my hand. "How do you feel about skipping dinner at the inn and getting takeout? We can hole up in the guesthouse and ignore the outside world for the next twelve hours."

"I think it sounds like you already had this planned out," I said dryly. "I guess I can live with the takeout. I want a bath, though. It's been a long day."

"I can make a bath work." His grin was flirty as he leaned forward and kissed me. "I'm still kind of mad about what you did. I expect I'll be over it by the end of the night, though. You smell too good."

"Ugh." I made a face as he helped me to my feet, dusting off the seat of my pants and leaning over to collect the files I'd been perusing so I could take them home with me. My gaze landed on Thistle, who had completely tuned out our conversation (I couldn't blame her) and was focused on the sheets I'd printed from Hannah Bishop's missing person file. "What are you looking at?"

"I recognize her," Thistle replied.

"Hannah? Yeah. She's the first person we found in the pool. Her photo has been all over the news."

"I don't recognize her from the television. I haven't been watching the news. I recognize her because she stopped in at Hypnotic a few months ago."

Landon, who was making a series of tickling inhalations against my skin, quickly straightened. "You talked to her before she went missing?"

"Yeah. I talked to her for a good thirty minutes or so. I was alone at the store because Clove said something came up — I'm betting that had something to do with the baby she's been hiding from us — when she came in. I didn't know her name."

"What do you remember about her?" Landon was all business now. "Did she say where she was going? Was she meeting anyone?"

"We talked about Hemlock Cove's history a bit. She said she was writing a book."

"That's definitely her," I agreed. "Her parents said she had big plans for the book."

"She seemed nice." Thistle was lost in thought as she tapped her bottom lip. "So often the tourists who come to town are annoying. She was the exact opposite. She had insightful questions and wanted to know about the town gossip. She thought Mrs. Little's store would make a funny chapter in her book because only a crazy person would sell porcelain unicorns."

I couldn't help but smile. "Well ... she wasn't wrong."

"She had a lot of energy," Thistle continued. "She was so excited to be here. She asked about a lot of places ... including Hollow Creek and the Dandridge. She wanted to know about the 'most magical' places." She used the appropriate air quotes. "I didn't tell her I knew about those places from firsthand experience, but she always seemed to have knowledge of them."

"Somehow she ended up at the campground," Landon pointed out. "Do you know how that happened?"

"No, but I do remember where she was staying. She might've left her stuff out there."

"Out where?" I asked.

"The Dragonfly."

"Of course." I rubbed my forehead. The Dragonfly was the inn run by our fathers. They'd only returned to the area a little more than a year ago. Our relationships with them were something of a work in progress. However, they would not be happy to see us darkening their doorstep again only because we were in search of information. "I'm guessing we have to go out there."

"We do," Landon confirmed. "I need to talk to them."

"They're going to notice I smell like bacon."

"Don't worry. I'll make sure they don't molest you."

I glowered at him. "You're a funny guy."

"I do my best."

THE DRAGONFLY WAS A BEAUTIFUL inn. It wasn't breathtaking like The Overlook — and our fathers weren't renowned as cooks like our mothers — but it was still a comforting place. That's why I was surprised when we walked through the front door and found my Uncle Teddy, Thistle's father, dealing with what looked to be some sort of frenzy in the lobby.

"We're doing the best we can, ma'am," he said, frustration evident. "I swear there's no ghost living in your room. We don't have any ghosts on the premises."

I exchanged a quick look with Landon, but didn't say anything. Teddy's eyes widened when he realized we were joining the fray.

"Hi, guys. I didn't know you were stopping by tonight."

"It wasn't exactly planned," Landon replied. "Um ... where is Jack? We need to talk to him."

"He's in the kitchen."

Landon linked his fingers with mine and gave me a little tug as he pulled me through the crowd. There had to be six people lined up in the small lobby, and none of them looked happy. "I'm so glad I don't have a job that forces me to work in customer service," he said.

"I kind of do ... although it's different. I ... hey!" I felt a hand on my bottom and swiveled quickly, my eyes going dark. A woman and man stood behind me and both had innocent expressions on their faces. "Did you do that?" I directed the question at the man because he seemed the obvious choice.

"Do what?" Landon asked, confused. "What's wrong?"

"Someone grabbed my butt."

The announcement didn't go over well with my boyfriend. "Excuse me?"

"Someone grabbed my butt," I repeated, annoyed.

"Are you sure it was grabbed? Could it have been an accident?"

"There was squeezing."

He growled. "Did you touch her butt?" he asked the man, his shoulders squaring.

The man's eyes went wide. "I didn't. I would never."

"Someone grabbed my butt," I argued. "I didn't imagine it."

"Maybe we should take this outside," Landon suggested to the flustered man. "We need to have a discussion about how you don't grab a woman's butt without invitation."

"I didn't grab her butt!"

"I grabbed her butt," the woman announced, causing me to take an inadvertent step back.

I wasn't the only one surprised by the announcement. Landon made a noise like a feral cat. "Excuse me?"

"It was me." The woman turned prim. "I'm sorry. It was an impulse. She smells like bacon. I didn't even know they made perfume like that. Is there a cologne option, by the way? I would like to get it for my husband."

"It's a personalized scent," I muttered, my cheeks burning.

"I'm truly sorry I did it," the woman offered. "I can't explain myself. I have a thing for bacon. I don't know how it even happened, to be honest."

"I'm right there with you." Landon's smile was sly as he glanced at me. "Usually I would defend your honor, but I can't beat up a woman."

I wanted to crawl into a hole and die. "We're going to have a talk about this later. This can't happen again."

"Yeah, yeah, yeah." He slipped his arm around my waist. "Try to keep your hands to yourself, ma'am. If you touch her again, I'm going to let her take you outside and you don't want that. She's tougher than she looks."

The woman's eyes gleamed. "Well ... that might be fun."

My mouth dropped open as Landon started chuckling and dragged me away. He didn't speak again until we were cutting through the dining room and heading toward the kitchen. "That was different, huh?"

"I can't even look at you," I groused. "This is totally your fault."

"I take full responsibility."

Dad and Warren, Clove's father, were busy overseeing dinner preparations when we entered the room. At first, neither of them acknowledged us. It wasn't until Dad noticed one of his kitchen aides staring at the door rather than focusing on the food that he turned in our direction.

"Bay, I didn't realize you were stopping in." He looked flustered as he wiped his hands on an apron and headed in my direction. "I'm so happy to see you."

"I'm happy to see you, too." I accepted the hug he offered. "I'm sorry we're dropping in on you like this. It's just ... we need to ask you about a guest who was here about two months ago. Hannah Bishop."

Dad's face reflected confusion as he pulled back. "I remember her. She left her bag and took off."

"Did you report her missing?" Landon asked.

"No. She was the sort of girl who had wanderlust. She took off in her car and never came back. I figured she'd decided to find another town. She was writing a book."

"Her car," I muttered. "We didn't think about her car."

"We really didn't," Landon agreed. "I mean ... I did at first and then I forgot about it. Her car is either still out here somewhere or someone destroyed or hid it. I can't believe no one has stumbled across it."

Dad stared at us a beat, blinking his eyes, and then he shook his head. "I'm confused."

"We need to see the things Hannah left behind," Landon supplied. "We pulled her body out of the pool at an old campground the other day. She was murdered. We need to figure out who did it ... and if you still have her belongings, that's at least a place to start."

"Her stuff is in the storage room off the library," Dad offered. "I have to finish dinner, but you're welcome to look through it."

"Thank you." Landon smiled at my father and squeezed my hand. "Maybe we're finally getting somewhere."

"Maybe," I agreed.

"Do you guys want food?" Dad called after us. "I can bring you plates in the storeroom when we're done. But you smell like bacon. You must have already eaten."

I glowered at Landon as he snickered.

"Plates sound good," Landon replied. "I, for one, am starving. I'm guessing Bay could use some nourishment, too."

"I'll bring them to you as soon as I can."

IT TURNED OUT HANNAH DIDN'T leave much behind. She had a simple suitcase — one of the smaller, carry-ons with rollers and a handle — full of clothing and toiletries. The only other items were a laptop and notebook. The laptop was password protected. The notebook contained a hodgepodge of ideas.

"She talked to a lot of people," I noted as I leaned against the wall and flipped the pages. "She was fascinated by Hemlock Cove. She talked to Mrs. Gunderson ... and Mrs. Little. She wanted to make an appointment with me."

Landon slid me a sidelong look. "I know what you're thinking, sweetie. You couldn't have saved her even if she did visit."

"You don't know that."

"And you don't know that you could've saved her," he pointed out. "What's done is done. We can't change it. You're the one always telling me that."

"Yeah. I guess." I blew out a sigh and rolled my neck. "She hit spots all over town. The downtown area was an easy draw. She went on a tour of the tanker, too."

"You're not saying you suspect Sam?"

I immediately started shaking my head. "That's not who he is. Even if he was, he didn't know about the camp. He'd never been there. If he was going to hide a body it wouldn't be under the pool cover at a camp he never visited."

"I'm glad to see you've given this some thought," he said dryly.

"I give things thought all the time." I flipped another page. "She mentions the stables and how she wants to ride a horse but she feels it's too cold. She went out to Hollow Creek. She says that she can 'feel' the magic there.

"She says she never really believed in that sort of magic until she visited Hollow Creek," I continued. "That's not the first time we've heard about strangers feeling the magic out there. Poet and the other people from the circus felt it, too."

"They did," Landon agreed. "Does she mention running into anyone out there?"

"No." I shook my head. "She doesn't mention many names. Hey, ... this is interesting. She went to the camp."

"We kind of figured that."

"Yeah, but she went to the camp and made it back to her room," I said. "She said that she saw it on a map and wanted to check it out. She took photographs, but I don't see any sitting around, do you?"

"They're probably on her computer," Landon replied. "I'll get a tech to unlock it remotely when we get back to the guesthouse. I'm guessing it won't be difficult because she's the type who would use standard passwords."

I continued reading. "She has a weird notation in here. One that doesn't make any sense."

"What does it say?"

"Just a name. Joey Morgan followed by a question mark."

Landon furrowed his brow. "Why would she be interested in a man who died a decade ago?"

That was a very good question. "I don't know. He was one of the people Vicky was uncomfortable around. Maybe ... maybe Hannah somehow figured that out. Maybe she was looking into Vicky's disappearance and didn't tell anyone."

"Why?" Landon was the pragmatic sort, so he needed a motive before he could get on board with an investigation. "Hannah lived downstate. Vicky lived in Traverse City. I've been through both their files and haven't seen anything that ties them together."

"I don't know. Maybe her parents could give us some insight."

"I don't know that I want to call them when they're grieving, but I guess I can shoot them an email. They asked that we email questions for the next few days as they prepare for the funeral. They're ... lost."

"I think they were good parents, and even though it was out of the norm for Hannah, I believe part of them was hoping she'd taken off on an adventure ... just like Vicky. Both of them had wanderlust."

Landon rubbed his chin. "I hadn't put that together, but you're right. Both of these young women wanted to travel, see other places, do big things."

"Do you think that's important to the case?"

"I don't know. It's another avenue worth searching."

TWENTY-FIVE

We stayed for dinner and a chat with my father. He felt guilty about not reporting Hannah missing. Landon assured him that she was probably already dead by the time he'd noticed she hadn't checked out, but that was little comfort.

We made the drive back to the guesthouse in relative silence. I couldn't stop running the idea that Hannah was investigating Vicky's disappearance through my head. On the surface, it didn't make sense. In my heart, I was convinced there was something there.

"Hannah's ghost isn't running around."

Landon, who had just pulled into our driveway, put his Explorer in park and looked at me. "What do you mean?"

"I mean that her ghost isn't running around," I repeated. "I haven't seen her. Only Vicky."

"So ... what does that mean?"

"I don't know. It's possible she didn't stay. Not all souls remain behind, even if their passing is traumatic."

He reached over and collected my hand. "I don't want you blaming yourself for this. There's absolutely nothing you could've done. There's nothing your father could've done. Although ... if he'd told us sooner we would've gone through her things and saw mention of the camp. There's a possibility we would've found her sooner."

"Only if you bothered to check the pool closely," I pointed out. "What are the odds of that?"

He leaned over the console and kissed my temple. "Your mind is going so fast it's a blur. Why don't you tell me what you're thinking?"

I slid my eyes to him. "I thought you were angry with me."

"You smell like bacon. I can't stay angry when you smell like bacon."

I chuckled. "That's good to know. Maybe I will look into having bacon-scented perfume made. I'll attract every man in a ten-mile radius when I wear it ... and some women."

He laughed, the sound low and warm. "That sounds like a fantastic plan." He killed the engine and pulled out his keys. "Let's finish this conversation inside, shall we? I have plans for you and I'm too old to carry them out in a vehicle."

"You have that trick knee," I agreed, gathering Hannah's journal and the files I'd been going through at the newspaper office to my chest. "Why do you think Hannah was interested in Joey? He died a full decade before she came here. There's no way she would've known him."

"You assume that," Landon countered as he hopped out of the Explorer and moved to the front of the vehicle, where he waited for me to join him. "Hannah was twenty-five. That would've made her fourteen when the camp closed. Kids that young spent time there, right?"

I slowed my pace as I did the math. "They did. I wonder if she was here that last summer. I mean ... that might be possible. She wouldn't have been with the last group of kids. That was Thistle and Clove's age group. That means the fourteen-year-olds would've been with the thirteen-year-olds a few weeks before."

"Would the same counselors have been utilized?"

"I don't know." The new information was giving me a headache. I leaned against the wall as Landon unlocked the front door. "I don't know what to think."

"Well, how about we take a bath and work things out? We still have to make up from our earlier fight."

I arched an eyebrow. "That wasn't much of a fight."

"That doesn't mean I don't want to make up."

I pursed my lips. "Will you stop being angry if we make up?"

"I'm not really angry. I mean ... I guess I was. I was more worried than anything."

"I wasn't in any danger."

"I know that. I met the guy. I agree with your assessment."

"You're still agitated." I knew his moods backward and forward and easily recognized that.

"I don't like it when you put yourself in danger," he clarified. "I love you, Bay. I want us to be together for a very long time. That won't happen if you get cocky and approach the wrong person. I know you can take care of yourself. This is my issue. I don't foresee simply being able to let you run headlong into danger without saying something. That's not who I am."

"Oh, I know." He was cute when he was explaining himself. "I should've called you before I headed over there. I did take Aunt Tillie. Honestly, there was no danger."

"I don't know that we'll ever agree that she's an appropriate sidekick, but I'm ready to let this go." His smile was flirtatious. "I was thinking we could take a bath, enjoy the delectable scent of bacon for a bit, and then have hot chocolate while going over everything from beginning to end."

"Like a team?"

"Definitely like a team."

I grinned as I stepped closer. "I can live with that ... but I don't understand how you can find bacon alluring after spending so much time with Peg."

He extended a warning finger. "I don't want Peg brought up in association with bacon again. I don't like it."

I chuckled despite his serious expression. "If you can get Aunt Tillie to lift this curse tomorrow morning over breakfast, I'll consider acquiescing to your demands."

"So ... just the one night of bacon-lovin' delight? I can live with that."

"You'd better get your fill now."

"That's exactly what I had in mind."

TWO HOURS LATER, WE SAT IN COMFY PAJAMAS in the living room. My hair was wild from the bath ... and a few other things ... but I'd long since given up worrying about bedhead when it came to Landon. He was a big fan of wild tresses and untamed waves.

"We need to go back to the camp office tomorrow," I said as I laid out the articles I'd found on Joey's death and adjusted my legs under the coffee table to get comfortable. "If Hannah really was there that summer that might explain a lot."

"Agreed," Landon said as he reclined on the couch behind me. He had Hannah's journal and was going over it again, from start to finish. "The thing is, even if she was worked up about something Joey did back then, he's gone now."

"That's why I don't believe he was working alone." I'd given it a lot of thought and this was the hunch I'd developed. "I think that Joey was working with someone else."

"Do you have the counselor sheets from that summer?"

"In the bedroom." I scurried back to the bedroom, which was a mess thanks to our earlier game. Landon referred to it as "Sizzlin' Bacon." I merely thought of it as the "Landon loses his head" game. When I returned to the living room, Landon had moved his attention to the articles on Joey's death. "What are you doing?"

"Reading." He patted the spot on the couch next to him. "Come up here and get comfortable."

That sounded like an iffy proposition. "I don't think that's a good idea because you'll insist on playing another round of bacon games."

"Bay, I hate to break it to you, but I can smell you when you're sitting on the floor. You're no less enticing with three feet separating us."

"Yes, but I'm less accessible."

"For now." He looked away from the article long enough to wink at me and then turned back. "We're not done yet."

"You're an animal."

"And don't you forget it."

I lost myself in the counselor list for a few minutes, putting the sheets of paper together so I could go over every name. When I was finished, there were ten names. "We've been assuming that if Joey had a partner and was doing something ... unfortunate, it would've had to be a man. What if we're wrong about that assumption?"

Landon slid his eyes to me. "You think he was working with a woman? I don't see how that works."

"Only because we've also assumed that the motive for killing these girls was sexual. What if it was something else?"

"I find a sexual motive as disgusting as you, sweetie, but what other motive could there be?"

"Well ... what if Joey was stealing money from his mother? Or, what if he was stealing from the other counselors? Vicky had a trip planned. She was going to travel and then return home before her sister gave birth.

"We know that Joey hated working and was deemed 'lazy' by pretty much anyone who had ever met him," I continued. "What if he decided to steal as a way to fund himself?"

Landon tunneled his hand through his messy hair and stared at the ceiling as he considered the suggestion. "I guess I could see that. The thing is, how much is he actually going to get stealing from camp counselors?"

"Maybe he was stealing from the kids, too. We never took anything of value to camp with us, but that doesn't mean other kids didn't."

"How would we find that out?"

I shrugged. "Maybe Chief Terry knows."

Landon flicked his eyes to the clock on the wall. "He's probably in bed with your mother. Even if she doesn't smell like bacon, I don't want to risk interrupting them."

I scowled. "I can't believe you just said that. I mean ... that is disgusting."

He smirked. "That's your payback for going to see a potential killer without telling me. I bet you won't do that again."

We both knew that wasn't true. I often leaped before I looked. I couldn't stop myself. "I thought the bacon curse was my punishment."

"The bacon curse is a special gift for both of us. You only pretend you don't like it because that's part of the game."

That's not how I looked at it at all. "How would you like it if I talked Aunt Tillie into cursing you so you smell like tomato juice and pickles? That might turn me on, but it wouldn't be a joy for you."

"I'd be fine with it."

"You would not."

"I would. I love it when you're turned on."

He said it in such a definitive manner that it was clear arguing would be wasted effort. "Fine." I rubbed my forehead. "I have ten names here. Hannah is one. Joey is another. Lance is a third. That leaves seven we need to run ... but I know four of the names on this list."

"Lay it on me."

"Samantha Bertrand was about three years ahead of me in school. She was a counselor for, like, four years in a row. She's still in town and married to Gary Lincoln, who works in the blacksmith shop."

"Any reason you can see her being a killer?"

"Not off the top of my head."

"Keep going."

"Patty Barton. She was my age. We graduated together. She was friends with Lila. I didn't even realize she was a counselor, so that must mean she only did it the one year. She wasn't smart enough to get into college even though her parents had the money to send her, which means she stayed behind when the rest of us left that fall. She married Trevor Kingston and they had a couple of kids. He's the manager of the grocery store. Patty is on several of Mrs. Little's festival committees."

"So ... she purposely spends time with Mrs. Little?" Landon queried. "I'm guessing that makes her evil incarnate or insane.

Nobody purposely spends time with that woman, so she must identify with the dark side of the Force."

I had to laugh at his geeky comment. "That's definitely a possibility," I agreed. "Nate Johnson is on here, too. He was only a counselor for one week that summer ... and he's listed on the week that Hannah would've been there – if she attended."

"Which we can't confirm until we head back to the camp tomorrow and go through the records again," Landon said. "I really wish we would've brought all the files back."

"I didn't realize we were going to need them," I admitted. "I thought the counselors were the ones we needed to focus on. I never thought the kids would be important."

"Fair enough." He moved his hands to the back of my neck and slowly started rubbing as he rolled so his legs were behind me, his chin on top of my head. "What about the fourth person?"

"Megan Dykstra. She's about two years older than me. She lives in Bellaire now. I think her husband owns a construction company. Her mother is still here, though. I've seen her visiting from time to time."

"Were you friendly with her?"

"No. Not even a little."

He pursed his lips. "Is there a reason you weren't friendly with her?"

"I know you find this difficult to believe, but most of the kids near my age didn't like us. Some of them were afraid because of Aunt Tillie. Others didn't like us because we were rumored to be witches."

"I have to tell you, if I heard a pretty girl was a witch when I was in high school I would've been all over her."

"Even without the bacon curse?"

His lips curved against my cheek. "Maybe I only would've been all over you. It's probably good we didn't go to the same high school. We never would've survived over the long haul."

He wasn't wrong. I happened to believe the same thing. "Timing is everything."

"It is." He kissed the top of my head. "I'll take the other names you've found and email them to the main office. We can have cursory background checks completed by lunch tomorrow. At least we'll be able to rule out anyone who isn't still living in the area. That's something."

"Yeah." I closed my eyes and groaned as he dug his fingers into my tense muscles. "That feels good."

"If you smelled like bacon all the time you'd get nonstop massages. Just something to think about."

I snickered. "Yeah, well ... ." I found my mind traveling to another issue. "What do you think about Clove being pregnant?"

"I think she'll make a good mother."

"I wasn't really talking about that. Of course she'll make a good mother. She's the most patient of all of us. I was talking about the part where she got knocked up before getting married. That won't go over well with our mothers even if she manages to keep it a secret until the wedding."

"I don't get that. Your mothers are all about female empowerment. Antiquated ideas about pregnancy shouldn't be an issue in your family."

"I hope you're right." I meant it. "There's always a chance that they only scared the crap out of us with threats about what would happen if we got pregnant in high school because they didn't want us to derail our futures. They might be perfectly happy with how things have turned out."

"But?" he prodded.

"But I still think there's going to be a meltdown or two," I admitted. "My mother and aunts are very 'do as I say, not as I do.' You probably figured that out from the way we reacted to Mom sleeping with Chief Terry on their first date."

He chuckled as he slipped down to the floor and wrapped his arms around me. "I remember the first time I spent the night with you. There were a lot of meltdowns. I was freaked out at the time, but I find it funny looking back."

"I don't find it funny."

"That's because you have a limited sense of humor."

"My sense of humor is legendary."

"Is that so?" He tickled my ribs to elicit a gasp. "I think your sense of humor needs some work." He kissed the ridge of my ear. "I also think I'm just the person for the job."

I had no doubt what sort of work he had in mind. "What is it with you and the bacon smell? You really do act like an animal."

"I can't help it." His lips fluttered lightly as he kissed my cheek. "You're everything I've ever wanted, Bay. The bacon smell somehow lifts you into the stratosphere. I don't know how to explain it."

I wanted to argue. We were supposed to be digging deep into the files, after all. I didn't have the heart, though. "Make sure you send your list of names to the main office and then we can go to bed. I expect you to get up early and actually work on the case."

"That's a fine idea." He gave me another tickle and then pulled me to a standing position with him. "Let's send that email together."

"You're just afraid I'll lock myself in the bathroom if you wander away."

"I'm not fearful of anything of the sort."

We both knew that wasn't true.

TWENTY-SIX

Landon and I woke at the same time. He was curled around me, his face buried in my hair, and he inhaled deeply as he snuggled closer. Then he made a pitiful groan.

"No, no, no. It's gone."

I knew what he was talking about and smiled to myself. Just like clockwork, Aunt Tillie's bacon curse had worn off. I was relieved. "It's okay." I absently patted his hand before stretching. "Maybe she'll give it to you as a special gift for Christmas."

"Christmas is more than six months away. I can't go that long without the bacon curse."

"Well ... I'm sure you guys can work something out." I rolled to stare at the ceiling, taking a moment to collect my thoughts. Then I remembered the email he sent right before we climbed into bed for the last time. "You need to see if your guys emailed you back."

He scowled. "What? I will. Just give me a second. I'm in mourning."

"I'm serious." I was firm. "Last night was fun, but we need to get back on the case. The only way to do that is if we manage to track down the information we need. Get to it."

"Ugh. You're such a taskmaster." He turned away from me and looked to the laptop plugged in on his nightstand. We'd thought ahead and left it there to charge overnight. "Hold on." He grabbed the laptop, which he had to leave running so a tech team could access it remotely, and rubbed the sleep out of his eyes as he focused on the screen. "Someone has definitely been on here," he said after a beat. "It's open and ready for me to access it."

"Great." I pushed myself to a sitting position and moved closer to his side. "Let's see what she was working on right before she disappeared."

"Chill out." He moved to her documents folder first. There was a long list. Everything filed neatly and in alphabetical order. Unfortunately, we had no way of knowing why she named things the way she did. "I don't know what any of this means."

"Give it to me," I instructed, reaching.

"Since when are you a computer expert?"

"I'm not, but I'm a woman who researches things and keeps files tucked away for a living. I might be able to find some reason in her files."

He shifted the laptop to me and watched as I navigated through the documents, arranging them by "most recent" instead of alphabetically. "This is the last file she was in." I double clicked on a file titled "Cove Camp" and started reading. "Hmm."

"Does it say anything about her attending the camp?"

"Not as far as I can tell. I'm still going to have to go out there and check."

"I think *we* should go out there and check."

"Don't you have other work to do?" I was serious. "I can take Clove and Thistle. It won't take long to stop in the office and scoop up all the files."

"Do you think you should be taking Clove anywhere in her condition?"

I hadn't considered that. "Oh, well ... I don't know. She's four months along. I don't think a simple trip to a campground will hurt her."

"What if someone attacks you?"

It was a valid question. "I doubt that's going to happen now. Besides, we warded the cabin. Once we're inside, we're fine."

"No offense to Aunt Tillie, but I've seen some of her wards fail. She's not infallible."

"I think you should tell her that."

"Please. If I tell her that, we both know I'll end up smelling like prunes ... or rancid cabbage."

I smiled at the thought. "Oh, that would be so fun."

"Really? There's no way you'd want to share a bed with a guy who smells like prunes."

"I'll make you sleep on the couch."

"Then we'll both be sad sacks." He poked my side. "Go back to reading. We'll talk about the Clove situation later."

"I want to talk about it now." He brought it up, so I needed to consider it. "Maybe she shouldn't be going on adventures with us. I mean ... she's probably not going to like that because she hates being left alone. She has the worst FOMO ever."

Landon stilled. "What's FOMO?"

"Fear of missing out," I replied. "It's when someone wants to go on a trip or to an event simply because everyone else is going. Clove has always had severe FOMO."

"Wow. I didn't even know that was a thing."

"You learn all types of stuff when we're together," I teased.

"I guess so." He rested his chin on my shoulder as I continued reading the file. "Is there anything in there?"

"There's a lot of stuff about Joey."

"Like what?"

"Like the fact that she didn't believe he was really dead. She was trying to prove he was still alive and hanging around the camp for her book. She thought it would be a great story to draw people in."

"But ... how?" Landon looked confused. "Why would she think he's still alive?"

"It doesn't really say. She planned to return to the camp to look for him again. Her first trip was a bust. She came up empty ... or she never had a chance to update the file and somehow found actual proof."

"She had to have a reason for believing he was alive," Landon pressed. "We need to figure out what that reason was."

"And if she was a guest at the camp when she was a kid," I added. "I think that's important."

"It's definitely important." He slouched down and cuddled closer. "I really miss the bacon smell," he admitted. "It's like when you take down the Christmas tree every year. There's a certain sadness permeating the room that's difficult to put a name to."

I was annoyed with the bacon talk. "Well ... you'll survive. You should check your email for searches on the other counselors."

"I won't get that information until noon at the earliest. I was more interested in getting into Hannah's files. I say we spend another thirty minutes going through them and then get ready for breakfast. If we don't find anything of interest, I'll hand the laptop over to a tech to dig into."

"I'll agree to your terms, but only if you don't bring up bacon for the entire thirty minutes."

Landon was clearly pained by the demand. "That's cruel and unusual punishment, Bay."

"Welcome to my world."

He heaved out a sigh. "Fine. No more talk of bacon. But you're going to owe me."

"I've already paid up ... for weeks. You got your money's worth — and then some — last night. I'm free and clear for three future fights going forward."

"I didn't agree to that."

"Yes, you did."

"No."

"If you don't agree, I'll ask Aunt Tillie to make you smell like prunes. I'm starting to warm to this idea."

"You're a cruel woman, Bay."

"I learned from the best."

"You definitely did."

. . .

THE BREAKFAST TABLE WAS packed with people when we let ourselves into the inn. We drove because it would be faster when parting for the day, but I hadn't been at the inn since the guests arrived and I was momentarily flustered when I saw the crowd of people milling about in the front lobby.

"What's going on?" I asked, confused.

"We're going on a tour of the town," one of the women replied. She was older, in her seventies if I had to guess, and she looked unbelievably excited. "We're going to meet some real witches."

"Oh, well, good for you." I looked to Marnie, who was working behind the counter. "Please tell me we didn't miss breakfast."

"There was an early breakfast for the tour group," she replied. "We're about to do another round in the dining room for the family. You're just in time."

"Good. Now Landon can have some real bacon and forget about me."

"Oh, that's never going to happen, sweetie." He slung an arm over my shoulders and grinned at Marnie as he prodded me toward the hallway. "We'll be waiting with bells on. I'm starving ... so don't be late. Winnie won't serve the food until everybody is present."

"Then you should get out of my hair so I can finish this." Marnie looked harried. "You're distracting me. You know how I hate distractions."

I definitely knew that. "We'll be in the dining room."

Chief Terry was already seated when we arrived. Clove and Thistle were also at the table, sitting at the far end, and they were making a big show of being involved in a conversation ... that absolutely nobody cared about.

"I think we should move the candle display to the east wall," Clove argued. "It's been on the west wall forever. A little variation never hurt anybody."

"We can't move the candles to the east wall," Thistle argued. "The sun hits those shelves every afternoon. The candles will melt."

"Oh, well, I didn't think about that." Clove gnawed her bottom lip.

"I still think we should move them. I want to put a crystal display on the shelf where they're located. Candles are so last year."

"You're just saying that because I made those candles."

"I'm saying it because it's true."

I rolled my eyes as I took my usual seat next to Chief Terry. "When you're done arguing about the candles, I need you guys to drive out to the camp with me this morning," I interjected, causing two sets of annoyed eyes to land on me. "It won't take long. It's a quick trip. I just need to grab a few of the files from the office. Landon would come with me, but he's got a list of people he needs to check on, so it would be easier if you two served as my chaperones."

"Why can't you go by yourself?" Thistle challenged.

"Because two people have died out there and no one is going to that camp by herself," Chief Terry answered for me, firm. "Do you want your cousin to die? Of course not. That means you can spare an hour to go out there with her."

"Wow!" Thistle made a face. "You're being awfully bossy for a guy who only started spending the night a week ago. Of course, you spent the night after the first date. Perhaps you have some magical powers we don't know about."

Chief Terry extended a warning finger. "Don't push me, Thistle. It's not safe for Bay to go out there alone. There's no reason you can't go with her."

"We'll go with her," Clove promised quickly. "We don't want to put her at risk."

Thistle was quiet for an extended beat and then she shifted on her chair. "What are you even looking for out there? I thought we got everything of interest the first trip."

"I did, too." I admitted, "but it has been brought to my attention that Hannah Bishop is the right age to have attended the camp. That last summer she would've been fourteen."

Thistle perked up. "Why is that important?"

"We don't know that it is, but it would at least give us a tenuous tie between Hannah and Vicky. I've managed to confirm that Vicky was one of the female counselors for that age group the final summer. Now we just need to prove that Hannah was there, too."

"I thought she was from Grand Rapids," Clove countered. "Why would she come to summer camp here if she lived down there?"

"I came to summer camp here and I lived in the middle of the state," Landon reminded them as he poured coffee from the carafe. "This area holds appeal for some people. Besides, you guys don't have enough locals to keep a camp running year after year. Kids would've had to come from other parts of the state."

"That didn't even occur to me," Chief Terry admitted, his expression thoughtful. "Perhaps Hannah was here researching Vicky's disappearance. She might've remembered her from camp and then heard about her going missing. She was at an impressionable age. Maybe it always stuck with her."

"We found her journal and computer at the Dragonfly," Landon said. "Thistle remembered last night that Hannah had been in the store and mentioned staying out there. Jack kept her items but didn't report her missing because he assumed she took off willingly. She had a vehicle ... and it's still out there somewhere."

"Oh, geez. We should've thought about that sooner." Chief Terry rubbed his neck. "I don't suppose you know what sort of vehicle she was driving?"

Landon nodded. "It was a Ford Focus. One of the two-door hatchbacks. I figure it's still out there somewhere, abandoned in the woods, or someone sold it to be chopped for parts. Those are the only two options I can accept. Someone would've seen the car if it was abandoned in a parking lot somewhere."

Chief Terry made a clucking sound with his tongue. "Did you find anything else of interest in her files?"

"Her journal and computer were both interesting," Landon replied. "She was apparently conducting research on Joey Morgan. She had a hunch that he never died, although why she believed that is beyond me."

"She believed it because half the town believed it," Chief Terry said, his eyes briefly flicking to the kitchen door when Aunt Tillie pushed her way through, Peg on her heels. "Tillie will probably remember that. Who started the rumor that Joey Morgan wasn't really dead?"

"That was Laura Preston," Aunt Tillie answered without hesitation. "I already told Bay and Landon about it at the campground the other day."

"She did," I confirmed. "I thought maybe there was a possibility she saw Joey's ghost. That's when I believed only one person thought he somehow survived the fire. Now you're saying half the town believed it. I don't get that."

"The town believed it because there was debate about the body," Chief Terry explained. "I mean ... the remains were burned beyond recognition. The coroner ruled that it was Joey, but there was never any proof."

"Wait ... what?" Landon's eyebrows hopped up his forehead. "How is that possible? Why didn't you run DNA?"

"Because there was no tissue left on the body. They tried drilling into the teeth, but the fire burned so hot we couldn't find a usable sample. Gertie was beside herself as it was. No one else in town was missing and Joey didn't pop up in the immediate aftermath to explain why someone else would be staying in his shed, so it seemed a foregone conclusion."

"Geez." Landon handed me a mug of coffee, his eyes conflicted. "What if he wasn't in there?"

"Who else could it have been? Where has he been all this time? How could someone else die and no one notice?"

"I don't know." Landon looked to me for help. "Do you have any ideas?"

"I don't know. I need to think about it." I flicked my eyes to Aunt Tillie. "Did you believe Joey died in the fire?"

She shrugged as she grabbed a leftover doughnut from the first round of breakfast and handed it to an ecstatic Peg. "I never really thought about it. Joey was never on my radar, so to speak."

"Yeah, but ... if people were seeing a dead guy walking around after the fact, it seems to me that would pique your interest," I pressed.

"I never thought about it," Aunt Tillie argued. "The kid was older than you guys and younger than your mothers. I had a hard enough time keeping up with the people you guys were friends with ... or hated. Why would I care about some random woman's kid?"

"Because he died under mysterious circumstances." I turned to focus on Chief Terry. "Is there any way we can confirm if that body was really Joey?"

"I can't think of anything off hand," Chief Terry replied as he stroked his chin. "Even if we got Gertie to agree to the exhumation, I'm not sure that today's technology is any better when it comes to extracting DNA."

"It's worth a shot," Landon argued. "If you're uncomfortable talking to her, I'll head over. She's going to have to understand that everything happening at that campground is important. I know she's still mourning, but ... if her son is alive that might explain a few things."

"Like what?" Aunt Tillie challenged. "Let's say Joey is alive. Where has he been all this time? Why has he been hiding? How has he been living?"

"Those are all excellent questions," Landon agreed. "Maybe he never left. Maybe he's been at the campground this entire time. Maybe he was a real-life Jason Voorhees ... without the face mutation. Or maybe he did leave and found a job someplace else. Maybe he created a new life away from his mother because ... I don't know why. Maybe they didn't get along or he simply wanted to be away from her. Maybe he returned recently because something happened and he had nowhere else to go."

"That's a lot of maybes," Chief Terry argued. "We need facts if we're going to get a judge to agree to exhume a body."

"Well, I don't have facts. I have a hunch."

"So, let's start building the theory," I suggested. "I'll go to the campground and collect the rest of the files. After, I'll drop Clove and Thistle at Hypnotic and head to the police station. We can start putting facts together one at a time once we have all the information."

"That's a good idea," Landon agreed. He leaned closer and kissed the tip of my nose. "I like working with you. It would be even better if you smelled like bacon, though."

"Don't push me."

"Don't push me either," Chief Terry barked. "I can't take it when you guys are all over each other. It makes me want to cut off your hands."

"You're zero fun," Landon lamented.

"That's not what Winnie said last night."

My mouth dropped open at the statement. "Did you just brag about having sex with my mother?" I was mortified. "Ugh. I'll never feel clean again."

"Suck it up." Chief Terry obviously wasn't in the mood to back down. "I've had to listen to you and Agent Romeo over here fall all over each other for a year and a half. Now it's my turn. You'll get used to it."

That didn't ease my nausea. "I kind of can't look at you," I supplied. "You're freaking me out."

"Oh, grow up." His smile was indulgent as he sipped his coffee. "I think I'm going to like this arrangement."

TWENTY-SEVEN

Mom met me in the front lobby when I was getting ready to leave.

"Can I talk to you for a second?"

That sounded like a very bad idea. Her expression was earnest, though, and I didn't see where I had a choice. "Listen, if you're going to apologize for what happened with Chief Terry, don't bother. It's not a big deal ... even if you did go back on every single thing you ever told us when we were growing up about sleeping with boys on the first date."

Mom's expression darkened, making me — not for the first time, mind you — wish I had kept my mouth shut. "I wasn't going to apologize for what happened with Terry. I'm not sorry for that – and you need to grow up."

"I'm plenty grown. That doesn't change the fact that you told us over and over that sleeping with a boy on the first date was wrong. Apparently it's only wrong if *we're* doing it. You can't pretend you're not a hypocrite on this one."

Mom's expression was withering. "I'm an adult. You were a child. I don't regret what I told you."

"Which means you said it merely because of my age." I thought of

Clove, what she was going through struggling with the notion of disappointing her mother. "What else did you guys tell us that's no longer true? I mean ... our faces really aren't going to freeze that way, are they?"

Despite the somber mood of the room, Mom cracked a smile. "Bay, you're an adult now. I'm sure you've figured out that most of the things we told you were specific to a certain age. Does it really matter? Are you unhappy with Terry's presence in the house?"

"No. I like him here." I meant it. "I simply don't like thinking about him doing dirty things with my mother. It freaks me out."

"Kind of like Landon's obsession with you smelling like bacon freaks everyone else out?"

I should've known. "I take it Aunt Tillie informed you about that one."

"Aunt Tillie likes to gossip." Mom's lips curved. "She had fun camping with you guys the other night."

That wasn't exactly how I remembered it. "She's looking for dirt on Mrs. Little. She didn't really care about spending time with us."

"That's not true. She says that she enjoys learning from a younger generation."

"Oh, please." I didn't bother to hide my eye roll. "We both know she didn't say that. She thinks we're dabblers of the utmost order. She hasn't learned a thing from any of us."

"She's a big talker. As for learning ... I don't know that she believes that's important. Merely spending time with you is enough to make her happy."

I didn't believe that for a second. Ultimately, it didn't matter. "You want something. What is it?"

"Is that any way to talk to your mother?"

"I don't have much time. I think it's best if we get down to it. What do you want?"

"I want you to take some time to tell Terry you're fine with this. He's nervous."

That wasn't the answer I expected. "You want me to tell him I am fine with you sleeping with him on the first date? Why would he care about that?"

"Bay." Mom folded her arms over her chest. "You know what I'm talking about. We're having a good time. There is a mild bit of stress for both of us, though, and that stress revolves around you."

I thought about messing with her a bit, but I didn't have the heart ... or the time. Besides, I might need her on my side when the truth about Clove hiding her pregnancy comes to light. She would have no choice but to aid us when I reminded her how gracious I was in her time of need.

What? That's smart, not manipulative.

"I'll talk to him later today," I said without hesitation.

"You will?" Now it was Mom's turn to be suspicious. "Just like that?"

"Just like that. It has to wait until after I'm done at the camp. I promised Landon I would get those records and take them to the police station as soon as possible. Clove and Thistle have to open the store for the tourists, so we have to go now."

"Oh, well ... that sounds fine." Mom offered up a pretty smile that made her look decades younger. She really was happy, which was a good thing. "I'm glad you see things my way."

"Yes, I love knowing my mother is a hypocrite." I smoothly evaded the smack she aimed at my arm. "We're going to talk about all the things you told me as a kid and see which ones still stand," I warned. "I'm going to make a list. You'd better prepare yourself."

"Just get going." Her eyes flashed. "I want a full report of your conversation with Terry before the end of the day."

"No problem. There's a murderer who killed two women over a ten-year period running around, but your love life takes priority." I flashed her a sarcastic thumbs-up. "I'm on this."

"You make me tired, Bay."

"Right back at you."

AUNT TILLIE INSISTED ON GOING with us. I should've seen it coming — she was nothing if not predictable — but I didn't have time for an argument.

"Fine. But you can't bring Peg."

"Twila is watching Peg," Aunt Tillie replied. "I have plans to spy on Margaret later this afternoon. You can't spy on someone if you have a pig. Didn't you know that?"

"I never really gave it much thought."

"Well, I didn't know it. People stare when you have a pig on a leash."

"Perhaps you should disguise her as a dog."

It was meant as a joke, but Aunt Tillie brightened considerably. "That's a great idea. I'll try that tomorrow. For now, I'm going to the camp with you and then you can drop me in town for the day. I've got everything mapped out."

"You mean you've got a full day of torture planned for Mrs. Little."

"I'm pretty sure that's what I said."

It took us twenty minutes to get to the camp. I parked in the lot, which had seen more activity in the past week than it had in a decade, and killed the engine of my car. "You guys can stay here if you want," I offered, turning to Clove and Thistle in the backseat. "I won't be long. I'm just going to grab all the files."

"Then we'll wait here," Clove said. "This camp gives me the creeps as it is. It's not like when we were kids. I used to love coming here back then. Now, not so much. You can feel the death hanging over this place – and I don't like it."

Aunt Tillie rolled her eyes so hard I thought she might fall through the passenger-side door. "Oh, geez. You're such a kvetch. Have you ever made it throughout a day without whining?"

"Have you ever made it through a day without ... being you?" Thistle challenged.

Aunt Tillie narrowed her eyes. "You're definitely on my list, mouth. Congratulations. You'll be my side distraction when I'm not thinking about Margaret this afternoon."

Thistle's expression remained defiant, but I didn't miss her hard swallow. "I'm not afraid of you."

"Then you finally supplanted your mother as the dumbest one in the family. Double congratulations to you." Aunt Tillie held Thistle's gaze for an extended beat and then slowly tracked her eyes to me. "I want to check the wards while you're grabbing the files. It won't take long."

"I thought the wards were just so no damage could happen to the campground," I challenged. "Why would you need to check them?"

"I might've added an extra dose of itchy ass to them and stamped Margaret's name on the wards. Sue me."

My eyebrows flew up. "Itchy ass? Is that a thing?"

"I made a new spell when I was bored."

"Oh, I totally want to learn that spell." Thistle leaned closer. "What roots do you use? Does it physically harm someone or do they literally have an itchy ass the entire time? I think that's a brilliant idea, by the way."

"Thanks," Aunt Tillie drawled. "You're still on my list."

Thistle's expression darkened. "Thank you so much for being my aunt."

"You're welcome."

Aunt Tillie and I exited the vehicle at the same time. I left my keys with Clove and Thistle so they could control the air conditioning and radio, and headed toward the office as Aunt Tillie moved toward the lake.

"You have ten minutes," I called out to her. "I have to get back to town. I promised Mom I would do something today and I would rather get it out of the way as soon as possible."

"Oh, she finally approached you to have the talk with Terry, huh?" She made a tsking sound as she shook her head. "I saw that coming. Terry is happy. His skin has never looked better. He's nervous around you, though. That's what she was afraid of. It's the reason they never dated when you were younger."

I frowned. "I'll make sure he's not nervous around me. That's not what I want."

"I know that. Your mother knows it, too. Heck, I think Terry knows that. You're the reason this is finally happening. You gave him the okay. Things will settle down in a bit. Our family likes drama. This is just the current bit of drama. In a few weeks something new will come along and this will be forgotten."

I had a feeling I knew what the incoming drama would revolve around. "Ten minutes," I repeated. "I don't want to waste the entire morning here."

"I've got it, whiner. You're not the boss of me."

"No, but I am your ride."

"Try to leave me," she suggested, a glint in her eye. "Just wait and see what you'll smell like if that happens."

"I have no intention of leaving you." I meant it. "There's a killer on the loose," I reminded her. "We need to stick together."

"Yeah, yeah, yeah."

The office looked largely as I remembered — files strewn across the floor, the undeniable odor of musty neglect permeating the air — and I immediately set about sweeping all the documents together. They would be a pain to sort through at the police station, but it was safer doing it there.

Once I collected all the files, I headed toward the old cabinet pressed against the wall. It was metal and rusted through thanks to the humidity, but it opened with a creaky groan. There were a few files left inside. I gathered those as well so there would be no need to return to the camp — I was starting to feel the creep factor as well — and then gave the office a long once-over. In truth, I found it sad that the camp had lost its former glory. I understood what Gertie and Earl were trying to build. They were too late. They made the attempt at a time when society was shifting. Had they tried twenty years earlier they would've made a real go of it ... and for a long time. Now, everything the camp should've been was shrouded in memory mist. In a few months, it would be completely gone, wiped from the earth.

The realization made me inexplicably sad, which is why I initially disregarded the hair standing up on the back of my neck. I waited until a tingling sensation — as if a thousand spiders were crawling over my back — caused me to shudder.

I felt a set of eyes on me before I turned. I expected to find Vicky watching — she had a habit of creeping up when she thought no one was paying attention — but Randy was the one standing in the doorway. The way he looked at me caused my blood to run cold.

"What are you doing here?" The words felt awkward tumbling out of my mouth, as if my tongue was suddenly too large. My heart rate picked up a notch as he glanced around the cabin and I couldn't help wondering what he had planned. "Chief Terry and Landon are looking for you. They know you were never hired to look after the camp."

Instead of snapping at me, which I expected, Randy merely shrugged. "I figured they would find out the truth sooner or later. Honestly, I'm surprised it took them as long as it did. How did they know?"

"We asked Gertie when we saw her here the night after the fire. Was that you?"

"Does it matter?" His gaze was challenging. "You've already made up your mind about me. I mean ... look at you. You're shrinking you're so afraid of me. You don't have to be afraid of me."

I didn't believe him for a second. "Did you kill Hannah Bishop?"

He balked. "No. Why would you ask that?"

"Because someone killed her, and it was someone who spent a lot of time around this campground. Gertie can't get out here on a regular basis like she could when she was younger. That leaves you, the man who claimed he was watching over the camp for money ... which turned out to be a lie."

"Listen ... ."

I held up a hand when he stepped in my direction. "Don't come any closer." I infused my voice with as much malice as I could muster. "I don't want to hurt you, but I will. If you come any closer I will make you pay in ways you've only imagined in nightmares."

Randy froze in his place, his eyes narrowing. "I just told you that I don't want to hurt you."

"And I don't believe you." I clutched the files tighter against my chest. "I don't understand why you would hang out in this campground if you weren't being paid to do it. Why would you care about this place otherwise?"

"I've been living here." He stated it as fact. "In one of the storage cabins across the lake. That's safer than staying on this side."

I made a grumbling sound deep in my throat. "I knew we should've checked those cabins. It seemed like a lot of work, but we definitely should've done it."

"I guess you should have," Randy agreed. "But it doesn't matter. I'm not a killer. No matter what you're thinking about me, it's wrong. I'm not who you think I am."

"You keep saying that. I can't wrap my head around why you would be living in a cabin without any power if you didn't have a reason for doing so."

"Poverty isn't enough of a reason for you?"

I shrugged. "Maybe you wanted to stay close to your victims," I countered. "Did you kill Vicky Carpenter? Was she your first?"

"How many times do I have to tell you that I'm not a killer?"

I ignored the question. "Were you a counselor here back then? I don't remember you. How did you meet Vicky? Were you already living out here before we were aware you were in town? I don't understand how that would work."

"I'll tell you how it would work," Aunt Tillie announced, appearing in the open doorway. She'd snuck up on us when we were focused on each other. For an octogenarian, she had light feet. She was like an evil cat that way.

Randy slid her a look. He didn't seem surprised by her sudden appearance. "Ms. Tillie."

"Joey."

My heart rolled at the word and my eyes flew to Aunt Tillie. "What?"

"Joey Morgan," Aunt Tillie confirmed, her expression thoughtful. "I didn't realize it was you until last night. It came to me out of the blue."

"You're smarter than most," Randy countered. "You're the only one to ever figure it out ... other than my mother, I mean."

"Your mother." A multitude of ideas collided in my head. "Does your mother know you're alive? Does she know what name you're operating under? I don't understand any of this."

"You're not meant to understand," Randy said. "It was supposed to be a secret. That's why I faked my death and ran. I left this place right after the fire. The goal was to start a new life, never look back. Things didn't work out exactly as I'd hoped."

"You faked your death to hide your culpability in Vicky's death," I surmised.

"Stop saying that." Randy's eyes fired with fury. "I'm not a killer. No matter how many times you say it, that doesn't make it true. I might've been a lazy kid. Heck, I might still be a lazy adult. I also might've run and taken the coward's way out. That doesn't mean I'm a killer."

"Okay." I was willing to play his game and at least listen. "If you're not a killer, who is?"

"My mother. She's been at this for a very long time."

I was astounded. "That is ridiculous."

"Hear me out."

I looked to Aunt Tillie. Her stance told me she was interested in the story. "Fine." I held up my hands in capitulation. "Tell me a story about your mother the murderer."

"You're dubious now, but it's the truth."

"Tell me."

"Well, it started with my father ... and my goal is to make sure it ends with Hannah Bishop. At least I think it started with my father. I have a few suspicions about my grandparents. But that's not part of this story."

"Just get to it," Aunt Tillie prodded.

TWENTY-EIGHT

Randy – or Joey, depending on how you looked at him – seemed to relish his tale.

"My mother is a horrible person."

"Well, you're claiming she's a murderer, so I think that goes without saying," I said dully.

"She's always been horrible," Randy stressed. "When I was a kid, she used to lock me in the closet if I was too loud. She said she got migraines and that I was the cause, and the only way to get rid of them was to lock me away."

I felt a tug of sympathy but it was mild. For all I knew, he could've prepared this story to lull us into a false sense of security so he could knock us over the head and dump us in the pool. "Is that your excuse? You were an abused child?"

"I'm not a killer." Randy's patience was obviously wearing thin. He flexed his hands at his sides. "My mother mistreated me my entire childhood. I never understood why she even wanted this place until I was older and watched her interact with the campers. She always picked one at every event and then tortured that kid until she made him cry ... or sometimes worse."

I balked. "I don't remember her being like that."

"That's because she was afraid of your great-aunt." He shifted his appreciative eyes to Aunt Tillie. "I heard her telling my father that she wasn't someone to be messed with and to stay away from her."

"Was your father a deviant, too?" Aunt Tillie asked. She seemed to be taking the story at face value. Of course, she was smart enough to play the game and attempt to lull Randy the same way I suspected he was trying to lull us.

"My father was ... something else. He was more lazy than hurtful. He never stepped in when she was mistreating me. In fact, he seemed frightened of Mother and did his best to stay away from her."

"He sounds like a lovely father," I muttered. "Are you saying he just sat around when your mother locked you in a closet?"

"That's exactly what I'm saying."

"And ... no one ever questioned it?" I felt as if I was grasping at straws, but it seemed too early to trust him. This was a man who had been living in the woods by himself, pretending to be someone else, for a very long time. How could I trust him? I would never hear the end of it from Landon and Chief Terry if I blindly fell for his tale of woe. "What about bruises? What about Social Services?"

"We had no family in the area," Randy replied. "We moved away from the family when I was small. I didn't understand it at the time — I really loved my grandparents — but I do now. She wanted to isolate me. She wanted to isolate my father, too.

"We moved up here and they bought this property for a really low price," he continued. "They knew the land would be worth something eventually. They simply had to figure out a business they thought would take little work and bring in easy money. They didn't need much to live on. They came up with the idea of the camp. The property served as a camp before they bought it. All it needed was a few tweaks."

"Why did they think a camp wouldn't be any work?" I challenged. "We're talking about kids and nonstop outdoor activities. Of course that was going to be work."

"I'm pretty sure they didn't think it out. They were notorious for that. It doesn't really matter. I was a teenager by the time this place was in full swing and I was already looking for a way out."

I tilted my head to the side, considering. "The rumor was you were lazy."

"Lazy? Probably. I learned my work ethic from them. I wasn't allowed to have a job. They wanted to make sure I was completely dependent on them. People would offer me things and I wanted to say yes, but I was instructed to say no. If I agreed to work for someone else, that would've gotten me out of the house, and that's not what she wanted. They even let me say yes a few times, but insisted I do a bad job so people wouldn't ask me a second time. They wanted word to get out that I wasn't worth hiring."

"You said your mother killed your father," Aunt Tillie pressed. "How do you know that?"

"I guess I don't know it for certain, but I'm fairly sure," he hedged. "They got in a huge fight one night and slept in separate rooms. I was an adult at this time – by seven years, which is sad when you think about it – I could hear my mother grumbling about him the entire next day. Then, out of nowhere, she made dinner for him ... and made sure that I didn't eat anything off the platter.

"He didn't make it thirty minutes after dinner before he was complaining about heart palpitations and holding his left arm," he continued. "I wanted to call for help, but she wouldn't let me. She basically sat in the chair — his favorite chair — and watched him die on the floor. He knew it was happening and didn't give her the satisfaction of hearing him beg. He cursed her until the very end."

"Didn't they perform an autopsy?" I asked.

He shrugged. "I don't know. I'm guessing they did a cursory examination, but my father was in his sixties and wasn't in the best of health. They probably didn't expect to find anything, so they didn't. I was hopeful they would, but it didn't happen and I had to let it go.

"After that she was worse, and I wasn't sure that was even possible," he said. "She was meaner than a snake and took to blaming me for my father's death. There was more work to do around the house than she could keep up on and she wanted me to do it. I was happy to do it as long as it kept her off my back. But that didn't last long.

"The first time I realized she was really mentally ill — I mean, crazy as a loon — was when she insisted I fill in at the campground because one of the counselors didn't show up. I was in my twenties then and looking for a way out, but I knew I had to be well prepared because I didn't want to be forced to come back once I ran.

"That was the first summer Vicky was a counselor," he continued, taking on a wistful expression. "She was a lot younger than me, but she was full of life. I remember looking at her and thinking that she was the sort of person I wanted to run away with. She planned on traveling all over the world, and I loved that idea because I desperately wanted to get away from my mother.

"My mother saw the way I was mooning over her and didn't like it. She made a big deal and attacked me at the house that night. She's small, but she's not afraid to use whatever weapon she can get her hands on, including a baseball bat or frying pan. She left bruises all over my back. I should've run then — it would've saved Vicky — but I didn't. I wasn't ready.

"The next summer Vicky came back and I had to fill in as a counselor again," he said. "I flirted with her every chance I got. She was nineteen, legal, and I thought maybe I could leave with her. She had plans to travel once camp was over. She was going to return to the area when her sister gave birth, but I had no intention of doing that. I was going to use her for a ride and to get away.

"My mother heard us talking one night," he explained. "I was trying to convince her to give me a ride. She wasn't keen on it because she didn't know me very well. I think she thought I was a pervert or something, that's why I kept looking at her. I just wanted to get away."

I pressed the heel of my hand to my forehead as things began coming together. "Your mother wanted to stop you from leaving so she killed Vicky."

"She did. She smacked her over the head with a brick after dark that last night. I was there. I saw her do it. I was terrified. I wanted to warn Vicky. It was already over before I could even get my wits about me, though.

"My mother dragged her to the pool and opened up the deep end," he continued. "She had the tool they used for the cover handy and just flipped up three of the hooks, rolled Vicky's body inside and then closed it again. The hardest part for her was dragging Vicky's body but she used a wheelbarrow. I swear she carried the entire thing out in ten minutes flat."

"What did you do?" Aunt Tillie questioned. "Why didn't you go to the police and tell them what you saw?"

"I should have. If you think I don't already know that, you're wrong. I should've gone straight to the police but I was afraid of her. I thought they might blame me because I had no doubt she would turn the tables and accuse me to save her own skin. I made a much more likely suspect, what with the entire town thinking I was lazy and stupid."

"Is that when you moved to the shed?" I asked.

"Yes," he bobbed his head. "I couldn't stay in the same house with her because I was afraid. I knew she would put up a fight if I tried to stay there over the long haul, but she had a migraine when she came back. I simply suggested it would be better if I stayed in the shed versus the closet for the night because it would make things easier on her.

"Once I was outside, I wasn't sure what to do," he continued. "I knew I wanted to run but I had to do it in a smart way. I wanted people to think I was dead so they wouldn't look at me. A fire seemed the easiest route, but I needed a body to hide in the shed to convince people I'd really died."

Now we were finally getting somewhere. "Where did you find a body?"

"The funeral home." His answer was easy, succinct. "They had three in there that weren't claimed from some accident. I took one of them, broke in and just took it because I knew they didn't lock the back door thanks to Brad Horton, whose father owned the place, and carried it back to the shed. I put the body in the shed, added some gasoline to the mix — really doused the body to get it good — and then lit a match.

"I watched from the trees across the road from the house," he continued. "I wanted to see her reaction. I didn't expect her to mourn me, but I wanted to make sure she believed. I had access to Vicky's car. She stupidly left it at the camp. I knew Vicky wasn't going to be using it, so I decided that I should take it for my escape.

"My mother was furious when she came outside and saw the mess. She ranted and screamed my name. It never occurred to her that I was inside. She didn't call the police. The neighbors did that. When they showed up with the fire department, they decided to let it burn out naturally because there was no chance of it spreading.

"I stayed in the woods the entire time and watched, even though it went late into the night," he said. "Once the fire was completely out they went inside ... and found the body. Up until then, I think my mother believed that I set the fire to mess with her. That it was some form of rebellion. When they found the body, though, they naturally assumed it was me."

"Did no one ever miss the body at the funeral home?" I asked, confused.

He shrugged. "I don't know. I didn't stick around. I took the few belongings I had, packed Vicky's car, and left. I moved to Detroit to get away from Walkerville. I had no intention of coming back.

"While I was down there, I kept an ear to the news reports because I wanted to make sure they never put it together that I was still alive," he continued. "I could've been charged with a crime for setting the fire and burning the body. I felt bad for whoever that was, but he was already dead and I just wanted to be free."

It was a stirring story. There were still a few holes in it, though. "You came back, though," I pressed. "Why did you come back?"

"Believe it or not, I didn't have any job skills." He was rueful as he rubbed the back of his neck. "I managed to find a guy who created a fake identity for me. Randy Weaver. The Social Security number belonged to a boy who died in infancy.

"I managed to find work in restaurants ... and construction ... and other places, but it was hard to eke out a living because I wanted to be paid under the table and it seemed everyone I approached was leery of that," he said. "Even more than that, though, I was curious. I made it five years before returning home.

"I looked different then. I'd taken to dying my hair darker and was used to doing it. I was a thin and underdeveloped kid, so I looked really different when I filled out. I was almost twenty-six when I left. I was thirty-one when I came back. I grew a beard, avoided my mother, and became Randy Weaver, jack-of-all-trades.

"The people in Hemlock Cove were surprisingly eager to hire me," he supplied. "Up here I could make enough money to survive and I knew how to keep a roof over my head at the camp. I picked the far side of the lake because my mother never visited that part of the camp ... and then I watched her."

"Were you planning on getting revenge?" Aunt Tillie asked, leaning against the doorjamb. She appeared perfectly comfortable with the conversation.

"I don't know. I didn't want her to get away with what she did, but I also had a lot of fear built up. Most people ignored me. They didn't question what I was doing out here. People knew me as Randy Weaver, not Joey Morgan. Joey was long forgotten. I wanted it that way.

"When someone did ask, which was rare, I told them my mother hired me to look after the camp. No one ever questioned it," he said. "The camp was nothing but a backdrop for a sad tale about a woman who had lost her husband and son. People felt sorry for my mother, which I hated, but I couldn't exactly tell them the truth."

"I can see that," I offered. "It sounds like your mother was a horrible person. The thing is ... you could've put her away a long time ago. All you had to do was tell the truth."

"Do you think the cops would've believed me over her? Be honest."

"I ... ." In truth, I couldn't answer that. "I think Chief Terry would've dug until he found the truth."

"I couldn't take that chance. I had one opportunity to get away and

I took it. I broke laws doing it, but I had to get away. You have no idea how horrible she was."

I was starting to get a picture. "What about Hannah? How did she end up in the pool?"

"I ran into Hannah when she was out here poking around one day. She surprised me. I ran the Randy Weaver story on her and she seemed to believe it. I was certain she believed it. She took a few photographs of the lake, waved as she got in her car, and took off. I didn't think anything of it until she came back the next day ... and this time she was armed with questions."

I thought about the notation I'd seen in her notebook. "She knew who you were."

He nodded. "She'd just researched my death and saw a photograph of me from the accompanying news article. I was fresh in her mind and she looked past the beard and added pounds. She addressed me by my real name."

"And then what?" I prodded.

"And then I told her the truth," he replied simply. "I told her about my mother, about running, and about why I came back. I told her everything. She was fascinated with the story and wanted to include it in her book. She filled a whole notebook with the things I told her."

I frowned at the news. "We didn't see that notebook when we found her things at the Dragonfly."

"Well, she had a blue notebook that she wrote in. Maybe it's in her car. It's behind the old paper mill on Wolcott Road. My mother moved it there after she killed Hannah."

"But ... why would she kill Hannah?" This was the part I didn't understand. "Say I believe you and accept that your mother killed Vicky to keep you from running away with her. Why would she go after Hannah?"

"Because she was a slut just like the first one and I had to keep my boy safe," a different voice answered, causing me to jump back as a shadow appeared in the doorway. "Hello, Joey. I just knew you wouldn't be able to stay away from your mother forever."

TWENTY-NINE

"Hello, Gertie." I managed to maintain my cool, but just barely. My stomach was knotted and for some weird reason I wanted to throw a chair at her and climb under the desk. That wasn't really my style — it was more Clove's style — but fear is sometimes an irrational beast.

"Hello, Bay." Gertie was calm. She had a gun in her hand, and even though she was outnumbered she was clearly in control. If she felt fear, she didn't show it. "I knew you would come back, Joey. I had no idea you were here the entire time — I never thought to check out Randy Weaver until Bay mentioned the name — but I know now. It's good to have you back."

Randy didn't return his mother's evil smile. "I'm not back."

"But you are."

"I'm not." He was firm. "I want nothing to do with you. I never did. I only came back so I could keep an eye on you. That backfired spectacularly, didn't it? I wanted to keep you from killing again, but you did it right under my nose. How?"

"And why?" I added. I had no doubt Randy was telling the truth. Gertie's cool demeanor — and the gun she had pointed directly at my chest — were dead giveaways. "What did Hannah Bishop ever do to you?"

"She stuck her nose where it didn't belong," Gertie replied simply. "I knew she was going to be trouble the second she showed up on my doorstep asking questions about Joey. They were rather pointed and phrased in such a way that made me realize he was still alive. Until she showed up, I assumed he'd died in the shed like everybody else. I was wrong."

"We were all wrong," Aunt Tillie agreed. "But why kill the girl? She wasn't doing anything but being curious."

"She was sticking her nose into things she had no right to ask about," Gertie hissed. "Joey was none of her business. Earl was none of her business."

"She must've gone to see Mom the night she accused me of being Joey," Randy mused. "I was so worked up I didn't think about what she would do next. I just took off and thought about what she said the entire night."

"She visited me." Gertie was smug. "She said that she had reason to believe that Joey was still alive. I thought that was nonsense, of course. A body was found in the shed. Joey had no reason to leave me ... and yet she was so sure of herself I couldn't stop myself from wondering.

"Then she started asking intolerable questions," she continued. "She wanted to know if Joey had reason to run away. She assumed his father mistreated him, that Joey was beaten and terrorized. She said she'd been doing research on certain personality types and believed Joey fit into a neat little box.

"I was so angry I wanted to kill her right there, but I didn't," she continued. "I kept my temper in check. I'm much better about doing that now, Joey."

"My name is Randy." He gritted out the words. "Don't call me that. Joey died in that shed."

"Someone died in that shed," Gertie agreed. "But it wasn't you. You're standing right in front of me."

I felt sick to my stomach. "You must've tracked down Hannah after the fact. You killed her out here."

"She should've stayed out of my business." Gertie's eyes flashed with malice and I couldn't help but wonder how I'd missed her lunacy the first time I'd met her. "I found her out here, on my property when she was supposed to be gone. She said she wouldn't bother me again, but she was out here."

"I was supposed to meet her." Randy looked forlorn. "I was late. I was doing some work for Mrs. Gunderson at the bakery. I needed the money. I figured Hannah would wait ... or leave a note and come back a different day. When she wasn't here, I just assumed she got tired of waiting. I didn't think to look in the pool."

"Why would you?" The sick sensation in my stomach grew. "You found Hannah out here and killed her, didn't you?"

"She accused me of all sorts of things." Gertie didn't look remorseful in the least. "She said I abused Joey, which was a lie. She said I killed Earl, also a lie."

"They're not lies," Randy hissed. "You did both."

"I most certainly did not." Gertie straightened her shoulders. "You were an incorrigible boy. I was a good mother, taught you how to behave yourself and not be a little snot like all those other kids in town. You were lucky to have me."

"Yes, I bet he thanks his lucky stars every night when he goes to sleep in a cabin without electricity," Aunt Tillie drawled, shaking her head. "You started the fire the night we were out here, didn't you, Randy? You were trying to scare us away."

"I knew the moment my mother lost her cool again because her space was being invaded that you would make targets," Randy admitted. "I figured she was probably angry because you found the bodies in the first place."

"Oh, I'm definitely angry about that," Gertie snarled. "This is private property. You and your boyfriend were trespassing. Don't think I've forgotten that little detail."

I swallowed hard. "You figured out Hannah was talking to Randy, learning things about your past, and figured she would out you to the police. At the very least she would make things you wanted buried public in her book. You came out here looking for her, got lucky and found her, and then killed her."

"Wrong! I came out here looking for Joey because I knew that little guttersnipe had been talking to him. She spouted a bunch of nonsense, said horrible things. You wouldn't believe the things she accused me of."

"I believe them." Randy briefly closed his eyes, regret lining his face. "She died because of me. I should've warned her. I should've kept her away. Hell, I should've known when she suddenly stopped showing up. I didn't believe anything bad happened to her until I stumbled across her car behind the mill.

"What were you thinking, Mother?" he continued. "Did you believe the cops would assume she'd been out hiking and got lost? Did you think they would chalk it up to accidental circumstances, like they did with Dad and me?"

Gertie merely shrugged. "I didn't really think about it," she replied. "There was no reason to trace the girl to me, especially after I took that filthy journal she was keeping. Once I read what she had in there I knew I did the right thing."

My stomach was so keyed up now that I was certain I was about to vomit on my shoes. I felt raw around the edges and wanted to lie down and forget this day. That wasn't exactly an option.

"Once you killed Hannah, you probably figured throwing her under the pool cover was the most convenient way to get rid of her," I noted, rubbing my stomach as I fought off the waves of nausea. "After all, it worked before, right?"

"It would've been fine if you and your boyfriend hadn't stuck your noses into my business."

"Yeah, well ... ." I broke off and pressed my hand into my abdomen.

"What is wrong with you?" Aunt Tillie demanded. "You're starting to embarrass me. We've been in worse situations than this."

"I don't know what's wrong with me." That was the truth. "I think I'm going to be sick."

"Oh, well, great." Aunt Tillie rolled her eyes. "We'll have to send you back to boot camp if you expect to be part of the WBI. I mean ...

seriously. You're acting like Clove, for crying out loud. I'm mortified by how you're reacting. You need to suck it up."

Clove? That's when I realized what was happening. Clove and Thistle were still in the car. Er, well, they were supposed to be in the car. There was every chance they'd realized something was wrong and came looking. There was every chance they were behind Gertie and she didn't know it.

"Come here." I grabbed Aunt Tillie's arm and jerked her closer to me. "Get away from Gertie."

"Don't tell me what to do." Aunt Tillie slapped at my hand. "I wasn't joking about you embarrassing me. This is undignified, Bay. I expected better of you."

"Next time," I offered with a bland smile.

"Oh, there won't be a next time." Gertie shook her head. "I'm afraid I'm going to have to put an end to things right now. I would put you in the pool, but that seems like a waste. Instead I'm simply going to end you, and then Joey and I will be on our way. We'll set down roots someplace else."

"I'm not going anywhere with you," Randy shouted. "And you're not hurting them. This is over, Mother. It's done. I'm putting a stop to it right now."

Gertie's eyes turned to glittery green slits. "Don't push me, boy. I won't be bullied. You've had your fun. Now it's time to rejoin the family. We need to get out of here. In fact ... ." Whatever she was going to say died on her lips as Thistle appeared in the opening. She had what looked to be a huge tree branch that she brandished like a baseball bat.

"Duck!" she ordered, her voice echoing.

I didn't have to be told twice. I grabbed Aunt Tillie and dragged her toward the ground. Randy instinctively did the same.

The branch hit Gertie solidly in the back of the head. Her reflexes weren't what they used to be so she didn't have time to react. Reflexively she pulled the trigger, but the bullet flew up instead of at us. Gertie hit the ground with a loud thud before Randy finished covering his head. Everything else played out in slow motion until I could get my bearings.

"Did you get her?" Clove asked, appearing behind Thistle. She had her hand on her stomach.

"I got her." Thistle was grim. "I can't believe Gertie was a killer."

That made two of us. "I think I'm going to throw up," I complained.

"Me, too." Clove's face was unnaturally pale. "I've been stopping myself from blowing chunks for the last three minutes."

"At least we're alive." I sat up and watched as Thistle kicked Gertie's gun away from her hand. "Is she dead?"

"No such luck." Thistle dug in her pocket. "I'll call for help. I guess we won't need to conduct that research after all."

Ah, well, a bright spot in an otherwise convoluted day.

LANDON AND CHIEF TERRY REACHED the campground within twenty minutes. They were both frantic messes as they checked each one of us over, ultimately letting us head outside while they sat Randy down for a long conversation and took his mother into custody.

We could have left — they knew where to find us if we wanted to head to town — but I opted to stay. Clove and Thistle waited an hour and then took my car. Landon would give me a ride to town when it was time. Now that I knew the truth, the campground wasn't anywhere near as creepy as it felt only hours before.

"Hey." Landon found me skipping stones across the placid lake. "How are you feeling?" He lowered himself to the ground and cast me a sidelong look.

"I'm fine."

"Randy said you were complaining about throwing up."

"Oh, that." I looked over my shoulder to reassure myself we were alone. Aunt Tillie was still running around and I didn't want to let Clove's secret out in front of her. "That was Clove. She was all nerved up when moving behind Gertie. She'll need to get that bit of magic under control if she doesn't want all of us to go through labor with her in five months."

Landon chuckled ... and then sobered. "You don't think she'd really do that, do you?"

"I don't know. I guess we'll have to wait and see. I'm still not sure if everything I've been feeling is because of her. It's possible it was a mixture of her *and* the ghosts. I guess I'll have to keep waiting that one out."

"Well, we'll definitely make her work on this. I don't want to know what it's like to give birth. That's the only reason I'm thankful I'm a man. Well ... that and I can pee standing up."

"Ah, small blessings."

He grinned as he leaned over and kissed my forehead. "You're okay?"

I nodded without hesitation. "I'm perfectly fine. I just never suspected Gertie. I don't know how I missed it."

"She's a sociopath, Bay. She hid who she was extremely well. That's what they do."

"I guess. Are you going to look into Earl's death?"

"Yup. We're also going to figure out how Randy managed to steal a body from the funeral home with nobody reporting it. I expect that to be a fun investigation."

"Good luck with that."

"Yeah." He gathered my hand and pressed a kiss to my palm. "I'm just glad you're okay. I was worried when Thistle called. I guess things could've been a lot worse."

"They didn't end well for Vicky and Hannah. I'll have to help Vicky cross over."

"Like I've told you numerous times, you can't help everyone. You can only do what you can do ... and today you fulfilled that potential to the utmost degree. You all did."

I believed him, yet I still felt deflated. "What's going to happen to Randy?"

"Well, he stole someone's identification, abused a corpse, set a fire, covered up for his mother in two murders and stole a car. He's going to spend some time behind bars."

I hadn't really considered that. "He just wanted to get away from her."

"And that will be taken into consideration. He won't get off without some time in jail, though, Bay. That's not how it works."

"Okay." I heaved out a sigh and rested my head against my knees. Suddenly I felt very tired. "So, this is it? The murder has been solved and the land will be free and clear in another week. That means Mrs. Little will be able to buy it."

"Not necessarily."

I shifted my eyes to him. "What do you mean?"

"I was just talking with Aunt Tillie about that very possibility out by the pool. She came up with an interesting suggestion and ... well ... the more I think about it, the more I like it."

"Ugh. Do I even want to know? If you're joining forces with Aunt Tillie, the world is clearly coming to an end."

"Or a beginning." Landon's smile was bright. "I've got some money put away. I've been making a good living and renting for a few years. Lately I've been paying your mother rent because I'm living in the guesthouse, but I still have a nice nest egg put away. It's not enough for this place, but it's a nice amount."

I was confused. "What?"

"Aunt Tillie also has a pretty penny put away," he continued, moving his hand to my back. "She's agreed to loan me whatever I need to steal this parcel from Mrs. Little. She's not even making me pay interest on the loan. In exchange, I've agreed to let her hang out here whenever she wants — including the big solstice party that's coming up about the time of Clove's wedding — with the stipulation that when we're ready to build a house she'll willingly retreat."

Things were happening fast now. "Are you saying you're going to buy this piece of property for yourself?"

"No. I'm saying I want this land for our future. It's perfect, Bay. It's a good investment. I should only have to take a small loan from Aunt

Tillie, and she's more than willing to give it to me because she wants Mrs. Little to lose.

"This is for down the road," he cautioned. "We need to save up money to build a house, which is going to be expensive. We'll still be in the guesthouse for some time. That doesn't mean we can't enjoy the land. We can camp here, turn it into a weekend getaway. How does Camp Nookie grab you? That would only be a temporary name until we build a house, but it's still fun. We'll probably want to fill in the pool, but I'll bet Marcus will be able to help me do that by the end of the summer."

I was stupefied. "You want this to be our forever home?"

"I do."

"But ... ." I exhaled heavily. Now that he'd said it, the idea seemed a good one. "It'll be years before we can build, but I've always liked the idea of living on the water."

He grinned. "Me, too. Plus ... this is where we met. I can't help thinking this is where we're supposed to grow old together. It's also close enough to the inn to eat there several times a week. And there's plenty of room for a dog when we're ready."

This time when my eyes pricked with tears I knew they were my own. "I like the idea of us being out here."

"I do, too." He slid his arm around my shoulders.

"I also like the idea of beating Mrs. Little."

"We all like that idea," Aunt Tillie barked from behind us. She'd obviously snuck up when we weren't looking. "I can't wait to dance naked under the full moon by the water. It'll be epic."

I bit the inside of my cheek and studied Landon's profile. He looked grim at the prospect. "That sounds like fun."

"It'll be legendary," she agreed, clapping her hands. "Now, come on. We need to get to the bank. Harry is handling this property. I have dirt on him if we need blackmail material."

Landon scowled. "We're not blackmailing him. This will be an above-the-board deal."

"Oh, you're so naive. Come on, Fed. We've got a battle to win. I can't wait to see Margaret's face when she finds out we've stolen this land. I bet she cries. If she does, I need to collect the tear, because I've created a new curse that requires tears from an enemy."

"It's not your itchy ass spell, is it?"

"You never know. Now ... come on! The future awaits. Let's make Margaret Little cry."

Ah, well, not all motivations can be pure. This one, however, was as close as we were likely to get.

Printed in Great Britain
by Amazon